THE MENTOR

By Ryan M. Shelton

Published by

Martin Sisters Publishing, LLC

www. martinsisterspublishing. com

ISBN: 978-1937273-99-6
Editor: Kathleen Papajohn
Christian Fiction/Young Adult
Printed in the United States of America
Martin Sisters Publishing, LLC

DEDICATION

For Dad, who taught me to love America's pastime. You were my first and greatest mentor.

ACKNOWLEDGEMENTS

I owe everything to God, from whom all blessings flow. I also owe a lot to my wife Angela who has had to become Super Mom so that I could attend to the particulars of the book. In addition, she has directly given countless hours to this book, and she is the person I bounce everything off of. I thank you for all your love and support. I thank my three wonderful children, Andrew, Ezra, and Neesa for being my inspiration in life. I would also like to thank my entire family for their love and support, especially my mom who has always believed in me. My family members have used their degrees and knowledge to help me with different aspects of this book, and I am ever grateful.

I wish to thank Melissa Newman and Denise Melton of Martin Sisters Publishing for their expertise and for taking a chance on an unknown. I promise to make it a good choice. I thank author Mark D. Williams, who has been a true mentor for me for the last five years. I don't know that I will ever be able to fully repay him for all the time and effort he has spent on me, though I will try. If you make it over to Oklahoma I promise to take you fishing. I also want to thank author and editor Kathy Papajohn who has taught me a lot about writing through the editing process. She was able to see past all of my manuscript's shortcomings and envision a much finer product. I would like to thank author Karen Robbins who offered a ton of helpful hints. I especially want to thank Rachel Rhodes who served for four years as my teen perspective. She is a budding writer herself, and it's only a matter of time before I'm seeing her work in print.

Jason Hicks of Jason J. Hicks photography is not only excellent at what he does, but anyone willing to wet-wade in northern Oklahoma river water in December to get the perfect photograph is pretty great, and I appreciate him. I would like to thank Ryan Burkett, computer guru, for helping me with all my computer questions, and for all my co-workers for all of their support. Brent

McCoy, a former DJ for The House FM, read over the radio scenes in this novel and let me know if I got the lingo right. My thanks go out to him. Finally I want to thank all the students I have ever taught. I can see "Vincent" in so many of you, so hopefully I have been your mentor when you needed it. For anybody I might have forgotten, please forgive me. I'll catch you next time.

Chapter 1

Vincent Preston never liked baked beans. He just couldn't overcome the texture. Covered in a brown ooze, firm on the outside, and mushy on the inside, no amount of Bar-B-Q sauce could improve his outlook. It was the same with oatmeal for Vincent. Back in grade school, the only breakfast item his mother kept on hand was instant oatmeal. Again, it was an issue of texture. Whether it was flavored with maple, cinnamon, or adorned with little dehydrated chunks of Granny Smith apples, the feeling of muck in his mouth was akin to stepping in quicksand. Once it was in his mouth, swallowing it was essentially a practice in suppressing the gag reflex.

Now at eighteen, the thought slapped him right across the face like one of his dad's backhands, two memories long ago repressed out of necessity. But before he could lose his nerve, he bravely scooped up four baked beans, dirt-brown sauce dripping off the fork onto what appeared to be a remnant of fatty pork on his plate, and he quickly shoved them in and swallowed without the slightest thought of mastication. If he were to ever be interrogated with the threat of baked beans held against him, and his life were at stake, he was a goner.

He looked over at the popular table just in time to see Bacon Bob scoop a mountain of beans into his mouth.

Someone at the table must have said something funny because his big mouth came open in laughter and a torrent of chewed up bean shrapnel exploded forth. It sent everyone ducking for cover.

Vincent knew that Bacon Bob Rogers would eat anything that didn't eat him first, but he loved baked beans the best. He once told the baseball team during pre-game stretches that he would swim in a pool of beans, especially Bar-B-Q beans. Bacon Bob also had a problem with flatulence. After having declared his love, he had reached down to touch his toes and released one so loud it sounded like it came over the loud speaker. Its resonance had reverberations past just the world of sound. And when the smell hit the inner-circle of starters (the very kids who were now sitting at the popular table) it sent the entire team to the infield turf, gasping for breath.

This memory made Vincent chuckle. Despite his idiosyncrasies, Bacon Bob was a good guy. He just hung around with the wrong crowd. Everybody loved him like a kid loves a puppy dog in a store window and persuades his mother to take it home. Vincent knew that sometimes this bothered Bob because he felt he could never be taken seriously, but it was the world Bob created and Bob had to live with it.

Vincent looked back down at his plate and pushed a solitary bean from one side of his plate to the other with his fork, leaving a trail of the brown ooze behind like a slug on a sidewalk. He impaled it and threw it in his mouth, choking it down only for its carbohydrate value, and chasing it with his iced tea. He needed all the energy he could muster for tonight. His hamburger was gone. He had eaten it up in a flash and would have asked for another had he not been concerned about it weighing him down for the big game. Coach Grey always said meat just sat in your stomach like a brick.

The Augusta High School Stampeding Herd baseball team was to play its first game in defense of its state title. Vincent wasn't much a part of that state title team. Oh sure, he was on the roster, but he seldom got the chance to prove himself on the field. The coach would substitute him in right field in the sixth inning when the game was out of hand so he could rest his starters. When given the chance, he got on base more often than not, but his lack of capability didn't sit well with the coach. During moments when the games' outcomes were foregone conclusions, Coach Grey could usually be found chatting with the starters on the bench, or glad-handing a parent or reporter. That was all going to change this year.

This year Vincent was a senior and he somehow managed to break into the starting line-up. This first goal accomplished, he set his sights on leading the team in batting average. He knew what Coach Grey thought of him. Coach Grey only cared about one person, his son Jimmy. Jimmy was Coach Grey's retirement plan. Coach Grey really couldn't care about the rest of the team. He liked winning, and as for left field, Vincent knew that Coach Grey was merely making the best of a bad situation by putting Vincent there.

At least Vincent had a strong arm. He could throw from the left field warning track, marked 297 feet on the monster fence, all the way to the plate without bouncing it once. In this regard, very few ballplayers could match his prowess, again, not that the coaches ever noticed. But his arm strength wasn't the problem. He had no accuracy. He was pure raw talent, with the emphasis on *raw*. Instead of a line drive, the ball took on a NASA trajectory and would land like space junk or a meteorite, usually half-way down either the first or third baseline. Vincent had worked on his skills since this first happened.

When others were out taking turns cruising Broadway on icy January weekends in Jimmy Grey's new Corvette, Vincent was toting his burlap bag of fraying baseballs to the fence. He would drag the concession stand trash can down the hill behind the backstop and place it on its side at home plate, open end facing the left field fence. He would then practice his aim, managing to hit the trash can one out of every twenty-five throws. He rarely put one inside the cylinder at all. No screaming fans, no newspaper reporters, no TV cameras, no encouragement. The only spectators to visit him were the bitter north wind and a hope that practice would eventually pay off. But by the time the first tulips were popping their heads out of the earth, Vincent was hitting the can more and more frequently.

The fact that he fell into the starting position by default didn't bother him. The glass had to be half-full for a regular kid with lethargic parents to be able to succeed in a town known for its loud, obnoxious... *caring* parents. Even when a fellow player's mom would scream from the stands to have him taken out for booting a ball, Vincent wouldn't let anyone else dictate who he was or how hard he tried. All he was concerned about was making the best of a golden opportunity and today the means to that end meant eating beans.

Vincent sat at a table littered with underclassmen, none of whom would see considerable playing time, none who dared talk. They all knew better. They all knew that if they appeared at all confident in themselves, it would be seen as arrogance, and Coach Grey had special punishment for players who thought they were better than the rest of the team. It involved railroad ties and lunges. It didn't take but one trip of lunges around the bases with a railroad tie on a person's shoulders to convince him that modesty was the only way to go. Vincent had wanted to sit at the popular table, *the varsity table,* Vincent corrected himself, but he lacked the confidence to sit with such a close-knit group of guys. They probably didn't even know his name anyway. Segregation was held in high regard with Coach Grey. He didn't like his starters having anything to do with the bench warmers.

Vincent looked across the banquet room at the community center. There was an excited buzz that ran the circumference of the room. The entire north wall was of a commemorative glass trophy case nearing its capacity. It was referred to as "Championship Row." The high school team had won nine state championships through the years. These trophies adorned the highest shelf, each with a brass plate stating the year and reading:

"Oklahoma State Summer League High School Baseball Champions."

All the trophies won from in-season tournaments sat on the lower shelves, bowing to the top shelf like peasants to a Caesar. The speaker's podium was placed right in front of Championship Row. On an empty table sat something big and cumbersome under a white sheet. Vincent knew what it was, and he could care less. After all, he had virtually no hand in winning the state tournament a year ago. He knew his legacy rested with the rest of the losers

NO! Non-starters! he had to remind himself

on the bench. Framed posters of past championship teams wrapped the other walls, complete with team picture, win-loss record, the scores of each game, and of course, the sponsors' names written in larger print.

Jimmy Grey and his buddies sat at one of the front tables cracking jokes and snarfing down food. Their loud voices could be heard above the rest of the crowd of players, parents, media, and happy community members who assembled not only for a good meal, but to hear the coach's first comments of the year.

Vincent didn't trust Coach Grey, who was never at a loss for words. Coach liked the sound of his own voice and was never too tired to talk to a member of the media or to fans. Talking to a bench warmer was another story.

The players at Jimmy's table were loose and confident, almost to the point of being cocky. They pigged out on hamburgers as Coach Grey sat at the radio media table, fork of beans in one hand and a microphone in the other. It was easy to see that he loved being the center of attention, and he managed to pass the quality onto Jimmy. Coach Grey's chest puffed out and he answered questions, taking no time away from his words to wink at one of the adoring parents at a back table.

Vincent looked back to his plate. Seventeen, eighteen, nineteen beans left. He impaled another and tossed it off much the way an old West cowboy would toss off a shot of whiskey, pretending to like it.

Milt Jackson, President of the Grand Slam Booster Club and father to Jake, the right fielder, walked up to the podium and tapped the mic with his hand a few times to make sure people could hear him. A feedback squeal emanated across the air and people covered their ears. From the back of the room, Jake's mom gave a thumbs-up sign, and Milt cleared the air.

"Ladies and Gentlemen, let me have your attention. Ladies, Gentlemen, please let me have your attention! We want to get this show on the road in enough time to get our boys out of here. They need to get ready for their game."

The crowd settled down. Those with their backs to the podium turned their chairs around, making horrible screeching noises across the polished wooden floor like 100 jumbo jets hitting their back thrusters while landing at LAX. Had the custodian been there, he would have turned green. Jimmy's table still had a few talkers, shushed down by Dusty Redenbacher, the third baseman. Jimmy kept on whispering.

"Okay. Thank you all for coming out this afternoon to share in our annual kick-off celebration. Before I get too far along, there are a few people we need to thank. Mildred Phillips spent many hours on the mountain of beans you see, or rather saw at the buffet table.

"Mildred, you gotta share your secret Bar-B-Q sauce!"

A middle-aged lady sitting toward the back of the room, in a blue knee-length dress pushed up her glasses and said, "You'll have to do a lot more than peer-pressure me, Milt!" and winked.

The crowd laughed as Milt blushed.

Vincent looked back at his plate. Fourteen, fifteen, sixteen more beans...

Milt collected himself and said, "Okay, okay. One of these years, maybe you'll tell us. Thanks Mildred! Also Dusty Sr. spent the last two hours burning the hair off his arms over the grill and we are thankful for him for that."

With the spatula still in his hands, Milt smiled and nodded.

Milt continued, "Also I would like to mention Myron's Meat Market and thank them for their wonderful contribution to tonight's feast. Seventy-five pounds of ground beef and we had to go back for more, so thanks to those good people. They wanted me to let you all know that they have new weekend hours. They are now open until 9:00 on Saturday nights for those last minute party needs.

"Okay, finally, thanks to all the parents who came here early and set up the tables. You are too numerous to thank individually. Okay. Um, this is always such a great night for me and for the rest of the community of Augusta. This is the thirty-fifth year we have started the season with a kick-off supper. I was here for the first one, as a fan of my older brother who was an all-state pitcher, but that's another story and I am sure I've told you all that before."

A few chuckles rose from the crowd, which appeared to be growing antsy.

"More special is the fact that for the first time in four long years, we are kicking the year off with a championship presentation. What lies under this cloth is a very special symbol of the hard work, dedication, and good attitude it takes to achieve such a grand, um... such a lofty goal. Would last year's seniors come up?"

Three young boys got up from Jimmy's table and made their way to the front.

The crowd of 100 plus people didn't just clap, but gave the three boys a standing ovation.

When the boys got to the podium and the applause died down, Milt said, "I'll let Brady Wright speak. Here you go son," and he handed the microphone to the tallest of the three boys.

The other two stood with their heads down, hands in their back pockets. Some of the crowd gossiped loud enough for Vincent to hear about how shaggy the three had let their hair get in college.

Brady said, "Well, I didn't have a speech prepared, since I've not ever been a part of this championship celebration," and paused, "but I guess I should say that last year was good. It was a fun time. Heck, we knew we had the talent to win, but it takes more than talent. It takes good, smart coaching to push the right buttons at the right time. Like when I was taken out in the seventh inning of the championship game and Jimmy came in and closed the door with three fastballs. Now, I would have stayed in, had I been given the choice, but that's why Coach is paid the big bucks!"

The crowd laughed.

"But seriously folks, this is the man who made this presentation possible. Please give a warm welcome to Coach Grey."

Everybody in the room stood, applauded, and whistled.

A tall, lanky man with a shock of black hair coming out the bottom of his blue ball cap with the big "H" on the front, sat in his chair for the first ten seconds until the applause got louder, or apparently loud enough to satisfy him. He stood, all six feet, four inches, and raised his index finger of his right hand in the air.

The applause got even louder. Whistles and cow bells appeared for the first of many times that night, and the place was alive with spirit.

Coach Grey slowly made his way to the podium, blue wind pants swishing with each step, giving a wink and a thumbs-up to someone on the front row, pausing just long enough for the local paper to snap a picture.

Vincent stood and applauded along with everyone else, but spent more time looking at his plate. Eight, nine, ten more beans...

Brady motioned for the crowd to quiet down.

Coach Grey stood with a jacket that matched his hat in both color and script. His pants matched the jacket to complete his tidy little ensemble. He kept his hands in his pockets, rocking up on the tips of his toes. His handlebar mustache had started to grey in the last few years, but remained silky black with the constant dye that, rumor had it, happened to find its way above his forehead as well.

"Thank you people," Brady said, and the crowd settled down. "Now Coach, as is tradition the year after winning a state championship, the seniors from the year before are to present the trophy." Brady reached down, pulled on the sheet and unveiled the tenth such trophy in the room.

Those in the room ooohhhed and aaahhhed. One untimely cowbell came out.

Picking the trophy up, Brady said, "Coach, thanks for all your guidance in helping us win this state championship," and he handed Coach the trophy.

The room erupted.

Coach Grey held the trophy high as flashbulbs illuminated the room. He hoisted it up over his head with both hands and smiled some more for the birdie. He was a good-looking man, appearing ten years younger than the big fifty his driver's license revealed him to be. He motioned for Jimmy's table to come to the front. The underclassmen at Vincent's table looked at each other in confusion, not knowing whether to get up with the rest of the team, or stay seated. They chose the latter out of fear. They were following Vincent's example.

I start left field, Vincent thought, and stood in purgatory before sitting also.

Jimmy stood near his father and the rest of the upperclassmen piled into the picture. The old folks said he was a direct reflection of what Coach Grey used to look like. Jimmy was still growing, now six-foot, two inches and in prime, slender shape. Jimmy had his blue ball cap pulled down low over his eyes, so he had to look up slightly to see the crowd. Coach Grey offered the trophy to Jimmy as father and son stood together in a room of admirers, each with a hand on the coveted prize.

The applause rose even more. The players behind Coach clapped out of respect.

Once things quieted again, Coach Grey let Jimmy hold the trophy and addressed the crowd.

With their notebooks and tape recorders, the small-town paparazzi knelt before the stage, poised.

"Thank y'all for comin' out. This is the reason I stay here in Augusta instead of moving on to a college coaching position or getting into professional managin'. It's you. So give yourselves a hand. C'mon!" and he clapped.

Another back-patting applause rose, and settled down quickly.

"There's a reason we don't add the state champ trophy at the end of the year. The kids all know this, because I harp on it all off-season. I harp on 'em during football season and I harp on 'em in the weight room. I do a lot of harping!"

Polite laughter and another cow bell rang out. Coach continued, "I harp on the fact that last year's last year and there's no reason to lament on what we'd done in the past because the past's the past and I'm a firm believer in the present and the future. We take this trophy tonight and place it on Championship Row to remind ourselves that that was last year and this is this year, and we are governed by the same goals's the year before."

People nodded their heads in agreement.

"What I see in the off-season is enough to make my heart explode. I continually saw a few of our players, even in the dead of winter, working on their mechanics, throwing, hitting, ya name it, out in the barren cold of our beloved stadium."

For a moment, Vincent thought the coach was talking about him. He was trying to figure out what to do when the coach called his name for a round of applause. Should he just stand? Butterflies invaded his lower stomach. A sickly fear pulled at his entrails and he became aware for the first time that he had to use the bathroom.

"Will you please give a hand to Coach Redenbacher's son Dusty, and to a ball player I think we all know puts in the extra hours to get it done, my son Jimmy!"

Vincent thought, *What!?! Are you kidding me!?!*

The crowd stood and applauded yet again.

Jimmy took off his hat and held it in the air for everybody as Dusty lowered his head, apparently out of embarrassment. Vincent knew why. While Vincent was out there every day, Dusty and Jimmy showed up just once, and their pictures were coincidentally caught by the newspaper photographer with a caption that read,

Dusty Redenbacher and Jimmy Grey show their dedication to summer baseball by putting in the extra effort in the winter. They exemplify the reason why Augusta won the State Championship last year.

Vincent stood with the rest of the bench warmers and just shook his head.

"Now before we do put the trophy away, my son Jimmy has an announcement." Coach stepped aside and Jimmy, who was still holding the trophy, took the microphone.

17

Without looking up, Jimmy said, "Hey everybody. I just wanted to let you know I decided on my college to play ball at next year."

The crowd all sucked in one collective anticipatory breath. Augusta's son. Jimmy All-American. Their hope for the future. The ticket to putting their great town on the map.

"California is a nice state and I liked Georgia just fine, but when it came down to it, I couldn't turn down the chance at a national championship while playing in my back yard. At least until I get drafted high enough, Coach Milford and the University of North Central Oklahoma over in Ponca City will pick up my tuition tab next year."

The crowd once again gave a standing ovation. More whistles came and the cowbells jangled. Had balloons been held in a net on the ceiling and confetti been prepared, things would have gotten messy.

Jimmy Grey was Augusta's son. Jimmy Grey could do no wrong. Jimmy Grey was what every parent hoped his and her kids would amount to. The perfect coach and the perfect son held the trophy together one more time for pictures and then turned to place it on Championship Row. None of the other players got a chance to touch it.

Having placed the Holy Grail up on Championship Row, Coach and son raised their arms in the air, index fingers lifted.

The crowd kept up the applause and cow bells for five minutes. Last year's seniors quietly exited the stage, keeping their hands in their pockets. The others on stage followed suit while father and son had their fifteen minutes of fame and glory.

The media kept Coach Grey and Jimmy for sound-bites.

The crowd left in anticipation of the night's big game with Woodward's AAA team.

Vincent left quietly, stopping by the trashcan to throw his empty paper plate in the trash.

Chapter 2

Less than an hour later, the starters, in full uniform, sat in a circle just beyond first base stretching and shooting the bull. Bacon Bob was in full form already, loaded with Mrs. Phillips baked beans. Bob knew his teammates were going to need some comic relief from the tension of the first game of the year, so he prepared himself to entertain.

The cottonwood trees beyond the right field fence that led downhill to the town's park were past the stage of budding and were now progressing toward their full summer coat. Mixed in front of the tall cottonwoods that had stood nearly 100 years was a stand of shorter white-barked birch. Spaced evenly planted every thirty feet in front of the birch were red buds, in full bloom. The view from home plate was breathtaking for fans and horticulturalists alike.

The stadium was at the pinnacle in town, carved out of Prospect Hill, the only hill in Augusta at that. The green course of the outfield spread to the chain-link fence, 330 feet in right, 375 in dead center and 297 in left. It was this left field fence that was a main attraction, its calling card around the state. Its creators back in the 1950's modeled it after the Green Monster at Boston's Fenway Park. Besides being not far from home plate, it was twenty-five feet tall, where the rest of the fence was only eight feet tall, just low enough for Jimmy to snare a would-be home run. The left field fence was no green monster, but line drives that were home runs at other parks were turned into doubles at the stadium.

Anyone who played at the stadium knew it as the "Little Monster."

Bob looked out toward the Little Monster and smiled. Nine wooden pennants adorned the top of the fence, marking the past championships. They started on the foul pole and worked their way south toward left-center field. People also called this Championship Row for no other reason than a lack of originality. A tenth pennant was covered up with a blanket and some ropes dangling down for the pre-game presentation. Carroll Avenue lined the monster's wall and crept the length downhill to the town's park and swimming pool. Before doing so, the fence curved back to the west toward right field and its neighboring forest.

Across the street stood a yellow two story house. It was a goal of batters to hit the house with a home run, but the only ones to do so in recent memory were "Clodhopper" Bill Jones, the present first baseman, and, of course, Jimmy Grey. Jimmy even broke the living room window once. Officials measured the shot at 411 feet and it was at this point that coaches from all over started ringing his phone off the hook.

On the third-base side behind the dugout was an area carved out of the hill, used as a pre-game warm-up area and a bullpen. After snowstorms would cancel school, kids would sled from the parking lot at the top of the grassy hill, down to the bullpen area in the winter. Many parents would watch the game from the top parking lot behind the backstop. It afforded a bird's-eye view of the entire field. The others who didn't get there in time to park in these coveted spots would have to park up the street and sit in the concrete stands along the first-base side. By high school standards, this was a beautiful field, especially after new sod was laid in the off-season.

Having won the state tournament the year before, they now had the right to host it this year with an automatic invite. This gave the team even more incentive to defend their state title, especially since they won it last year on their arch-rival's field.

Seiling's field consisted of land donated by an oil company that made spills a part of its business. So not only did home run balls bounce off oil rigs, the infield was hard and oil-stained and was an infielder's nightmare.

Bob, and the whole team, knew to wear their athletic supporters and cups to keep from singing soprano after a bad hop. And sliding was totally out of the question.

As the guys stretched, Vincent jogged laps around the outfield fence. Bob had made little notice of this last year, but now that Vincent was a starter, he took note.

Bob knew that most of the players didn't even know his name, but now that he was a part of the starting lineup, Bob hoped they accepted Vincent. After all, team chemistry was important. There were only two open spots after graduation last year, second base and left field. Brady Flowers played left when he wasn't pitching, and Kenneth Gonzales played second. Both graduated and the third graduate, Francis Gothinger, never played at all.

Eleven boys stopped their stretches to watch Vincent make his way past the 375 sign in center.

"Man, what does he think he has to prove?" Jimmy broke the silence. "We already know he doesn't have a car and has to run to practice. So why does he have to run around the outfield and make us all look bad?"

"Maybe that's how your dad noticed him, by his work ethic," Dusty Redenbacher said. Dusty's dad was an assistant coach, usually the first base coach in charge of mundane tasks like hitting fly balls to the outfielders.

"No, it's to make him feel special. Now that he cracked the lineup he has to act all macho," Jimmy insisted.

Bob didn't like what he was hearing, so he took this time to unleash. *fuuuuuurrrrrttttttttt!*

The entire team recoiled as Bacon Bob took center stage.

"CB! Can't you hold it in long enough to spare us?" Quentin Albany asked.

Bob liked Quentin a lot. Quentin didn't talk much, but when he did, people listened. He was on the fast track to college, literally. He had accepted a scholarship to run track at the University of North Central Oklahoma, the 100 meter and the 200 meter. His 100 time was nearing the low ten second mark. In baseball, Quentin was a natural short stop. His smooth motions and heads-up play landed him a spot on the all-state team along with Jimmy. There were only about four black families in town, and the team had two of the kids: Quentin and "Clodhopper" Bill Jones. Both Quentin and Bill were respected in their baseball family, but they were only two of a handful of black kids who managed to break the racial code in town.

Bob gave this topic some thought and concluded that the townsfolk weren't racist, but there was still a small contingent of important people who pulled the strings, and they didn't make life very easy for anyone who wasn't white. For a minority to be accepted by everyone, he had to be a terrific athlete at his respected sport.

Bob also had a lot of respect for Bill Jones. Bill had a bunch of nicknames, but "Clodhopper" was his most publicly recognized. He was six feet, seven inches tall and weighed 285 pounds. Everyone in town called him Clodhopper, and Bob knew Bill didn't mind because there was a funny story behind the name.

During a high school game Bill's freshmen year, in his first high school at-bat no less, he came off the bench during a blowout and forgot to lace up his size sixteen shoes when he got to the plate. On the first pitch, he belted it into the trees beyond right field. He went into his slow, emotionless trot, and when he rounded first, his right shoe came flying off, hitting the first baseman right in the hands. He stopped, turned around, thought about what he should do next, looked at second and finally went back toward first where the first baseman handed him his shoe, much to the crowd's heavy laughter. But as soon as he pushed off with his left shoe, it came flying off also!

The home crowd laughed even harder while Bob and his teammates were rolling on the ground in the dugout. They got such a kick out of Bill picking up his clodhoppers and carrying them both around the bases that the nickname stuck.

Jimmy, who was already a starter at that point, called him Chocolate Thunder for his ability to mistreat a ball with a bat. Bill appeared comfortable with this nickname around them. It seemed to ease the racial tension, but Bob knew that secretly Bill just wished he could blend in and not be singled out, praise or scorn.

"Sorry guys!" Bacon Bob blurted out. "When they come, they come. You want me to hold them in? I'll burst and cover you all in liquid blubber!"

The whole team recoiled again. If there was one thing Bob Rogers knew he was good for, it was a laugh. They called him Bacon Bob because he once made the regrettable mistake late at night after a game of saying that he could go for a pound of raw bacon, right then and there.

Bacon Bob was a freshman at the time, and loved by the seniors, as evidenced by their willingness to kid him mercilessly. The nickname was born and stuck. For as big as he was though, he could run pretty fast and the first baseman didn't want to get in his way when he came barreling through the bag because it would take forty feet of landing strip to slow him down.

The year before one first baseman from Stillwater had the misfortune of reaching for a poorly thrown ball from the third baseman and about the time the ball hit leather, he found himself in the baseline.

Bacon Bob hit him and the poor sucker went flying into Dusty's dad in the first-base coaching box. For this same reason, Bob was an all-state selection in football at center and nose guard.

Bob was normally pretty quiet. He figured that he was sort of like having a pet around, for entertainment purposes. His bleach-blond hair was always kept short in a crew cut and his cheeks looked like two red water balloons being squished by a constant smile- one of those grins that lets you know he either did something he shouldn't have, or he was about to say something funny. He had two chins. The top one had a circular patch of blond hair he kept neatly trimmed. The bottom chin resembled another balloon, though this one was much larger, much more defined, and pushed his goatee up his face. He would joke around sometimes about having a cantaloupe stuck in his throat. It always made the kids laugh, but Bob sometimes wished he were just another person.

Jimmy held his nose and spoke, "Dad said he didn't have a choice but to put that grease stain in left. He didn't want to hurt the pitchers' arms by making them throw the ball from the fence." And as Vincent slowed to a trot in front of the starting lineup stretch circle, Jimmy said, "Here, let me prove it. Hey! Vince! Come over here and join the team!"

*

Vincent, with his hands on his hips and catching his breath, walked to the circle. Nobody moved out of the way to let him in, which bothered Vincent.

Vincent knew that Coach Grey made it a point to separate the starting lineup from the backups, even in stretching, making the backups stretch out by the right field fence. Coach Grey was afraid they would infect the starters with bad luck. Vincent was secretly happy to move up to the starters crowd.

Vincent stood there waiting for someone to move for him so he could join the circle, and when nobody did, he said, "Hey, what's up guys?"

"Yeah," Jimmy said with a wry grin, "you excited for the first game? Woodward isn't a pushover. They're triple-A. Besides, with our pitching staff, you're liable to get plenty of action in left." One of the pitchers pulled some grass and flung it at Jimmy.

The wind caught it and peppered Bacon Bob, who immediately sneezed and at the same time farted again.

Vincent cracked a smile with the others and replied, "Well, I reckon I'll be ready. Just gotta loosen up my legs."

Jimmy smiled. "Yeah, can't be too loose." A few guys snickered and looked at Vincent, as if to wait for a retort. Vincent knew Jimmy was just waiting for the right moment to pounce. When Vincent didn't say a word, Jimmy drew his sword.

Jimmy looked directly at Vincent and said, "You know, my legs are a little tight. Will you show me the proper way to run a lap in order to get the blood flowing. Will you do that for me? Model another lap?"

Where is this going? Why is he singling me out? Vincent's thoughts were in a turmoil.

Everybody looked at him, and he looked at Jimmy.

Jimmy's expression never changed. He was as serious as Bacon Bob with a bad case of constipation.

Vincent felt estranged. This was the first time Jimmy Grey had ever talked to him. "Well, you just... jog, ya know?" Vincent said, shrugging.

"No, I don't know. I don't waste my energy unless it's to rob a home run or hit one. But then again, I guess that's why I have been a starter for four years and have a scholarship next year. I guess that's also why the Red Birds have been ringing my phone off the hook." Jimmy thought a second and said, "No, it's because I am not a loser. Hmmm. Jog you say? Well I gotta good idea. If you aren't going to jog a lap for me, for us starters, why don't you just jog over to that circle in right field where you belong, because even though you're starting in left field, you are still a loser in our book."

Vincent just stood there. He couldn't tell if Jimmy was joking or not. When nobody said anything, Vincent did an about-face and jogged to the silent underclassmen circle to stretch. His face turned red. On the way he heard Bacon Bob let out another audible *fuuuuurrrrrtttt.* The guys couldn't contain themselves.

What a bunch of jerks, Vincent thought. *Don't let it affect you. You are the right man for the job. You'll show them! Just do your job. Jimmy is the coach's son and is untouchable. If you lose your cool, you'll be off the team. You'll show them on the field! You'll show them tonight!*

Dusty and a few others didn't laugh, didn't find that the least bit funny. Vincent turned around and saw Dusty's face turn as red as his hair in embarrassment.

Vincent wondered why Dusty didn't stand up for him and say something to stop Jimmy's harassment. Leaders like Dusty weren't supposed to let this kind of stuff fragment the team.

Vincent wanted to say something, just one thing to Jimmy like, "C'mon, Jimmy! You've got a gift. You will someday be playing professional ball, and you drive around in a Corvette for cryin' out loud. Do you have to be a big jerk also?" Of course, Vincent didn't say anything. The sound of an approaching diesel engine kept the thought from becoming words.

Everybody turned toward the Little Monster to peer at Carroll Avenue. A big red bus motored up Carroll Avenue and into view.

*

At the same moment Coach Grey walked up to his starters. He had been in the parking lot behind the bleachers making friends with his whiskey bottle and a few of his buddies on the local newspaper staff. "What is going on here? I count ten guys. I see all my pitchers, which means we're missin' a position player. Who we missin'? And for cryin' out loud! What in the tarnation is that smell?"

"Bob's beans," someone said and everybody started laughing again.

Coach chuckled inside, then caught himself and said in a gruff voice, "Well that answers one o' my questions, but who's missin'? Who's going to be runnin' laps after the game for being late?"

Jimmy spoke up. "That would be your starting left fielder. He decided he's too good for our group. He was late and just snuck in with the other group," and he pointed toward the right field fence where the others sat without talking. "Not much of a team player if you ask me."

Coach Grey looked out toward the right field fence and saw #58, Vincent, sitting with his back to the infield, doing the butterfly stretch. Every few seconds Vincent turned around and looked at him. "Hmmm," Coach Grey said, "Once a loser, always a loser. You guys see that? That's right. That's not a team player. You need to let him know that kinda behavior won't be tolerated! I trust you'll do the job?"

"Yes Coach!" most of them barked in unison.

Coach Grey cupped his hand to his mouth to make sure the mouthwash covered the smell of his whiskey. He eyed the outfield group again and clapped his hands together. "Starters! Take the infield. Let's get some B.P. in before those guys from Woodward get off their bus. This is our field! Fuzzy! You're playing left tonight!"

"Yes, Coach!" Fred Fingers barked. He was the third pitcher in the rotation. Coach only used him on windy days because he was a knuckleballer. His knuckleball pitches would baffle the opposing hitters, dancing all over the place as the surface area of the non-spinning ball reacted with the air it plowed through. He only threw fifty miles an hour tops, but that was more than fast enough when the batters' eyes turned fuzzy trying to look at what appeared to be two or sometimes three balls floating, rising, and dropping.

"Well, let's get a move on!"

"YEAH!!!" the guys yelled and jumped up.

Coach looked out toward right field to see Vincent running in, apparently to join his teammates. Coach stopped him at first base before Vincent could get to the dugout.

"Son, where have you been?" Coach Grey questioned Vincent. "The other boys have been stretching and getting ready to play a ballgame."

"Coach-" Vincent began, but was cut off short by his coach.

"I thought you'd take this opportunity a little more seriously, but I guess I was wrong. Start runnin'."

"But Coach-"

"What did I just say? You want to play on this team, you better take off. Run till I get tired!"

"Yes, sir!"

*

By 5:30 Vincent noticed that all the spots in the preferred parking lot had been filled for an hour and the latecomers (5:30 was late for a 6:00 game) were filling in the stands. Others who didn't want to be disturbed by the incessant chatter of others laid their respective blankets on the sledding hill and enjoyed a panoramic view of the field.

The loudspeakers blared the oldies from KBAL, the local AM radio station. Presently Simon and Garfunkle were belting out "Bridge over Troubled Water." The infielders whipped the ball around the infield simulating double plays in silky smooth fashion.

5-4-3,

6-4-3,

4-6-3,

3-6-1

"Greasy" Gabe Conway with his deft sliders and tight curve balls got the start pitching. He moved into the #1 pitching slot after Brady Wright vacated it last year when he graduated.

Gabe ran to first to complete the difficult 3-6-1 double play, Jones to Albany to Conway, and the infield looked to be in mid-season form.

Coach Grey looped fly balls to the outfield who came up gunning to second base.

Jimmy caught one behind his back which led to oohhs and aahhs from the crowd and a proud smile from Papa.

And behind the outfield fence ran the penitent Vincent Preston, watching the whole scene.

The temperature spiked at the start of the game, a balmy ninety-five degrees with eighty percent humidity. Vincent, following the coach's orders, looked over his shoulder toward left field where Fuzzy clumsily heaved the ball from the warning track toward second base, hopping it three times and ten feet off to the third-base side of the bag. He didn't have a strong arm at all. That's why he was a knuckleballer.

Woodward's players, dressed in all red, leaned against the fence with hands and fingers curled into fists, waiting to take the field.

Coach Grey kept his team on the field until 5:47 before he waved them into the dugout with the rest of the backups. Gabe took the bullpen mound and Bacon Bob warmed him up. Not after being on the field for three minutes, KBAL stopped in the middle of Elvis' rendition of "Suspicious Minds" and the announcer came on.

"Test, test, test, 1...2...3...- this thing working? Okay, welcome to another year of the defending State Champion Augusta Stampeding Herd Baseball!"

Cheers erupted from the crowd.

"Tonight's game is sponsored by Joe's Petro. Remember Joe's for all your automotive needs. Joe is running a special this week: one free bratwurst with every oil change. Sign up at the concession stand. Joe is proud to sponsor Stampeding Herd Baseball. That's Joe's Petro. Alright, for tonight's starting lineup. First for the Woodward Angels, leading off in left field..."

Vincent finished his tenth lap, and he felt that he was visibly exhausted. Besides running a mile to the stadium from his house, and his warm up laps, he was now forced to run because of a misunderstanding, all on account of Jimmy Grey.

And none of the other starters stuck up for me, Vincent thought.

Vincent felt the sweat drip down his chest and under the sleeves of his grey uniform. His hat, saturated, had been taken off five laps ago. His cleats clacked on the pavement behind the stands as he passed them, fighting his way through a thick crowd again. He passed the stands and looked up the rows again. No sign of his parents. He scanned the parking lot and saw no trace of his parent's wood-paneled 1985 Ford Station Wagon. He had had plenty of laps to look.

Vincent burned inside. *My first start and they still won't come. Just as well. Looks like Coach forgot about me.*

Now behind the dugout, he looked over to see Coach lecturing his players. Some sat, intent on his words, while others, including his son, talked and even seemed to be laughing.

The P.A. announcer continued, "The Angels come into this ballgame with a 5-0 record, fresh off a championship at the Ulysses, Kansas Pre-season Invitational. And now ladies and gentlemen, what you've all been waiting for: the starting lineup for YOUR STAMPEDING HERD!"

More cheers erupted and a cannon went off somewhere in the vicinity of the water tower behind the upper parking lot. Horns honked. A few babies started crying.

"Leading off, your right fielder with a three ten average and eighteen stolen bases last year, a guy with blazing speed and a golden glove, double Oh, JAKE JACKSON!"

Vincent heard the crowd cheer.

"In the two hole, playing third base, he was a .421 hitter last year with twelve home runs and sixty RBI's, number thirty-three, DUSTEEEEY REDENBACKER."

Vincent heard even louder cheers.

"AND OUR STAR, A PLAYER WHO REALLY DOESN'T NEED AN INTRODUCTION, HE'S YOUR CENTER FIELDER. HE BATTED SIX TEN LAST YEAR WITH *TWENTY-TWO* HOME RUNS AND *SEVENTY-FIVE* RBI'S. HE WILL BE PLAYING FOR THE UNIVERSITY OF NORTH CENTRAL OKLAHOMA NEXT YEAR, *NUMBER ONE ON HIS BACK AND IN OUR HEARTS, JIMEEEEEEEEEY GREY!!!*"

Vincent heard the sound of cow bells and whistles, applause and more applause coming from the home team crowd.

A cannon blasted again.

The parade lasted the better part of a minute, in which time Jimmy stepped out of the dugout to wave to the crowd, an encore move usually reserved for home run applause.

The crowd didn't seem to care about his breach in etiquette. Vincent understood that the crowd probably didn't know better. They cheered on lustily as the Woodward players stared in disbelief and hatred.

Vincent figured Woodward's players had to be mad as Vincent's teammates shagged fly balls and made routine plays, not giving their opponents any time to warm up. Their head coach even seemed to be taking notes in the dugout.

Vincent, who was beyond the right field fence for the eleventh time, suddenly fell to his knees and vomited the remains of the hamburger and those detested baked beans. He didn't know if it was from the running, the heat, or from Jimmy. Probably all three, but he couldn't get up.

"Batting clean-up at the catcher position, he hit a team-leading twenty-five bombs last year, number ninety-nine, 'BAAAAAAACON BOB ROGERS."

The crowd applauded.

"Batting fifth, he hit three thirty-three last year with seventeen home runs, first baseman, number forty-four, 'CLODHOOOOPPPPPEEERRR' BILL JONES."

The crowd applauded each player as he was introduced, but the crowd's enthusiasm was starting to wane and the applause got less and less strong as each remaining player was announced.

"Batting sixth, the starting pitcher, number five, 'Greasy' Gabe Conway.

"Seventh, with twelve stolen bases, short stop, number twenty-three, Quentin Albany.

"Batting in the eighth spot, second baseman, number twenty-one, Seth Short," and without pausing for applause, "and batting ninth in the line-up in left field, number fifty-eight, Vincent Preston."

At this Vincent looked up, grass in his hair, only to be disappointed.

"Correction. Batting ninth in left field, number forty, 'Fuzzy' Fred Fingers."

The crowd applauded this correction. Vincent put his head back down, narrowly missing his own vomit.

The P.A. announcer said, "Now if everyone would look toward left field we have a very special presentation." The crowd quieted.

Vincent realized that everybody, even the announcer prescribed to Coach's unsportsmanlike attitude. This was an apparent attempt to throw the visitors off their rhythm. "Under the Little Monster is Milt Jackson, the President of the Grand Slam Club. With no further ado, the championship pennant of the Oklahoma State Summer League High School! Your State Champions, the Augusta Stampeding Herd!" Everybody stood, clapped and rang cowbells. Milt gave a swift yank on the tarp and unveiled the tenth wooden pennant to adorn the top of the Little Monster. Ten cannon booms went off in succession. In big, bold letters it read:

AUGUSTA SUMMER LEAGUE

HIGH SCHOOL STATE CHAMPIONS 2012

The poor Woodward left fielder looked like he didn't know whether to shag a fly ball or turn and salute. On another day, Vincent would have cared.

"Now, would everybody rise for the singing of our national anthem by Miss Sabrina Morris," The P.A. announcer said, and everyone in the crowd stood up.

The Woodward players were still on the field practicing double plays. They hadn't had a chance to take batting practice and weren't half-way done with infield practice.

The hitting coach behind home plate, getting ready to swing the bat to hit his infielders a ground ball, turned in disbelief as a pretty young blond in blue jeans and a white blouse strolled over to him with a microphone. He moved for her reluctantly.

The Augusta players were already in a single-line formation along first base, and the Woodward players searched for the flag beyond the center field fence. Some of the players even forgot to take their hats off in the confusion.

"Ohhhhh Say Can You See..."

At that moment, an underclassman ran up to Vincent's heaving body and stopped, turned, put his cap over his heart, and said, "Vincent, you gotta get up now! Coach wants you in the dugout!"

Vincent slowly rose.

"Ohhh Saaaaay Does That Star Spangled..."

Vincent, with his hat already in his right hand, placed it above his heart, and then bent over and dry-heaved.

Vincent looked at the underclassman. He put his fist to his face and looked to be suppressing the gag reflex.

"AND THE HOOOOOOOOOME OF THE BRRRRRAAAAAAAAAVE!"

At the close of the national anthem, the crowd applauded politely.

The underclassman grimaced and said, "Dude, you alright?"

Vincent gave it some thought.

If I could get my hands around Jimmy's neck I would be really good. Maybe even bash Coach's head into Jimmy's a few times. That would be nice.

While bent over, Vincent re-tied his left shoe. "I'll be fine. You say Coach wants me over there now?"

"That's what he said, and something about not being on the team if you don't get over there now. Seemed pretty mad!"

At this point, Vincent thought, *I don't really care.*

The Stampeding Herd took the field, kicking-off the opposition. Woodward's hitting coach threw the bat he was holding toward his dugout and started in with the umps, prompting the head coach to take to his feet too.

The umps looked bewildered, checking their watches and putting their arms in the air, as if to say, *I don't know?*

The crowd of five hundred caught on fast and started booing the two opposing coaches.

The Woodward players slowly walked off the field, turning every-so-often to yell something else.

Vincent made his way to the dugout. He still had grass stuck to his right cheek from lying in the grass after running as long as he could.

He walked past Coach Grey, who was up on the steps of the dugout with his arms crossed at his chest, observing his players. This was Coach's normal look when he was trying to be critical.

When Vincent sat down, one of the underclassmen pointed to Vincent's cheek, and he wiped it.

Woodward was good. In fact, they were very good.

Vincent knew it was Coach Grey's intention to play mind games with the Woodward coaches and players. Get them ticked-off. Not giving them enough time for infield and not giving them any batting practice.

Vincent also knew that the coach's tactics were just beginning.

Coach Grey made an appeal at each of the three bases throughout the first game. He accused the Woodward players of leaving early when tagging-up on sacrifice fly balls. He accused the second pitcher in the fifth inning of throwing spit balls. Five pitches later, he accused him of scuffing up the ball with a nail file. He was merciless and got into a shouting match with Woodward's head coach right on the pitching mound.

After the opposing pitcher practically had to strip in order to show that he had no foreign objects with which to scuff up the ball, the game proceeded.

The Augusta fans all agreed that they were proud to have a coach who was savvy enough to watch for anything those cheating Woodward players and coaches tried to pull.

And it worked. Augusta won the first game 5-3, mostly behind Gabe Conway's complete game and his curveball.

Conway let a few get away, and he gave up a two-run monster shot that landed in Carroll Avenue and bounced into the front yard of the yellow house.

Besides a sacrifice fly (one that Coach Grey argued, saying the kid tagging up had left third base too early) and a few other scattered hits, Gabe pitched a gem.

Vincent watched the whole game from the dugout, woozy and weak. He watched Fred Fingers limp the ball into the infield on the sacrifice fly that tied the game in the sixth, a throw he knew he could have made.

Of course, there was Jimmy. Jimmy stole the show going 3-3 with a home run. He was intentionally walked in the seventh inning of a 3-3 tie, only to see Bacon Bob crush the next pitch over the center field fence for the dramatic win.

Between games, the players mingled with their girlfriends or parents in the stands while Vince went up to the concession stand to get a hot dog.

Despite his illness before the game, he was starving and felt weak. None of the spectators parted way for him so he could get his food and get back to the field, but as soon as a girl announcing herself as Jimmy's girlfriend showed up, the crowd parted like the Red Sea to let her get to the front. Even Vincent moved for her, not wanting to start an argument he wouldn't win.

By the time he got the hot dog and stuffed it down his face, the players, minus Jimmy, were back in the dugout and stretching out their arms.

Vincent looked up and saw that Jimmy sat up in the stands with his blond girlfriend, casually finishing his hot dog, taking time in-between bites to steal a kiss. When the players took the field for game two, Vincent was still on the bench. He chose this time to talk to Coach.

"Coach?" he asked as Coach Grey took his normal position on the steps. Coach Grey didn't seem to hear Vincent, so he beckoned again.

"Coach, can I have a word with you?"

Coach Grey looked pained to have to turn around and talk to a non-starter. "What do you want, slacker?"

Vincent was astounded by the coach's words. *Slacker?!*

Vincent took this in stride and said, "I would like to prove to you that I can play."

"And just how do you plan to do that?"

"On the field."

"Just why do you think you have the right to be on the field? See those guys out there? They all put in the time and effort, they all work their tails off, and this is their reward. I thought I would take a chance with you, but you proved my instinct wrong and I don't like to be wrong. Do you like making me look like an idiot?"

"Coach, I don't know what I did wrong!" Vince said, his voice rising.

"Don't you take that tone of voice with me son! I'll kick your little butt off this team faster than you can run, which isn't very fast to begin with!"

Vincent was thinking, *Do you know what I would like to kick, my dear loving Coach?*

"Coach, I don't mean no disrespect, but I didn't do anything wrong. I just want to get out there and play."

Coach turned fully around at this. Everybody in the dugout was watching with full interest. Coach chuckled. "You just don't get it, do you? I was going to get you into this game to give you a second chance, but after this show of disrespect to me, now I'm thinking a certain cocky player of mine needs to grab a railroad tie and show this crowd how to do lunges."

"If it'll get me in the game to prove myself."

CRACK! The ball went sailing to deep center field and all you could see was Jimmy's numbers on his back.

Coach turned around.

Jimmy ran to the fence and in full stride, stuck his left foot into the fence to cushion the blow, reached up with his left hand to make a terrific grab, and robbed the batter of a sure home run.

The stands went wild.

Coach Grey turned around to Vincent and said, "Now that's what becomes of a young man who applies himself. You should take Jimmy as an example to follow. Now you'll sit right down on that bench and shut up if you know what's good for you!"

Vincent sat back down and sulked. It just wasn't fair.

His dad had once told him that life wasn't fair. That was his dad's idea of a pep talk. He said it once while clumsily trying to take off his belt with one hand. He couldn't quite manage, so he had to put down his bottle of cheap bourbon to more effectively use both hands. Once the belt was off, his father showed him that little Vincent Preston, eight years old, was old enough to be able to pour a glass of milk without spilling it.

At that point, his father had asked Vincent if he thought that he was made of money.

Vincent had braced for the worst, and hoped for the best, which would have been possibly seeing his dad slip on that spilled milk.

Instead of his father slipping, Vincent remembered his father's words.

You want to talk about fair? Life isn't fair, boy. Your mom works hard for the money we have so you can drink that milk you just wasted! WHACK! My back hurts constantly because I had to take that crap job working on the street crew so you could be born. WHACK! Babies aren't cheap! Diapers WHACK! Formula WHACK! Jars WHACK! of WHACK! baby WHACK! food. WHACK! You cost me a lot of money and my back, boy! WHACK! And you almost cost me my marriage! WHACK! Now, take your medicine, boy.

Vincent took it in stride, much like everything else. He learned not to cry. To cry meant to be weak, and his father didn't want to raise a weak boy. Not a Preston, no siree Bob! The belt was part of life, and life wasn't fair. When Daddy drank from the bottle and got angry, it was a part of life to see the belt. That was all. Bad boys had to be punished. Catching his breath, his father would clumsily put his belt back on, inevitably missing a loop every time, not that Vincent would point that out. He had made that mistake once.

Now you'll shut up if you know what's good for you! was his father's response.

No, life wasn't fair. His father was spot-on with that little nugget of wisdom.

The game progressed in slow fashion. Each inning sagged time a little bit.

The thought made Vincent think about that Dali painting where these blue clocks were

Now what's the right word? Gelatinous. Yes, that seemed to be the word. Like gelatin. Blueberry.

In any case, these crazy clocks seemed to be melting off the side of a counter top, on a tree branch, and in places where clocks shouldn't be, not that melting clocks were the norm anyhow. And on some of the clocks were ants. His senior English teacher, Mrs. Dean, called it Surrealism. She was easily the best teacher he had ever had. It's not that she did wacky things like merge art and language. Sure, that made things interesting. What separated Mrs. Dean was that she *cared.* Twelve years of schooling, and she was the only one who seemed to want to help. A lazy fly ball sailed to mid-left field where Fuzzy caught it to retire the side. An easy play that Vincent was sure he could have made also, given the chance. It made him wonder why he was thinking about Mrs. Dean or English.

*

In the fourth inning "Nasty" Ned Gasser ran into trouble. All he had were two pitches: a fastball clocked at eighty-five miles per hour, and a change up that was much slower. His only saving grace was Bacon Bob.

Bob cracked himself up. He had been at this game for a long time and knew just how to get to a batter when a pitcher was losing his stuff. Bacon Bob sat behind the plate and tooted at the appropriate moment to disrupt the batters' concentrations. This didn't go over well with the home plate umpire who got onto him more than once. Heck, what could he do about it? Nature calls, you dig?

Still, some batters managed a half-hearted swing, trying to stifle their laughs. Nothing like flatulence to break one's concentration.

Ned had a no-hitter working through the first three innings as the Woodward batters couldn't catch up to him, but in the fourth, Bacon Bob was running out of fumes and Ned was getting clubbed. He lost some velocity off the fastball and the batters started timing him.

Coach Grey finally called time-out after Woodward put four runs on the board and loaded the bases. He called the infield and the outfield to the mound for a conference.

"Ned, you got a second speed on that arm of yours?"

"Sorry Coach," Ned said. "I'm throwing as hard as I can, but they're timing me. They seem to be picking up my change up too. I don't know what to do."

"Bob?" Coach Grey questioned as he turned to his catcher.

Bob could feel himself turning red. "Yes Coach."

"You know darn well what. Are you calling a good game, mixing it up?"

"Coach, they got Ned's number."

Coach Grey looked over his starters in contemplation.

Bob peered over at the dugout, saw Vincent, and secretly wondered what he could do if given a chance. Bob looked at Vincent's face and saw what appeared to be a pitiful kid sitting there.

Coach Grey looked at Ned, who was rubbing his shoulder.

Bacon Bob knew Coach Grey's first option was Jimmy, but Bob knew exactly how Jimmy felt about pitching in relief from the losing side.

"Jimmy, your arm warm?"

"C'mon Dad! You want me to pitch from four runs down? That's what a relief pitcher does, not a closer. You get our guys to start hitting and I'll close the door on them."

Bob glared at Jimmy. Jimmy was 0-2 in this game, so who was he to be pointing fingers?

Coach Grey looked at Jimmy and then took off his hat to scratch his head. He had only one option left and Bob knew Coach hated to do it. There was about no way to save face, but maybe Coach could seem merciful in the process.

"Nasty," Coach said, "take a seat and put some ice on that shoulder. Fuzzy, warm your arm up." The players took their positions again.

Coach Grey looked back toward the dugout.

Bob knew the two options were to either go with Vincent in left field since Fuzzy was now on the mound, or pick a random underclassman. Ned was done for the night. Coach couldn't stick him out in left. Sighing, he pointed and Vincent sprung out of his seat as if shot from a cannon and sprinted to left field. Coach didn't even look at him.

*

Fuzzy got the job done. It wasn't pretty, but coming in with the bases loaded, he got the batter to ground into a double play to end the inning.

The next two and one-half innings went much the same way on offense. Jimmy was still hitless, partly because he was now getting intentionally walked. The Stampeding Herd had managed to eek out one run from Bill Jones' first home run of the season, but Vincent still hadn't had a chance to bat since being put in left field. That would change in the last inning. Vincent knew that, and he knew that Coach knew that.

In the top of the seventh, Fuzzy was getting into trouble. Two guys singled and with one out, runners were on the corners. The ball hadn't been hit to Vincent since he got into the game. This was another thing that was about to change. On an 0-2 pitch, Woodward's cleanup hitter popped one up to mid left field. The runners on third and first tagged-up.

Vincent pulled up under it and called for the ball as Jimmy came rushing hard from center field. Vincent snuck a quick peek at the runner on third who was still tagging. Out of the corner of his eye he saw Jimmy and, called out, "BALL!"

Jimmy veered, just in time to keep from running right into Vincent.

Vincent caught the ball, took a crow-hop toward home and with a grunt, let it fly. His eyes played tricks on him. Bacon Bob, standing right on top of the plate, turned into a big, fat trash can, and Vincent looked deep into the trashcan as he released the ball. The ball whizzed through the air on a frozen rope to home, beating the runner by two steps.

Vincent thought, *You are so out, dude!*

As Bacon Bob caught it, the runner took his final two steps and with a full head of steam, bounced right off Bob's chest, but not without accomplishing the goal. The ball somehow came squirting out of his mitt and hit the ground. The runner, on the ground, reached for home plate and slapped it with his right hand.

You gotta be kidding! Vincent thought.

"SAFE!" the umpire called.

In the meantime, the runner on first advanced to second.

Vincent shook his head. It was a perfect throw. A one out of a hundred shot to land right in the barrel, and it was wasted because Bacon Bob couldn't hold on.

"Hey idiot! You have to throw that to second base to keep the runner at first!"

Vincent was shocked. *You talking to me?*

Vincent turned around to see Jimmy berating him.

Vincent quickly caught his temper. "It was a perfect throw!"

"Hey, next time just step aside and let me catch the ball. Don't you EVER call me off again!"

Words failed Vincent.

Jimmy patted Vincent on the butt with his glove, making it look good for the fans, and ran back to center field.

When Fuzzy finally closed the inning out, the runner on second base had scored to make it 6-1.

The Stampeding Herd dogged their way into the dugout, except Vincent who had been sprinting ever since he got in the game, despite how tired he really was.

Before he got to the dugout, Coach Grey grabbed Vincent by the jersey and lit into him.

"What do you mean throwing home and lettin' the runner advance to second like that? Were you born stupid or do you have to work at it because I've seen some dumb plays in my life and that one ranks right up there!!! What were you thinkin'?!? If we lose by one run, I'm blamin' you!"

Vincent again couldn't believe his ears and thought, *Yeah, you would. I think the word is scapegoat, maybe patsy.*

"Uh, ah…" was all that Vincent managed to get out.

Bacon Bob stepped in. "Coach Grey, it was my fault. I shoulda held onto the ball. He threw it perfect."

Coach Grey let go of Vincent for the moment and stared at Bacon Bob. "Bob, are you the coach? Then butt out. We have some runs to score." Then Coach Grey turned back to Vincent. "Now back to you. If you don't get on base, you can just sit the rest of the season. You got me?!?"

Vincent shook off the coach and grabbed a likely looking bat and helmet. He stepped into the batting circle and loosened up his arms with a few swings. One thought bugged him. Bacon Bob had stuck-up for him. Nobody had ever stuck-up for him. It was a weird feeling to coincide with a weird day.

Vincent couldn't remember having had so many emotions in one day. First he was a starter, then he wasn't and was running laps and puking. Then he was a bench warmer, and now he was in the batter's circle hoping to start a rally. His luck was improving.

Vincent's teammates had managed one hit off the opposing pitcher, Bill's home run, and Woodward's coach took the kid out and put in their closer. Vincent had watched this guy pitch a number of times, had taken notes on him at the AAA State Tournament the last few years (unlike any other of his teammates.) The pitcher had a fastball that reached the mid-eighties, and no other pitch. He relied wholly on the fastball and always tried to throw the first one for a strike to get ahead in the count. Vincent knew exactly what to expect.

Vincent looked over toward third base for Coach Grey's sign, but he wasn't there. He was still in the dugout yelling at the other players. *Just as well,* Vincent thought. It took some pressure off him. He looked at first base to where Coach Redenbacher stood oblivious to anything in his own little world. It appeared he was looking past right field into the trees. Was anybody going to give him a sign? Should he swing away? Bunt? Finally Coach Redenbacher looked his way, looked toward third base, and looked into the dugout for Coach Grey.

"Let's go batter," the umpire said.

Vincent looked back at Coach Redenbacher who held his hands up as if to say, "I don't know?"

Vincent looked over the outfield and saw they were playing him pretty shallow. They didn't respect his power.

Vincent stepped into the right hand batter's box and tried to focus. The memory of the group of starters before the game making fun of him, and of Coach Grey making him run laps, and of eating those nasty beans just to throw them up, and Jimmy's insulting words, all of this infuriated him. Vincent looked down at the plate and picked out a speck of dirt on the otherwise clean, white pentagon. He pulled his bat across the plate to remove the speck, and a thought raced through his mind. He traced the length of the plate crosswise to complete the sign of the cross like he had seen other players do. Even though he didn't know what it meant, he did it and suddenly felt powerful, confident. Everything went quiet except his own thoughts.

I'm gonna show them!

In the background he heard himself mutter, "Break-on through to the other side." The music of the Doors was faint in the receding airways of his conscious mind. The catcher looked up at this weird kid, shook his head, and ordered up a fastball with extra mustard.

The pitcher went into his windup. Just as expected the fastball came and to Vincent it looked as big as a volleyball.

He heard himself think again, *Break-on through.*

Vincent wasn't even aware that he swung. He didn't hear the clank of the ball against the metal bat. All he was aware of was that in the next moment the bat was suspended over his left shoulder and a slight electrical tingle graced both hands. He looked up and saw the ball getting smaller.

I hit it!

He took-off toward first and a few steps down the line he looked up again toward the Little Monster to see the ball hit the brand new wooden pennant with a loud SLAP.

Everyone in the dugout was quiet, as they apparently couldn't believe Vincent creamed it.

If it weren't for the Little Monster, the line drive would have put a hole in the yellow house's steel siding. It was an F-14 taking off from the runway and not getting up high enough to clear the trees.

The sound of the ball hitting the pennant would be etched in Vincent's memory forever.

Coach Redenbacher swung his arm for Vincent to round first and go to second, but Vincent had already made that determination. He rounded the bag and saw the left and center fielders still running toward the fence. As shallow as they were playing him, it would take some time to get to the ball. He hoofed toward second and peered over toward third base to where Coach Grey should have been coaching him, telling him whether or not to advance.

Break-on through!

He rounded second and grunted with determination, his cleats digging into the soft infield dirt as fast and hard as he could pump his already-dogged legs.

Break-on through, Vincent!

By this time the center fielder, having made up some ground, had the ball and a laser for an arm. He heaved it toward third. Without a third-base coach, Vincent didn't know whether to slide or not.

The ball's gotta be coming! Vincent thought.

He looked up at the third baseman who was getting his glove ready to catch the ball.

Slide Vincent!

Vincent flopped head-first, arms reaching out for the bag and cradling it like a pillow, and at the same time, the third baseman caught the ball about waist-high. Vincent felt the glove smack him in on his backside, well after he had touched the bag.

I'm Safe!

"YER OUTTA THERE!"

Vincent turned around and saw the second base umpire making the call from well-behind, the worst possible angle to see the play.

WHAT??? Vincent thought.

"WHAT???" Vincent screamed.

"I said you're outta there! Don't be arguing my call, boy!"

BOY!?! Vincent thought. *Why does everybody keep calling me BOY??? What am I, a cart horse to whip?*

The third baseman whipped the ball to the second baseman and the infield took it around the horn.

Vincent looked to the home plate umpire for an overturn, but he said nothing. Vincent laid there with his arms up in the air. "You gotta be kidding!" He looked toward his dugout to see Coach Grey standing on the steps with a hand over his mouth. It appeared he was masking a smile.

"Son," the umpire said, "you say one more word and you're outta the game!"

Vincent looked into the dugout again and saw Dusty talking to Coach Grey. Dusty's arms were open wide, apparently pleading, but Coach just stood there.

The crowd was silent, silent when the ball hit the fence, silent when Vincent was called out at third.

Vincent picked himself up, refusing to dust off, and slowly jogged toward the dugout. As he passed the mound, the opposing pitcher said, "That was a heckuva hit."

"Thanks," Vincent said under his breath with his head down.

He passed Coach Grey on the steps and Coach said, "Got in over yer head going for third. That was pretty stupid. We could have used the base runner."

And with that, he yelled to Dusty, "Dusty, go coach third if you think you can." Dusty walked past Coach into the batter's circle to wait his turn, silently. Dusty was supposed to be a leader, but leadership duties on this team were unclear.

Vincent, after pausing for a moment beside Coach Grey, made his way to the end of the bench. The eyes of the dugout were shifting to the Little Monster where hung the remains of their brand new pennant, just christened a few hours ago. It broke down the middle in two pieces, both hanging from the single ties that held each top corner.

*

Woodward earned the split.

Dusty managed the third hit of the game, a little blooper into shallow right field, but the immortal Jimmy Grey grounded into a fielder's choice to end the game, going 0 for 3 in game two.

Coach Grey called his players into right field where he berated them for twenty minutes, not minding if the crowd, reporters, or God Himself heard his colorful words. Most of the time he talked about how coaches coach and players play and how his authority should never be questioned and that anybody who wanted to question him could find a different team to play for. Pretty tough in a one-team town. Coach Grey didn't so much as look at Vincent or say a word to him. Their season-opening double-header was ruined, and it was easy to point a finger at the cause, but Vincent figured Coach thought it better to let the kid know he wasn't even worth talking to. One of Coach Grey's old coach's maxims was "When the coach stops yelling at you, he's given up on you." That spoke volumes to Vincent.

Coach Grey made the radio people wait the twenty minutes he was with the team, and then basically repeated his performance about the players overstepping their bounds. Vincent overheard every word.

Vincent took his time gathering his gear and taking off his spikes and waited in the dugout, watching over the empty field until everybody was gone. He tried not to look up at that broken pennant, lest he smile. He figured others on the team, starters from last year's team, felt the same way.

Dusty and Quentin were the last two to leave. Dusty patted him on the shoulder and said, "Nice hit Vincent," and walked up to the parking lot, cleats click-clacking on the concrete steps.

Quentin waited until everybody was gone and went up to Vincent. "Don't let them get you down! You stand up and keep fighting, you hear me?"

Vincent nodded his head, looking down, embarrassed. Quentin looked like he wanted to say more but instead left. He had fought the same battle Vincent fought now. In fact, Vincent wondered if Quentin still felt like an outsider.

Vincent looked up at the broken pennant, and when all was clear, smiled. The smile was cut off short when the lights went out and the field joined the dark sky.

He walked up the hill past the water tower to the parking lot. The only cars left were Jimmy's Corvette and a Ford Explorer back by the elm grove. He stayed in the shadow of the trees when he saw something suspicious, three guys, one in a baseball uniform, passing around either a cigarette or a joint.

An older bald man walked up to Jimmy and slipped him something while shaking his hand. Vincent was too far away to hear their conversation and couldn't tell anything in the darkness of the street lamp farther up, but he did see Jimmy reach into his pocket without flinching. A moment later there was the brief light from a lighter and a puff of smoke.

The bald man and the two other guys got back into the Explorer and drove off, leaving Jimmy alone with his joint.

Not wanting to see anymore, Vincent snuck down through the trees without being detected and once out of sight, walked home.

Chapter 3

Vincent had more than a few thoughts roaming around in his head but had nobody with which to share them when he got home.

Vincent's father had already gone off to the Rusty Nail, a popular tavern for the town's drunks, shifty women, and all-around general losers. Though he was a mean drunk, the guy hadn't hit his son in a few years, not since Vincent had grown stronger than the old man and bared his knuckles in retaliation.

That should have been a glorious night for Vincent, but it wasn't. It was just survival. His dad had come home hammered and, as usual, looking for his favorite target to wail on. For no reason whatsoever, with no provocation, he had yanked his son out of bed by the collar of his T-shirt, the fabric shearing in a grotesque zipping noise. The light had come on. When his dad turned around, Vincent cocked his right arm and waited.

What Vincent's dad saw through his bleary vision was a grown boy with both his fists raised. No tears, no fears. Nothing. Then he looked into his son's eyes. Vincent's stare was determined.

As for Vincent, it was merely fight or flight. His fists chose to fight. His dad stared at Vincent. Vincent was not making a move to advance, but not backing down either. Even in his drunken stupor, he could see the determination in his grown boy's eyes. His fist dropped down to his side and he turned to the door, side-stepping to catch his balance. He didn't know what to think of his boy's courage.

Vincent knew he made his point. He knew his father would want to seek revenge, but Vincent saw a fear in his father's eyes when he stood up to him. A cornered animal has everything to fight for, nothing to lose. Instead, Vincent's father cut-off all communication with his son. It was easier than giving up the bottle. It continued to this day.

Not a word had been spoken in the exchange in Vincent's bedroom that night. It wasn't until a few minutes after the elder left that Vincent lowered his right fist. Truth to be told, Vincent didn't even notice his torn shirt hanging in shreds off his shoulders. What he did do was lay back in bed and fall asleep. It was the best night of sleep he had had for quite some time.

Vincent's mom was still at work, naturally. She worked the third shift as an aide out at the state hospital a few miles out of town, assisting the security personnel. She wouldn't be off until eleven. Then when she got home, she wouldn't want to talk. She didn't talk much to begin with. She hung-out in a daze most of the time.

She didn't take drugs, prescription or other. She didn't smoke or chew. She had no vices except her love for her abusive husband, and a secret bottle she kept stashed away in her purse to make him more tolerable. Surely a few punches to her skull rattled a few brain cells and helped them slide right out her ears.

She was in a constant state of depression and apparently wanted nothing to do with her son when she normally got home. She wouldn't even check on Vincent to make sure he was in bed asleep. She would walk in, drop her purse on the bedside table, and go to bed.

Despite his parent's flaws, Vincent still loved them both. He wasn't totally desensitized. He felt it was only natural to seek praise from his parents. He wasn't used to praise, and wasn't used to doing anything worthy of it. He wanted to talk to them, to share his exciting news about his first hit of the year, and about the ball breaking that stupid pennant. He hoped the nasty parents in the stands were just sick about that. He also wanted to ask advice about the situation he witnessed after the ballgame in the rear of the parking lot. His dad would surely be a wealth of knowledge on that one. But even if they were there, he probably wouldn't have talked to them. It was just too hard to bring up a conversation when you knew you would be shot down, rejected.

Besides being messed up, his parents also had no idea how to love a kid. They were of the opinion that they raised him to a certain point and it was his life now, to sink or swim. He guessed that point came around his seventh birthday. There would be no more birthday parties, no more parent-teacher conferences, and no more hot meals waiting for him at home, as evidenced by tonight.

He was also going to get no help for college from them, if he went to college that is.

He didn't exactly excel in his studies, especially math. He hated math. Thankfully all he had to pass was Algebra I and Geometry I, both of which he had to repeat through his junior year. Science was another dead-end proposition for him. He finished General Science and Biology with D's. He enjoyed his history classes and his English classes and even managed to pull an A in Senior English. He and his English teacher Mrs. Dean became really close throughout his senior year and he came in twice a week in the mornings before school for tutoring. Having slept through most of his underclassmen English courses, he had a lot of catching up to do, and Mrs. Dean was kind enough to excuse him for his past failures and push him to his capabilities.

Elna Dean was elderly, shriveled with grape-grey hair and glasses as thick as double-paned bullet-proof glass. Everybody figured she would retire any time.

Vincent knew that most of the students couldn't stand her and her structured classrooms, and that the underclassmen every year hoped that year was her last. For four years Vincent listened without comment to all the boys hoping for a pretty, young thing, fresh from the silly pedagogical theories of college - somebody easy-going, someone who hadn't figured out that a student will take whatever he can get from a teacher.

He had new teachers say things like, "Now Johnny, you hit that boy and broke his nose. I would like you to open up and talk about your feelings with me. No, your conscience will be your punishment. Do you need a hug?"

But Mrs. Dean had a soft heart for a hard case, a fact most students never knew. When Vincent came along begging for help, she said, taking off her glasses, "You have come to my class with quite a reputation for being a slacker. The only reason I would help is if I knew your intentions were honorable, that is to say that you were serious about not wasting anyone's time, especially mine."

Vincent looked at her in shocked disbelief. She spoke so bluntly, but truthfully, and his resolve was greater than his apathy or pride. With his head lowered, he said, "Mrs. Dean, I hope I can tell you I am serious about doing better than I have in the past, but all I can really tell you is that I will try harder than anybody you've ever had." He did, but not before she made him look her in the eyes.

He came in before school at seven o'clock promptly on Tuesdays and Thursdays, and true to his word, worked harder than anybody she could remember. Despite her gruff appearance,

Vincent knew that she couldn't help but like him. In their mutual respect, they found in each other qualities that others overlooked.

He earned that A the hard way, and his grade point average his senior year was 3.5, the first year he ever earned better than a 2.4. Vincent knew Mrs. Dean was never more proud than when watching her unceremonious protégé walk the stage and receive his diploma. She helped Vincent find brains he never knew he owned.

Unfortunately, his overall high school GPA was 2.11, and with an ACT score of eighteen out of thirty-six, no colleges offered him academic scholarships. He simply waited too long to get serious, and his parents' laze faire attitude did him no favors. But in all truth, he was basically on his own before he entered his ninth-grade year. Having two parents who didn't care about him toughened him as much as his father's beatings had. It made him stronger.

His summer job of teaching baseball skills to tee-ballers during morning summer recreation and cutting grass in the afternoons wasn't going to pay for college tuition, much less room and board and a car to get him there. There was high school baseball and the hope of some college coach seeing him play and offering him a scholarship. An athletic scholarship to play baseball in college was Vincent's greatest and only hope, one, he figured, that Coach Grey sought to dash.

He couldn't fathom digging ditches for the rest of his life, out in the hundred degree heat of summer and the freezing temperatures of winter, blistering his hands on a shovel and dreading waking up every morning. That's what his father did until he found a loophole in the system, a rather big loophole, and started receiving a check from the government every month to fuel his growing addictions. Vincent decided that no matter what, he was not going to be his father.

His father was unemployed and hung around the house all day doing basically nothing. Everybody knew the old man's back was okay. The neighborhood mothers would stare out their front windows on an idle Tuesday and catch him drunk, mowing the weeds or sawing down a tree in those duct-taped cowboy boots of his.

Mr. Preston became the neighborhood joke and earned the nickname Tape Boot Willy. Always in the background was his tape player crooning Roger Miller.

The neighborhood children even started a song about him. They modeled it off one of Tape Boot Willy's favorite songs that he blared when he was drunk and attempting to do yard work.

Oh Tape Boot, Tape Boot,
They Oughta take a rope and hang you
From a branch in your front yard tree.
Hey y'all, I'm faking!
Du du du du du du do do do do doa

They would sing it as they rode by the Preston's corner house on their bikes, while playing football in the street, or anytime in general that the mood to be mean hit them. Vincent was glad that none of the neighborhood kids were anywhere near his age. They were all in grade school, but at times Vincent would feel like a prisoner in his own house, fearing that if he went outside to shovel snow or out back to shoot hoops on the makeshift basketball goal he nailed into the tree with the air conditioning filter screen for the backboard, that he would be mocked by the neighborhood children.

It's not that he didn't care, because he did. He truly cared what other people thought about him. It's just that he had a way of brushing all the negatives away and focusing on the positives. That is most of the time. At times, his pressures would surmount and he would feel like blowing his stack.

More than once he felt like taking that shovel and practicing his baseball swing on the first little monster to open his mouth. But he never did. No matter what rude comment a schoolmate would say, what teacher would tell him he was no better than his dad, or when either of his parents acted like he didn't exist, he always held it inside.

From what he gathered, his father never wanted children, but his mother wanted a girl. After four long years of trying, Vincent came along. Since his mother wanted a girl, his parents tried for another seven years before they finally gave up. The rest was up to Vincent.

He had to enroll himself in Little League. His parents never went to his games, even when he told them both he was starting that night. It was this last point that hurt the most, even more than his father's blows.

Jimmy and two others he had never seen before were smoking what Vincent figured was marijuana back in the trees after the game when they thought everybody was gone. There was no question that any teen could get pot if they knew where to go and had twenty bucks. Who were those two others and that bald man, and what did he slip Jimmy? Was he paying Jimmy for going 3 for 3 in game one, or even worse, was he paying him for going 0 for 3 in game two? Could he have been giving Jimmy drugs?

These were questions that Vincent didn't really want answers to. Walking by the scene after the game was enough to make the hair rise on Vincent's neck. Besides the alleged illegal activity, there was something that made Vincent scared for his life. If he would have been caught peeping, who knows what would have happened to him. He may have been found in a culvert somewhere out in the countryside.

Vincent walked over to the fridge and poured a glass of milk, looking over his shoulder while doing so. He drank it with the gallon still in his right hand and promptly refilled. He was parched, no doubt in regard to his punishment.

He threw his baseball uniform in the washer and went straight to bed. He fell asleep instantly, but was awakened all night by bad dreams.

*

Two seven round bursts from an M-16 machine gun rang through the night and tore up the ground all around Vincent. He jumped to the left and hit the fresh dirt. He didn't know where he was, but all he had for shelter was an elm tree that didn't even cover his shoulders. He was dead meat.

He peeked around the tree and saw his perpetrator. It was a man with male pattern baldness and glasses. He wore a light blue jacket zipped down all the way and slowly lifted the gun to his shoulders to finish the job. The third burst from that gun was what woke Vincent. He threw himself out of bed and ducked for cover. The phone rang, and the cold fear that a man feels in his last seconds before death slowly left, his nerve endings feeling like thousands of needle pricks. Vincent's heart pounded as the phone rang again, and he realized it was only a dream.

The phone rang seven times before Vincent was able to run to the kitchen and grab it. "Hello?"

"Oh, Vincent, I'm sorry if I woke you up. It was such a nice morning that I just had to get up and stretch my limbs. Besides, I couldn't wait any longer to congratulate you."

The voice on the end of the line sounded familiar, but it was out of context and Vincent was still in a war with the bald man in his mind. It was a voice he had heard many times before, but never over the phone. Vincent stretched his mind but couldn't figure it out. It was a Saturday morning, and Vincent hadn't planned on getting up before noon.

He looked at the microwave and saw the time read 9:03.

"Ma'am?"

"Yes Vincent, I'm still here."

"Ma'am, may I ask who's calling?"

The voice on the other end of the line chuckled. "I really did wake you up, didn't I? Well, I'm sorry. Kids your age need the sleep. It has to do with their hormones, I think I read that somewhere. It's amazing you got out of bed this past school year at all to come see me. I guess I should consider myself lucky."

"Mrs. Dean?" Vincent asked and scratched his disheveled hair.

"That's right, son. At this point, since you have graduated I'd normally let you call me Elna, but it appears I've got more work to do on you. So it'll have to remain Mrs. Dean to you, if you don't mind."

Vincent ran a hand through his messed up hair. Was this a dream and the former real life? He quickly threw that notion away, but this was strange. His English teacher-- no, make that his former English teacher-- was calling him on a Saturday morning just a week after graduation.

Something didn't make sense. What did she want with him? Was there an incomplete that lowered his grade to a B? Was she going to accuse him of plagiarism on the research paper? Did she want him to enter a writing contest? Doubtful. But here she was calling him during his summer vacation saying she had more work to do with him. Vincent's heartbeat rose again.

"Vincent?"

"Yes, Mrs. Dean."

"Vincent, I was wondering if you would do me a favor?"

"Of course, Mrs. Dean. What can I do for you?"

"Well, do you like spaghetti?" Mrs. Dean asked.

"Mrs. Dean?"

"Spaghetti, son. Do you like it?" Mrs. Dean asked again.

Vincent took the phone away from his ear and stared at it, not sure if it was going to turn into a snake next. Maybe it was a dream. If not, then this was the single weirdest phone call he had ever received, despite not getting many in his life anyway.

"Yes, Mrs. Dean. Spaghetti is good, but I don't like those sauces with chunks of onions," Vincent answered.

"That is helpful information. Thanks, Vincent. Here's the favor I need from you. I need you to come over to my place for dinner. Around sixish? Do you know where I live?"

Vincent stood there for a moment longer and realized he really had to go to the bathroom something bad. The memory of the two tall glasses of milk before bed was now haunting him. He crossed his legs, "Did you say dinner at your place?"

"Yes, around six," Mrs. Dean replied.

Vincent was hopping on one foot. "Uh... is this a date???"

For the second time in the conversation Mrs. Dean was laughing, only harder this time. She took five seconds to compose herself.

"Oh, my dear boy! I am truly honored that you would think that way about me, but I am sorry if I misled you. I should have revealed the purpose of my calling. How rude of me. I would like you to come to dinner tonight so I can introduce you to my husband."

"You're married?" Vincent asked, more confused than ever.

"You do call me, "Mrs.," don't you?" was her reply.

That was a good point. Vincent felt embarrassed. He wanted to take the time to explain to her that he had no romantic feelings for her, but his desire to use the bathroom was overpowering.

"Your husband? I didn't realize you had a husband. I don't think I have anything planned." In all reality he knew he didn't have anything planned. He was eighteen, it was going to be a Saturday night, and he had never had a girlfriend to spend that kind of time with, much less friends. His Saturday nights included homework and lugging the burlap bag of baseballs to the stadium.

"Well then," Mrs. Dean said, "we'll be expecting you."

Vincent felt weird accepting an offer to dine with his English teacher. What happened if the guys on the team found out? Vincent would be laughed at, but then he was always getting laughed at. That was nothing new to him.

"We live on 1015 Park Street. Six o'clock. Don't be late, and by the way, you don't have to bring anything except your ball glove," Mrs. Dean said.

"My ball glove?" Vincent replied.

"Yes, son. It was a pleasure talking to you and I look forward to seeing you tonight. Good bye."

She hung up before he could say another word.

*

All reason told him to stay home, but what was he to do there? Naturally, his father still hadn't come home from the Rusty Nail and his mother was going to work. He'd have the whole house to himself, but the Prestons didn't even have cable television. What was there for him to do? As sad as the proposition was, it was the best proposition he had gotten in a long time. He couldn't figure out for the life of him what Mrs. Dean would want with him and his baseball glove. A baseball glove? Surely he was half-asleep and just misunderstood her.

He arrived at her house five minutes before six. He could remember her lecturing once in class about how the applicant should arrive to a job interview no later than five minutes early and no earlier than five minutes early. Vincent heard it, remembered it, even if the rest of the class was sleeping and he was now utilizing it in the real world.

He didn't know what was about to happen, because it sure felt like a job interview. Just to be on the safe side, he made sure he showered and shaved and wore the nicest clothes he owned, a pair of second-hand khakis and a button-down shirt with a collar. He didn't have any dress shoes, so he put on his old sneakers.

The house wasn't much to look at. It was a small ranch-styled house, white with deep ocean blue trim and appeared to be in need of a paint job as flakes were peeling off. Vincent felt a bit relieved he wasn't entering a mansion. He visualized having trouble determining which fork to use for the salad and whether or not he could put his elbows on the table. After all, his family used plastic cutlery. They washed and reused plastic cutlery for that matter.

He rang the doorbell which made an obscene buzzer noise that reminded him of a New York City apartment door buzzer. Mrs. Dean promptly appeared, opening the screen door with delight. "Vincent! It's so nice to see you, and you're five minutes early!"

"I'm sorry if I'm early Ma'am," Vincent replied, looking at his shoes.

"Well, it appears you didn't listen in class," she responded. "Don't you know it's polite to be five minutes early?"

"Yes, I remember you said that," he admitted. "No more and no less."

"Well, maybe you were listening. Come in! Come in! Dinner will be ready in a minute." She led him into the front room of the house, and the first thing that caught his eyes were all the picture frames. The coffee table, end tables, curios, they were all full of pictures, and most of them black and white to match the general decor of a room that was inspired during black and white times.

Ornate China graced the top of one cabinet. Squeaky wooden floors were waxed to a mirror shine. The furniture looked very antiquated. The inside of the house didn't match the outside appearance. Overpowering his senses was a lemony smell that he assumed came from anything made of wood, which in this room, constituted everything from the floor to the ceiling. He stood there trying to remember which commercial it was that promoted their product to smell so "lemony-clean" that one shouldn't confuse it with fresh lemon slices in one's iced tea.

Whatever the answer, the heat of the day, the long walk from his house and his long-sleeved button-down shirt caught up to him and made him sweat profusely. He now craved an ice tea, with lemon.

Mrs. Dean called to him, "Go ahead and have a seat, and I'll call my husband. He's out back working in his wood shop." She walked through the oval door entry into the kitchen and through to the back porch where the screen door banged shut.

Vincent sat on a green couch that looked as if it belonged in a museum or on the bottom of the North Atlantic with the rest of the Titanic. It was beautiful, and very ornate, but not very comfortable. Not much stuffing.

He took his glove out of the back pocket of his pants. It was very flexible, had been broken in some ten years ago to where it resembled a rag. He had probably outgrown the glove by now, but that was just another cost that he couldn't afford. He could afford leather strips to re-string his glove, which he did on a regular basis. Besides, he loved the glove and doubted he would ever get rid of it.

Waiting, his curiosity got the best of him, so he walked over to the curio and peered through the glass at the pictures.

Old students? He thought. *No.*

The first one that caught his eye was a picture of none other than Frankie Duke! Frankie Duke was a short stop for the Oklahoma City Eagles back in the sixties. He wore a big smile and had his arm around another guy, a white guy with black slicked back hair, a mustache and a tie.

At that moment he heard the porch screen door bang shut, so he quickly resumed his seat on the couch, lest he be caught snooping. Mrs. Dean came in helping an elderly man with a cane. The guy had a full head of silver hair, slicked back and wore a mustache to match. The aroma of garlic came wafting in from the kitchen and competed with the lemony-fresh floor for Vincent's appetite. Vincent stood at attention.

"Leonard, this is the young man I was telling you about," Mrs. Dean said. "Vincent, I want you to meet my husband, Leonard."

"It's a pleasure to meet you Mr. Dean." Vincent took out his right hand and Leonard, after taking his left hand off his cane, nodded without speaking and shook Vincent's hand. It was awkward since Vincent held out his right hand, but upon closer observation, he noticed that Mr. Dean's right arm was shriveled and useless.

"Shall we go to the table? The sauce is just about right."

The three sat down to dinner and Vincent had to constantly watch for clues to how these people acted and the proper table etiquette to use.

Before they ate, Leonard gave the blessing, not the first prayer Vincent had ever heard, but then he could probably count the number of prayers he had heard in his life on two hands. After all, he wasn't what one might refer to as *religious*. His parents were never into that *stuff*. Consequently, he wasn't either.

He couldn't understand the words well because Mr. Dean spoke in a very raspy voice. Vincent knew people who were *religious*, but had never discussed *religion* with anyone. He wanted to ask why they prayed and what the old man said, but Vincent held his tongue.

The meal was the best Vincent had ever had. Much better than his annual Thanksgiving turkey pot pie. He never knew he liked tomatoes until he found a red chunk in the sauce. He tentatively bit into it and a rush of flavor filled his mouth. The bread was heavy on the garlic and butter and melted in his mouth. He felt selfish asking for seconds, but Mrs. Dean beat him to the punch, loading up his plate again without asking.

Vincent was looking for an artful way to compliment her meal, so he said, "Mrs. Dean, thank you for inviting me over for dinner. It was very delicious. What brand of spaghetti sauce do you use?"

She tilted her head as Mr. Dean chuckled and then started to cough. She answered, "Vincent, I don't use store bought sauce. I make my own spaghetti sauce. It's a recipe that's been passed down through the generations."

Vincent smiled and said, "Well, it's the best spaghetti sauce I've ever tasted! I was hoping I could buy it and make it at home."

"Well, if you play your cards right, I might pass the recipe down to you," she laughed.

Mr. Dean chose this time to speak for the first time. He rasped, "How long have you played ball, kid?"

"Ball? You mean baseball?" Vincent asked, ignorantly.

Mr. Dean responded curtly, "Is there another kind?"

"Most of my life, sir. As long as I can remember. I guess I started in Little League and worked my way up," Vincent said.

Mr. Dean continued, "Elna tells me you have a heck of an arm."

Vincent was caught off guard. How did she know how he played baseball?

Before Vincent could ask, she apparently read his mind and said, "I stopped by the stadium to watch your games last night, Vincent. I was very impressed with your play."

"Well, thank you ma'am," Vincent said. "That's very nice of you to say." Vincent normally wouldn't have been so polite with his "yes sirs" and "yes ma'ams." After all, it wasn't the way he was raised. But he felt an obligation to the one woman he truly respected. After all, she tutored him in as many hours of manners as she did composition. He knew he was her project.

"I assume you got a chance to look at the pictures out in the front room?" Mrs. Dean asked him.

"Well, I got a peek," Vincent admitted.

"Recognize anybody?" she asked him.

"Yes, ma'am," Vincent responded. I saw a picture of Frankie Duke with someone else I didn't recognize."

"Yes, dear. That was Frankie with Leonard. When was that picture taken?" she asked her husband.

"Long time ago," Mr. Dean whispered, stifling a cough.

"That's you with Frankie Duke?" Vincent asked, again showing his ignorance.

"Yes, dear," Mrs. Dean answered for her husband. "You'll see Leonard with quite a few famous people in those old photographs. You see, Leonard was a scout for the Eagles organization for, what was it, about thirty years?"

Leonard nodded and kept eating.

She continued, "Now he didn't find Frankie. Frankie broke into the majors in 1954, when Leonard was with the San Antonio Coyotes organization."

"Had 117 R.B.I. in 1965," Mr. Dean interjected and then started coughing.

Mrs. Dean continued, "But he found a lot of rough talent and helped mold them into the history books. He discovered many of the great players of that era. He found Ed Rankin who threw a few no-hitters. He helped Ryan Adams, Zachary Sutters, mostly pitchers, but the list goes on and on. We spent many years on the road when we were young, enjoying the sights of the country on the way to a left-handed hurler in Seattle, or a catcher in Boulder, or a shortstop in Florida. If you name the state, we visited it. After time we settled here and Leonard took to the road once or twice a month while I taught. But I learned a few things about baseball while touring the country, like how to spot a diamond in the rough."

"Wow! How cool!" Vincent said. "Did you play baseball yourself?"

Mrs. Dean answered for her husband again. "Uh, Leonard played a little before he was called to duty in the Second Great War."

"Oh," Vincent said and looked down again.

"You're probably wondering why I asked you over here tonight for supper, and I'm sure you're dying to ask why you needed a glove," she said.

"I am curious," Vincent admitted.

"Well, it's simply because I can spot a diamond in the rough," she said.

Me, a diamond in the rough? Vincent blushed. He wasn't used to receiving compliments.

Mrs. Dean continued, "But I want you to know that even though I am impressed with your playing ability, the little that I got to see last night, your diamond is a little rough. It needs some polishing. Do you understand what I mean?"

"Ma'am?" Vincent said.

Mrs. Dean continued, "I told Leonard about you early on in the school year. I was impressed by how hard you worked to achieve the grades you earned. You *did* earn that A in Senior English. But in a day and age when it seems youth is so irresponsible, it's nice to be able to spot someone with drive, someone who is willing to work hard to achieve goals. I could have retired years ago, but for some reason I hold on. I'm getting up in the years, I don't mind telling you. The older I get, the crankier I get, and the less mature my students become, but now-and-then I find a student with drive. I checked out your standardized test scores before you got into my class. They didn't exactly match up with your class grades. I know why you worked so hard in my class this year, coming in all those mornings for tutoring. But the question is, do you?"

Vincent said, "Sure, I wanted to pass your class, and I needed all the help I could get."

"Well, that's not entirely true," she corrected him. "There's another reason why you worked so hard. It's because you have a bigger goal. College. Any colleges beating down your door?"

Vincent looked down at the floor for a third time. "Well, no ma'am. My grades weren't all that good before this year."

"Exactly," she snapped. "You just slipped your way through life until something lit a fire under you. I don't know what that was, but I was glad to see it. I hear teachers talk about which students to abhor, which students I'll love, and about which students might be, uh, how do I put it nicely... misrepresenting their talents. You were one of those they talked about negatively. But luckily for you, I didn't listen to them. I like to make my own decisions about a student's worth." Vincent listened with full intent, now putting his fork down.

She continued, "So here's the problem. You want to go to college, but your parents, ahem... aren't exactly going to pay your way. Am I correct?"

Vincent nodded, looking at his shoes. He hadn't totally divulged his infamous past with his parents to Mrs. Dean, but he figured she could guess most of it.

"Am I also correct that you have no academic scholarship offers?" she asked. Again Vincent nodded. She continued, "So, that leaves baseball. You need a baseball scholarship to make your dreams come true. Have you thought about a major yet?"

"Uh, I thought about English."

This made her smile. "Oh, you humor me. Even if you're undecided at this point, it matters not because it's important to get your prerequisites out of the way early. After the basics, you can decide on a major that befits you, even English if you so dare."

Vincent shook his head and said, "Mrs. Dean, that sounds all good and stuff, but I don't have any college baseball coaches talking to me either."

"Did you talk to Mr. Bellamy, the counselor?" she asked.

"He told me to get a job after high school."

Mrs. Dean looked mad. "Never mind what he said. You're more than capable of earning a college degree. You see, it doesn't take brains to graduate college."

"Ma'am?" This was a direct counter-point to everything Vincent had ever heard about college and how tough it was.

Mrs. Dean clarified, "No, it doesn't take much brains. It takes willpower. And to get there, you need a baseball scholarship. That's where we come in. Do you work in the summer?"

"Yes, ma'am. I work rec at the park in the morning."

Mrs. Dean looked at him thoughtfully. "Sounds like you can make it here by say, six in the morning."

Vincent was confused. Why did he need to come here? Were they offering him baseball lessons? "Mrs. Dean, I'm confused. Why do you want me to come here?"

She smiled and said, "So Leonard can have a shot at you."

A shot? thought Vincent.

"Surely you don't doubt my husband's ability to teach the sport of baseball?" Mrs. Dean questioned him, looking over her glasses at him.

"No, not at all! I just don't know why you would want to help me, unless—"

Mrs. Dean stopped him in mid-sentence. "No, we don't want money from you. Our services are free of monetary charge. I saw something special in you this year, and I saw something special in you last night, and I am willing to stake my reputation with my husband to vouch for you. All I want in return is to see you succeed. I am a teacher. So is Leonard. This is what we do. What we're doing with you we haven't done in a very long time, but we have our reasons, reasons we aren't going to share with you right now. Maybe I will sometime in the future, but they're honorable, let me assure you. Do you trust me?"

"Yes, of course I trust you Mrs. Dean," Vincent said.

Mr. Dean wiped his mouth with his napkin and got up.

"So we'll make it Tuesdays and Thursdays again?" Mrs. Dean asked and smiled at him.

Vincent smiled back. "Tuesdays and Thursdays at six AM. Thank you for this chance."

Mr. Dean got up awkwardly and slouched at the shoulders, and gave an awkward wave with his crippled arm for Vincent to follow. "Don't forget your glove, son," he rasped. Vincent followed excitedly.

Once in the backyard, Vincent beheld a mound of dirt with a pitcher's rubber on top and a home plate flush against the worn grass by the woodworking shed. Vincent walked it off, counting his steps silently.

Sixty feet, six inches.

Against the shed wall were old bed mattresses. Mr. Dean caned his way into the shed and produced a heavy bag with a handle that had the Eagles logo on the side. The bag was very old, but very official looking. It was pretty dusty, evidence that it hadn't been used for a while. It was everything the old man could do to lug it.

Seeing this, Vincent ran over and took the bag from Mr. Dean. "Put it on the mound, son," the old man rasped.

Vincent ran it over to the mound and came back to Mr. Dean. He was bent over in obvious pain. In between sharp breaths, Mr. Dean said, "Grab this chair."

Vincent grabbed the folding chair Mr. Dean pointed to and followed him to the mound.

Once seated, Mr. Dean said as best as he could in an effort to keep from coughing, "Son, I don't have a lot of time to B.S., so I hope you'll listen and listen good. You're curious about the arm. It happened in World War II over in France. Long story short. Ask Elna, and she'll tell you more about it. It's an old story, and I don't want to tell it. After I came back I was a scout for the Eagles and I have trained professional athletes, specifically pitchers. See that mattress with the box?"

Vincent looked at the mattress behind home plate that was laying on its side against the wall of the shed and saw a black box taped onto it with electricians tape. "Warm-up your arm," Mr. Dean ordered. I wanna see what you got."

"Sir," Vincent started to speak, but he held his tongue. The guy didn't know he wasn't a pitcher.

"Like I said," Mr. Dean rasped, "I don't have a lot of words left, so don't make me repeat myself. Warm your arm up and hit the square."

"Yes, sir."

"Oh, by the way, they call me Grandpa Dean."

Chapter 4

Monday evening the team practiced for Tuesday's doubleheader with Alva, a club in the same class as Augusta. Before practice, Coach Grey talked down to the ball club about responsibilities.

He didn't come right out and say it, but he blamed the last game on Vincent, and his inability to be prepared for the game was what jinxed the whole team and kept them from sweeping Woodward.

Vincent kept his head down during the entire speech.

Another issue Coach Grey raised was responsibility. Responsibility was a key issue, and it was known that each player would be responsible for his own position and not concern himself with what was not his business.

Of course this wasn't what Vincent wanted to hear, not after working with Grandpa Dean. Vincent was still smiling when thinking about his meeting with Mrs. Dean and Grandpa Dean.

Grandpa Dean was a very quiet, but wise man. He showed little if no emotion as Vincent threw pitches for him.

Vincent shagged the fly balls Coach Redenbacher hit to him in the outfield and replayed the scene in his head, Grandpa Dean doing all the talking.

You want to throw that same pitch over again, son?

Grandpa Dean would look at his radar gun each time.

Again.

Again.

Again.

Grandpa Dean put the radar gun down, shook his head, and caned over to him to show Vincent the proper motion. Grandpa Dean looked very awkward, but illustrated well enough. Vincent had never been shown how to pitch, all the movements, the exaggerated gesticulations, the leg kick, the follow-through.

Vincent listened very carefully to Grandpa Dean's instructions, and on the next windup, looked over at the back window of the house to see Mrs. Dean looking out and smiling.

Whiff went the pitch.

Grandpa Dean shook his head each time Vincent threw.

After his last pitch, Grandpa Dean said, "Your arm hurtin', son?"

The youth responded, "No, sir."

Grandpa Dean took a deep breath and said, "Put the ball down and take a look." Vincent dropped the ball and walked over to Grandpa Dean. Vincent read the gun.

90 MPH.

"Holy cow! I can throw ninety?"

"Don't get cocky kid," Grandpa Dean said and spit. He was just starting to find his voice. "You have a long way to go before you're big league material. We gotta get that arm under control and get it in rhythm with the rest of your body. Right now you look like a giraffe trying to take a squat."

Vincent was still beaming and asked whatever he wanted. "If I work at it, how fast do you think I could throw?"

"That's not for you to worry about right now," Grandpa Dean responded. "You groove ninety mile-an-hour fastballs consistently and any hitter can catch your timing. We have much more to work on before you're ready to even show your coach what you can do. Tuesday morning then?"

Vincent walked away with a smile that wouldn't quit. Ninety miles-per-hour! Visions of pitching in The Show at all the big ballparks danced in his head. He was so excited that he had to run home, though there would be nobody there to tell.

*

After Vincent left, Mrs. Dean came outside acting ignorantly, as if she hadn't been watching the whole scene take place from the window.

"Well?" Mrs. Dean asked as her husband walked through the kitchen and straight to the fridge for some cold water.

"He's got it."

A tear ran down Mrs. Dean's cheek and she smiled. "How long will it take?"

Grandpa Dean took a drink of cold water from a bottle with a pristine mountain stream on the label. It made him cough.

"It better be before the summer's over."

"Doc's been wrong before," she said.

"No, he's right."

Mrs. Dean turned, and a tear rolled down her cheek. She composed herself long enough to ask one more question.

"Are you sure this is what you want?"

"You said he needs help."

"Yes," she responded.

Grandpa Dean paused then said, "Greater love has no one than this, that he lay down his life for his friends."

As if second nature, she recalled the verse. "John 15: 13. You are a wonderful man."

"Think of it as a penance."

"Doc could be wrong." She wiped the tear from her eye with her apron and left the room.

"No, he's right" Grandpa Dean said. "But that's neither here nor there."

*

Coach Grey asked Vincent to stay after practice. The other guys got into their cars and sped off as soon as they could after that tongue-lashing. None of the guys spoke to Vincent, and he didn't speak to them. Vincent was on cloud nine all practice. Nobody would rain on his parade. He made pin-point accurate throws from left field and hit the ball very well. He was a man on a mission, playing with a confidence he had never had before.

When Coach Grey had him alone, he said, "Vincent."

"Yes, Coach."

Putting his hands on his hips, the coach continued, "Did you learn anything from the other day?"

Vincent had to think hard about this one. It was a stupid question, but he needed to come up with the perfect answer that Coach wanted to hear. He could tell that Coach needed to be placated. "Yes, Coach."

"And what lesson was that?" Coach Grey inquired.

Vincent's thoughts wandered. *That you need your ego stroked.*

Vincent looked him straight in the eye and said, "That you're coach and that I am a player and what you say goes, sir." The lie came out easier than Vincent imagined it would.

Coach Grey grinned, stroked the hairs on his long chin. "So why were you grinning all practice? Was there something funny you were thinking about?"

"No Coach. I was just happy."

"About what?" Coach Grey inquired.

Vincent couldn't tell Coach about his private practice. Grandpa Dean forbade it; said Vincent wasn't even close to being ready to show his pitching skills.

Vincent again responded with confidence. "I guess I was just having a good day."

"Hmmm," Coach Grey paused. "That has to be it. Because I thought you might be grinning about breaking our brand new pennant. I bet that made you feel all high and mighty, didn't it, since you weren't really a part of that championship team last year."

The thought almost made Vincent smile, but he repressed it. He could see that Coach was egging him on, trying to get him to lash out, looking for a reason to can him.

Vincent looked at the Little Monster and saw that the pennant hadn't been replaced yet. He imagined the booster club members were probably working day and night. They probably lost sleep over it.

Vincent again side-stepped his coach's volley and said, "No, sir. I would rather the ball landed in the street."

It appeared Coach Grey didn't even listen to Vincent's response before saying, "Well, I don't want you getting cocky on us. It was a lucky hit. You closed your eyes. That's right, I saw it. So don't think that you're bigger than the team. I don't care what you do right in practice. No one player is bigger than the team. You got me?"

That irked Vincent. *What a hypocrite! That's not what you say about your son in the newspapers!*

"Of course, sir. I will try my best to help out the team in any way you see fit."

Coach Grey looked sideways at him. Surely this was not the reaction he was expecting? Surely he was expecting Vincent to lash back. From the look on Coach Grey's face, Vincent figured the coach thought Vincent was mocking him.

Coach Grey's neck loosened from the vice grip that held it, and he said, "If that's the truth, then good. I'm glad we had this talk. Now get outta here and don't be late tomorrow!"

"Yes, Coach."

Vincent took the long walk home and Coach watched him ascend the hill. Vincent felt his coach's stare in the middle of his back the whole time.

Vincent snuck a peek behind and saw Coach Grey talking on his cell phone.

*

Vincent showed up early for the game, a full twenty minutes before the first car entered the parking lot. By the time any of the other players had made the field, Vincent had run his warm-up laps and sat in the place reserved for the starters to stretch. Vincent didn't stretch before anyone else got there for fear that he would be seen as an individual rather than a team player, he didn't lay back and relax for fear that Coach would think he was lazy, and he didn't stand for fear that Coach would take it for arrogance. Vincent knew he had to walk on egg shells.

He sat with his hands cupped under his knees. Jake Jackson was the first to join him.

Jake plopped-down across from Vincent and nodded as he threw his bat bag down. There was an uncomfortable silence before Jake spoke up.

"You know, you're pretty fast."

Vincent was taken aback by this. Another compliment. He didn't know quite what to think, so he just nodded and lowered his head.

Jake continued, "You know, I woulda never gone for third."

"Huh?"

Jake turned his head toward the dugout and saw a few more players descend the hill and take the field. "You know, the other day when you tried to stretch that double into a triple. I woulda never gone for third, but I guess you didn't have a third-base coach."

"But you would have made it. I mean, you're our leadoff man. What is your forty time?" Vincent asked.

Jake looked into his bag and found some atomic balm and started applying it liberally to his right shoulder. He looked up at Vincent, back at the others approaching, and back at Vincent and said, "That's the point, Vincent. I'm gonna run track next year in college and I wouldn't have tried that. Yet you did, and you made it, despite what that ump said. What does that say to you?"

Vincent never had a chance to answer.

Quentin Albany slapped Jake on the back. "Double J, how's it hangin'?"

"Not bad Q Dog!" Jake replied. "Who's your sidekick?"

"You can call him Mighty Mouse!" Quentin said as Seth Short shoved him in the ribs and they all laughed.

Seth was short, only five feet, five inches, but was a very capable second baseman. The year before he saw limited action, but now as a junior was the full-time starter. He batted in the number eight slot normally and wasn't relied upon for his hitting. It was his defense that secured his starting spot.

Seth and Quentin sat down and both reached into their bags, apparently for the same reason Jake had just before. Vincent watched these seasoned pros and felt left out. He didn't have any hot cream to rub on his elbow or shoulder. He didn't need to, despite working with Grandpa Dean that morning and throwing fifty pitches. Grandpa Dean told him that it was of the utmost importance to keep track of his pitch count that way he didn't injure his arm.

Quentin looked up at Vincent and saw that he wasn't rubbing like the rest of the guys. "Yo Vincent, you want some?" Quentin held up a white tube with red letters on it.

Everybody looked up at Vincent.

"Uh, me?" Vincent responded.

"Yeah, you want some?" Quentin asked again.

"Uh, sure, I could use some." Vincent opened the tube and smelled it. He had never used the stuff. He was about to pour some cream into his right hand when Jake stopped him.

"Whoa! Vincent, you're right-handed, right?"

"Yeah," was all Vincent could think to say in return.

"Then rub it in with your left hand if at all possible, Jake continued. "If you get the stuff on your right hand the ball might slip out on a throw. It makes your hand sweat."

"Oh, thanks." Vincent felt stupid for not knowing, but put a pea-sized amount on his left hand and rubbed it on his shoulder. He didn't feel it at first, but after a few minutes his whole shoulder started to feel warm. It was a good feeling. His arm was so empowered that he felt he could throw a baseball all the way to the water tower, maybe through it. He flexed his arm and saw a vein on the inside of his forearm bulging out like when he lifted weights.

One by one the rest of the guys filed in and the two groups, starters and backups, segregated just like Coach had taught them. Bacon Bob and Jimmy were the last to show up, just before Coach Grey.

The team sat in a circle and stretched. The usual banter rose from guys, each laughing at the other. Coach Grey stood on home plate talking to reporters, giving the sound-bite. The team was half way through their stretches before Jimmy decided to stir up the hornet's nest. "So Vincent, you were in the weight room this past winter, weren't you?"

Vincent was wary. He didn't want anything to do with this guy, but nodded in reply and reached for his toes.

"Is that how you got your warning-track power?" Jimmy asked, then snickered.

The guys all looked back toward the Little Monster and saw that the pennant had been replaced just in time for Alva's ball club to come to town and see it.

"I guess so," Vincent replied. He wasn't going to give Jimmy a hook to bite on. He saw that Jimmy was looking for a fight, and Coach Grey was looking for any reason to kick Vincent off the team. After all, it wouldn't be Jimmy who would take the fall.

"So you know the story behind the Little Monster, don't you?" Jimmy continued probing.

Vincent reached for the other leg and shook his head.

"Back in the day it was considered too easy to hit a home run, so they put up the Little Monster to keep the junior high boys in the park. Looks like it was designed for you too."

Quentin about spoke up when Dusty grabbed Jimmy by the arm and said, "Dude, he hit it so hard that it broke the pennant. If the fence weren't there, it would have sailed right through the yellow house. Probably would have broken your record."

"Ooooo!" the guys said collectively as Jimmy turned red. Vincent sat there and kept quiet. He wasn't used to people standing up for him.

"Yeah, but it didn't because he couldn't lift it over the fence. I, on the other hand, put one out there, didn't I?" Jimmy yelled.

Jake spoke up. "This weekend I was watching a Charleston Demon's Game, and Omar Santos hit a rocket shot that wouldn't have cleared our fence either, but it still went over 400 feet. "Jake looked right at Jimmy and continued, "Santos wouldn't have gotten a double out of it had it hit the fence, and Vincent almost stretched a triple. Heck, he did stretch it cause we all know the ump missed the call!"

Vincent kept stretching, hiding his smile. Other people were sticking up for him for the first time in his life and it felt great.

"Yeah!" Quentin said. "And Vincent hit it harder than Santos did. That was the hardest hit I ever saw."

"It was nothing," Jimmy said and stared at Vincent.

This was more than Vincent could take. Memories of his father's childhood beatings, the snot-nosed little neighborhood

81

kids mocking him, the fact that neither his mom nor his dad loved him, all this came rushing violently into Vincent's eyes. Vincent looked up and everyone stopped breathing. He knew they saw the fire in his eyes, the bulge of the V shaped vein in his forehead. If looks could kill! He felt all the rage, all the flak he had taken over the course of his life, not just his parents, but the uncaring teachers, the pushing and taunting at school, and now this from Jimmy. It all came boiling up as the V began to pulse with the rapid beat of his heart. He knew he would punch Jimmy out by the end of the season, if he made it that long. That was how it usually shook out when people picked on him.

Vincent knew he was an easy target because he was unpopular. Once in school his freshmen year, three seniors off the football team jumped him. He didn't win. He ended up on the floor and got the boot treatment, but not before two of them left with black eyes. When self-preservation was an issue, Vincent could find that inner-strength. And now, that the coach's son was hassling him, it was all he could do to keep it in.

Jimmy looked surprised and a bit scared and this was something Vincent had never witnessed from the great Jimmy Grey. Jimmy reached for his lower abdomen as it gurgled.

Bill Jones chimed in, "So Vincent, how did you hit that thing so hard?"

Vincent kept his stare on Jimmy and said, "I closed my eyes."

Everybody sat there waiting. Finally, Vincent's stare turned into a slow, sly grin and the steam fled from his ears.

Jimmy tried to stare back at Vincent, but he just didn't have it. Jimmy Grey was not so insurmountable as Vincent thought, and he suspected that everybody now knew it. Jimmy was not the alpha-dog. Vincent waited for Jimmy to say something, but only bits and pieces of syllables came out.

"Guys, do I have to rip one to lighten the mood?" Bacon Bob spoke up, but nobody seemed to hear him. They were all fixed on

Jimmy and Vincent. Bacon Bob said, "Okay, I warned you," and jumped onto Jimmy's lap. Its purpose achieved, everybody let loose with the laughter again. Jimmy and Bacon Bob wrestled on the ground.

The only one who didn't laugh was Vincent. He felt his pulse slow in small increments. His breath turned cool again, and he finished his stretch.

Coach Grey and Coach Redenbacher came over yelling.

"Do you boys take nothing serious?" Coach Redenbacher said.

Coach Grey took over. "Get your butts off the ground and take the infield. Ned, get one of those underclassmen to warm you up."

Jimmy hopped up and whispered something in his father's ear. Coach Grey looked toward left field and then back at the team members slowly rising from the turf, and as an afterthought, said, "Fred, you're starting in left." Vincent looked up in disbelief as the guys got off the turf and ran to their positions. Jimmy looked back at Vincent and smiled and the vein popped out again.

*

Alva was outmatched. Ned lived up to his name as he threw gas right by the opposing hitters before Coach Grey took him out. Vincent kept his cool and watched the blowout from the bench without so much as a word. The home team jumped out to an eight-run lead after four innings before Vincent was finally inserted into left field for Fred who pitched the rest of the game. The top part of the inning was uneventful as the change in pace from Ned Gasser's fastballs to Fred Fingers' knuckleballs was enough to make pitching look easy, and Alva look pathetic. Vincent wondered if he might have the same effect if he were pitching. It was the bottom part of the fifth inning where things got interesting.

Coach, even with an eight-run lead, seemed reluctant to take out any of his starters. Vincent knew Coach's philosophy: that leads could vanish in the blink of an eye. They could always catch

Fred's rhythm, or his knuckleball might not knuckle and would then turn into a meatball sandwich. No, Coach had to leave his starters in long enough to make it official. After all, they already cost him his perfect year the week prior.

The inning started off innocently enough as Jimmy singled to left field. The pitcher intentionally walked Bacon Bob and Bill Jones to load the bases with no outs. Vincent looked up at the crowd as the hometown fans were laughing at the audacity of walking two players with no outs.

Alva changed pitchers to some right-handed runt with a very slow curve ball. With the wind out of right field, it put some pretty fierce break on the ball. And the next few hitters didn't even touch the bat to the ball, striking out. With the bases loaded and two outs, Vincent stepped to the plate.

He moved some dirt around in the batter's box and looked to third for a signal. Coach Grey talked to his son, not even paying attention to Vincent. Vincent waited until Coach Grey looked at him, exhaled out of frustration, and flashed a few signs that meant absolutely nothing. He seemed unconcerned.

Vincent felt slighted. *Thanks for the attention, Coach.*

Vincent nodded as if the coach had actually given him a sign, stepped into the box, and everything around him went quiet. The thoughts of the other day entered his mind and he tried to remember exactly what he had done right. Of course then he was facing a fireballer, not a junk ball pitcher like this kid. He hadn't even hit a curveball in practice. He decided to let the first pitch go by so he could get a good look at it.

The wind kicked up some dust from the baseline and blew it directly into Vincent's eyes as the first pitch came in low and outside. Vincent never saw it. He stepped out and cleared his eyes, but they were very blurry. He looked back at Coach who was still unconcerned.

Vincent figured, *Guess I'll have to do it myself.*

Stepping into the box, Vincent managed to clear his right eye. The second pitch landed in the same spot as the first had, and though he felt a huge desire to swing, he held up. At two balls and no strikes, he didn't even look at Coach. It didn't matter because he wasn't paying attention anyway.

Vincent made the sign of the cross with his bat on the plate for good luck. Whatever it meant, it worked last time and he knew superstition had a great hold on the sport. He looked up at the pitcher with two clear eyes. He could feel the pulse in his forearms again. It was a feeling of confidence, as if he could do no wrong. His grip on the bat seemed but an afterthought. The bat was an extension of his arm now. He had tunnel vision.

At the end of the tunnel was a boy with a few blond whiskers that were meant to constitute a goatee. The face shook a few times and the eyes scrunched. Vincent could pinpoint every little feature of the boy's face, and it was almost as if Vincent could read his mind. Vincent knew he had him. He knew the guy wanted another chance to throw the curveball and that he and the catcher were in a mental tug-of-war between a fastball and the curve. Apparently, the pitcher won out. The face smiled and the body got set.

Now Vincent smiled. *Don't have much of a poker face, do ya? Okay, curveball it is. Let's see it.*

Vincent took a step toward the pitcher in the batter's box so he could catch it before it broke out of his reach.

Jimmy took a safe lead from third and stood directly on the white chalk of the third-base line with his hands on his hips. He wasn't looking at the pitcher or the third baseman. His gaze appeared to take his mind to the stands, perhaps to his little blond ditz.

The dugout stopped chattering, and the players concentrated on Vincent.

The pitch came very slowly. It started at his head and Vincent immediately recognized the red dot right in the middle of the ball that the two prior curveballs had made from the effect the spin had on the seams. The ball slowly broke across his body in a tight arc, and directly into the strike zone.

Vincent's left leg kicked up like Grandpa Dean had shown him in pitching practice and settled in the dirt, turning with a transfer of energy from his hips. Through the tunnel Vincent saw the ball hit the bat and the energy that was transferred from his hips into in his extended arms transferred into the ball, which shot out at a bullet's velocity, straight down the third-base line.

Straight at Jimmy.

Even if Jimmy would have been watching, he wouldn't have had a chance.

The players in the dugout heard what sounded like two popcorn kernels popping back-to-back. The former was the *clank* from Vincent's bat, and the latter was a deep *thud*. It took Jimmy by surprise, right in the belly button.

"BLUGH!"

He went from standing to curled in a motionless ball on the ground in one movement.

"RUNNER'S OUT! RUNNER WAS IN THE BASELINE!" called the home plate umpire.

Vincent sprinted down the first baseline. He hit first base with his left foot and looked back to see a lump on the ground right by third base and Coach Grey on his knees right beside the lump. The umpire was running over to the lump and the stadium was silent.

As Vincent walked back to the bag, he realized what had happened. It had to be a foul ball because if the lump on the ground was Jimmy, surely he would be smart enough to be standing in foul territory, that way it would just be a foul ball. But when Vincent replayed it in his mind, he knew the truth. He blistered the ball and it was not going foul. Vincent's beautiful swing was for naught, because Jimmy didn't know better than to be out of the way, and his dad, as third-base coach, never told him.

The Alva players walked off the field, all looking down at the immortal lump when they passed him on the way to the dugout.

Coach Grey took Jimmy to the hospital and left Coach Redenbacher in charge. Vincent heard whispers abound and wondered if the crowd all agreed that #58, this newcomer, was a threat to repeating as state champions.

Vincent had quite the auspicious start, first breaking the pennant, then breaking Mr. All-World.

A line of cars followed Coach and son to the hospital like a funeral procession, leaving the stadium seats half-empty.

The boys held on to win the first game 8-0, but lost the second game 1-0 behind an uninspiring performance. Alva was inept at scoring runs, but a suicide-squeeze in the last inning was all it took to leave with the split.

Vincent went 3-3 in the game with three singles, but he was about the only one who could figure out the Alva starter who pitched a complete game, five-hitter.

The air seemed deflated from the Stampeding Herd, and a weak pep talk from Coach Redenbacher didn't help matters any. Nobody spoke to Vincent. He didn't mind. After all, it wasn't his fault that Jimmy was stupid enough to stand on the baseline. That was a rule Vincent had learned way back in Little League, never to stand in fair territory when leading off from third. But this was the first time he had seen a runner drilled. The fact that it was Jimmy made it all the more sweet.

As Coach Redenbacher dismissed the team, Jimmy and his dad pulled up in Jimmy's Corvette. The remaining crowd had been waiting their return and cheered when Jimmy stepped out of the car in his undershirt with an ace bandage around his stomach and raised his left hand in a wave. He still had the black smudges under his eyes, although they were smeared, maybe from tears.

*

The concerned crowd flocked Jimmy, and he and his dad answered any questions, the media's first. And as an added bonus, Channel 2 from nearby Enid was there to get highlights and instead got the leading sports story of the night. They captured every moment on tape. All concerned people of Northwest Oklahoma, Grandpa and Mrs. Dean included, found out that night on the ten-o'clock newscast, the injuries were minor with some possible internal bleeding, and that the doctor would be in close contact with Jimmy over the next few days. Grandpa Dean knew that Jimmy got the wind knocked out of him. That was it, and that was all.

Grandpa Dean and his wife sat on the couch watching the newscast, and when they saw the replay, he laughed himself into another coughing spell. "Serves the idiot right for standing in fair ground. What's this coach teaching these kids anyway?"

Mrs. Dean smiled politely.

Vincent's name was withheld, and the sportscaster summed it up by saying, "We'll all have our eyes on Jimmy as he and the rest of the defending state championship team plan to prepare for this weekend's Stillwater Invitational." Chants of *Ji-mmy, Ji-mmy, Ji-mmy,* echoed in the background as they went off the air.

*

Vincent had to walk past the mob to get home. He received angry glares, but nobody said a word to him. Vincent noticed that Coach Grey even looked up during the TV interview to shoot a glare out at Vincent as he walked by.

In the back of the parking lot was a Ford Explorer, the same one Vincent had seen from the night of the Woodward double-header, with the same bald man leaning across his hood, smoking a cigarette and staring at the mob. His eyes were as sharp as a hawk's as he watched the scene unfold. He looked down at his watch and then up at Vincent who went by. Vincent quickly looked away.

He kept to the alleys on the way home doing his best to blend in with the shadows.

Chapter 5

Vincent arrived at Grandpa Dean's house early Thursday morning, five minutes early. The two men sat down to bacon, eggs, and toast with black coffee. "A real man's breakfast" as Grandpa Dean called it. Vincent had never tasted coffee before, but decided he liked it. Mrs. Dean was her usual pleasant self, sliding a few more eggs onto Vincent's plate and refilling his coffee. Grandpa Dean didn't finish his breakfast. He left half his plate untouched and put a toothpick in his mouth.

Once outside, Vincent trudged a trail through the dew-laden grass to the mound and warmed up his arm. Grandpa Dean had to yell at Vincent a few times not to rush it, not to throw too hard until his arm was warm, lest it, "fall off." At 6:30 in the morning, the air was already alive and static with the looming threat of a hot day to come. Beads of sweat stood out on Vincent's forehead. The early-morning temperature hit eighty-three on the outdoor thermometer and the humidity neared ninety percent.

Grandpa Dean invited Vincent to sit down beside him. When comfortable, Grandpa Dean held up one of the old, ragged balls with his good hand and said, "Vincent, this is a baseball. What do you notice about it?"

"Sir?" Vincent responded.

"Don't say "sir" like I just asked you a question about astrophysics. What do you notice about this ball?"

Vincent looked it over really well. "It's round."

Grandpa Dean waited so Vincent continued.

"Uh, it's white, or at least it was. It's got these red stitches ..."

"EXACTLY!" Grandpa Dean said and started to cough. He studied it, moving his fingers from one side to the other. "Son, these stitches are your best friend. These stitches are the reason Sacramento's Sonny Giles's curveball drops like it does. These stitches are the reason nobody can see Francis Brando's slider. They are the same reason Shawn Love's fastball moved like it did. If a baseball didn't have stitches, everybody in the majors would bat over .500. You see what I'm sayin', son?"

"Yes, sir."

"These stitches use friction to react with the air, and depending on how you hold the ball, you can make it do anything you want: curve, drop, rise, even plunk someone in the stomach." Grandpa Dean smiled and looked at the boy who understood the inside joke. Grandpa Dean continued.

"Now, it's a trick to figure out how these stitches work. That's why I'm here. You gotta learn from what others say. They've failed and found ways to succeed so you don't have to go through the same failures they all go through. I want you to listen very carefully, boy, because I'm about to give you some secrets I don't normally give out. Most coaches don't know how to teach pitching and a kid's arm and career suffer because of it. Now how were you gripping the ball the other day?"

"I don't know," Vincent admitted.

"Exactly," Grandpa Dean snapped. "You don't know, and that's why your balls fly all over the place. Even though speed is important, movement is even more so. And how you put your fingers on the ball dictates what kind of movement the ball will have. That means you can have one pitch, the fastball in this instance, and make it move in different directions to baffle the hitters. Now what is your best pitch?"

Vincent thought for a moment. "Uh, all I can throw is a fastball."

"EXACTLY! That is the only pitch you need."

"Just one pitch?" the younger asked.

"Just one pitch," the elder replied.

"Then why do most people have at least two pitches, if not three or four?" Vincent questioned.

Grandpa Dean frowned. "Son, if you want my help you'll listen to me."

"Yes, sir."

Grandpa Dean continued, "Your fastball is your main pitch. Other pitches are effective only when you establish your fastball. But you're not ready for any other pitches yet. Odds are, I won't pollute your mind with the idea that curve balls and sliders are important, cause they're not."

Vincent sat there in silence waiting for instruction. He had learned better than to talk back. Grandpa Dean, satisfied that his pupil wasn't going to ask a question, kept talking.

"Now, there are different forms of the fastball, each one beautiful, each one with its own purpose. I'm not gonna show you how to throw with movement today. I'm gonna show you how to throw a straight ball. This will also help your accuracy from the outfield, which we both know you can use."

Vincent smirked, but then frowned, wondering how Grandpa Dean could know he had accuracy problems in the outfield. So far in the games his throws had been pretty much right on.

"Now when it comes to the fastball, Grandpa Dean said, "there's the two-seam, the four-seam, the split-finger, the cut, you name it."

"What does each one do?"

Grandpa Dean sighed. This kid needed a lot of help and he hoped the kid was a fast learner. "Take for instance the four-seamer. This is what we'll work on today. This is your most basic fastball." Grandpa Dean held the ball out in front and Vincent studied it. "Grip the ball with your middle and index fingers across the two widest seams, maybe a half inch apart. You release the ball just like you would when you make your throws from the outfield, letting the ball rotate off your fingertips with backspin. When you grip it right, the ball goes right where you want it to. That's great if you're in the outfield, but not so good if you overuse it as a pitcher."

Vincent paused for a moment, then said, "I had no control whatsoever the other day when I pitched for you."

"Control is the easiest part. All you have to do to hit your spot is to remember not to aim," Grandpa Dean said.

"Don't aim?" Vincent asked.

"That's right," Grandpa Dean said. "A pitcher never aims. He uses hand-eye coordination. There's a difference. You look the ball to the glove. It's that simple. Wherever you look, that's where the ball goes. You were looking all over the place, not concentrating on one spot. That's why you weren't hitting the strike zone with any consistency. Wherever you look, that's where the ball will go. That is unless you start thinking. You have to have total concentration on the glove, never letting your mind wander. Notice I said *total concentration*, not *over-concentration*. When you think too hard, you start double-guessing yourself. But we'll talk about that later. Throw some four-seamers for me."

Vincent got on the mound and went through a quick wind-up and tossed the ball over the mattress. It met the corrugated metal of the shed with a loud clang.

"Good grief, boy! That was the ugliest pitch I've ever seen!" Grandpa Dean got up and hobbled over to the mattress where his square strike zone was taped. He took out some black double-sided sticky tape from his pocket, bit off an inch-long piece and lightly tacked it directly in the center. He backed up from the plate one step, took the chewed-up toothpick out of his mouth and said, "Hit that piece of tape."

Vincent waited for Grandpa Dean to move, and when he didn't, he said, "Are you gonna move outta the way?"

"Son, I'm in the batter's box. If you hit me you'll just be doing me a favor. Anybody can hit this strike zone without a batter up there. Question is, how good is your concentration?"

Though unsure, Vincent responded, "Pretty good, I guess."

"Good." Grandpa Dean moved another half step closer to the plate so that his pants obscured the inside line of the strike zone from Vincent's view. The toes of his shoes were on the plate.

"Uh, Grandpa Dean …" Vincent started.

"THROW THE STUPID BALL!" Grandpa Dean yelled.

Startled, Vincent went into his windup and threw the ball about two feet outside and about fifty miles-per-hour.

"Now what in tarnation was that?" Grandpa Dean yelled, his voice cracking.

"I don't wanna hit you!"

Vincent looked toward the house and saw that Mrs. Dean was about to emerge from inside with a tray of tea, but held still by the screen door. She bowed her head.

Grandpa Dean composed himself. "If you listen to me, you won't hit me. I don't have much breath left, so what I tell you I expect you to take to heart. Don't make me repeat myself again. Look at that piece of tape!"

Vincent stared at it and back at Grandpa Dean.

"DON'T TAKE YOUR EYE OFF THAT TAPE!" Grandpa Dean repeated.

Vincent refocused on the tape, and he could feel that vein in his forehead pop out again.

"Now when you go into your windup, you don't take your eye off the tape. Throw the ball, follow through with your arm, and watch the ball all the way to the tape. You're going to hit the tape. I guarantee. Don't think. Concentrate!" Grandpa Dean stared at Vincent.

Vincent stared at the tape until that was all he could see. He could no longer see Grandpa Dean standing just five short inches away.

All was silent as Vincent's body went through the movement that he was accustoming himself to. He saw a white blur come in from the right side of his peripheral vision when his hand silently pushed through the vortex of air. In the next moment, the tape disappeared from the mattress. He looked up at Grandpa Dean who was still standing there with that stern look on his face and down at the ground where the ball rolled away with a black piece of tape stuck to it.

"I hit it!"

Grandpa Dean placed the toothpick back in his mouth and said, "Now that you can concentrate, we need to work on that awful windup of yours."

"The ball went right where I aimed!"

"Wrong!" Grandpa Dean corrected him. "You didn't aim. You never aim. You concentrated. All you did was reach out and touch that piece of tape with your mind. That's nothing more than hand-eye coordination."

Mrs. Dean exhaled and came out the back screen door with sunshine and a smile. "Who's ready for some tea?" Grandpa Dean gave her an irritated glance.

She placed the tray on the picnic table by the house and asked, "How's it going?"

"I hit a little piece of tape on my second try, Mrs. Dean!" Vincent beamed.

"That's wonderful son," she said with a smile and went back in the house.

Vincent felt like he could do no wrong. In a world where everything he did was worthless, he was finding self-worth very gratifying. And when Mrs. Dean called him "son," he wished for a moment that he was her son.

"Forget about that tea. We have to work on that windup of yours. Now stand like this." Grandpa Dean took his place beside the mound. He looked awkward with his shriveled right arm tucked into his side, but bent over at his waist and stared at the box, hanging his left hand loosely toward the ground like an ape.

Vincent turned it over in his mind so that he was seeing it right handed, copied the look, and felt stupid.

"You feel that?" Grandpa Dean asked.

"Feel what?" Vincent questioned.

"Feel the blood rushing into your forearm?"

"Yeah, I do," Vincent said. "That's what it feels like when I get up to the plate."

Grandpa Dean said, "That means the blood is *concentrating* in your arm. Concentration. It's a feeling of control, confidence. With the power in your arm like this, you can do anything. Throw 100 miles-per-hour with pinpoint accuracy, hit a home run, you name it. Now grab the ball with the four-seam grip." Vincent looked at the ball in his glove to feel it.

"What did I tell you about taking your eye off the catcher?" Grandpa Dean scolded him.

"Sorry, sir."

"Concentrate, Grandpa Dean reminded him. "In the windup you never take your eye off the catcher. That's why God gave you feeling in your fingers. Always place the ball in the glove with the four seams perpendicular to your fingers so all you have to do is grab it and throw it. You're smart enough to know where the seams are by feeling them."

Vincent tried it again.

Grandpa Dean said, "Now with your hand positioned on the ball and both still in your glove, bring your glove over your head like this." He modeled the position for Vincent and continued. "Now as your glove comes down, your leg kick comes up to meet your glove half way. Remember, you keep your hand in your glove so you don't give the hitter any chance to pick up on the ball any earlier than he has to. Show me."

Vincent brought his glove over his head like shown and then went into the leg kick.

"NOW STOP RIGHT THERE!" Grandpa Dean commanded.

Vincent stopped at the top of his leg kick and almost fell over before catching himself with his left foot.

"Now, you were leaning too far forward which is why you fell, Grandpa Dean explained. "You have to have balance or you'll have a harder time with your hand-eye coordination. If you're in the right position you will be perfectly balanced on your right foot. Your thigh will be parallel to the ground. All your energy should be balled up in your hips, ready to unleash like a bolt of lightning. Try it again."

Vincent tried it three more times before he was able to catch his balance. He still looked awkward, so Grandpa Dean insisted Vincent keep going into that position and holding until he felt totally comfortable. He never did.

"You're locking your knee, Vincent," Grandpa Dean explained. "You have to keep it slightly bent and flexed. That eighteen-year-old thigh should be strong enough to hold up your weight. Balance is everything. Each pitching element must be executed the same way on every pitch in order to gain control. Your motion has to be robotic. Now try it again." Vincent tried it again and this time it worked. "Hold it there."

Vincent held the pose for fifteen seconds before giving out. "That was pretty good, Vincent. Now it's time to unleash the lightning. You have to transfer all that balled up energy into the stride. It can't be too short or you won't use all your energy. It can't be too long or you'll overextend yourself and waste the energy somewhere in the process. It has to be comfortable. Something in the middle. Land on the ball of your foot and your arm will naturally follow across your body. Now start from the balance position without the ball."

It took Vincent three tries to get it just right, following through with his arm in slow motion. It felt natural which surprised him.

"You ready to throw your four-seamer now?" Grandpa Dean asked.

"You bet I am!" Vincent was full of energy. Besides the balance thing, he felt total confidence. He went through his new and improved windup and the throw landed a foot outside the box.

"You keepin' your eye on the target?" Grandpa Dean asked.

"Sorry." Vincent tried it all over again and on the follow through hit the square right in the middle.

Grandpa Dean hid a smile. "Like clock-work. Did you hear it?"

"Hear what, sir?"

"Hear the thunder," Grandpa Dean said. "Did you hear it?" Vincent looked up at a pale blue sky. A few cirrus clouds curled many miles up, not threatening a hair on his head.

"Not in the sky, Vincent! What did I tell you was in your arm?"

"Lightning?" the boy asked.

"That's right. You got lightning in your arm. When a storm approaches what happens first? Do you see the lightning or hear the thunder?"

"The lightning," Vincent responded with confidence. "The thunder comes later."

Grandpa Dean went into his point, "So think of it in those terms. Your windup is balled up electricity in a cloud waiting to be released, your stride and follow through are the bolt of lightning you unleash, and the sound of the ball hitting the catcher's mitt, or in this case the mattress is the thunder that resonates afterward. If you think about this on every pitch, you'll never aim, and you'll never double-think yourself out of a strike. The pitch will just throw itself right. Pitching is that simple. Concentration. The closer the lightning is, the faster the thunder claps. The harder you throw, the faster you hear the thunder. You ever seen lightning and hear the thunder at the same time?"

Vincent wiped the sweat from his brow and exhaled. "Sure, a few times. It was enough to scare the pee out of me."

Grandpa Dean laughed out loud. "Which is exactly how batters should feel when they are in the box. Now let's see some more four-seamers before we touch that tea."

Vincent smiled. The idea of his arm possessing lightning built his confidence toward the level of his potential. After twenty-five pitches, in which he hit each corner of the strike zone when asked, he sat down with Grandpa and Mrs. Dean to some iced tea. Vincent was a confident pitcher with pinpoint control.

Mrs. Dean looked at her husband who was physically worn out, to the point that he didn't even try to drink his glass of tea. He looked up at her and winked as his wife wiped his brow with a handkerchief. She smiled back, a knowing smile as this young boy, the boy they never had, gulped glass after glass of iced tea before leaving to go to work.

Chapter 6

"Can you hear me?"

"Roger. You're coming in loud and clear."

"So we're coming in after the PSA, correct?"

"Yeah… It should be the Smokey the Bear one. Hey, don't forget to go straight into the Station ID after your intro. It'll be exactly two after the hour. Got it? What time you got?"

"Right-E-O. I'm reading 10:01 and thirty-three seconds."

"Roger that. You're all set to go. Have a good broadcast Sol."

"Thanks, Paul."

"Ten seconds."

"You ready Joel?"

"I'm dying up here, but ready for your cue."

"Five, four, three, cue intro."

"Now, a 1230 KBAL Tradition for the past sixteen years, it's Augusta Stampeding Herd baseball! Brought to you by Fischer Plumbing. Your number two is their number one. By Rowdy's Food Market, open seven days a week. They're your food source for quality and a friendly smile. And by your local merchants. And now, Augusta Stampeding Herd baseball with The Sultan of Swat, Solomon Smity, and Joltin' Joel Richards."

"Hey, all you back in Augusta, like our intro suggested, this is the Sultan of Swat, Sol Smity with Joltin' Joel Richards bringing you Augusta Stampeding Herd baseball. But before we get too far along, let's pause for station identification."

"Bringing you the best of the golden oldies, this is 1230 AM, KBAL, Augusta."

"A very good morning to everyone listening out there. It's gonna be a scorcher today. Temperature here in Stillwater is a balmy eighty-five degrees. There's not a cloud in the sky and the weatherman is predicting conditions to be high and dry for this Saturday to kick off the 32nd Annual Stillwater Memorial Day Invitational. Before we go any further, I'd like to introduce my colleague, the best color man in the business, Joltin' Joel Richards."

"Thanks Sol. It is indeed going to be a scorcher today as the leaves on the nearby trees look like they're about to curl up and die. The heat waves are so thick that the trees out beyond the right field fence of Diamond Number Nine look like a mirage. If you forgot your water jugs, bring plenty of cash cause at two dollars a bottle, the Stillwater Merchants are cleaning house. We haven't had any rain in Northwest Oklahoma in a while, and I know I don't have to tell the farmers in the area about that. Can you remember a summer when all the cuttin' in the area was completed by the end of the first week of June?"

"No, Joel, I can't recall. It's been hot and dry and reports coming in say we're averaging eight to ten bushel of wheat per acre, one of the saddest harvests I can remember in recent history."

"Right you are Sol, and speaking of sad, we need to talk about that second game of the twin bill with Alva the other night."

"We'll get to that and other stories before we're done here. By my watch, it's 10:05 A.M. Our Stampeding Herd drew the early game, which is great considering they can get one under their belt before the heat of the day really sets in."

"Darn right. The sun will be murderous on the kids today. We'll find out how fit these boys are today."

"We are twenty-five minutes out from the start of the Stillwater Tournament. Augusta is the defending champion of this prestigious early-season tournament, yet they didn't get the number one seed, much less one of the four first round byes as they are slated to play the Ardmore Golden Bears in the first game, a tough AAA ball club that went to the state tournament last year."

"We'll get to that story and a few others like the health of our superstar, Jimmy Grey. As you know he was drilled in the stomach during the first game against Alva by a wicked line drive off the bat of a newcomer to the lineup this year, Vincent Preston. We'll talk about both of those boys and give an astonishing fact that you've probably overlooked. Plus we'll talk to Coach Grey about the preparations he made for this tournament and how he plans to bounce back from that disappointing 1-0 loss to an Alva team that quite frankly isn't that good. All those things and more when we come back from commercial. This is Stampeding Herd Baseball."

"And we're out."

"That coming through all right, Paul?"

"Straight down the line."

"Is it as hot back in Augusta as it is here right now?"

"We got air conditioning in the station Sol. You need to get in more often."

"Well up here in the press box it's about 120 degrees and those idiots forgot to put sliding windows in here so there's not a bit of breeze. The sweat is dripping off my body and soaking my socks. What a pit. It's like looking straight into a furnace and seeing Shadrach, Meshach and Abednego dancing around. I'd like to step in front of that hose they're spraying on the infield."

"Who?"

"Never mind."

"Twenty seconds, guys."

"Hey Joel, let's start with the Jimmy section before moving onto the record. If we got any time left after Coach Grey, we'll get into this new kid."

"Maybe bring it up during the interview."

"Five, four, three,"

"And we're back. We'd like to remind our good folks out there that the gas you put in your car is a direct reflection of how you feel about your car. Love your car with super-clean Petro gas. That's Joe's Petro. This week with every full tank of gas you'll get to choose between a fresh order of cheese nachos or a free Joe's Petro keychain. That's Joe's Petro. So, what's on tap first, Joel?"

"Sol, let's talk about the injury to Jimmy Grey first."

"Right. I, along with everyone else in town was speechless during the fourth inning of the first game against Alva when a blowout turned into a major blow for Augusta. Unless you've been camping in a cave the last three days, you know that Jimmy was drilled by a sharp line drive off the bat of Vincent Preston, reserve left fielder. Jimmy took a lead from third and never had a chance to get out of the way. To add insult to injury the Umpire called Jimmy out, saying he was in fair ground. I think we all know that wasn't the case."

"Right you are Sol. The blue really blew that call."

"Poetically speaking, nice call Joel. It put the brakes on a good Augusta rally. We had the bases loaded, but more importantly, it put Jimmy in the hospital. Thankfully tests came back negative yesterday and Jimmy has been given the green light to play this weekend, but will he be up to it? Joel, what is Jimmy's condition?"

"Sol, I ran into Jimmy about an hour ago in the bathroom, and he assured me he was a warrior and that it would take a shot to the head to keep him out of the game."

"Sounds like Jimmy is in good spirits. He exemplifies all the qualities of a natural-born leader. He's sort of a throwback, isn't he?"

"Sure is. He's old-school in the fact that he's willing to play injured because he knows the team is better with him in the lineup. That's a lesson for all you kids out there. Pain is temporary, but pride is forever."

"Well put Joel. I get nauseous just thinking about it, much less watching the replay on TV. Will it affect his play today?"

"We'll have to see. That's the million dollar question. His swing might be a little tight with his bruised stomach muscles and he might be a little stiff and slow, but I'm willing to bet the farm he comes out and surprises all the nay-sayers out there."

"Farm might not be worth much this year Joel."

"Yep. Feels like the *Grapes of Wrath* out there this year."

"Yeah, it's so bad that I saw a family walking down the road with all their belongings in a wheelbarrow. They were heading west, presumably for California. Isn't there gold out there?"

"That's what I heard. Apparently they're tripping on the stuff out there. Well, the grounds crew has just finished watering the field and the Ardmore Golden Bears are taking infield. We'll talk about what a tough first round battle this will be with Coach Grey who is making his way up to our booth right now. So we'll take a short break. You're tuned into Stampeding Herd baseball on 1230 on your A.M. dial."

"We're off."

"Check out the grimace on Coach's face, Sol."

"Ha! Yeah. He doesn't have much to be happy about right now. Good thing Jimmy's already signed that letter of intent, huh?"

"Darn straight. Here he comes- Hey Coach, how's it going?"

"Go a lot better if we'd be seeded first like we're supposed to be. Those jerks from Stillwater really put the screws to us. No first-round bye, making us play out here in the boondocks. What field is this, number nine? Feels like unlucky number thirteen. May as well not come back next year if we're going to get treated like this. Plus it's hot up here!"

"You don't have to tell us that. I can smell Sol from over here."

"Funny. Here's your headphones, Coach."

"You guys both smell like an outhouse."

"…three,"

"And we're back with the head honcho of the Stampeding Herd, Coach Grey. Coach, the first question on everybody's mind is about Jimmy. What did the doctor say at the hospital?"

"He was cautious. That was a pretty good shot that Jimmy took to the stomach. It missed the ribs so the next question was whether or not there might be some internal bleeding, but it appears Jimmy has a stomach of steel, something he got from eating his mother's cooking all these years."

"Ha!"

"He only has a small chink in the armor. The bruising will go away. We just had to be cautious."

"Coach, that's good to know. You just put a lot of people's worries to rest, especially Coach Milford over at UNCO. Are we going to see Jimmy on the mound any at all?"

"Not unless we have to. I'd rather not push our luck with his stomach muscles, but just keep them from stretching any more than they have to. We have three capable pitchers who can sustain us and Dusty is ready for spot duty if need be."

"Just a few minutes ago Coach, Joel, and I were just talking about the challenge before the team today having to play a first round game versus a tough Ardmore ball club that made the AAA State playoffs before bowing out in the first round. Coach, tell us the difference between AAA and AA. Is there really a difference between the toughest class and the class that we play in?"

"Well, that's a good question, Sol. You know, some years I think we've had the pitching that could run the tables at the AAA

State tournament. I think we could have won it last year because we all know hitting wins games and pitching wins championships. You don't see many Providence Wildcat teams win the World Series without three solid starters."

"Very true Coach. The Wildcats are known for their great hitters like Smith, Manson, Godfrey, Jones, and into the modern era with Jackson, Jacobs, and Jerrell, but behind all these hitters is a competent staff that keeps their series' ERA's in the low twos. Don't have to score many runs when you've got pitching like that. What can you say about our pitching thus far?"

"Good question, Joel. We really miss Brady this year. So far we've been inconsistent at best. Greasy Gabe Conway has been our number one starter without a doubt. He's had the luxury of pitching on windy days, and that junk he throws has baffled the hitters. He's only given up one earned run in two starts. Nasty Ned hasn't come around yet. That fastball of his has been too concise-he's putting it across the plate too often and has paid the price, especially in the Woodward game where they found the street beyond the Little Monster on a few too many occasions. Now Alva couldn't catch up to his fastball, but I'm sure Ardmore will be able to today if he doesn't work the corners a little better, even with this wind blowing in."

"So you're starting Ned. What can you say about Fred Fingers so far?"

"Fuzzy has been a good set-up man for us, but so far he's pitched more innings than I would like to see him throw. That's the good thing about a knuckleballer. He can put in as many innings as you need him to and all you have to worry about is a cut cuticle!"

"Ha! Ha! That's pretty funny."

"But seriously, I don't like knuckleballers. I trust the knuckleball about as far as I can throw it cause it's such an inconsistent pitch, but Fuzzy has come around for us and done what we've asked without complaining. As you know, he's been playing some left field, a position he'd never played before this year."

"That brings me to my next question, Coach, and the Joe's Petro Fact of the Day. Can you tell us who has the highest batting average on the team right now? You probably keep pretty good stats on that."

"Actually I've been a little preoccupied with trying to fix our problems to concern myself with numbers just yet, cause it is early, as shown in our record, but if I were to guess, I would say, hmmm... Jimmy had one bad game... I would say it's gotta be Dusty."

"You're close. Dusty has the second best average on the team right now with an amazing .667 average, but one player's higher than that yet. Anymore guesses?"

"Uh, you got me there. Clodhopper?"

"No, Bill Jones is right there with a .476 average, good for third. Would you like to know?"

"Quentin?"

"Nope. Believe it or not, the person with the highest batting average on the team right now is your number nine hitter and reserve, Vincent Preston."

"Vincent? How many at-bats does he have, Sol?"

"So far he's 4-5 in three games for an .800 average. Ironically his only non-hit was the line drive that hit Jimmy in the gut."

"You don't say? Well, with only five official at-bats I don't think we'll consider him in the running for MVP yet."

"Coach, Vincent was projected as the starter in left field, but he's not seen much action yet."

"Vincent has been in my doghouse so far. But before you ask, it's something we're keeping in-house. We're dealing with the problem and expect to move on."

"Coach, on all five of Vincent's at-bats he's hit hard line drives. I heard some people in the stands the other day say that he purposefully hit the ball at Jimmy, that he was upset at Jimmy, and that he has that kind of accuracy swinging a bat. But he bat a measly .210 last year in mop-up duty. Is there any truth to this rumor, and has he improved that much over the off-season?"

"That's the most outrageous thing I've ever heard. I've never met a player who could direct his shots that well before, except in slow-pitch softball. If there were an ounce of truth to that, I'm afraid young Vincent would be watching from the stands. We wouldn't tolerate that kind of behavior on our team. We all get along. We have to. This is a team sport and each player depends on each other to get his individual job done. We live as a team and die as a team. Besides, I think his average is inflated. Vincent's not that great of a hitter. If he gets a quantity of reps in, you'll see that average drop back down under .300. Trust me."

"Coach, you've done your scouting report on Ardmore. Who on their team scares you the most?"

"I don't think one player from their team scares me. We won't be stealing many bases this game cause their catcher has a heck of an arm and a bat to boot, and is just a junior this year, but I think we can match up with them pretty evenly."

"So which is the team to beat at the tournament?"

"Well, we are. We're the defending champs, so as far as I am concerned, it's our title until someone takes it away from us. We're the only AA squad to ever win this tournament, and we're not about to give back that trophy yet. We have a good following today. I see a lot of blue and white in the stands and at the end of the tournament, I think you'll see us on top."

"Coach, I've saved the best for last. I know you need to get back down to your team. It looks like Coach Redenbacher has them looking good on the infield right now. Everyone wants to know, is Jimmy 100% for today?"

"Well, that's a question for Jimmy. As a coach I'll never get the truth out of a player of Jimmy's caliber when he's hurt. A great player who's hurt will try to play no matter what. And Jimmy is a great player. As a parent I definitely know he won't tell me anything. But he says he's ready to go, so I'm ready to see what he's got."

"Coach, as always a pleasure. We wish your team the best of luck today against Ardmore and hopefully we can get this first one outta the way and advance in the winner's bracket."

"Thanks Sol. Say Joel, we gotta catch up on some of that golf one of these days."

"You got it Coach. Take care. Coach Grey, ladies and gentlemen. Coach and I try to play a round of golf with each other at least once a month at Nine Pines. Nine Pines Golf Course, the best nine-hole golf course in the state, located a mile west of Augusta on Eighth Street overlooking scenic Jack's Creek and State Hospital. Play where Coach Grey plays. Nine Pines, where everybody is on top of the leader board."

"Right on Joel. We're going to pause a few seconds for a commercial break. When we get back we're going to sum up this pre-game show with a review of Ardmore's ball club. You're listening to 1230 KBAL, Augusta."

"We're off."

"Man Joel, Coach really took exception to your questions about the Preston kid."

"You ask me, there's something going on there that he doesn't want anybody to know about. You see that look he gave me? I didn't think it was that bad of a question, but apparently I hit a sore spot."

"And when has he ever wanted to keep something in-house?"

"That's the point. He's never withheld information about a player or a performance before. I usually can't shut him up!"

"Maybe we've never asked the right questions."

"Apparently."

"Guys, you got twenty seconds."

"Say Joel, where'd you spot that john this morning?"

"The big building in the middle of the four main fields."

"There's nothing out here?"

"Just those woods beyond right field."

"Tempting. I might just have to pour out my pop and use this cup before the end of the first. I have to go so bad, it's leaking out my ears!"

"Dude, that's sick!"

"four, three,"

"And we're back. This is the Sultan of Swat Solomon Smity here with the one and only Joltin Joel Richards and you're listening to Augusta Stampeding Herd baseball. The captains are making their way to home plate right now to flip for home field. We are about four minutes shy of official game time and before we get to the line-ups, here's Joel with the specifics on the weather."

"Thanks Sol. The temperature will play a big part in this game. It's already up to eighty-eight degrees. The wind will also play a big factor on hitting. Our first game will be played on field number nine. The right-handed batter will be pulling the ball directly into the wind, which is whipping the pennants along the outside of the field at roughly twenty miles-per-hour. The weatherman is forecasting temperatures to soar to 105 degrees with a south wind twenty to thirty miles-per-hour and gusts up to thirty-five with no chance of rain. Right now is the best weather we'll see all day."

"Thanks Joel. And now for your starting lineups, courtesy of Joe's Petro. Joe's Petro, where you can trade in your old battery for twenty percent of its original value and receive your very own Girls of Petro Calendar free. That's at Joe's Petro in Augusta. And now for our lineups."

*

That was the most ridiculous thing Grandpa Dean had ever heard. He considered turning the radio off, but kept it on out of morbid curiosity of what that arrogant coach was going to say next. Sure, Grandpa Dean knew Vincent's average was inflated. There was no way he would keep it around .800 and would probably have a tough time with .400, but to come out and say that your player wasn't that good, not even the old time managers were that mean just for the sake of being mean.

Grandpa Dean sat in his big overstuffed armchair and adjusted the tuner on his stereo so the reception would come in better. He plugged in his headphones and put them on so Elna wouldn't have to listen to the stereo as loud as Grandpa Dean liked it. He wasn't deaf yet, would never get the chance to make it there.

Putting on the headphones was like taking a trip back in time, back to when he was a Lieutenant Radio Operator on a B-17 flying missions out of England into Germany during WWII. The hand dial on his home stereo was much nicer than the antiquated piece of machinery he worked with back then. But as irony would have it, over fifty years later he was listening to a baseball game on AM.

One of Grandpa Dean's jobs during the war was to transmit and decipher Morse Code. He could transmit fifty words a minute back then. Grandpa Dean looked down at his shriveled right hand. His flashbacks were nearly non-existent for the past thirty years, but sometimes, something would jar his memory. This time it was the radio dial. Other times it would be something else like a sonic boom or a car backfiring. It was the same thing that other vets went through. Grandpa Dean swore to himself that he wouldn't let it rule his life. But his arm was an everyday reminder of that time spent behind enemy lines.

He grabbed yesterday's newspaper and turned to the sports page as the first inning came over the airwaves. The tournament bracket spread before him. He checked out the seedings:

Stillwater Memorial Day Annual Invitational
Single Elimination Tournament Seeds
1. Stillwater Giants (AAA)

2. Topeka, Kansas Reds (Maj.)
3. Emporia, Kansas Blues (Maj.)
4. Guymon Dodgers (AAA)
5. Augusta Stampeding Herd (AA)
6. Stillwater Bronchos (AAA)
7. Joplin, MO Black Sox (AAA)
8. Enid Cubs (AA)
9. Ulysses, Kansas Tornadoes (AAA)
10. Stillwater Jackals (AA)
11. Seiling Pirates (AA)
12. Ardmore Golden Bears (AAA)

Grandpa Dean coughed under his breath. *The Stillwater Giants got the number one seed. There's a big surprise. Looks like we're the number five seed? Sounds about right to me, with teams from Topeka and Emporia in the tournament. Coach Grey should be happy he got seeded where he did as bad as his kids are playing!*

Mrs. Dean came into the sitting room with a tray in her hands.

"Time to take your pain medication, Pa."

Grandpa Dean ignored her, so she gently took the earphones off his head and repeated herself.

Grandpa Dean looked at her and said, "I don't hurt."

"Honey, you know that if you don't take them right now you'll regret it later."

Grandpa Dean finally relented. "Okay." He grabbed his pills and the glass of water. His wife just stood there watching him.

"You don't have to stand over me like I'm a little child. I'll take them."

"So show me," she said.

He knew she knew his little tricks. "Look, if I take them I'll fall asleep before the game is over. Please just let me take them in the fourth or fifth inning?"

Mrs. Dean sighed and walked back to the kitchen without a response.

*

The fourth inning had passed into the fifth and Grandpa Dean still hadn't taken his meds. His back was aching and he was coughing up some yellow stuff with little black specks sprinkled in. It went along with the territory. He had been going through two handkerchiefs a day lately. But that didn't seem to matter much because he was lost in the moment. Grandpa Dean was steaming that Coach still hadn't put Vincent into the game. The annoying announcers had commented on it once or twice, and it became a relevant topic for conversation in the fifth.

"Well, Joel, we're in the bottom of the fifth inning and we still haven't seen that Augusta offense kick in. This marks fourteen straight innings, scoring just one run, going all the way back to the first game with Alva on Thursday."

"Sure enough Sol. We knew Boxberger would be tough and hoped we wouldn't have to face him. I guess we foolishly thought they might try to hold onto their ace for the second round, but here we are."

"Yep, here we are scoreless going into the bottom of the fifth; it's 3-0 Ardmore leading. Ned Gasser has had great stuff today, but Bret Boxberger from Ardmore has one-upped him. Boxberger has thrown four perfect innings and his fastball slider combination has been enough to baffle the Augusta hitters. Only one ball has left the infield, a lazy fly ball to left that got held up in the wind. We gotta hope the kid runs out of gas, because he's looking as good as advertised. Mississippi Tech sure has a dandy in this kid."

"One thought that's on my mind right now, Sol, is the status of Vincent Preston. As we mentioned earlier, he's 4-5 on the year in reserve duty. Does Coach need to make a change and get him in the lineup?"

"Well, I'm not sure, but what I do know is that we need some kind of a spark right now. Up to the plate is our number eight hitter, second baseman, Seth Short."

The pain was too great for Grandpa Dean. He reached and grabbed two blue diamond shaped pills and one red horse pill filled with liquid and put them down with water. The effect was almost immediate. He sank into his chair, a comfortable man. The last thing he remembered hearing was, "Strike three retires the side."

*

Grandpa Dean was running through the rolling hills at night. In the distance he heard a dog barking over toward a farmstead with a solitary light in one of the windows. Behind him was the faint sound of artillery. Down the hill he ran toward a ravine, looking back to make sure he wasn't being followed. He was cold and wet and was happy that the rain had finally stopped. He vowed to find a restful spot in the morning that was both secluded by cover and that had enough sunlight to dry him out. He wanted to ball up for warmth, but knew he had to keep on the move. It was too dangerous to move in the sunlight. "Maybe just tonight," he said under his breath. "The straw in the barn would feel nice and warm." But the barking got louder and louder and his feeling of security left him. He must get on the move again.

Just then he was shaken awake by his wife. She looked strange to him, like a character in a dream, but slowly his senses came back to him, and he remembered where he was. The newspaper still lay on his lap, the headphones neatly placed on top.

"You missed it!" his wife yelled in excitement. "You have to turn on the radio right now!"

"Wha…" Grandpa Dean started when his wife interrupted him.

"The end of the game! I listened to it in the kitchen. Vincent did it. Quick, turn it on!"

Grandpa Dean reached over and unplugged the earphones from the stereo and it came to life, louder than Mrs. Dean liked.

"…DRAMATIC WAY TO START OFF THIS TOURNAMENT AND SEND US INTO THE SECOND ROUND!"

Mrs. Dean quickly turned the volume down to a tolerable level.

"What can I say, Sol? Words have left me. There's no way a ball could leave the ballpark in conditions like this with the wind blowing in at thirty miles-per-hour, but Vincent Preston has done it. In case you're just tuning in, you missed one of the most dramatic finishes I can remember in Augusta Stampeding Herd History! Ardmore ace Bret Boxberger took a perfect game into the seventh inning, but with fielding errors and a walk to Quentin Albany to load the bases, Coach pulled the trigger on Vincent Preston, inserting him in as a pinch hitter for Fred Fingers, and Preston took the first pitch slider over the right-center field fence into that dense stand of trees for a grand slam to break up the no hitter and win the game in dramatic fashion. Holy cow! I can't take much more of this!"

"And you want me to add another log to the fire, Sol? If my statistics are right, that was Preston's first home run, not just of the season, but of his entire career! It doesn't get any more dramatic than this!"

"Whew! Let me catch my breath. The team is jumping up and down around Vincent at home plate. What a sight! I have never seen a bigger smile on a kid's face. We need to take a break. You're listening to Augusta Stampeding Herd Baseball!"

Grandpa Dean smiled and turned off the radio. His wife looked lovingly at him and said, "Isn't that just wonderful? You know, you're giving the boy so much confidence working with him. When do you think he'll be ready to pitch?"

"Give me a few more weeks with him," he replied. "I want that coach of his to give the boy a fair shake, not dismiss him. I'm going to go back to sleep. Wake me up when they start game two, will you?"

"Sure thing, honey," Mrs. Dean said.

Thirty seconds later, he sat there slumped in slumber with a smile to match Vincent's.

*

Two members of the team, both with the last name of Grey, didn't join in the celebration. Father stood in the third-base coaching box with a perplexed look on his face. He scratched his mustache. Son sat on the bench with his face buried in his glove.

Coach had clearly given Preston the take sign. The boy was supposed to watch the first pitch go by. Instead Preston gave himself the green light and powered a rocket over the fence to win the game. What was Coach to do?

Essentially the boy had usurped his power. He disobeyed the head coach's sign, and now the boy was the hero. Was he to yell at Vincent for not obeying his command? Play it off because the team needed the emotional win? Take credit, saying he gave Vincent the green light so that he doesn't lose authoritative face with the fans?

He couldn't have this anarchy on his team. His players had to respect his authority. He wondered if maybe Vincent was too dumb to understand the sign. He knew that Vincent took a risk and easily could have ended the game with a pop up or ground ball. The kid had gambled and won. Surely he wouldn't be so lucky next time, and there would have to be a next time.

Coach Grey saw that the kid was the hero, the team was starting to respect him, and the fans were starting to love him. It wasn't a good PR move for Coach to discipline the kid. It was more of a tightrope than Coach was used to walking. To add another log to the fire, Coach Grey had a specific arrangement with a local "businessman" who wasn't going to be too pleased with the end result of the game. What had seemed like a fool-proof way to earn some extra cash ended up back firing. Coach Grey didn't want that to get out to the public. He would lose his job, the respect of the whole community, and worse yet, his son would never forgive him for mixing up with the kind of people he had always told Jimmy to stay away from. After all his son was an innocent kid who didn't know about the horrors of the real world and how things really were.

Visions of famous scandals raced through Coach Grey's head as he twisted his mustache some more. He would have to do whatever necessary to protect Jimmy's innocence. It was a lot to consider. Coach stood there pondering his next move.

*

As for Jimmy, he didn't celebrate. He sat on the bench not moving an inch. He had flinched when he saw the ball take off from the bat hoping, praying.

Please hang up! Please hang up... Uh oh.

Jimmy watched a few of the players awkwardly attempt to carry Vincent off the field, and his dad yelled at them to put him down.

Jimmy grabbed his glove and bag and looked toward the stands. The same bald man from the parking lot the other night stared back at him, looked toward the trees beyond the right field fence, and started walking.

Jimmy gulped. *Oh, man.*

Jimmy's dad gathered the kids in the valley between fields nine and eight for a meeting. He gave a weak congratulatory speech, praising their "never-say-die" attitude and mentioning a few facts about their upcoming opponent, the Guymon Dodgers AAA squad who got the four seed.

Jimmy saw Vincent smile from ear to ear as the occasional hand patted his back. It made Jimmy want to punch the interloper. He was repulsed at Vincent's innocence.

Jimmy kept glancing toward right field with a worried look.

The five minute speech felt like an hour. When Jimmy finally slipped away to the trees outside of right field afterward, he was greeted with a sour look.

"That was $400 I just lost. $400! What do you have to say?" the bald man asked.

Jimmy pushed a piece of bark with his cleat and peered back toward the field. Nobody was coming. "Deuce man, what can I say? I did everything I could. I didn't get on base, I didn't throw anybody out, nothing. In fact ..."

"SHUT YOUR MOUTH BEFORE I SHUT IT FOR YOU!"

Jimmy stopped abruptly. He was genuinely scared.

"Don't talk to me like I'm one of your little followers! I could care less what you say you are in charge of and what you can't handle, and I could care less about your precious little scholarship. I could end you right now! I got people to answer to also! We had an agreement. When I bet against you, you lose and you get all the free grass you want. It's that simple. When your team wins, my boss blames me and then I have to blame it on somebody. Since you're my little partner, the blame goes directly on you."

"But-" Jimmy tried to squeeze in his excuse, but was promptly cut off.

"There are no buts." Beads of sweat dripped off Deuce's forehead and onto his glasses. He took his glasses off, cleaned them, and wiped his forehead. "You not in control anymore? Do you need some encouragement?" He lifted the front of his red t-shirt to reveal the handle of a 9mm handgun. He quickly lowered his shirt.

Jimmy nearly lost control of his bowels.

"You got a problem with our little arrangement now?"

It took a second for Jimmy to catch his voice and he uttered a nervous, "No, Deuce."

"Or maybe we should just let your father know what you're up to?"

This scared Jimmy worse than the handgun. He couldn't have the shame of his father knowing what he had gotten himself mixed up with. "No Deuce. Please don't tell my dad! I'll do anything you want."

Deuce was amused that he could keep father and son from knowing about their existences in this little charade. As bad as things appeared on the outside, there was always a silver lining, a way that a loss can be turned into a gain.

Knowing he had Jimmy right where he wanted him, he continued. "At four-to-one odds against I should have raked up! Now I owe $400, and you're going to earn it back for me. You guys are underdogs the rest of the way, so I can't bet against you. So you're going to have to sell your way back into my good graces. You're in my pocket now." Deuce zipped open his backpack and threw a freezer bag full of marijuana at Jimmy.

When Jimmy recognized what it was, he dropped it like it was a deadly virus.

"Man, you crazy?!?" Jimmy said. He looked around to make sure nobody was watching and kicked it behind the trunk of a Chinese elm. "I'm not a drug dealer! I'm barely a recreational user! I don't know how to sell the stuff!"

"PICK IT UP!"

Jimmy picked it up and awkwardly stuffed it in his baseball bag.

"You know what the stuff's worth. Get rid of it before the end of the weekend. And I better not catch you pocketing any of the profits!" Deuce growled.

"But ..."

"You like that little scholarship to North Central Oklahoma?" Deuce continued. Because if you don't, I can always come clean with the cops and then introduce you to a few guys in the big house who would love to make your acquaintance. They like them nice and prissy, just like you. You understand what I'm sayin'? You're in the big leagues now, kid! You are now officially in my debt." Deuce lifted his shirt and stroked the butt handle of his gun and walked back toward the field.

Jimmy waited five minutes for his heartbeat to settle before heading back to the diamonds.

*

Thirty yards away, Vincent came out from behind the thick evergreen he was using for a toilet. He couldn't hear from all the wind, but what he saw was enough to confirm some of his suspicions.

*

What neither Vincent, Jimmy nor Deuce knew was that Bacon Bob also witnessed the entire scene from an obscured view in the parking lot. He couldn't ever remember feeling so sick.

Chapter 7

"We are back with our good friend Coach Grey up in the booth. Well, Coach! Congratulations! That certainly was an exciting way to start off the tournament! What are your thoughts about the first round game?"

"Thanks Sol. I must say I am happy about coming away with the win. It was looking a bit iffy there for a moment. Ardmore is a good team and Boxberger is one heck of a pitcher. MTU got a good prospect in him. He pitched six perfect innings against our club of bashers. That's hard to do. He's the toughest pitcher in the tournament. There's no doubt about that. It gives our kids great confidence, knowing we can beat any pitcher here."

"Coach, not only did you break up the perfect game in the seventh with Bill Jones' grounder that the third baseman bobbled, but Boxberger still had a no-hitter going right up until Vincent Preston took that first pitch over the right center field fence."

"Yeah, Vincent's an aggressive hitter, and I didn't want to put the handcuffs on him. The way I figure, might as well go down swingin'."

"Absolutely Coach. A gutsy move giving Preston the green light in that situation. Babe Ruth once said, 'I just keep going up there and swinging at em,' and that's what you did."

"Well Joel, sometimes you just have to break with what the statistics tell you to do and go for it."

"Well, it certainly worked out well for us. Also, that grand slam broke a sixteen-inning near scoreless stretch, the longest I've seen in years and amazing given the firepower we have on offense."

"Well, like I always tell my guys, you gotta poke a small hole in the dam to get any water out. Once we have that hole, the floodgates slowly come open. Clodhopper got us started with his hustle and the floodgates slowly opened."

"Coach, what is your feeling about Jimmy's health? To us he looked a little tight and hesitant, definitely not the Jimmy we're used to seeing."

"Jimmy's going to come around. Good pitching beats good hitting. If you noticed, nobody else on the team hit today either."

"That is except for Vincent Preston who is now batting five-for-six for an .833 average. He is off to a stellar start. His eyes are keen on that ball right now."

"Well Joel, I think I'm going to give Vincent a little more playing time next game- see what he can do with a few extra at-bats. It's nothing more than a good start. You gotta remember, he came in fresh and ready to go. He hadn't had a chance to get tired or worn out like the rest of the players had. Sometimes it's good to put someone in there for a fresh look. If nothing else, it makes the pitcher over think."

"Your next opponent is the crafty Guymon Dodgers who enter this game with a tough 8-2 record. Their only losses have been to this tournament's number-one seed, the Stillwater Giants, and a team from Amarillo. They took fourth place in a tough tournament down in Amarillo last weekend. They have plenty of experience under their belts. We've only played five games now. What is your plan this afternoon against Guymon?"

"Well, the game's not until 2:00 so the first thing we're going to do is make sure the kids have eaten a good lunch, nothing to bog them down, get plenty of fluids in them, and hunker down in the shade. The hungry dog plays better. I'm not sure who Guymon is going to throw against us, but they have three good pitchers returning. We'll have to be prepared to out-hustle a team who hasn't had to deal with the sun and wind."

"Finally, what are your thoughts about the Stillwater Giants? They won that tough Amarillo Tournament and will be your next opponent if they get past Enid and you can get past Guymon."

"Sol, I've decided a long time ago not to look past the next opponent. Ask me that question after the next game."

"Coach, as always, a pleasure. We wish you good luck this afternoon. That was Coach Grey and his Stampeding Herd has won its first round match against Ardmore on a two-out grand slam in the seventh by reserve outfielder Vincent Preston who apparently will get the start next game. Folks, it doesn't get much more exciting than this! For Joltin' Joel Richards, I'm the Sultan of Swat, Sol Smitty wishing you a good morning and afternoon. We'll be back at 1:55 to broadcast the next game. This is Stampeding Herd baseball."

*

They were only two words, but they meant the world to Preston. They got his heart pumping, got the butterflies moving around a bit in the pit of his stomach. "Left field," was all Coach said as he walked past him.

Coach Grey's arrogance was enough to make Vincent want to vomit. Coach had apparently come to his senses and seen that Vincent was indeed worthy of a starting spot, the same one he was supposed to have at the beginning of the season, but Vincent saw that Coach couldn't bring himself to be civil to someone who was obviously beneath him. Vincent knew he was a *sirrah* to Coach.

Vincent had learned the word in Mrs. Dean's class while reading *Romeo and Juliet* and cringed whenever an arrogant character called a servant *sirrah*. Coach needed his *sirrah* though. Vincent knew that. Vincent figured everybody knew that and couldn't figure out why nobody had ever stood up to Coach.

The team just wasn't as good as everyone said it was going to be. Vincent now knew that it was because Jimmy was throwing his performances on purpose. Why would Jimmy do such a thing? If ever there was a sure bet for the pros, it was Jimmy Grey. It was easy for Vincent to see that Jimmy had the skill and confidence to go all the way. He also had a full ride to one of the best baseball schools in the nation with a free education, all because he was good at a kid's game. It dawned on Vincent that Jimmy might not be the only one on the team working for someone else. Jimmy and his father were everything that was wrong with baseball, a total disregard for ethics and principles.

Coming into a game in the fourth inning was one thing, but starting, that was another. And since Vincent had been robbed of his first start in the Woodward game, he felt a personal vendetta. He had to prove himself all over again, but he knew he must keep his cool. He must not become complacent.

After the post-game mob earlier that day, and Coach's comments to the team, fans came up to Vincent to shake his hand. It wasn't but four or five good-natured Augusta fans, but it meant the world to him. Phrases like, "Boy, you really can smoke a ball!" and "It's good to have you on our ball club!" pervaded the morning air.

Vincent had looked over at Jimmy who was getting mobbed like always. Why, Vincent wondered? He went 0-3 in the game. Since signing with UNCO, Jimmy didn't seem to care much about doing well. Of course, Vincent now knew why. In fact, as the team took the field to warm up, neither the immortal Jimmy Grey nor his Corvette was anywhere to be seen.

Coach Grey posted the lineup on the dugout clipboard. Vincent saw that he was batting last. That was fine by him. He knew he should still get in at least two, if not four at-bats against Guymon.

Jimmy's spot was penciled in on the lineup, but he was still nowhere to be seen. Vincent saw Bacon Bob look over his shoulder at the parking lot as the two were normally inseparable. Vincent figured Bob was more worried than Jimmy's dad.

Finally, when the coin hit the dirt behind home plate, Jimmy ripped into the parking lot, bringing up a cloud of dust that drifted past the stands and the infield, causing Vincent to fan the air.

Jimmy came running with his bat bag slung around his shoulder and only one cleat on.

He hopped on one foot into the dugout and received a sideways glare from his dad. He threw his bag down in frustration. A few players chuckled.

"Take the field guys," Coach Grey said and the players, except for Vincent, assembled into their positions. Vincent hung behind with the bench warmers, hoping to find out what Jimmy's problem was.

Fuzzy Fred Fingers walked out to the mound with a smile on his face. Since they were playing on field two, the wind was reversed. It now blew out to straight center field. Vincent and the whole team knew Fuzzy's knuckleball was going to dance all over the place against a thirty mile-per-hour wind. Sure, he would have his walks. It would be impossible to control it in this wind. But with an aggressive team like Guymon, Fuzzy would also get his strikeouts and pop-ups.

Jimmy was still wrestling with his shoe when his dad lit into him. Coach Grey pulled Jimmy aside from the bench warmers.

Vincent leaned in to hear Coach Grey say in a low voice, "Just where in the world have you been?"

127

"Lay off it dad. I don't need to hear it right now." Jimmy looked into the stands briefly, intently.

"Don't you tell me to lay off it. You need to get here to warm up just like the rest of the team. How's it look when I show favoritism toward my son, when I would bench anyone else for the same infraction, even less? You know, I could have yelled at you in front of the team, jerked you from the lineup. Would you like that?"

"And who would you play in my place? We both know you need me. This team sucks without me."

A few bench warmers scooted down the bench to get out of earshot, leaving Vincent as the only one close enough to hear everything.

Jimmy ripped into his bat bag and searched furiously for his glove and then closed the bag suspiciously.

Jimmy reached into his bag blindly, found his glove, zipped his bag, and threw it way under the bench. He ran out to center field just as Fuzzy was finishing his warm ups. Vincent took this time to run out to his position. He looked back and saw Coach Grey glare at his son, apparently unaware that Vincent was late getting out to his position as well. Then the coach turned around and started yelling at the bench warmers.

*

Grandpa Dean woke up in a pool of sweat. His wife was across the room humming to herself while dusting. She walked over to him and wiped beads of sweat from his forehead with the bottom of her shirt.

"More dreams?" she asked.

Grandpa Dean turned away and coughed.

"What were they about?" she probed further.

"More of the same."

She resumed her duties around the room, watering her airplane plant. The tendrils stretched their long, skinny arms all the way from the pot on the end table to the ground where they curled up like a cozy dog in front of a fireplace. "You know, he's going to figure it out one of these days."

Grandpa Dean just sat there in silence and looked at his watch. When it read 3:10 he quickly switched on the stereo.

"...just fathom what the Guymon coach could have been thinking."

"Well, it's just a simple case of underestimating an opponent, Sol. Different coaches have different philosophies when it comes to which pitcher to use in a tournament. Those with guts will leave their ace on the bench for a later round against what should be tougher competition, but I would think it would be at least in the back of a Coach's mind that Augusta is the defending champion of this tournament and defending AA State Champions. The team is practically intact from last year, and if anybody were to guess a sleeper team, it was Augusta. Seeding them number five was obviously a mistake."

"As Guymon just found out. They used four relief pitchers in the first inning against the Augusta Stampeding Herd. Forty-seven minutes and three outs later they were looking uphill at a seventeen-run deficit! Well, I've seen some great offensive innings in my time, but that might take the cake!"

"Sol, I know it's easier to look in hindsight and say they should have started Powell against Augusta, but the fastballer was looking straight into a thirty mile-per-hour wind. That eighty-five miles-per-hour looks more like seventy against the wind, just perfect for breaking a hitting slump."

"Joel, I don't know if Guymon could have done anything. They just ran into a buzz saw. And we were due after such pathetic performances. Maybe Vincent Preston is the lucky rabbit's foot. He kept us afloat with that grand salami against Ardmore while the other players were bogged down in a slump."

"Let's run down some stats. Augusta took out the Guymon Dodgers AAA ball club twenty-three to nothing in a three-inning run-rule game."

"Look, the whole compound is buzzing! News of the shellacking is reaching everyone, and the entire Stillwater Giants team even sat down in the grass outside third base to see what they couldn't have expected!"

"Well folks, as you can see we are very excited, so excited that Sol interrupted me in the stats."

"Sorry, you may continue."

"Fuzzy got the win and improves to 2-0 on the season. He was nearly unhittable against this wind, striking out nine of the ten batters he saw. One batter reached base on a squib infield single. Otherwise Fuzzy was perfect. Jules Jefferson took the loss for Guymon. Augusta scored twenty-three runs on nineteen hits. We never had a chance to commit an error, but Guymon committed eight! Man, when it rains, it pours!"

"Boy, that's for sure, unless you're talking about the weather."

"Individually everybody on the team had a hit, led by Jimmy Grey who broke out of his personal slump, going four-for-four just missing the cycle. He tried to stretch a double into a triple on his last at-bat and was thrown out by a mile. But he wasn't the only one who hit a home run. Bacon Bob had one, Clodhopper had one, Quentin rocketed a line drive over the center field fence that took all of two seconds to leave. But the story remains to be Vincent Preston. Batting last in the lineup but finally getting the start, he went three-for-three with not one, but two home runs and a double off the fence that missed being a home run by mere inches. It was that close to a hat trick!"

"Struck the Petro sign on the left field wall."

"Sure did. He has a knack for hitting signs on fences. If you'll remember, back against Woodward he broke the brand new state championship pennant on the Little Monster. Sol, what's his batting average up to now?"

"Three-for-three today makes him eight-for-nine on the year and ripping it up with an .888 average and three home runs."

"That's just incredible Sol. I know Coach said he's going to cool off, and we aren't dumb enough to think otherwise cause he's not a robot, but this hitting display is pretty impressive. It's a great way to start off the season. If he wants to hold off his slump for a while, I won't mind."

"Darn right, like hold it off through August. We can't say enough about this welcome addition to the lineup. Well, as much as I would like to just sit around and reflect on this amazing show, we are running out of time. Augusta will be playing the number one seed in the tournament and host team, the Stillwater Giants AAA ball club at ten o'clock tomorrow morning. We will come on at nine-thirty for the live broadcast on the Grandstand field for the first semi-final. In the bottom half of the draw is a team we're very familiar with, the Seiling Pirates AA team, the number eleven seed who took out the six seeded Stillwater Bronchos AAA team in the first round 2 to 1, and the three-seeded, Emporia, Kansas Blues, 3 to 1 in the second round. Clearly they have earned their semi-final the hard way, with good pitching and timely hitting."

"Question is, will their arms be healthy tomorrow? They used their two best pitchers today."

"Well, that doesn't mean much when it comes to Seiling. They always seem to find a way to win."

"They will be playing the number two seed, a team many think is the best team in the surrounding states, the Topeka Reds."

"Topeka will be tough to beat. They throttled a tough Joplin, Missouri team in the second round 15 to 0 after receiving a first-round bye. They could have sleep-walked through that game."

"Well folks, tomorrow could prove to be very interesting. Two of the three AA ball clubs in this tournament have made it to the semis. Both are playing Goliaths, but something tells me that isn't going to make any difference. We'll find out tomorrow."

"Again, Augusta has made the semis of one of the toughest tournaments in the state by beating Ardmore 4-3 dramatically in the seventh inning, and later this afternoon, by wrecking a tough Guymon squad 23-0. This is the Sultan of Swat, Solomon Smity, for Joltin' Joel Richards telling everybody to stay cool in this heat. Tune in tomorrow at nine-thirty for more Augusta Stampeding Herd baseball!"

Grandpa Dean slowly switched off the radio and turned toward his wife. "Elna, why didn't you wake me for the game?"

Gobs of dust bunnies fell from the blades of the ceiling fan, like paratroopers jumping out of planes deep in German-occupied France. His wife looked awkward, standing on an old milk crate. Before she could answer him, the second wave of drowsiness from the pills hit him. He was sound asleep in seconds, a smile obscuring his pain.

Chapter 8

Vincent and the guys sat in a circle beyond first base and stretched. The morning's dew had long dried up in such arid circumstances. A church bell off in the distance chimed "Onward Christian Soldiers" before hitting nine bells. Vincent was indeed feeling like part of the group and felt comfortable having a conversation with anybody. He really preferred Quentin Albany's company.

Vincent knew that he and Quentin both felt like outsiders and had to work their way into the inner circle through their feats of labor. Neither would be given a chance at the honor of popularity if he didn't produce on the field. Quentin, because he was black, was accepted only on merit of his play. Vincent never was popular, and being exiled at the beginning of the season by Coach Grey didn't help matters any.

Though Vincent wanted to talk, he still felt ill at ease for fear of saying the wrong thing, so he listened. He had decided that he would be respected more for what he didn't say. Everyone else spoke freely and loosely and there was only one person missing, Jimmy Grey.

Bacon Bob came by himself, which Vincent found strange since Bob normally rode with Jimmy. Bob walked amongst the players, and for the first time was silent.

Vincent thought Bob looked about ready to explode. Bob walked up to Vincent and said, "Hey, dude, how you doing?"

Vincent answered without looking up, "Couldn't be better."

Bob tapped Vincent on the shoulder and asked him to follow him.

The two jogged to the fence to warm up their legs. This made Vincent smirk.

Bob, you jog?

Vincent turned around and saw that the whole team was staring at the two of them.

Vincent's curiosity caught the better of him. "So, Bob, what's on your mind?"

"Well," Bob started to say, but apparently the words were hard to form. Vincent knew Jimmy was Bob's best friend, had been since grade school, and Jimmy's weird behavior must have been a strain on him.

As Bob sought to formulate the words, he scrunched up his face in apparent mental torture, then he simply said, "Vincent... I am happy... you're starting. You're a good ballplayer."

This caught Vincent off guard, but he simply replied, "Thank you. You're a good catcher."

"Vincent," Bacon Bob said and caught him by the arm to stop him. Bob bent over to get some air and held up one finger. Vincent waited. Finally, Bob said, "Vincent, sorry about dropping that ball in the Woodward game. It was a darn good throw."

Vincent smiled. Bacon Bob might have bad taste in friends, but he was a good guy. He didn't even have to dig deep down to find that out. The man emanated laughter and smiles. "That's alright Bob. We'll hook up again this season."

"I'll hold on next time," Bob said. "Next time I'll lower a shoulder and knock the guy backward!"

"I believe you could do that," Vincent replied.

They stood mid-way to the fence and an awkward silence fell. Finally, Bob told Vincent, "Well, if you ever want to talk about anything, just let me know."

"Sure." Vincent gave Bacon Bob a peculiar look but passed the moment on like two strangers on an elevator who just happened to talk about the big league baseball game from the past Sunday, just to fill-in time waiting for the doors to open to their respective floors. The conversation ended there as Bacon Bob walked back to the infield, sweat pouring off him. Vincent was perplexed at Bob's weird conversation and figured he better probe a little deeper.

Sweat dripped off of Vincent's nose also and fragmented upon hitting his right forearm. If there was one thing he hated, it was sweating. His uniform didn't make it any easier for him. He would have preferred to be wearing shorts and flip-flops in the morning's glare.

He took his cap off and wiped his forehead with the inside bill. Just as he was about to flop it back on his soaked hair, something caught his eye. On the inside of his bill, and in fancy font was penned:

Phil. 4:13.

He had to look twice to make sure his eyes weren't tricking him. On the back of his hat was embroidered the number 58. It was his hat indeed, but was there someone named Phil who was playing a trick on him? Was this his new nickname, some other player writing it in when he was up to bat? And what did 4:13 mean? He thought about asking if someone was playing a trick on him, but decided to wait until he was out of the intimidating group setting.

Vincent looked toward the dugout and saw Coach Grey standing on the steps of the doorway with one arm bracing his weight against the concrete wall while fielding questions from the reporters who stood just inside the baseline.

Coach Redenbacher hit ground balls to the infield.

The outfielders stood in two lines, twenty yards apart from each other, one side throwing hard ground balls while players on the other side would scoop them up and in one motion burn it back, taking the crow's hop just as Coach Grey had taught. Vincent was loose and confident.

Jimmy Grey still hadn't shown up, and the game was due to begin in the next five minutes.

Vincent watched Coach Grey, now pacing back and forth in the dugout nervously as he cut off the reporters with the wave of a hand. They dispersed as Coach continued to pace.

Across the field to the other dugout sat a Stillwater team, listening to a pre-game speech from their coach. Coach Grey didn't even seem the least bit interested in the game at this point.

In the outfield Vincent opened his glove, captured the ball, and in one motion whizzed it back to Jake Jackson. He had never said a word to Jake outside of their one brief conversation, and Jake never spoke to him either.

Jake was the fastest player on the team and the most unselfish. He wasn't afraid to take a base-on-balls if the pitcher was going to give him one. He still batted over .300 and was the most selective hitter on the team. As the lead-off batter, he got on base over half the time, .580 to be exact, which was a luxury Vincent knew that Coach Grey valued, when Coach cared.

Vincent also knew Jake was a bit embarrassed by his father Milt. Mr. Jackson was the President of the Grand Slam Club, and it was obvious to Vincent that Jake's dad lived his life vicariously through Jake. Though Jake resented his father for it, Vincent couldn't help but wish his own father cared as much.

Everyone could hear Milt above the rest of the crowd anytime the umpire missed a call. Vincent knew Jake would never approach his father, but wished his dad would just shut up. Coach Grey whistled and the outfielders jogged in. Vincent and the others sat down on the bench, except for Bacon Bob who strapped on his shin guards. Coach Grey paced the dugout, and when Coach Redenbacher whispered something in his ear, he shook his head and kept walking.

Vincent sat between Jake and Quentin and got up the nerve to ask about the strange writing on his hat. "Hey Quentin, look at this and tell me what you see."

Quentin brightened up immediately and said, "Ah! That's a good one!"

Now Vincent was even more confused. "I beg your pardon?"

"It's a bible verse," Jake interjected without looking over at him. "Philippians Chapter 4, verse 13."

"Do you know what it means?" Quentin asked.

Embarrassed now from his lack of faith, Vincent shook his head. His parents never took him to church a Sunday in his life. He had never felt the need to go, but never gave it much thought either.

Jake looked at Vincent, square in the face, and said, "Deep inside you, it pushes you to be the ball player you are, and many more things in your life."

"So why did you write it on your hat if you didn't know what it means?" Quentin asked.

"Well," Vincent replied, "to tell you the truth, I didn't. I just found it there this morning."

"What about the sign of the cross?" Jake asked.

"The what?" Vincent asked.

"You know," Jake explained, "what you do with your bat on home plate every time you go up to hit."

"What's that called?"

Jake explained, "The sign of the cross. We Catholics make the sign of the cross as a sign that we believe in God."

Jake made a cross with his right hand, extending from his forehead to his chest and then from left shoulder to right shoulder, repeating the words as he did it, "In the name of the Father, the Son, and the Holy Spirit. You see, God is divided into what is known as the Trinity. He's the Father of our world. He gave his son Jesus to us, and He's all around us with the Holy Spirit. Every time you go up to the plate and make the sign of the cross, you are asking for God's help to be the best you can be. Without God we are nothing. We wouldn't have the skills to do what we do. God gives us our strength. That's why you are doing so well. I don't know where I would be without Him." Jake said more in one paragraph than Vincent had ever heard him speak before and he said it with such conviction, such seriousness.

Vincent felt like he was an incoming member of a special club and started to get goose bumps on his arms. "I don't know. I've never been religious."

Jake smiled and patted Vincent on the knee. "Vincent, there's a big difference between being 'religious' and being a Christian."

Quentin walked over to his bat bag and brought it over to Vincent. Quentin pulled out a tattered bible with black vinyl and pages that had worn off the gold tip long ago. "Look it up yourself," Quentin said. "There's a lot to learn. Philippians 4:13 is the perfect verse for you." And then as if to drive the point home, he said again, "There's a lot to learn."

The goose bumps became stronger. Vincent regarded the Bible as something of a delicate relic, too afraid to open it up and look in it.

Finally Jake opened to the table of contents and ran his finger down the list of New Testament books until he found Philippians. "Page 872."

Commotion overtook the dugout as Jimmy appeared, just as the night before, a minute before first pitch.

Vincent was the only one not to notice him. He was intrigued. The goose bumps ran all up and down his body. In a lifetime of never feeling loved, he felt more love from these two teammates he hardly knew. He didn't know why they cared. Just as Vincent was about to open to page 872, fingers trembling in anticipation of a gift, Coach boomed, "Alright y'all, we got home. Let's take the field. Fuzzy, you're in center."

Everyone stopped short and stared at Coach. Vincent wondered if Coach was actually taking his son out of the lineup?

Jimmy paused a step up from the dugout floor and looked blankly at Coach Grey. "Jimmy," Coach Grey said, "you're on the mound."

Jimmy maintained his poise and just stood there.

The other players filed past Jimmy, each patting him on the back with his glove.

Coach Grey didn't even look at Jimmy, just paced toward the other end of the dugout where Vincent, Quentin, and Jake were still sitting. "YOU GUYS WANT TO PLAY OR NOT?"

"Just hold onto this for a while," Quentin said and patted Vincent on the knee. With a wink, Quentin's face returned stolid and he hit the field.

Jake took the Bible from Vincent and put it in Vincent's bat bag. "Quentin is Southern Baptist, and I am Catholic; we believe the same things. We just worship in different ways. The great thing is that we confide in each other for strength. I'd like to tell you more later."

"GENTLEMEN?" Coach glared trying to keep his patience.

"Yes sir," Jake said and he and Vincent ran past him and his son to take the field.

"Coach, you got a pitcher?" the umpire yelled from behind the plate.

"Sure thing, Blue. He's heading out right now," and he looked at Jimmy for the first time. Jimmy grabbed the glove out of his bat bag and without a word, walked out to the mound.

*

Jimmy threw hard without warming up a bit.

The first Stillwater batter came to the plate, but Jimmy wasn't thinking about baseball. After a night of pushing, he was tired. Finding people to sell to on a Saturday night was easier than he imagined, but he still had to win this game. Was it out of submission to his dad? Was it pride, knowing he could beat this team and rub it in Max Grossman's face?

After his episode with Stillwater's third baseman last year, Jimmy liked the idea of exacting a little revenge. He didn't know what was driving him, but he felt great. His sleep-depravation headache was gone. He was catching his second wind. His fancy sports sunglasses hid his bloodshot eyes.

He peered to home plate where Bacon Bob, a worried look on his face, gave the first sign. Fastball, inside.

No problem, Jimmy thought.

The crowd of Stillwater parents and fans faded into Jimmy's background, a blur of faces around a crystal-clear tunnel that included a catcher and his mitt. The windup was effortless, exact. The ball slapped against the leather after a stride and a grunt.

"STEERIKE ONE!" the umpire called.

Jimmy read the radar clock on the scoreboard. 89 MPH.

The batter backed out of the box and cut a few more swings to refocus.

Jimmy knew this kid was as unprepared for the heat of the pitch as the crowd was. Jimmy stood on the mound, a picture of perfect concentration.

The crowd of Stillwater fans, having seen the scoreboard, leafed through their programs until finding out that number one was the great Jimmy Grey.

Seeing this made Jimmy smirk. As the chatter picked up about this coaching move, Jimmy let another one unleash, slapping leather on the inside portion of the plate again.

"STEERIKE TWO!" the umpire called.

The batter again backed out of the box, this time looking confident. Jimmy turned around, and again the scoreboard read 89 MPH.

Stepping back into the box, the batter took a few more cuts.

Jimmy looked out to left field and saw Vincent smirking. It irked Jimmy, but he turned his attention to his catcher.

Bob gave three fingers and patted his right thigh.

Jimmy shook his head. He wasn't going to mess around today with junk. It was pure fastballs.

Bob shook his head and gave one finger, again patting his right thigh. A stride and a grunt later, a bat swung through the path of the ball a split-second late and the umpire rung him up. "THREE!"

Augusta fans, outnumbered at least four to one, cheered with lust. Again the scoreboard read 89 MPH.

The second batter strode to the plate, this one a southpaw.

Jimmy shook off numerous signs from Bacon Bob, each time settling on a fastball, and each one whizzing right by the next two batters. Nine pitches, nine fastballs for strikes and three outs later, the Augusta fans were happy and the Stillwater fans sat down dejected. Jimmy knew he was overpowering, each time hitting the same mark on the radar screen.

In the bottom of the inning, the Stillwater pitcher struck out Jake, Dusty and the indispensable Jimmy Grey.

Nobody said a word to Jimmy. Baseball is a superstitious sport, and these players were no different. He was as avoidable on the bench as he was untouchable on the mound. Jimmy knew that the team, fearing they would jinx his zone, stayed as far away from him as possible. Nine pitches and three strikeouts against the top of the Stillwater Giants' order? That was plenty unbelievable and nobody was going to infringe upon his zone. He knew the Stillwater players treated their pitcher the same way. It was a sign of respect.

Due up at the top of the second inning for the Giants was their cleanup hitter and third baseman, Max Grossman. He and Jimmy hadn't gotten along in the past. The year prior when Max was playing for the AA Stillwater Jackals, the two had gotten into a fight in the parking lot after the game. It was more of a one-sided fight. Jimmy had his arm around Max's girlfriend after the game. That was all it took for Max to punch Jimmy, leaving him lying on the ground with a bloody nose.

Jimmy never talked about it, so everyone had no choice but to believe that he went down swinging. Jimmy had seethed over the ordeal, and now was his chance for payback.

Max stepped into the batter's box, all 250 pounds. He didn't take any warm up cuts, just stared back at Jimmy with a crooked smile on his face.

Bacon Bob gave Jimmy three fingers and patted his right thigh again. This time Jimmy nodded. But what came out of Jimmy's hand was not a slider.

Bob set up about six inches outside the plate. Jimmy went into his windup. He strode forward and let forth a loud grunt. He put everything he had into it. A fastball with tailspin started inside, rose, and just as Max turned his back, the ball plunked him right between the shoulder blades with a loud THUD.

The crowd of Giants' fans rose to their feet in anger. Big Max sank to his left knee in pain.

Jimmy watched from the bottom of the mound, not looking around at anything that might disturb his moment of bliss, just watching Max writhe in pain now. A thin smile played about the corners of Jimmy's lips.

The umpire stepped toward the mound and said, "Jimmy, that's your only warning. Anything else inside and you're walking. You got me?"

Jimmy didn't acknowledge the ump, only looked past him to where Big Max was rising off his knee, bracing himself with the bat still in his left hand. He took three steps toward the mound, still with the bat in his hand until Bacon Bob tackled him from behind.

The Stillwater bench erupted, running out onto the field to get the catcher off their best player.

Dusty ran from third base to home and joined the mêlée. Bob was gang tackled by the group off the bench, which infuriated the Augusta crowd. Within five seconds the whole infield was picking the Giants' players off their catcher.

After it was all said and done, no punches were thrown on the field, and the umps managed to break it up. Besides the outfielders who couldn't run fast enough to join in time, the only player not involved was Jimmy, who stood in the same spot at the bottom of the mound, staring at Max Grossman on the bottom of the pile. Jimmy's best friend was being mauled by the opposing team and he never flinched, despite the fact that Bob saved him from a sure beating by tackling the big oaf.

The coaches from both teams were in the pile, trying to sort out the mess, but the real fun was in the stands. Milt Jackson stood over some proud father from Stillwater who had apparently said the wrong thing. He looked like a boxer standing over somebody he just knocked out in the first round and pounding his chest. It made Jimmy laugh. Security was called, and Milt was promptly taken away, kicking and screaming.

In al,l ten minutes were lost in the game and the perpetrator of the ordeal got only a brief warning. The ump called both coaches to the plate and let them know that he had no patience left for anymore horseplay.

With a little encouragement, Max took his place at first base and immediately took a lead.

Smiling, Jimmy watched Max the whole time, oblivious to the rest of the world. Jimmy finally turned his attention toward his catcher. Just as he was about to put his right foot on the pitching rubber for the next pitch, he turned and fired the ball to Bill Jones at first base. Max was slow in diving back and Bill easily tagged out Big Max, adding insult to injury.

Max laid twelve inches from the base where he tried to dive back, clutching dirt in his left hand. The first base umpire had to walk Max back across the field to his dugout to ensure there would be no more trouble.

Smiling the whole time, Jimmy stared back at Max, not saying a word. His actions had spoken loudly enough. Six pitches later Augusta strode off the field with their heads held high, and a classic grudge match was on.

*

There are certain unwritten rules in baseball. Probably the most consistent unwritten rule is revenge for plunking a player. It doesn't matter what the umpire says. If the team whose player got plunked had any respect for themselves whatsoever they would exact revenge. It was just a matter of whom they would bean, and when. Vincent knew someone was going to get it from the opposing pitcher. What Jimmy did would have repercussions. Vincent had his money on Jimmy, but Jimmy wasn't due up for a while.

When Vincent reached the dugout he walked to the far end with his bat bag and pulled out the Bible Quentin had loaned him. Being last in the lineup Vincent wasn't due up for five more batters, or so he thought. He flipped to page 872 and then a few pages later he found Chapter four. Scrolling his hand slowly down the page he saw verse thirteen.

I can do all things through Christ which strengtheneth me.

Strength. He'd never given much thought to a higher being controlling him, helping him, aiding him along, giving him strength. Vincent knew Jake and Quentin believed in the power of this book and of God, a concept so foreign and vague that it just couldn't be real. Could it? Still Vincent couldn't shake the goose bumps everytime he thought about the topic. Reading the Bible, just having it in his hands gave him the cold chills, as if he were being spoken to directly. He read a little further.

But my God shall supply all your need according to His riches in glory by Christ Jesus.

"Who's supposed to be on deck?" Coach yelled at the players on the bench. Vincent looked up. Seth read the lineup.

"Vincent's next." Vincent looked at the batter. Bill Jones was at the plate. Vincent earmarked the page and put it back in his bag and ran to the lineup card, clipped to the wall of the dugout above the bat rack. He was moved up to number six in the lineup this game! He grabbed a helmet and bat and ran out to the on-deck circle.

Hurriedly, he took some cuts and watched the pitcher, looking for his mechanics, pitch choice, expressions on his face, and anything else that might give away his poker hand. Lucky for Vincent, Bill fouled off four pitches before striking out, giving Vincent plenty of looks at the pitcher.

The only flaw Vincent could see was that the pitcher shook off his catcher every pitch. To Vincent, that meant either the catcher was incompetent, calling the wrong pitches, or the pitcher was arrogant enough to think he knew his pitches better from the mound. Given that he threw five straight fastballs to Bill, Vincent knew it was the latter. This guy had to be just as arrogant as Jimmy and neither the catcher nor the coach was man enough to have a conference with him to lay down the law.

As Vincent and Bill crossed paths, Bill said, "Look fastball."

With two outs, Vincent stepped into the back of the box, hoping to give himself enough time to catch up to the 88 MPH that kept flashing on the scoreboard during Bill's at-bat. But first Vincent had to play a little psychology. He readied himself and watched the pitcher's face. As soon as the pitcher shook off the first sign, Vincent called time-out and stepped back out of the box.

This had the effect Vincent was hoping for. The pitcher threw his hands down in anger. The guy was in a groove and Vincent knew he had to disrupt his timing.

Vincent stepped back into the box and studied the guy's face once again. Tunnel vision took over and the rest of the world ceased to exist. His vision became more acute. He began looking at the eyes, checking for an unnatural wrinkle which might give away his hand. But one thing caught Vincent's attention more than anything. The guy had a pimple right on the end of his nose that was forming a disgusting whitehead. A bead of sweat slowly rolled down the bridge of his nose and suspended on the end of the whitehead before dripping onto the guy's glove. And then Vincent's concentration became so great, the tunnel became so focused, that the pitcher's face became one big, giant pimple, just about to burst, a dehumanization that turned the world into simple, basic thoughts of nothing but the electrifying connection of aluminum and stitched white cowhide. Nothing else of the world existed. All was good.

Vincent could feel the blood rush to his forearms and make them rock hard. No sounds entered his ears. The aroma of the hamburgers smoking off the grill at the concession stand was a long-ago forgotten memory. It was just Vincent's bat and Mr. Pimple and the longer Vincent looked at it, the more he wanted to hit the ball right at the pimple to pop it. Of course this progression of thoughts ran through his brain way too quickly, never making English syllables in his mind. They remained the inner-most thoughts that go by too fast to be deciphered into a language understood by anything but the specific area of the brain in which they center.

Just as his conscience started to wonder if he might be going crazy thinking such thoughts, the pimple went into the windup and the game was on. Vincent watched the ball come out of the pimple's hand moving in slow motion.

The bat raised off Vincent's shoulder, he brought up his left knee, let his foot drop to the earth in a solid plant, twisted his hips toward the pitcher and brought his weight forward. But the ball did not take the trajectory Vincent had anticipated. The ball was heading right for his head.

Vincent's inner-mind said in a loud voice, CURVEBALL! HOLD, HOLD, HOLD, but then he saw that the ball didn't have the little red dot in the middle of it that a curveball has just as it is about to curve, and in the same instant he knew that it was going to get him good. But as fast as the inner-mind made the connection, the body paled in comparison.

Halfway through his swing and totally exposed to Mr. Pimple, Vincent had just enough time to tilt his chin down, a reflex that probably saved his life. One micro-second he knew he had a home run. The next, darkness.

*

The crowd, both dugouts, and everyone in the general vicinity jumped to their feet after hearing the most disturbing CRACK! Vincent lay flat and cold on his stomach after spinning to his left and his cracked helmet bounced and rolled a few feet away, making a hollow rattling noise. It came to a rest in the dirt, open end to the sky in supplication.

A moment later the entire Augusta dugout sprinted for the pimple and World War III was on. Dusty Redenbacher, being one of the slowest on the team was the first to tackle the pimple, using correct form he learned in football, getting his head across the midsection, driving from the hips, and planting the pimple into the dirt like a daisy. It felt so good to Dusty to level the pitcher. He gave the guy two punches to the side of the face before he was doubled back over by one of the opposing players, whose dugout was also cleared of its bench warmers. The Giants' infield wasn't far behind.

The two sides' players met with vicious collisions on the mound, right on top of Dusty, the pimple, and the others who had tackled Dusty. Dusty figured that it resembled a medieval battlefield. Maybe there was even glorious theme music in the background. Through the gouging, biting, punching, and yelling, Dusty could hear the crowd cheer on lustily, as if at a hockey fight. Dusty's teeth met with someone's fingers and an odd thought occurred to him.

I wonder where Jimmy is?

*

The only Augusta player who stayed planted on the dugout bench was Jimmy Grey. He wasn't going to defend Vincent, though Jimmy was the chief reason Vincent was out cold behind the plate. But Jimmy didn't sit for long as Max Grossman ran right past the scrum and into Augusta's dugout to seek out Jimmy. Jimmy had nobody to protect him this time and nowhere to run.

Coach Redenbacher was now with the unconscious batter, and Coach Grey was in the middle of the pile up. Jimmy made it to the top of the dugout steps before Max tackled him. Jimmy never had a chance.

The mad man on top of Jimmy outweighed him by 100 pounds and the weight of each punch found its mark despite Jimmy trying his hardest to deflect them with his hands covering his face. Jimmy's only saving grace was to bring his foot up between Max's legs as hard as he could, which seemed only to infuriate Max further. To make matters worse for Jimmy, apparently nobody from the stands could see him getting the woodshed treatment because nobody came to save him. Everyone else must have been preoccupied with the battlefield.

The fight lasted a few minutes. Afterward, apparently nobody noticed Max Grossman, jogging back across the field to join his fellow players who were retiring to their dugout.

The indomitable Jimmy Grey was balled up in the corner of his respective dugout looking more like Beetle Bailey after Sarge is done pounding on him. Out of his good eye, he saw parents from both sides on the mound, sensibly trying to break things up. It never dawned on him that others, players and parents alike, had bloody noses and black eyes.

*

Vincent lay flat on his stomach with arms outstretched while Coach Redenbacher mobilized his head and backed everybody else away.

The ambulance arrived ten minutes later.

Smelling salts were brought out by the paramedics, which made Vincent wake up rather unpleasantly. He was groggy and didn't know where he was and why all these strangers were standing around him. The only thing he could remember were the words:

I can do all things through Christ which strengtheneth me.

With that, things slowly started to come back to him and he tried to get up, but the paramedics made him sit back down. They took him to the hospital for precautions and Coach Redenbacher rode with him.

*

"Now that's how baseball is played!" Grandpa Dean said between coughs and had to put his handkerchief to his face to catch what came out of his lungs.

Mrs. Dean looked at her husband and smiled. "I guess you don't see many fights in baseball anymore. I just hope Vincent is okay." A commercial for the local supermarket featuring three singing pigs aired over the radio.

"Heck no you don't!" Grandpa Dean agreed. "Back when baseball was a real sport, you didn't have to worry about the ump turning it into a pansy game. Real men played, one pitcher would flip a batter and it would escalate from there. Nowadays you don't see your pitcher protecting his batters like that."

"You think Vincent is alright?" she inquired.

Ignoring the question, Grandpa Dean continued his rant. "If you're going to flip my batter, I'm going to flip yours. It's that simple. You gotta clear the benches at least once a month to keep the players sharp. Ballplayers are too lethargic these days. They're like those pansies who grew their hair out long and smoked weed during the Viet Nam War. If you don't invest nothing, you shouldn't have an opinion." Grandpa Dean started coughing more violently now, trying to suppress it as the radio personalities came back on the air.

"Wow, you folks listening at home are not going to believe what just happened! Joel, go ahead and inform the audience listening at home what just happened. I'm going to step out back and throw up!"

"Well, shocking turn of events here in Stillwater. First off, the ambulance took Vincent away to the county hospital, but we just received word that he was coherent and even tried to get up and walk. But he will have a headache for a while. They suspect it's a nasty concussion. They're going to run some tests as a precaution, so that's good news on Vincent Preston, we hope. But that's not the bad news that has Solomon so upset. Solomon actually left the booth. I think he's going to give these umpires a piece of his own mind. We'll see.

"Anyway, what you missed during the commercials was a flurry of activity. The umpires conferred on the mound and decided to kick the entire Augusta team out of the tournament for

150

involvement in the fight that just occurred. Folks, I'm not making this up. The Stillwater Giants will play the championship game later this afternoon courtesy of their hometown umps.

"In case you're just tuning in, Vincent Preston, recently moved up to the number six spot in the lineup, was hit in the head by a pitch, obviously a retaliation for Jimmy Grey hitting Max Grossman in the top part of the inning. Both benches cleared and met at the pitcher's mound, and personally, I think our guys won the fight, but that's not important. The umpires have now kicked our Stampeding Herd out of the tournament for involvement in the fight and the only guy who was kicked out from Stillwater's side was Nick Castle, Stillwater's pitcher. So now Stillwater will meet the winner of the Seiling-Topeka Reds game later this afternoon. Unbelievable. Coach Grey gave the umps a piece of his mind after the ruling. He looked eerily reminiscent of Kolby Kimbrell in the early eighties, rushing out of the dugout at Wildcat Stadium in the infamous spitball game. The only difference was that there was nobody there on our side to hold Coach back.

"The umpires are now being escorted off the field by the security personnel, and boy, our fans are giving it to them. And ladies and gentlemen, looks like our own Solomon Smity is in the middle of the ruckus. Wow! In all the years I've been around baseball, I've never seen such a home-job. Unbelievable.

"Well, it looks like our Augusta team, possibly the hottest team in the tournament right now, is going to leave unceremoniously without this year's championship trophy, and the hometown team gets a free pass into the championship game courtesy of three incompetent idiots. You know it's one thing if both teams were ejected. I would be upset about it, but at least it would be fair, because both teams were involved in the altercation and some of our boys are going to come away from this with headaches, and black eyes, not to mention Vincent Preston who is the real victim here. In fact, I'm looking at Jimmy Grey right now, and boy-oh-boy, he really got it! He has blood all down his chin, down his jersey, and it looks like his right eye is swollen shut! Man, he must have been the first one out there to defend Vincent! Well, what can you expect from a team captain? He goes out there and mows down the opposing batters in his first start of the year, and he's right in the middle of the fight to avenge his brother-in-arms. A heck of a guy Jimmy Grey is! They sure broke the mold when they made him. It looks like Sol is making his way back to the booth. Give me a few seconds as you're listening at home… Sol, what is it like down there? Sorry for those listening at home, we have to get Sol's headset on."

"It was crazy Joel. Those umps know they made the wrong call and they're going to hear about it for a long time. I don't think many are going to forget this day!"

"Sol, did you happen to see Jimmy's face up close? What can you tell us about our superstar?"

"Joel, I didn't pay much attention."

"There he is right there."

"Holy cow! Ladies and gentlemen it looks like Jimmy was right in the middle of the ruckus. He must have really stuck his neck out. What can you say, I love that kid! We'll really miss him next year. Just what you would expect from a team captain! Was he the one who led our troops to the mound?"

"Sol, it happened so fast that I don't really know. It looks like Dusty might have taken a few shots too. Other than that, I don't see any injuries to our players. Our guys are slowly loading their gear into their bags and vacating the dugout. What a way to exit the tournament."

"Well, I guess there's not much more to say here. Augusta will be going home without even having a chance to play for the trophy. I was really looking forward to seeing an Augusta-Topeka Reds showdown. I think that would have been a good matchup, maybe the toughest competition we would see all year, but that isn't going to happen now. What can I add Joel?"

"I don't think there's anything we can add. It's just a disappointment. I doubt we will be asked back next year after this, but knowing Coach Grey, he will be talking to tournament officials about this travesty. Unfortunately, there's nothing can be done now. The head umpire's call on the field is final, right or wrong."

"Well, we're going to end this broadcast. Next time you hear from us will be next Saturday when Augusta takes on our hated arch-rivals, the Seiling Pirates who now have an open door to win this tournament without us in it. Augusta exits early from the 32nd Annual Stillwater Memorial Invitational via corrupt umpiring. For Joel Richards, this is Sol Smity. See you next week."

"This has been a proud broadcast of Augusta Stampeding Herd baseball, on AM 1230, KBAL, Augusta."

Grandpa Dean switched off his stereo. He didn't say a word. He was more disappointed than anybody.

Mrs. Dean wiped her hands on her apron, "Gosh, I hope he's alright."

*

Coach Redenbacher took Vincent home that night. All tests were negative. The doctor told him he had a concussion and to take it easy for a few days before picking up a baseball. When he got home, there was a plate of chocolate chip cookies on the doorstop and a note that read,

You had a good tournament. Get your rest. -Mrs. Dean

He picked up the plate and went straight to bed.

Chapter 9

Tuesday morning Vincent was at the Dean residence at 5:55 promptly. A few thin cirrus clouds stretched the eastern horizon of the sky, welcoming the sun to burn them off shortly. The dew was as thick as ever on the Dean's fescue.

Vincent pulled the cord on his old mower three times before it sputtered to life. He had planned to pay for the lessons he was receiving one way or another, and it seemed Grandpa Dean was too sick or old to mow the grass himself. It was the least Vincent could do. He didn't know what was wrong with Grandpa Dean, but Vincent didn't feel good about it.

The front window was already illuminated, but now Mrs. Dean's figure appeared in it, probably wondering who on earth could be cutting her grass at this time of the morning.

Vincent had made one loop around the outside boundary, giving him just enough room to turn around so he could cut it in straight lines. He wanted to give it the baseball field look with all the cross cuts, but the grass was so wet that he had to bang the mower to the ground time and time again to clear the grass from under the decking.

Mrs. Dean looked at Vincent and appeared worried. She came out onto the front porch and tried to get Vincent's attention, but he only waved at her and kept mowing. She threw up her hands and went back inside.

Vincent joined them shortly after 7:00.

After coffee and some cholesterol, Grandpa Dean picked this time to speak.

"What did the doctor say?"

Vincent grimaced, then smiled. "Said I have a hard head."

All three laughed. Both his elders seemed concerned, Elna more than Grandpa. Vincent knew that Grandpa Dean came from the old age where if you were spiked while trying to turn a double play and the blood was running down your pants, you rubbed dirt on it to stop the bleeding. Still though, Vincent knew the noggin wasn't anything to mess with.

"I see you brought your glove," Grandpa Dean said to keep the conversation going.

"Thought if you weren't too busy you would teach me the two-seamer-" Vincent exclaimed.

"Or the split," Grandpa cut him off. "I would love to today, but I am sure Elna would break my good arm if I tried to put you through a practice with what happened to you yesterday."

"Really," Mrs. Dean interrupted her husband, "I could skin you alive for cutting our grass. What on earth made you think you could get out of bed this morning anyway? I'm sure the doctor told you to rest."

"Oh, it was just a concussion," admitted Vincent who again smiled.

Mrs. Dean shook her head, "Oh, Goodness me! I'm glad I never had to raise boys. Look, you don't have to mow our grass in the first place."

"Mrs. Dean, I figure it's the least I could do for payment."

Mrs. Dean shook her head as if that fact weren't enough. "Well, at least let me pay you for it. What's a job like that go for nowadays? Twenty-five dollars?" She walked to the hallway to find her purse.

"Mrs. Dean, please," Vincent stopped her. "I want to do at least that for you. I don't want paid. I just want to learn more about pitching. Would a contract make you feel better?"

Mrs. Dean stopped in her tracks and Grandpa Dean whispered to Vincent, "You better do what she tells you to. Trust me; I've been married to her for a long time."

She turned around and said, "No, we don't need a contract. But what we do need is for you to go back home and go to bed. Let me give you and your mower a ride home."

"I was going to edge around your sidewalk too, if that's alright?" Vincent asked.

Mrs. Dean finally had enough. "Okay, son! That's where I draw the line. You go home this instant and get some sleep. You may do whatever you want to tomorrow, if you're alive, God help you."

Vincent smiled. "Deal. Then can we work on the two-seam tomorrow?"

Grandpa Dean smiled back and said loud enough for his wife to hear, "If she says it's alright," and then whispered, "Bring your glove over anyway."

*

It was a good thing Vincent went home because a few hours later he felt nauseous and went to bed, not waking up except for answering the phone when Coach Redenbacher called to check up on him. Woozy as he was, he took this time to ask Dusty's dad for a favor.

"Sure kid, what can I do for you? You need me to bring you something hot to eat."

"No Coach," Vincent said. "Nothing like that. It's much bigger."

"Okay, kid. What do ya need?"

"Well, I'm going to ask you at the beginning of practice tomorrow," Vincent said with confidence.

Coach Redenbacher paused for a few seconds. Vincent could hear breathing on the other end of the phone and wondered if this was such a good idea. .

Finally, Coach Redenbacher replied, "Sure kid. Depending on what it is, I'll see what I can do."

When Vincent hung up the phone, he reached into his shorts pocket and pulled out a slip of paper. He opened it and read it.

The LORD is my light and my salvation; whom shall I fear?
The Lord is the strength of my life; of whom shall I be afraid?
-Psalms 27: 1

He studied the verse, reading it twice and scratched his head. He was really feeling woozy now and put the scrap of paper on his nightstand and slipped under his covers. The verse from his hat entered his mind:

I can do all things through Christ which strengtheneth me.

Within seconds he was fast asleep.

*

And just like Old Faithful, Vincent was at the Dean residence at 5:55 the next morning with his weed eater spewing cheap plastic string and blades of grass everywhere in a cloud of dirt. By the time he finished twenty minutes later, it looked like it had been done by a pro.

He sat down to breakfast and somewhere between buttered toast and the Denver omelet, he realized he never really sat down to breakfast with his family before. Usually his dad was in bed sleeping off a hangover and his mother was at work or just getting off, in which case she didn't really have time for anything but a drink and bed.

During a lull in the conversation it was on the tip of Vincent's tongue to ask them if they had been giving him the Bible verses, but his confidence swayed and he decided to hold off. He didn't really know how to approach such a foreign subject. But still he couldn't shake the presence he felt everytime he thought about Philippians 4:13.

When they finished breakfast, and directly after Mrs. Dean gave the okay with reluctance, Vincent and Grandpa Dean were out the back door.

Vincent warmed up his arm, and Grandpa Dean made sure Vincent hadn't forgotten the basics of his windup and, more importantly, his concentration by barking orders at Vincent. As far as Vincent could tell, he seemed to show no ill effects of getting beaned in his noggin, and the goose egg was going down. After grooving his fastball with consistency for ten pitches, Grandpa Dean went to work.

"Let me see the ball," he said as he caned over to the mound. "Before I show you the two-seamer, we need to get things straight. I don't want you to do anything, I mean *anything* different in your windup and stride, unless I tell you to. Got that?"

"Yes, sir."

Grandpa Dean continued, "Okay, show me your four-seam grip."

Vincent obliged.

Grandpa Dean said, "Now turn it in your hand until your middle and index fingers are on the narrowest seams."

Vincent again obliged.

"Okay," Grandpa Dean continued, "you got the grip. I want you to throw the ball just like you have been."

Vincent looked at him as if waiting for some more directions.

"Well, go ahead and throw!" Grandpa Dean yelled.

"What do I concentrate on, sir?"

Grandpa Dean smiled. "Very good, Vincent. I want you to concentrate on the middle of the box."

Vincent turned into a machine with his stare directed at the box taped on the mattress. He looked for something within the square to more closely focus on and found what looked like a little smudge just left of center, maybe ink. He went into his windup and never heard Grandpa Dean telling him to stop. Vincent let the ball go and followed through. It whizzed through the air with a slightly different sound before hitting the tape on the outside of the box, a good six inches outside his target. He stood there and couldn't believe he missed his target. He had been hitting his target perfectly before. He had the concentration. He never took his eye off his target. How could he have missed that badly? He saw a hand wave in front of his face and the outside world came back to him with sounds of robins and blue jays fighting with squirrels in the pear tree by the house. A hint of perspiration trickled off his brow.

Grandpa Dean was trying to get his attention. "Son, aren't you listening to me? Are you there?"

"I'm sorry?" Vincent asked, breaking his trance.

"I yelled at you to stop right in the middle of your windup. Didn't you hear me?"

Vincent blushed. "Sorry, sir. I guess I blanked you out."

Grandpa Dean smiled. "Wonderful. That's called concentration. Major leaguers have to get all junk like booing fans, organ music, and railway cars out of their ears and hear nothing but their own thoughts. You couldn't do that any better."

Vincent was confused. "Then tell me how I missed my mark so bad!"

Grandpa Dean looked Vincent in the eyes and said, "What did you concentrate on?"

"That little black smudge left of center."

Grandpa Dean peered hard and couldn't for the life of him see what the kid was talking about, but took his word for it. The kid had young eyes. Good eyes, so Grandpa Dean continued, "Well, what were you wanting the pitch to do?"

Vincent replied, "Hit that mark."

"What pitch did you throw?"

"The two-seam," Vincent replied and a light came on in his head. He figured it out before Grandpa Dean could say anymore. Grandpa Dean continued anyway, "That means you put more pressure on your middle finger than your index. The two-seamer will glide whichever direction you direct it. If you put more pressure on your middle finger, it will glide left, just as if you put more pressure on your index, it will glide right. You see, you threw with the same velocity that you were throwing with the four-seamer, maybe a little faster, because there is less friction with two seams. But do you think the batter will be able to figure out why the pitch that looked exactly like the last and went just as fast as the last ended up six inches from where he expected it to go? Does this help you understand why you don't need a curveball?"

"Wow! So I threw it right," Vincent exclaimed.

"Well, pretty much," Grandpa Dean said. You threw it without knowing where it was going. If you can figure out where your pitch is going, you can really baffle a hitter. You will know this time which direction it is going, won't you? Try it again, only this time, put a little more pressure on your index finger."

Vincent was already in his concentration mode. He took a look at that black smudge and the only thought that entered his mind was *index finger*. He went into his windup automatically, strode forward, and released with a grunt.

The ball whizzed through the air and this time slithered far to the right and rose a few inches to boot, and if Grandpa Dean had been standing in that right hand batter's box, he would have been taking a dirt nap. For the second time Vincent stood in disbelief.

Grandpa Dean stared stupidly at where the pitch went. "Well, that definitely moved."

"Was that good?" Vincent asked.

"Well, you would have a runner on first," Grandpa Dean replied, "but that was quite a bit of movement. Throwing that pitch inside to a right handed batter is tough, but very effective. The barrel of the bat gets smaller and it's almost impossible to hit. And when the batter actually does hit the ball, what happens is a little squibber, and in the majors, a broken bat. How's your head feel?"

Vincent said, "I feel great."

"Okay, let's work on that some more," Grandpa Dean said.

Vincent threw for another twenty minutes until his pitch count hit fifty, and Grandpa Dean made him quit. At one point Vincent looked toward the back door of the house and saw Mrs. Dean through the screen, a worried look on her face.

When Vincent asked if he could come back tomorrow, Grandpa Dean grimaced in pain and agreed.

As Vincent left the house with the trimmer in one arm, the trimmer's brace around his neck, and his glove in the other hand, he reached into his pants pockets and came up empty-handed. He was a little disappointed until he looked at the webbing of his glove and found yet another slip of paper. He read it.

For in the time of trouble He shall hide me in his pavilion; He shall set me up upon a rock.

-Psalm 27: 5

*

A dirty red Corvette pulled onto the gravel driveway at Davison Motors on the south end of town. Dust from the back roads caked its exterior and nobody would have guessed by looking at it that it was actually red. It kicked up a dirt storm all the way to the rear, passing under the Davison Auto Salvage sign behind the dealership and into the past.

Jimmy had learned the dirty history of the operation in the past year and wondered how Deuce kept his little secrets.

The whole operation was an eyesore from Oklahoma State Highway 45 where motorists passed everyday on their way to work at any of the industrial plants south of town. Visitors from other towns would be greeted by this distortion of the natural landscape as they arrived to visit relatives or sight-see the 1800's sod house or the wildlife at the Great Salt Plains Lake.

The operation located itself in the inside elbow of land created by the juncture of the Eagle Chief River and Jack's Creek which collided just behind the salvage yard through the thick brush and cottonwood trees.

John Davison started the operation when it was still legitimate upon returning from the South Pacific in WWII and ran a respectable business on the twenty-five acres of land between the two waterways. He was known to close up shop in a heartbeat if he caught word that the catfish were biting behind his property on the hole locals referred to as "the mouth" of the creek. It was even rumored that he once stopped in mid-sentence, right in the middle of a sale, and excused his patrons from the premises, which gave him a dubious reputation. It prompted men in town to lament on the old days before the world was changed forever by a madman from Germany, and on that twenty-five acres which used to look so good sewn with winter wheat right up to the cottonwood trees that lined the banks.

Those men, being old, still lamented, but for another reason. When John Davison died in 1977, he left it to his son Dan, a man everyone in town just knew was a rotten apple.

Jimmy stepped out of his Corvette and slammed the door. He surveyed the scene. Davison Motors was getting in a new shipment of used cars direct from Mexico. Whether they were hot or not was of no importance. Jimmy knew Dan might sell the cars, and then again, they might get stripped and added to the rusting piles out back.

A couple grease monkeys in Stetsons and overalls were working the hydraulics, lowering what appeared to Jimmy as ten worthless pieces of junk.

Dan stood by the wooden steps leading to a dingy white trailer home on cinder blocks. It doubled as his office and residence. After his dad had passed on, Dan had decided to venture into an alternative business. New shipments came in from Mexico once a week.

While finishing the paperwork, Dan gave an irritated glance toward the dirty Corvette sharing his driveway and a mean glare to its occupant. He turned around and said something in fluent Spanish before signing a white paper on a clipboard and shaking the third grease monkey's hand.

Grease Monkey number two took off his overalls and gloves and laid them on the front seat of the semi-truck cab. He busied himself moving from car to car, lining them into a nice row.

Jimmy looked at the car being lowered to the ground and wondered how much marijuana was stored in its radiator, the oil pan, the muffler, and other places he couldn't even conceive. Maybe even the gas tank. A big pickup truck with a twenty gallon tank would hold a lot of weed.

Before Jimmy could contemplate the exact numbers, Dan looked back at Jimmy and fingered him to come forward. Jimmy felt a lump in his throat and his legs didn't seem to want to move. Dan ascended the three dirty steps and entered his office. Jimmy followed.

Once inside Jimmy first noticed the place didn't look much better on the inside than it did on the outside. The carpet was a gold, green, and orange shag mix with stray pieces flaking up with each step like the dirt flung up by horse hooves at the Kentucky Derby on race day. The furniture that constituted the front room matched all three colors of the carpet and all pointed to a television that, if any bigger, wouldn't have fit through the front door. Jimmy also noticed that a video game unit with its hand-held controllers lay strewn on the floor.

The window unit blew ice-cold air and still only managed to cool off a five-foot section that included the couch and mini-refrigerator.

Dan's abode was decorated in the early seventies. The decorator had died since, and his belongings had never been replaced.

When Jimmy took another step forward to the bar that acted as the room divider between the front room and the kitchen, he was knocked over by a horrendous smell.

"Dead rabbits." Deuce pointed to the trashcan, and Jimmy saw what was causing the odoriferous emanation. Two or three skinned rabbits lay in a heap in the office trashcan. Looked like they had been there for a few days and really drew the flies. "The Jews used to take a cloth and dip it in rabbit's blood and cocaine. That way when the dog would smell the cloth, it would strip it of its sense of smell temporarily. Made it that much harder for the Nazi's to find the people they were looking for. Cleans out your sinuses. That's for sure."

Jimmy giggled nervously, "Well, Deuce, that's good to know. Next time I want to hide something, I'll just go out and get some cocaine and shoot a rabbit."

Smiling a magnanimous smile, the operation's owner continued, "See kid, learned that in school. Kept it all these years. When you go away in August, make sure you listen real good in class. You never know when you'll end up using something in real life. What happened to your face?"

"Got in a fight."

"Over what I gave you?" Deuce asked.

"No. At the game."

Deuce smiled. "Yeah, that was a nice brawl. Looks like you head-butted some guy's fist. Only I don't remember seeing you in the middle of that pile."

Jimmy just stood there, not wanting to answer.

"You got what I want?" Deuce asked.

Trying to play off his initial reaction to this sty and Deuce's backhanded comments, Jimmy said, "Nice big screen, Deuce. Probably get a bunch of friends together to watch football on Saturdays, huh?"

"Well, if you have what you better have, I might just invite you over for the opener. But otherwise, since you're a few days late in seeing me, I'm going to guess you wouldn't be stupid enough not to bring the money."

Jimmy took another step forward and threw a manila envelope at Deuce who caught it in one hand while mixing a drink with the other. "It's all there and then some," Jimmy bragged. "I know it's late, but I remembered some punks who are graduating next year that I played football with. I invited them out to the Garfield River Bridge and collected a flat fee per head. You came out a little better than you might have guessed. They were more than willing when I told them where it came from."

"WHAT DO YOU MEAN YOU TOLD THEM WHERE IT CAME FROM?" Deuce yelled.

"No, not from you, you know man!" Jimmy tried to explain. "I told them it was from Costa Rica or Guatemala or somewhere down there and was really good stuff."

Deuce pulled out his cash box from under the bar and ripped open the envelope.

Jimmy wondered what else he had under that bar.

Deuce started counting. "It's from Mexico, but who cares, right? Hmmm, looks like over 500 here."

"521 dollars to be exact. I didn't mooch off it or pocket any of the profits, and even made you a little more than you expected," Jimmy bragged again.

Jimmy expected some praise from Deuce, but the businessman kept on counting, not seeming to care much about what Jimmy was saying. It was a dead silence that made Jimmy a little less comfortable. Jimmy chose this time to try to weasel out of the office. "So, I guess that's it, huh?"

Deuce kept on counting, stopping to go over a few bills to make sure they weren't stuck together and when finished, said, "521."

"Just like I said. I wouldn't cheat you, Deuce."

"Who said anything about cheating?" Deuce asked. "You did a real good job, kid. If this baseball thing doesn't work out, you know how you can make a living. Maybe I'll even cut you a commission, other than what goes up in smoke. You just gotta keep in good with the greedy little kids around town."

"Well," Jimmy said, looking away from Deuce, "I like baseball just fine."

"Yeah, a kid's sport. I never played baseball. Dad kept me pretty busy here in the backyard. I keep forgetting you're just a kid. You talk a big game and have even fooled all the town, and state for that matter. Boy, if they only knew what you were into. Mmmm, that'd be a shame, huh?"

Jimmy felt woozy at the thought. "Well, if it's all the same to you, we'll just keep this little business venture a secret and nobody will be the wiser."

"It wasn't a business venture kid, and we ain't any kind of partners. You owed me a favor. You want a drink? A smoke?" Deuce pointed to the fridge. "Got more than just beer in there. I'll even let you have some special rabbit's blood!"

Jimmy squirmed a bit. "Yeah thanks, but nine o'clock's kinda early in the morning for me. Besides, I think I'm thinking about quitting that kind of stuff."

Deuce chuckled. Takin' the high road, huh? Why? Feel in over your head right now? Afraid you might end up like those rabbits?"

Jimmy squirmed a little more. "Don't get me wrong, Deuce. It's a good business and you are a good businessman and make your money, and I'm not trying to say I'm better than you, because I'm not, but ..."

"Kid, get your nose out of my butt and tell me what you're trying to tell me." Deuce put his glass to his lips and drank what appeared to be something stiff because he exhaled deeply and coughed a few times.

Not knowing the next step, Jimmy said, "Well, I guess I don't have anything to say. So I guess I'll just be leaving. Nice knowing you Deuce."

Deuce chuckled and lit a cigarette from his Zippo and clinked it shut. No matter how much Jimmy hated and feared Deuce, there was still a small part of him that admired this awful human when he did something cool like clink his lighter open and shut. It was stupid, but true.

"What do you mean you'll be seeing me, boy? I've got more work for you!" Deuce said.

Click.

Jimmy stopped short in his steps when he heard the hammer pull back on the 9mm. The sound made him lose control of his bladder.

"You're not thinking that you're clear of your debt, are you?" Deuce asked to Jimmy's back.

Jimmy stood there. It was quite the dilemma. Just when he thought he might have to make a break for the door, Deuce asked, "Who do you play Saturday?"

It took Jimmy some control to talk without wetting his pants all over again. He was too afraid to turn around and see what he figured was pointing at his back. "We play Seiling. Doubleheader."

"Who's pitching the first game?" Jimmy arched his neck and saw that Deuce was turning the gun over and over, admiring its blued appearance.

"Uh, probably Gasser, or Conway. Probably Gasser."

Deuce calculated the odds. "They won the Stillwater Tournament didn't they?"

"Gasser and Conway?"

"No you idiot. Seiling. Seiling won the Stillwater Tournament, right?" Deuce asked.

"Yeah."

"Hmmm, and the game is here, correct?" Deuce asked.

"Both."

Deuce uncocked the hammer and put the gun on the bar, still pointed at Jimmy. He still hadn't fully turned around.

"They beat that Topeka team and the Stillwater Giants, huh? Doesn't matter. You'll still be favored if it's here." Deuce said.

"Deuce, maybe if you didn't gamble with your boss' drug money, you wouldn't have to worry about losing it."

Deuce looked sideways at Jimmy. After five tense seconds, Deuce laughed and reached under the bar. He pulled out another bag and threw it at Jimmy. It hit Jimmy on his right foot and he leaned over to pick it up.

"Push this bag," Deuce said.

Deuce blew out a plume of smoke as Jimmy stared at the bag in his hands in disbelief. He couldn't believe he would have to go through that again. Staying up all night and talking to total strangers, sleep deprivation, having to throw parties to get rid of the stuff, stress, cops.

"Oh, and by the way," Deuce said, "make sure you lose the first game and win the second, no matter who's pitching. Got me?"

Deuce poured another drink as Jimmy nodded and walked out the door. Jimmy jumped in his Corvette and ripped out of the parking lot.

*

The next day Vincent was his usual punctual self. After trimming the grass around the Dean's house and garage, Vincent enjoyed his coffee, which he was really starting to rely on. The caffeine buzz made him feel like king of the world from on top of that mound in their back yard. He observed the two friendly faces at the table and could read nothing in their eyes. He now knew they were the ones slipping him the bible verses, but why? Before he struck up the courage to ask, Grandpa Dean ushered him outside.

Vincent repeated his performances with the four and the two-seam fastballs and when showing excellent control with the two-seamer, he swore up and down that he hadn't been throwing any outside of these little practice sessions with Grandpa Dean. Vincent repeated Grandpa Dean's sentiments about not overdoing it, since the overhand throwing motion was not natural, and hence easily overdone.

"Can I learn the splitter today?" Vincent asked once it wasn't immediately after breakfast.

Grandpa Dean chuckled at the kid. "Pretty impatient, aren't you? You got something to tell me? Something you're hiding from me?"

Vincent lowered his head. Somehow Grandpa Dean saw right through him. "Well, sir," Vincent began, "with your permission, I was thinking about throwing for Coach Grey tonight at practice to see if he'll let me pitch a game."

"And you think you're ready for this?" Grandpa Dean inquired.

"No, probably not. But there are other guys on the team who are starting pitchers that have only two pitches. One of our guys only has one, and he hasn't lost yet."

Grandpa Dean chuckled again and felt his chest tighten into a ball before he coughed it away. "Well that's pretty impressive. What pitch does this kid throw?"

170

Vincent replied, "He's a knuckleballer."

"Waste of time," Grandpa Dean said under his breath. "How many knuckleballers are there in the majors right now? One, maybe two? The knuckleball is a waste of time. If the conditions aren't just right, the knuckleball is like a meatball sandwich. You'll never see me teach you that cursed pitch!"

"Of course not, sir," Vincent stammered. "I don't want to throw a knuckleball. I just want to pitch in ballgames this summer, before it's too late."

"And you think you're ready?"

"No, probably not," Vincent admitted.

Grandpa Dean frowned. "Show me how to throw a four-seamer out of the stretch."

This caught Vincent off guard. He had been throwing everything out of the windup, but he didn't consider what he would do if someone got on base. He looked at the rubber and kicked the dust off the top with his sneakers and went into an awkward stretch. He came up and delivered a pitch just outside the strike zone.

"Balk!" Grandpa Dean shouted.

"I balked?"

"You balked."

Vincent paused and went over his motion. Not coming up with any answers, he asked, "Okay, what did I do wrong?"

"Well," Grandpa Dean said, "for starters, you didn't pause at the top for a full second. Second your foot was on the back of the rubber, which is considered not being on the rubber at all. You want me to continue?"

"No sir. Can you teach me to throw out of the stretch?" Vincent said quietly.

Grandpa Dean knew the kid was anxious to show off his stuff, but he wanted him to be ready when he did. That guy would try to burn him down the first chance he got, so he needed Vincent to be prepared.

Grandpa Dean grabbed the ball from Vincent and shooed him away from the mound. "If you have to do this tonight, watch me closely."

Grandpa Dean looked more awkward than ever with his back hunched over. "You never touch the rubber unless you're ready to make a motion of some kind. You never place your front foot on the rubber, only your back foot, and then if you want to step off for any reason, whether to throw a runner out or to refocus, you gotta step off the back of the rubber like this," and he demonstrated for Vincent.

Grandpa Dean continued, "Next, you place your foot in this groove in front of the rubber and lean over to get your sign from the catcher. Leave the ball in your glove like I showed you with all four seams facing you. And remember, what should you be doing all this time?"

"Concentrating," Vincent replied like a good student.

"Exactly" Grandpa Dean said. "Now you have the sign, you have to come up. Concentrate on putting your fingers on the ball still in your glove without looking at it. What should you be staring at?"

Vincent replied with confidence, "The catcher's mitt."

Grandpa Dean corrected him, "That is true, almost. If you're in the stretch, you have to acknowledge the base runner. Let's just say a runner is on first. Now that you're up and your weight is perfectly balanced on both legs, you have to give at least a glance at the base runner by turning nothing but your head and neck. If you turn a shoulder toward first without stepping off the back of the rubber, that's a balk. If you make any motion whatsoever toward first base without taking your foot off the back of the rubber, that's a balk."

"Okay," Vincent said.

"Now when you look at the runner, don't make it sneaky," Grandpa Dean continued. "Do it the same way each time so you bore the runner to death. You want him to know that you looked at him. The base runner is your catcher's responsibility. He will give you the sign to throw to first base, so if you're coming home with a pitch, just give him the same glance, but don't worry about him one bit. If he's going to run, it's your catcher's job to either give you the sign to throw over to first, or throw the runner out himself when he tries to steal. It's not your job at all to worry about. Your only concentration is on that glove, so when you look over to first base, he may think you're looking at him, but in actuality, you're thinking about where your catcher placed his glove to receive the pitch.

"So you're coming home with a fastball. You look back at your catcher and concentrate on that glove, but unfortunately you don't have all the time in the world to concentrate on your mark like when in the windup. If you do, the runner will pick up your ritual and steal on you. No coach has patience for that. So you have to use no more than one second to refocus your concentration on the glove before you go into your leg kick and heave it home," Grandpa Dean finished up and stopped. "Pretty simple, huh?"

Vincent looked at the ground and pawed the tip of his sneaker at an old ant pile. "Sounds like it needs to be kept as simple as possible."

"Exactly," Grandpa Dean agreed. "Keep it simple. If you take care of the batter, what difference does it make if the base runner steals second and third? You'll just strand him in scoring position. See what I'm saying?"

"Yes sir."

"Give it a try." Grandpa Dean flipped the ball to Vincent and crutched over to first base. "Now, put your foot on the rubber. Remember, you can't throw to a base if your foot is on the rubber.

In fact, I'm not going to even teach you to pick off a runner today. We'll save that for another day. Get your sign."

Vincent stepped onto the rubber and leaned in to read his sign from the mattress.

"Four-seamer, outside corner, low," Grandpa Dean said from first. Vincent kept his concentration on home and came up, placing his hand on the ball just as Grandpa Dean had suggested. He felt a bit awkward, but caught his breath and looked over at the old man who was standing on first base now. He looked back at the box on the mattress, found the bottom outside corner of the strike zone, and with a big leg kick let it fly. The ball hit its mark.

"Not bad, kid."

Vincent shook his head in disgust. "It felt like I threw it slower though."

"Well of course you did," Grandpa Dean confirmed. "You're pitching out of the stretch. Nobody can throw as hard out of the stretch as they can in the windup. It's just not possible to unleash as much energy. Try it again."

Vincent went through the motions again and hit the corner again. Concentration was on. He was looking pretty machine-like.

"Again. Perfect practice makes perfect," Grandpa Dean said.

Vincent threw again and again, each time hitting his mark well. After twenty-five pitches Mrs. Dean came out with iced tea and they decided to take a break.

Sitting down to a refreshing tea, Vincent waited until it wasn't immediately after they sat down and said, "Well, what do you think?"

Grandpa Dean slurped down half his glass before answering. "I know you're not ready to pitch in a game yet."

"But what do you think about practice tonight?" Vincent asked.

Grandpa Dean put the ball back in Vincent's court. "Do you think you're ready?"

This time, instead of saying no, Vincent replied with confidence. "I think I have enough to show the coaches so they can consider me."

Grandpa Dean took another deep swig of his tea and Mrs. Dean came out with a plate of shortbread cookies.

"Elna, sit down," Grandpa Dean said. She obliged with curiosity. Grandpa Dean asked, "Do you think Vincent is ready to show the coaches his pitching tonight?"

"Well, that's kind of your area," she replied.

"Can you grab me a piece of paper and a pen from inside?" Grandpa Dean asked.

Mrs. Dean obliged and Grandpa Dean leaned in close to have a serious word with his young prodigy. Grandpa Dean felt his chest tighten again and had to breathe in and out deeply a few times to loosen it. Each day was worse than the one before.

"Okay kid," Grandpa Dean started, "ordinarily I would tell you no and leave it at that, but this isn't ordinarily. I'm going to try to get you everything you need, when you need it, but I am going to have to do it expeditiously for reasons you'll find out later."

Grandpa Dean paused and took another drink. "Go ahead and show them your heater and throw a little movement in there if they ask for it, but don't give them too much to look at. Keep it to yourself as if your arm is something they need, instead of the other way around. Don't be cocky about it. Just let them have a taste and if they want more, give them a little more. Just concentrate and do it like you know you can. Consider it practice if you will."

Mrs. Dean came out with paper and pencil and handed it to Grandpa Dean who scribbled on it as he went on. "I'm tired and need to go in for the day. Come back tomorrow morning to let me know how it went." He folded the piece of paper three times and placed it in the webbing of Vincent's glove, and Mrs. Dean helped her husband into the house.

For the first time that morning Vincent realized just how bad Grandpa Dean looked and it worried Vincent. He looked at his glove and back up at the closing screen door. He drank the last of his iced tea and took a peek at the piece of paper in his glove. He unfolded it and read it.

Psalms 27: 14. Look it up.

*

The evening air radiated. The heat seemed to pass Vincent's face in miniature invisible clouds. It felt like trying to breathe while enveloped in a swarm of gnats.

Vincent looked around. The kids acted particularly lethargic, but this apparently went unnoticed to Coach Grey who seemed to be preoccupied.

Vincent knew everyone was probably concerned about him, especially Coach Grey, and that worried Vincent. Why would Coach be the least bit interested in Vincent? Then he found out why. Coach Grey told everybody to take the field and asked Vincent to stay behind. Vincent felt particularly vulnerable alone with the dictator.

Coach Redenbacher looked at Vincent and instead of waiting around, went out into the field to direct practice.

"Vincent, how's that noggin of yours?" Coach Grey asked.

Vincent wondered, *Has he finally seen how valuable I am?*

Vincent looked out in the field and saw the outfielders shagging fly balls and wished he were out there with them.

Vincent finally found the right words. "I feel fine sir."

"You sure?" Coach Grey continued. "That was a heck of a shot you took. That would put most people out of commission for the season."

Vincent finally figured it out. *Aha! Coach is trying to get me to quit! How pathetic! Am I taking the spotlight away from his precious son? If only the proud daddy knew about innocent little Jimmy.*

"Well sir," Vincent started, "I felt a little lightheaded for a day, but the doctor said I would be ready to go in three days and I was ready in two. Either I have a hard head, or that helmet was very good." He looked up at Coach Grey who was studying him with his head cocked at an angle and his right hand up to his chin. Vincent didn't like what he saw in Coach's eyes.

"Well, do you have a release from the doctor?" Coach Grey asked. "You know, I can't play you without a doctor's release."

Vincent reached in his back pocket and saw Coach's expression change to bitterness when he produced what he asked for. Coach appeared to read it over twice before finally convinced. "Well, it looks like there's nothing keeping you on this bench, but my concern for your health. You sure you want to go out there? I'm not a doctor, but I know a bad shot when I see it, and you had a bad shot."

Vincent caught himself smirking. *And you're not a nice man, but you sure are trying to impersonate one.*

"Yes sir," Vincent replied. "I'm ready to get back into the groove of things. Seiling's a big game this weekend and I want to be sharp, given your permission of course."

Coach rolled his eyes and stuffed the piece of paper in his back pocket. "Well, you better get out there then."

Vincent jogged to the outfield smiling. The verse Grandpa Dean gave him earlier that day going through his head over and over again: *Wait on the LORD: be of good courage, and he shall strengthen thine heart.*

On the way to left field, he said to Quentin, "I got your Bible here."

"Hold onto it for a while," Quentin replied as he fielded a ground ball and side-armed it to first base.

Coach Grey took over the infield and instructed Coach Redenbacher to work with the outfielders. There were no fancy speeches about the big fight the other day with the Giants, no looking down his nose at the kids. In fact Coach Grey mentioned how proud he was of the way his team responded.

Vincent had heard rumors about how Jimmy valiantly jumped in the pile to protect him. It was questionable if Jimmy was even going to be able to play by Saturday. Between his ribs from the Alva game and the dugout-clearing brawl the other day, Jimmy sure was having a rough senior campaign.

Vincent looked out in center field and saw Jimmy struggling to find his depth perception. More balls found the ground than his mitt. He told the team at the beginning of practice that his left eye had been closed shut until he woke that morning.

Vincent knew that a damaged eye was the kiss of death in baseball, great eyesight being what separated weekend warriors from the pros. Despite not liking Jimmy, Vincent was a bit worried about him.

Toward the end of practice, the position players played pepper games against the Little Monster in left field under Coach Redenbacher's supervision while the pitchers worked on their stuff, Coach Grey measuring each pitch on the radar gun. Vincent pulled aside Coach Redenbacher.

"Coach, are you willing to do that favor for me now?" Vincent asked him.

Coach Redenbacher frowned, but relented. "Sure Vincent. What do you want?"

"I would like to throw a few pitches for you and Coach Grey from the mound."

Coach Redenbacher took a step back. He stretched, looked toward the infield, and asked, "Well, can you pitch?"

"Not bad," Vincent replied. "Coach, the reason I am asking you is because I know Coach Grey would never let me, the way he feels about me. I was hoping you could convince him."

Coach Redenbacher exhaled and said, "Well Vincent, I will ask him. I can't promise anything, but I will ask him."

Coach Redenbacher looked to the other players and said, "Attention everybody! Keep working on pepper, I'll be right back." The kids barely turned their heads to acknowledge Coach. Pepper games were something all the players looked forward to, and as soon as Coach Redenbacher jogged into the infield, they started making their little variations to make things more interesting, even taking bets on the side. Jimmy sat it out and rested with his back against the Little Monster.

*

Coach Grey was having a conversation with Ned Gasser when Coach Redenbacher approached him. "Can I have a word with you, Coach?"

Coach Grey was irritated. As they walked to the dugout, he said, "Can you believe Ned went water skiing and his right arm hurts too much to pitch today! What on earth could these kids be thinking? I'll have you know that in my day I wouldn't even dream of doing anything that would interfere with baseball or my ability to play the game. Coach Wolf would have kicked my butt out into the street and told me to stay gone."

"Well Coach, pitching is sort of on the lines of what I was wanting to talk to you about," Coach Redenbacher said. "I have a favor to ask you."

Coach Grey eyed his assistant with suspicion and let him go on. "I know it sounds silly, but we're already short on pitchers and now with Ned coming up gimpy, there's another player who wants to give pitching a try."

"Yes?" Coach Grey asked.

"Well, if you could just let him pitch a little, look him over."

Coach was getting irritated with this dialogue. "Well, who is it? Jake? Quentin?"

Coach Redenbacher exhaled and said, "Vincent."

Coach Grey laughed out loud. "You gotta be kidding me?"

"He really wants to give it a shot. The way I figure, what do you have to lose?" Coach Redenbacher pleaded.

Coach Grey thought it over.

The kid was getting really cocky now! He won't even be able to find the strike zone. But if we put him on the mound for everybody to see, maybe he'll make a fool out of himself in front of the whole team and pop that big head of his.

Coach Grey smiled finally. "That sounds like a good idea. In fact, I'm going to make an announcement."

He looked out to left and saw most of the kids on their backs laughing with Bacon Bob right in the middle squatting and making faces. He didn't even want to know what was going on.

"EVERYBODY BRING IT IN!" Coach Grey yelled.

The kids filed their way to the infield, Jimmy pulling up the caboose.

When Coach Grey had everybody's attention, he said, "Okay guys, I'm holding an open tryout right now for anybody else who wants to break into the rotation." Coach Grey stared at Ned Gasser, who looked up with shocked surprise. Coach Grey hoped that Ned was worried about losing his starting spot.

"Anybody want to step up and try their hand at pitching?" Coach Grey continued.

Coach Grey saw everybody look around at each other. He knew they weren't used to such an aberration in the practice ritual. Coach Grey was so strict on what went on and stuck to his schedule down to the minute. He even used an egg timer for drills.

He looked around while everybody was silent. Finally, Vincent raised his hand.

Coach Grey smiled. "Okay Preston, take the mound. Bacon, grab your mask and get behind the plate.

Bob tooted.

A few giggled.

"Sorry Coach," Bob said.

Vincent walked to the mound and Coach Redenbacher caught up to him. The two spoke briefly and Coach Redenbacher patted him on the back and joined Coach Grey behind the backstop in the media booth.

*

The other players all filed over to the bench and sat down. Quentin sat at the far end of the bench and was joined by Dusty, who patted Quentin on the back.

Dusty watched Vincent stretch out his arm on top of the mound. He looked over to Coach Grey, who seemed to be disinterested.

Something didn't sit right with Dusty, so he cleared his throat and whispered, "Hey Quentin, does something seem off here?"

Quentin loaded his mouth with sunflower seeds. "What do you mean?"

Dusty really didn't know where he was going with this. "You know, just off. Like Coach Grey."

Quentin spit a shell out of his mouth and leaned back. "You mean more than normal?"

Dusty felt the implication. His dad was the assistant coach, and really didn't have any say in anything involving the function of the team's affairs, but Coach Redenbacher was guilty by association. Dusty by association to his Dad.

"Coach Grey is…" Dusty started and didn't know how to finish the sentence. Quentin finished it for him.

"Corrupt? Arrogant? A jerk?"

Dusty lowered his head. "Yeah, all of those."

Quentin looked at Dusty and said, "This just now dawning on you?"

"No," Dusty began, "I don't think so. I guess I've known all along. The way he treats the bench warmers. The way he talks down to us. The way …"

"The way he treats Vincent?" Quentin interrupted.

"Yeah, that's really bothering me," Dusty said.

Quentin spat out a few more spent shells and said, "Look, Dusty, we're seniors. We've almost made it out of here. At the end of the season we will all go off to college and we will never have to worry about Coach Grey again."

"Yeah?" Dusty asked.

"Well," Quentin continued, "what about Vincent?"

Dusty's sick feeling made sense. He was worried about Vincent's future. Dusty didn't know if Vincent had any prospects, but Dusty assumed it was pretty bleak. "I don't know, Quentin."

"Well," Quentin continued, "You asked if something was off. Well, something most definitely is." Quentin's voice started to rise. "Don't you see what Coach Grey does, man? He is nothing more than a bully! He picks on the weak in order to make himself feel better."

A few of the other players looked over at the two, so Quentin lowered his voice to a whisper. "And don't think he cares about us, man. There's only one person he cares about other than himself, and that's his little moneymaker."

Dusty looked over at Jimmy who was sitting by himself, seeming to be in his own little world.

"You 'bout ready, boy?" Coach Grey yelled out to Vincent.

Dusty listened to the tone Coach took with Vincent and was disgusted. "It's true," Dusty said to Quentin. "Coach Grey is just a bully. In fact, I wonder if he's planning on making fun of Vincent?"

Quentin shrugged and spit out another spent shell. "Guess we'll see."

Dusty looked out at Vincent who appeared to be the model of concentration out on the mound. Dusty lowered his head and said a little prayer.

*

Coach Grey picked up his radar gun. "This ought to be comical," Coach Grey remarked loud enough for Vincent to hear. Coach Redenbacher just sat there, expressionless.

"What pitch are you going to throw?" Coach Grey asked Vincent who stood at the base of the mound.

Vincent replied, "Four-seamer."

"Four-seamer? You mean fastball?" Coach Grey asked.

"Yes sir."

"Okay," Coach Grey yelled loud enough for everybody to hear. "Fire away. Everybody, watch Vincent. We'll have a critique session after he's done."

Vincent placed the ball in his mitt just the way Grandpa Dean had shown him and stepped up to the rubber. Vincent stared at Bacon Bob's mitt which was centered over the plate. This was the first time he had thrown to a real live person, and it was a bit different than that old stained mattress, but he focused on the mitt and finally found what appeared to be a hanging stitch in the webbing.

Philippians 4:13 came to his head again. *I can do all things through Christ which strengtheneth me.*

"C'mon! Let's go! Whenever you're ready!" Coach Grey yelled from behind the backstop.

Concentrate! Vincent thought to himself. *You're not in their world anymore.*

Everybody waited in anticipation as Vincent took his sweet time. The players chattered amongst themselves, as Vincent sought to fade them out with his own thoughts.

Lightning and Thunder, Vincent! Lightning and Thunder!

Vincent took a step back and started his windup, fingers securely on the stitches, eyes on that dangling thread in Bacon Bob's mitt.

All was silent. The world was just the ball and the hanging thread from a catcher's mitt. The rest now was just a blur that

Vincent didn't concern himself with. Just as fast as the lightning struck, thunder followed.

Bob's mitt made a *Clap!* sound. Or maybe it was a clap of thunder. Vincent wasn't sure.

The ball deflected off Bob's mitt and bounced away to the backstop.

Vincent took his stare off Bob's mitt and saw all the kids' eyes jumping from Bob to Vincent like they were watching a tennis match, and not a one of them said a word. Vincent saw Quentin and Jake both smile, as did Dusty.

Vincent turned his attention to behind the plate where Coach Grey was stone silent as Coach Redenbacher exclaimed in a big voice, "Holy Cow!" Coach Grey gave him an irritated glance and all the players looked over at them.

"How fast was that?" Dusty finally asked.

"None of your business," Coach Grey responded and Coach Redenbacher exclaimed the same sentiments. "Holy Cow! Is that right?" Again Coach Grey glared at his assistant.

Coach Grey glared out at Vincent and said, "Throw that pitch again."

Bacon Bob stared at Coach. "Well, throw him the dang ball back Bob! What are you waiting for?"

Bob ran back to the backstop, grabbed the ball, and heaved it back to Vincent who refocused.

Vincent knew how fast he was throwing, or at least thought he knew. He still had no idea that Grandpa Dean led him to believe he was five miles-per-hour slower than he really was.

"What pitch?" Coach Grey asked.

"Four-seamer," again was Vincent's response.

"It's called a fastball!" Coach Grey shouted. Coach Redenbacher looked at the screen of the radar gun again.

"Had to be a bird, or something," Coach Grey said and glared back at his assistant.

"What in tarnation kind of bird flies that fast?" Coach Redenbacher asked.

Coach Grey didn't answer.

Vincent saw that now even Jimmy was watching from the end of the bench.

Everybody was talking loud enough for Vincent to hear, but he tried to fade back into his own little world now, an alternate universe where everything was perfect.

Vincent focused on the thread in Bacon Bob's glove again.

Vincent silently coached himself up again. *Concentrate! Lightning and Thunder!*

Vincent cleared his head of everything and went into the windup with an even bigger leg kick.

The ball sling-shot out of Vincent's arm and popped the pocket of Bacon Bob's mitt, only this time the ball took the mitt clean off his left hand.

"Whoa!" Bob said as he fell backward and came to a rest on his butt. He rolled over onto his back and let out another fart, only this time nobody laughed. The coaches were both silent.

Coach Grey stared at the radar gun and yelled to Vincent, "Again."

A few players tried to sneak around and get a glimpse of the radar gun from behind, but Coach gave them a glare and they backed off. The scene made Vincent chuckle to himself.

His teammates whispered again.

Vincent readied himself again atop the hill as soon as Bob got his glove back on. The pitcher went through his windup and delivery and popped the leather again.

Again, Bob dropped the ball.

"Bob, can you hold onto the darn ball?" Coach Grey yelled down at his catcher.

"Sorry Coach. I'm tryin'! It's just commin' in so fast I can barely see it!" Coach Grey shook his head and prompted Vincent three more times to throw the same pitch and three more times the results stayed consistent.

Beads of sweat stood out on Vincent's forehead and he wiped them with the bill of his baseball cap. He saw the verse again and meditated.

I can do all things...
POP!
through Christ...
POP!
which strengtheneth me...
POP!

Coach Grey appeared mad. "Bob, outside corner." He moved his glove to the outside corner and Vincent nailed it perfectly.

POP!

"Inside corner," Coach Grey yelled.

POP!

Vincent was oblivious to everything outside of his kinship with the ball and the hanging thread in Bacon Bob's glove.

Coach Grey scratched his head. "You got any more pitches, or you going to throw fastballs for an entire game?"

Vincent was so focused on Bacon Bob's glove, he barely heard Coach Grey talking. When his not entirely-unwilling catcher finally put his glove down, Vincent broke the trance and looked up.

"Hello! Are you listening?" Coach Grey shouted to Vincent. "Have you any other pitches?"

"How 'bout a two-seamer?" Vincent asked.

Vincent peered over to the dugout and saw his teammates all looking at each other in confusion.

"A what?" Coach Grey asked.

"A two-seamer."

"You mean another fastball?" Coach Grey asked again.

"Yes, only with movement."

"Okay," Coach Grey said. "Bob place your glove outside."

Bob did as instructed and Vincent took another ten seconds to recapture his focus. He fired, and the ball tailed where he wanted it.

The other players apparently couldn't stand it anymore and got behind the backstop. Jimmy joined the rest of his teammates, Coach Grey at this point appeared to not even notice.

"Inside, Bob," Coach Grey prompted.

POP!

"Oohs" and "Aahs" came forth from the players-turned-spectators.

"Okay Vincent, can you change speeds now?" Coach Grey inquired. Vincent looked at the thread once again and this time grunted. Vincent knew it came out even faster that time.

A smile came over both coaches' faces. The kids directly under the press box kept peering up at Coach Grey who would give them dirty looks.

"Okay, you can throw hard. You got any other pitches?" Coach Grey asked.

Uh-oh. Here it comes, thought Vincent.

Vincent looked up at Coach. "I don't have anything else ready yet."

"What do you mean you don't have anything else ready yet? Do you have any other pitches?" Coach Grey asked again.

"None of my other pitches are ready yet," Vincent said again. "I still have to work on them."

"Well, how many other pitches do you have?" Coach Grey asked, appearing more amused than irritated now.

Now Vincent was getting irritated. "None that are ready."

Coach Grey scratched his five o'clock shadow with the back of his right hand and looked at the radar gun again, just staring at it.

"Can you pitch out of the stretch?" Coach Grey asked.

Vincent responded confidently. "Yes."

"Show me," his coach prompted him.

Vincent exhaled. He wasn't as confident out of the stretch. He placed his foot on the back side of the rubber just like Grandpa Dean said.

Vincent repositioned his foot on the front side of the rubber and leaned in for his sign. Bob didn't give a sign, so he threw a four-seamer.

POP!

The mitt might have made the same noise, but Vincent knew he had lost some velocity on that last pitch.

"Well, that's more like it," Coach Grey said out loud. A few kids poked their heads over the ledge and one got bonked by Coach Grey's hand this time.

Coach Grey smiled, gave a good stretch and said, "I've seen enough. Jimmy, get up on the mound."

"What? C'mon Dad! I can barely see!"

Vincent stepped off the back of the rubber like he was taught so he wouldn't balk and walked to the dugout, his mitt carried in his right hand and his hat off. He was looking at a good Bible verse.

Jimmy grabbed his glove and met Vincent in the dugout on his way to the mound. Vincent put the ball in Jimmy's glove.

Jimmy said, "You see my face. This is all your fault!"

Vincent only smiled and thought, *My fault huh? That's rich. The bump on the side of my head is YOUR fault, you jerk. There are a lot of things that are your fault, and your kingdom is falling down around you.*

Jimmy attempted to nudge him with his shoulder, but depth perception being off, missed entirely and looked awkward in the process.

Vincent didn't even acknowledge Jimmy formally, but just sat down on the bench and waited to see what Jimmy had. Vincent wasn't going to be an arrogant jerk. He would just take care of business and let the cards fall where they may.

Just before Vincent sat down, his keen eyes caught a motion in the woods beyond the right-field fence. He thought he saw an elderly lady peer from behind a tree, but thought he must be mistaken. Not thinking anything of it, he quickly turned his attention to the great Jimmy Grey.

*

Coach Grey watched his son slowly trudge to the mound. When Jimmy stepped on the rubber and squinted at Bob, he broke concentration and said, "I'm not even warmed up yet!"

"You've had all practice to warm up that arm," the elder said. "Give me a fastball."

Jimmy shook his head, obviously upset at his dad, but Coach Grey didn't care. He had a plan working in the back of his mind.

Jimmy went into his beautiful windup and strode forward, releasing the ball with an audible "Ummph!"

The ball climbed and Bacon Bob wasn't fast enough to bring his glove up to catch it. It skidded off the top of his webbing about six-foot high and hit the backstop, prompting everybody behind to duck out of reflex.

Coach Grey knew it was an ugly pitch, but fast. Both coaches looked at the radar gun.

88 MPH

"What's his best again?" Coach Redenbacher asked.

Coach Grey responded, "Ninety."

"Looks like the radar is pretty much right on then," Coach Redenbacher responded, pausing, then adding, "But how could Vincent …"

"Shut up," Coach Grey told his assistant and his assistant obeyed. Coach Grey didn't want to hear from anybody how much faster Vincent was than his own son, the pride of Augusta.

"Coach, how fast is Vincent throwing?" Dusty asked.

Coach Grey stood up and turned off his gun, ignoring the question. "That's enough," he said to his son, who stood on the mound in disbelief.

Jimmy threw the ball down in anger. It projected off the front of the mound and rolled to the plate. Coach Grey winced, reminded of the type of temper tantrum Jimmy would throw when he was three.

Bacon Bob took off his mask and picked up the ball and turned around. "It was fast!" he told the players.

Coach Grey looked the players over and pondered what to say.

Somebody asked again how fast Vincent had thrown.

Coach Grey growled. "None of your business. Listen up. We were embarrassed in Stillwater last week. Everybody knows we were the best team there. And I think you all know by now that Seiling ended up winning the whole dang thing. And by coincidence we play Seiling in a double-header on Saturday. This we all know."

Coach Grey thought for a bit longer, trying to decide what to do about the pitching situation. He thought it through for a few seconds and knew there was only one answer.

Vincent is not ready, Coach Grey thought. *If Vincent flounders, he will lose popularity and the rest of my players will start to rally around Jimmy for leadership again. That has to be what is wrong with Jimmy. Vincent is stealing his thunder so my son is acting out. That is the only possible answer for Jimmy's change in behavior. Yes, Vincent has to pitch. It is a win-win situation.* "We've had some players take it upon themselves to put the team second, and gone out and done some stupid things between the weekend and now," Coach Grey began. "Hear this once and for all. The team always comes first. That means if you're going to get a sunburn swimming, stay home. If you're going to stub your index finger playing tiddlywinks, wear a glove. And if you're going to hurt your arm skiing, for cryin' out loud, drive the boat instead. We are the best team in the state in any classification and we are a measly four and three! That is embarrassing! That's why we need to kick it in high gear and sweep Seiling on Saturday. To show that their championship trophy means nothing. Game one starter will be Vincent."

Coach Grey looked over at his son who now looked sick to his stomach.

Refocusing, Coach Grey continued. "Game two starter will be Gabe. Vincent, I expect you and Bob to get together between now and then to get your signs straight. Got it? Everybody else, get your rest. Dismissed."

Coach Grey watched as nearly all the players huddled around Vincent and congratulated him, asking him all sorts of questions. Coach Grey hoped his little plan would work. There was a lot more at stake than just a stupid ballgame. He couldn't stand to watch the spectacle anymore, so he turned and ascended the stairs.

Jimmy and Coach Grey were the first to leave, both in different cars in different directions.

Chapter 10

"Now, a 1230 KBAL Tradition for the past sixteen years, it's Augusta Stampeding Herd Baseball! Brought to you by Cartwright Insurance, protecting farmers for thirty years. They're your hometown heroes when hail hits. By Coulter Floral, your one-stop shop when you're in the doghouse with your wife. And by your local merchants. And now Augusta Stampeding Herd Baseball with The Sultan of Swat, Solomon Smity, and Joltin' Joel Richards."

"Hey all you Augusta Stampeding Herd baseball fans, this is the Sultan of Swat, Solomon Smity here with my sidekick, a man who had garlic bread with his spaghetti for lunch today and won't be saying much if I have any control of the situation, Joltin' Joel Richards."

"Ha, Ha. Very funny. We won't talk about that escargot episode you had. People, here's a little known fact. Sol can really snort down those snails. It's one sick display, let me tell you."

"Well, if you're curious as to where you can find great Italian food like what we just ate for lunch, look no further than

Michellini's Deli on the corner of historic 8th and Main, right across the street from Birch's Mortuary. It's a short walk away just in case you overeat on Wednesday's all you can eat supper buffet. Michellini's even delivers and caters. That's Michellini's Deli for your Italian appetite. Well Joel, you know what today is, don't you?"

Yes, it's coming one week later than we had hoped, but it's Seiling Day! Ladies and Gentlemen, the Seiling Pirates come to town fresh off their tournament championship at last weekend's Stillwater tournament as the number eleven seed. In case you've been camping for the last few weeks, Augusta and Seiling were on a collision course for the championship game in what many consider the toughest tournament in the state when Augusta was unceremoniously shown the door. After up-and-coming star left fielder, Vincent Preston, was beaned in the head by a pitch, the Augusta players ran out onto the field to defend their star, and after the melee was cleared up, the umpire decided to eject the whole Augusta team for fighting and declare the hometown Giants victors via default, despite Stillwater's involvement in the fight. I must say I have never been so disgusted in my life. Seiling went on to win the tournament, narrowly defeating the heavily favored Giants behind what has been their staple for years, strong pitching and timely hitting with a touch of small ball added in. So to make a long story short, we got jipped out of a grudge match with Seiling last week, but lo and behold, we get our shot at them today."

"Or rather they get their shot at us. Remember, we are the defending state champions."

"Right you are Joel, and here's a breath mint. Well, we promised ourselves that we wouldn't spend much time complaining about what happened last weekend, but rather concentrate on the here and now. It's thirty minutes to game time and we're watching the good guys warm up on the infield while the bad guys have the outfield, and I couldn't help notice that a few of them seem mesmerized by all the pennants adorning the Little Monster."

"As they should Sol. How long has it been since Seiling has won the state tournament?"

"Have they ever? Actually I know the answer to that, but that's not important. During the show we will talk about star Vincent Preston and discuss that shot he took to the head with Coach Grey, plus we will go over the Seiling lineup. Seiling's much like Augusta; they just reload every year. It seems like there's always someone ready to fill a vacant spot. Anyway, when we come back from break, we'll hit these headlines and more. We'll be back in one minute with Coach Grey. This is Augusta Stampeding Herd Baseball on KBAL 1230 AM, Oldies Radio."

"And we're off."

"Do you see Coach Grey anywhere?"

"I haven't seen him pull in yet. I wonder what's going on. Not only that, but where's Jimmy? He's been coming in late to the last two games, and this makes three. You don't think there's some family emergency, do you?"

"Ah, speak of the devil, there come the two down the steps and it looks like they're ticked off at each other. Well, at least Jimmy is here before game time today. Must have gotten a push from his dad."

"Well, he needs it. Ever since he announced he's signed with North Central he's been another person, really... I can't come up with the word."

"Fifteen seconds, guys."

"I know what you mean. I thought it was me. It's almost like he's become a... gosh, I don't know the word either."

"Five, four, three-"

"And we're back. Grey is busily working with his players, and it looks like we can get to the Seiling lineup before he gets up here. We talked to Dalton Creek before the game. He's been Seiling's head coach for the last, oh I don't know, few decades. Anyway, the guy's been around forever and it's always interesting to talk to the man that can't sit in the same room with Coach Grey without a fight breaking out. Anyway, we had a chance to talk with him when we got to the park, and he gave us the starting lineup. Take it away, Joel."

"Thanks, Sol. Just like us, Seiling has a senior-laden team with lots of starters coming back. They only have two newcomers to the starting lineup. If you will remember, they took second place at state last year. Batting leadoff is senior center fielder Tag McNugert, a three-year starter who's very fast and very dangerous. They say he got his nickname from elementary school. Tag isn't his real name, but it seems to be a mystery that he isn't going to give away. It's probably something funny, like John Denver's real name."

"What was John Denver's real name?"

"Man Sol, I was hoping you could remember. It's something really long like Leonard Somethingorother. Oh well, that doesn't matter. When Tag would play tag with the other students, nobody could catch him. Well, nothing's changed. He's still very fast and very dangerous. He was also a wide out for their football team and has signed a letter of intent to play football with Tulsa State next year."

"Burned us twice last year on fly routes."

"Man, don't remind me. In the number two spot is senior second baseman, Steven West, who's always getting a bat on the ball and has long-ball capabilities when he gets the bat around. In the three hole is the ever-dangerous senior shortstop, Jas Foster, who not only is a threat to get on base everytime he's up, but also has been drawing all sorts of attention to his fielding. It seems nobody can get a ball through the left side of the infield. He's still undecided on his choice of college, but it sounds like plenty of universities are giving him looks. He's one of the reasons that Seiling is only giving up two runs a game this year on average."

"Yeah, I hate to say anything good about Seiling, but this kid sure is the real deal."

"Sure is Sol. Batting cleanup is senior first baseman Shawn Parker. He's not the most loved of the players when he comes to town. He was involved in an altercation last year with Brady Wright. Brady was running out a grounder and Shawn not only caught the ball from their second baseman, he figured he should swipe his glove across Brady's face. It was in response to a brush-back pitch Brady threw earlier in the game, but the play was uncalled for. Expect the crowd to boo him today. Nobody likes him. I've heard that his own mother doesn't even like him, but I can't confirm that. He's known for his awesome power and already has eight home runs on the young season. Given that Seiling has played in eight games this year, that comes out to one home run per game. Something else! He's also headed to Tulsa State on a football scholarship, and he's every bit as big and mean as you can imagine.

"Batting fifth is probably the best player on the team, or at least the most versatile, senior pitcher/catcher Lew Lassiter. That's right, he pitches and catches. One of Coach Creek's philosophies is that his pitchers should be able to catch a game so that they can become better from the mound, seeing the world from both sides."

"It's a philosophy I agree with Joel, but there's one flaw. Catching over a period of time ruins a person's knees."

"That's for sure. This Lassiter kid will make Jimmy a great teammate at UNCO next year, but if I were his parents, I would be worried about his knees. Batting sixth is junior right fielder Hershell Price, another starter from last year. Batting seventh is the first of two newcomers to the starting lineup, sophomore third baseman Conrad Thomas. Conrad started on their football team last fall as fullback and had a 1000 yard season. Pretty impressive as a sophomore, though I think I could have ran for 1000 yards behind that line they had."

"Average starting weight on that line was 285, Joel."

"Well, you're just full of timely, yet useless information, Sol. The second of the two newcomers is sophomore catcher Luke Houska. He will catch first game for Lew Lassiter and sit the second game. Sol, I don't know much about this pair of sophomores."

"Well, we're going to find out a lot today."

"Batting last in the lineup is senior left fielder Ray England. You really gotta watch out for this kid's bunts."

"I stayed and watched the championship game last weekend and saw the kid put down three perfect bunts down the third base line. Even with the infield playing in, they couldn't throw him out. In fact, he scored two runs in that win."

"Yeah, with him at the end of the lineup, it's kind of like having two leadoff hitters with speed. Finally, in game two junior Jerrad Daniels will get the start at pitcher and bat in the number eight hole for Luke Houska as the versatile Lassiter catches."

"Well, Coach Grey is in booth. Welcome Coach. How are you doing?"

"Well, guys. It's Seiling Day."

"Yes it is. Are the kids excited?"

"Well, if you can't get excited for Seiling Day, you don't have a pulse, now do you?"

"Well put Coach. We won't keep you long, because you have to get down to your kids, I realize, but there is one topic I want to hit on, and that's Vincent Preston. Now as everyone listening at home knows, he took a nasty shot to the head by a malicious fastball last weekend. The rumor going around town is that he's not only okay, but that he's pitching today. Can you comment on any of this?"

"Yes, that's all true."

"Wow! I guess we have a lot of questions. For starters, how long has Vincent been a pitcher, and what does he throw?"

"Well Sol, I've been wanting to keep Vincent a secret for some time. You know he started off the year in my doghouse, and I have slowly let him work his way back into my good graces."

"And a good thing too!"

"Well, Coach Redenbacher and I have wanted to hold him until a special day, like today. He's a little rough around the edges, but he's got a good fastball. I don't know if he's ready yet, but I figure what better way to get your first start than against your arch rival. Once again, if you can't get up for Seiling Day, you don't have a heartbeat."

"Coach, you said that he has a good fastball. Does he have any other pitches?"

"Well, I'm going to just leave that a little secret. We don't want to give away too much."

"Fair enough, Coach. And Vincent is feeling no ill-effects from the bean ball?"

"No Joel, the doctor released him with a clean bill of health."

"Well Coach, it's starting to become somewhat of a tradition to ask you if you know who's leading your team in batting average."

"Sol, I know the answer to your question today because I just updated the stats this morning. Obviously, Vincent is leading the team at .888. Right?"

"You're right on Coach. He's eight for nine. Nice little start. It seems hard to get him any at bats when he gets plunked in the head."

"Well guys, he's 100% today, so we ought to see what he's made of. He still has a small lump on his forehead, but I think he'll be just fine. The true test often comes on Seiling Day."

"Last question, Coach. How's Jimmy doing? We know his left eye was swollen shut from that altercation the other day against the

Giants as he valiantly fought for his fallen teammate. Is it better, and has that affected his fielding or batting?"

"Well, that's a good question. I'm sure we're going to find that out today. He seemed a little shaky at practice Wednesday, but the optometrist has also given him the go ahead, so we'll just have to see."

"Fair enough, Coach. Hey, good luck in the games today!"

"Thanks, guys."

"That was Coach Grey discussing his two biggest stars, Vincent Preston and his son Jimmy. We'll see how Vincent does in his first pitching assignment of the year and how Jimmy does with his eye. We'll be back in one minute to discuss the Augusta starting lineup."

*

Vincent warmed up on the bullpen pitching mound. From time-to-time Vincent peered over at the opposing dugout and saw that the Seiling players and coaches were keeping an eye on him. He knew that they had by now heard of him and what he was accomplishing on offense. Seiling had no idea what he had in store for them today though.

Vincent kept it simple, throwing only the change up Grandpa Dean had taught him a few days before. Vincent didn't want to give Seiling a real taste of what he had.

Since Vincent had gotten the nod from Coach Grey to pitch today, Grandpa Dean told Vincent that he would teach him the change up, but wouldn't dare try to instruct him on how to throw a splitter, for fear of overload.

Throughout his pitching practice with Grandpa Dean, Vincent became more and more worried about his mentor. Each day Grandpa Dean had only thirty minutes or so before he would have to go in and lie down, usually by his wife's suggestion. Vincent knew the old man was proud and couldn't admit when he was overdoing it. Vincent supposed that was what Mrs. Dean was for.

Each day Grandpa Dean would leave Vincent with another verse from the Bible and Vincent would go home and read. Vincent found a love for reading in Mrs. Dean's class, and now he had been shown a good book to read. Vincent was making his way through the book of Exodus, and had to look no further than Moses to see strength.

Grandpa Dean had become more of a father-figure than Vincent had ever had before. He knew something was wrong with Grandpa Dean, but Mrs. Dean was keeping it very hush, hush. It worried Vincent, angered him.

Vincent fired a fastball by accident and the underclassman managed to catch it somehow. Vincent looked over and saw a few players in the Seiling dugout whispering to themselves, and Vincent knew he had warmed up enough.

When Vincent got to the dugout, Coach Grey was giving the pep talk.

Coach Redenbacher motioned at Bacon Bob. Bacon Bob left the dugout and took Vincent by the arm and led him aside.

"Look Vincent," Bacon Bob began, "we gotta be seeing eye-to-eye on everything. I have to know what pitch is coming, or else we're going to give a lot of free bases to the Seiling players on passed balls. Now you throw very hard. I can catch that straight ball of yours, but I'm having a little trouble with your two-seamer. So when I give you two fingers, I'll pat my thigh where I want the ball to go. Just nod if you agree."

Bacon Bob crouched down to demonstrate. "For example, if I pat my inside thigh and then my middle, I want you to start the ball inside and move it out over the plate. Now I'm going to be keeping track of who's up to bat, and I've caught against this team many times. I know what most of them look for. Just trust in me. Okay?"

Vincent smiled. "Sure thing."

Bacon Bob continued. "Okay, two fingers for two-seamer, four fingers for four-seamer, and three fingers for the change up. Right?"

"That's right," Vincent confirmed.

"Relax, you'll do just fine!" Bob said nervously.

Vincent looked down and noticed he himself was dancing in place from side to side out of nervousness. The stands were packed. He felt the need to urinate and crossed his legs.

"Okay guys, take the field," the umpire called and the Augusta players strode to their positions.

Vincent stopped at the top of the steps to the dugout and looked up in the stands. The hometown faithful came to their feet and cheered on their boys. Some Seiling visitors, who made up nearly half the occupancy, booed and drew sharp criticism from the Augusta fans. This made Vincent chuckle.

Forgetting about his bladder, Vincent walked to the mound and was already in the zone. He couldn't hear anything but the muffled sound of his own breathing and his innermost thoughts, basic as they were.

He threw his eight warm-up pitches, all change ups, and watched the infielders take the ball around the horn. When the ball got back to him, he steadied himself at the bottom of the hill and watched the first batter come to the plate.

The loudspeaker rang out, "First to bat, center fielder, Tag McNugert." That was the last thing Vincent heard as he found his zone of concentration.

*

Tag kicked some dirt around in the box and looked down. "Bacon Bob."

"Tag. How's life?" Bob asked, trying to be nice.

"Oh, same as always. Winning becomes such a bore. I guess you can't relate."

The comment didn't faze Bacon Bob. "Ha! That's pretty funny. Did you learn that at the state tournament last year?"

Tag looked back at Bob and mouthed a bad word at him.

"That's enough," the umpire remarked. "You are both going to get yourselves thrown out of the game if you keep this bantering up."

"Sure thing, blue," Bob told the umpire. He looked out at his pitcher who appeared to be in his own little world. He watched Vincent staring at his baseball cap in his hand and wondered what might be going through his mind.

Focusing on more important things, Bacon Bob said, loudly enough for his opponent to hear, "Well, which of Vincent's eight pitches should I pick first? Let's see," and he paused.

Tag kicked a little dirt Bacon Bob's way.

"You know Tag, I just can't decide," Bacon Bob toyed with his opponent. "Perhaps you can choose for me? What pitch would you like to see, Tag?"

"You just tell him to throw that weak little fastball he has," Tag responded.

"Boys!" the umpire yelled at the two.

"Sorry, blue" both responded.

*

Vincent took his cap off and wiped his forehead with the bill and read, "Phil 4:13" now faded through sweat and use. He recited his verse and breathed in through his nostrils and out through his mouth to try to steady the beating of his heart, augmented by three cups of coffee that morning that had never really worn off.

Vincent looked to the dugout one last time at Coach Grey who stood on the second step of the dugout looking out to center field. Vincent automatically turned around and saw that Jimmy was playing about ten steps in and wondered, *For what reason would he be playing in so far?*

Vincent shrugged it off and stepped to the rubber. He looked in for the sign.

Bacon Bob gave four fingers.

Vincent let his inner voice calm himself down. *Concentrate! It's just me and a catcher's mitt.*

Vincent went into his windup and delivered a strike right down the pipe.

"STRIKE ONE!" yelled the umpire.

Tag took a step out of the batter's box and practiced a couple of swings.

Vincent watched the batter intently and saw him smile.

Vincent knew he let up a little on that one, probably in the mid-eighties.

Tag stepped back into the box and Vincent's acute eyesight helped him notice that the batter had dug in six inches further back, probably to compensate for Vincent's fastball.

Vincent studied his catcher now.

Bacon Bob held three fingers and patted his outside thigh.

Vincent nodded and went into the windup. He delivered the pitch using the same motion and follow through, but using the circle grip Grandpa Dean had taught him. The ball floated in there and Tag swung ahead of it as planned, cleanly missing it and looking stupid in the process.

"STRIKE TWO!"

Like that change up? Vincent thought.

Vincent stepped back up to the rubber and steadied himself. He hadn't given much away yet.

Vincent noticed Tag got back into the box in the same spot.

Bacon Bob must have noticed too because he gave Vincent four fingers and patted his inside thigh.

Vincent nodded with a smirk that he quickly wiped off, lest his enemy see it and read his hand. Vincent went into his windup and delivered with a grunt.

Lightning!
Thunder!
"STRIKE THREE!" the umpire called.

Vincent kept his stare on Tag, who looked back at the umpire, then down at Bacon Bob who was smiling as he fired the ball to Dusty at third to take it around the horn. Vincent didn't stare too long so as not to rub dirt in Tag's face, but turned around to watch the ball fly around the infield. He looked at the scoreboard to refocus, wishing it would tell how fast he was throwing.

PA announcer's voice echoed, "That's one away. Next up, second baseman Steven West."

Vincent turned back around in time to see Tag say something to the next batter.

When Steven stepped into the box, Vincent noticed the batter's back foot was on the far-back line of the batter's box. Any further back and he would be automatically out for stepping outside the batter's box. The batter obviously wanted to have a bit more time to see the pitch.

Vincent watched his catcher say something inaudible to the batter. After no response, his catcher looked back at Vincent and gave his sign.

Three fingers outside.

Sure, thought Vincent. *I can throw another off-speed pitch. It's just a walk in the park...*

Vincent nodded and delivered, and the kid swung for all he was worth, way out in front of the ball.

"STRIKE ONE!"

So far, Vincent hadn't had to throw the two-seamer and had been mixing speeds well. Vincent's batter got back into the box and took a few swings from the same spot. Bacon Bob gave the same sign. Vincent found himself singing inside his head.

Sittin' in the morning sun,

Vincent threw the pitch, but this time though, the kid made contact with the ball and sent it sailing out of play into Carroll Avenue, a monster shot.

"FOUL BALL!" the umpire shouted.

Vincent stared at the ball, now rolling down the street. *Okay,* he thought, *maybe a tune that will liven things up a bit. A bit more uptempo.*

Vincent knew he got away with one there.

Bacon Bob must have felt the same way because he gave a sign for the two-seamer.

Vincent knew he had to get this one to move inside. There was no sound in his ears but the beat of his heart and the rapid fire of his breath. He wanted this ball to be filthy. His mind raced to find a fast song. ACDC was the first band to come to mind.

"It was cold in the middle of a railroad track. And I knew there was no turning back."

Vincent delivered with a grunt and the second baseman started his swing before seeing the ball move in on him. The batter tried to hold up, but the bat went around and he looked ridiculous.

"STRIKE THREE!" shouted the umpire.

Vincent smiled. *"You've been THUNDERSTRUCK!"*

Vincent heard a roar and came out of his trance.

The Augusta crowd came to its feet.

Bacon Bob whipped the ball to Dusty at third and the players took the ball around the horn again. Vincent took off his hat and wiped the sweat from his forehead and repeated the verse to himself again.

Seiling's number three hitter, Jas Foster, stepped up to the plate, and Vincent knew the guy liked hitting pitches inside. Vincent hoped Bacon Bob knew likewise. His hope was satisfied when Bob called for a four-seamer outside.

That-a-kid!!

Vincent delivered the pitch and hit the mark perfectly.

"BALL!"

Vincent got the ball back and gave it some thought. Just a bit outside. Jas was a smart hitter and wouldn't let a regular fastball off the mark fool him, no matter how fast it was traveling. He had to think this one through. He had to either blow it by him, or move it across the plate. Bacon Bob showed two fingers and moved his hand from inside to middle. Vincent knew this was going to be a tough pitch because he would have to stare at the guy's knees to get it where it needed to go. The guy was already standing close to the plate.

Okay, just a bit outside. Jas is a smart hitter and a regular fastball off the mark isn't going to fool him, no matter how fast it is traveling. I have to think this one through. Concentrate!

Vincent wiped the sweat from his brow. *I either have to blow it by him or move it across the plate.*

Vincent looked at his catcher who showed two fingers and moved his hand from inside to middle. Vincent frowned and thought, *That's going to be a tough pitch because I am going to have to stare at the guy's knees to get it where it needs to go. Besides, he's already standing close to the plate!*

Vincent then remembered Grandpa Dean's first lesson in concentration. *The guy isn't even standing there. All I am doing is throwing at a mattress.*

Confident, Vincent went into his windup and put the ball at the guy's knees. It peeled back over the plate as easily as a yo-yo comes back up when it hits the end of the string. Jas jumped back in surprise and was even more surprised when the umpire called it a strike.

Vincent was now back in rhythm. *"Sound in the drums."*

"What? You gotta be kidding! It almost hit me in the knees!" the batter yelled at the umpire, plenty loud enough for anybody on the infield to hear.

Vincent forced himself not to smile and looked back at the stands. The Seiling crowd now jumped to its feet in protest and the opposing fans started berating them. It appeared to Vincent that a fight might start between the parents at any moment.

Vincent refocused his attention on his catcher.

Bacon Bob called for the same pitch, so with pinpoint accuracy, Vincent put it in the same place with the same result.

"STRIKE TWO!"

The music continued in Vincent's mind. *"Beating in my heart."*

Vincent watched as Jas stepped out of the batter's box and stared at the umpire. Vincent studied the batter and noticed he was stumped. Vincent knew Bacon Bob saw this as well, and called the pitch: change up, outside.

Vincent nodded and delivered with a fake grunt and Jas took an exaggerated cut, trying to slow down with the speed of the pitch. The batter's effort was to no avail. He had been thinking fastball and missed it by a foot.

The umpire rang the batter up. "STRIKE THREE! HUSTLE IN, HUSTLE OUT!"

Vincent smiled. *"Thunderstruck!"*

Vincent walked to the dugout and looked up at the stands. The Augusta fans were cheering wildly for him and he suddenly felt self-conscious, looking to the ground in embarrassment. Any praise from the fans made him feel very uncomfortable and he did not know why.

When on the mound he felt perfectly at home. It was just him and Bacon Bob playing catch. The rest of the world might as well cease to exist. The wind didn't blow, the sun didn't blaze a path across the sky, and time just stopped when he stepped on top of that mound. He was just a boy, enjoying the national pastime that legions of children before him had enjoyed countless times. No worries. No worthless parents. Nothing but unadulterated joy.

Vincent cracked a smile, but put his glove in front of his face to hide it.

This Augusta crowd who seemingly couldn't care less about him a few weeks ago was now his biggest ally, though he knew they were fickle and only supported a winner.

Coach Grey stood on the steps of the dugout, not showing any emotion.

The players all patted Vincent on the back, but when he got to Coach, he stopped Vincent and Bacon Bob and said, "That second change up 'bout got away, didn't it? Let's not get cocky in our pitch selection, or I will be calling the pitches from the dugout. Got me?"

"Yes Coach," Bacon Bob replied.

On the way to his seat, Vincent looked at the lineup and saw that he was still in the number six spot. He sat on the far end of the bench and closed his eyes.

Jimmy sat next to Vincent and stared at him, but Vincent ignored Jimmy.

*

Grandpa Dean sat uncomfortably in his armchair. His feet were kicked up and his pain was fading, thanks to his medicine. He listened to the radio personalities praise his pupil.

"We're back. It's the bottom of the first inning with Augusta up to bat, but we gotta say more about Vincent Preston! We knew he was a hitter, but what a pitcher! Ladies and gentlemen, he threw a total of ten pitches in the first inning and with the exception of the change up Steven West took foul, Vincent was untouchable. According to my radar gun, Vincent's fastball was hitting the mid-nineties, with his fastest pitch coming in at ninety-five miles-per-hour! Where has this kid been all this time? When Coach Grey said he was keeping the kid a secret, he really meant it! Ninety-five miles-per-hour! Unless my gun is off, and I'd like to think it's accurate, he's throwing as fast as most major leaguers right now.

And that's not to mention the fact that he seems to be putting movement on his pitches. That ball he threw to the third hitter, Jas Foster, moved at least six inches, and it wasn't a slider or a curve. That's going to be tough to hit. I just wonder how long he will be able to keep his velocity up. I know I sound like a broken record, praising him, but he has the look of a polished pro out there! It's amazing to watch!"

Grandpa Dean was content, though he wished he could have had at least two more weeks with Vincent before giving him the go ahead. Grandpa Dean was not surprised that everybody was salivating over Vincent. His pupil had legitimate big league talent, something he knew the town had never seen before, something he suspected the coach's son could have if only he wanted to work at it.

Grandpa Dean only wished he could be there. He felt good that at least Elna was going to be able to give him a report. To this point he hadn't let her miss so much as a practice, something they were keeping from Vincent. Before Grandpa Dean finished this last thought, he coughed a few times and fell fast asleep in his easy chair.

*

Vincent didn't have much time to relax. The inning ended with a Jimmy Grey strikeout, three up, three down.

Before Vincent could leave the dugout, Bacon Bob got a hold of him and said, "Vincent, this next guy, Parker, nobody really likes him much, so if you don't mind, we might flip him a little, if you know what I mean, kind of mark our territory. Let's take advantage of that inside heat, huh? Let him know we mean business."

Vincent smiled and replied, "Sure, you're the boss."

Vincent wasn't dumb. He knew the history between the two ball clubs, knew there was bad blood. He knew that sooner or later someone would take exception to a pitch he threw, but he must establish the inside part of the plate, lest he be bullied by the batter. Right now he was in control, and he wasn't about to relinquish that power. If his catcher wanted to flip the next guy, then flip him he would. It wasn't personal. It was business.

Vincent watched Shawn Parker, all 275 pounds of him, step up to the plate and the Augusta crowd started booing him. Vincent looked up to the crowd to see that one creative kid held up a sign that made the crowd laugh:

"PARKER IS A PORKER!"

Vincent turned his attention back to Seiling's cleanup hitter. As Shawn was digging in, he spat on Bacon Bob's shin guard. Vincent thought about charging the guy, but kept his head cool.

To Bob's credit, he didn't appear to say a thing, only pour some dirt on his shin guard, but Vincent could easily see that Bob's cheeks were beet red and a vein bulged in his forehead.

Everyone knew Bob disliked this guy more than anyone. Vincent, like everybody else, was very aware that Bacon Bob and Shawn had a long history of beating on each other in football.

Bob played center and nose tackle while Shawn Parker did the same for Seiling, and all through junior high and high school, these two butted heads every play.

This one's for you, Bob, Vincent thought. *Time to go to the office, Vincent. Let's get nasty with Mr. Ugly!*

Bob called for a two-seamer, high and tight and Vincent delivered. The ball started inside and kept going, and Shawn Parker flopped to the dirt to keep from losing some teeth.

Shawn jumped up and threw down his bat in anger, his helmet already rolling away. He flared out his nostrils and his chest bulged in hatred toward Vincent who didn't smile.

Vincent just waited for the ball with a stare that could pierce sheet metal. It wasn't personal. It was just business.

The umpire stepped in front of the Seiling cleanup hitter and instructed him to back up.

Seiling's third-base coach helped his cleanup hitter back to the plate.

Vincent knew that if Grandpa Dean were listening, he would be proud.

The umpire, apparently having seen enough, had Parker go back to the on-deck circle and called both head coaches out to the plate.

Vincent stepped forward close enough to hear the conversation.

"Okay, Coach Grey," the umpire started, "I'm well aware of what happened last weekend, and I'm well aware of this rivalry. This is the only warning, and it goes for you too Coach Creek. If I see another inside pitch, I'm starting with the pitcher and I will kick every player out of this game if I have to. Do I make myself clear?"

"But that's hardly fair!" Coach Creek argued. Coach Grey stood there with his hands crossed in front of his chest and smiled. "You expect my guy to just take that? Kick that pitcher out of the game, for cryin' out loud! We both know it was intentional." Coach Creek gave Vincent a dirty look.

The umpire held his ground. "Look, you've both been warned! Back to your dugouts, before I kick you out of the game."

Coach Creek kicked up some dirt and walked back to his cleanup hitter.

Vincent watched Seiling's head coach whisper something in Shawn's ear and walk back to the dugout. Whether Parker heard it or not, Vincent couldn't tell because he kept his stare on Vincent the whole time.

Vincent heard the Augusta crowd boo Coach Creek until he sat down. Some opposing fans shared words before things simmered down.

Vincent walked back to the rubber, turned, and waited for his sign.

The batter stepped in and crowded the plate, still staring at Vincent. Vincent didn't care and looked to Bacon Bob, who called for a four-seamer, inside corner. Vincent put it there perfectly.

"STRIKE ONE!" the umpire called.

The batter didn't flinch, or step out of the box. He stood there and waited for his next pitch, never taking his eyes off Vincent.

This didn't faze Vincent. He had only the drums pounding in his ears, louder and louder.

Vincent got his sign and delivered a two-seamer that started over the plate and moved outside.

The cleanup hitter swung for the fence and his helmet came flying off for the second time as he missed.

"STRIKE TWO!" called the umpire.

Vincent gave one more look at Shawn's feet and noticed the guy had moved even closer to the plate. The tips of his shoes were over the obscured chalk line.

Bob called for another four-seamer, inside corner.

Vincent went into his windup and delivered.

The batter leaned in and took the pitch off his shoulder without so much as a grunt. The ball rolled to the Augusta dugout as the Seiling crowd jumped to its feet in outrage. Parker took a step toward first, still staring at Vincent.

The umpire jumped up and yelled, "BATTER'S OUT! BATTER WAS OUT OF THE BATTER'S BOX. ONE OUT!"

"WHAT?" Parker screamed as he turned around.

"YOUR FEET WERE OVER THE LINE. YOU'RE OUT. SIT DOWN!" The umpire shouted.

Parker took a step toward the umpire, who wasn't backing down.

The Seiling coach came out of the dugout for the second time that inning and had a heated conference with the home plate umpire, shoving his finger in the guy's chest and kicking dirt on his black shoes. The whole while Parker had turned his glare to

Vincent who was at the base of the mound, watching the whole scene without so much as an expression. Stone Cold.

Vincent took a peek over at the Seiling team, who were all staged at the steps of the dugout, ready to step onto the field. Vincent could hear yelling in the stands, but didn't dare take his eyes off Shawn Parker, keeping the rest of Seiling's team in his peripheral vision.

When Coach Creek was finally escorted out of the park, the game commenced and Vincent mowed down the side.

The game went on much like that. Lew Lassiter tried to brush Vincent back, but his fastball didn't scare anybody, and it wasn't his best pitch anyway. The very next pitch Vincent took a hanging curveball over the Little Monster for a 1-0 lead, his fourth homer of the year.

The crowd noise was deafening to Vincent, and he was mobbed at the plate by his fellow players.

Only three Seiling players put the ball in play, two groundouts to Seth at second base, and a short pop out to Bill at first. No Seiling hitter had yet gotten the ball out of the infield and Vincent had an amazing twelve strikeouts after five innings.

Vincent took a perfect game into the sixth inning. The pressure built inside of Vincent with every pitch.

With two outs, Seiling's number-nine hitter laid down a perfect bunt along the third baseline. Dusty charged the ball, and barehanded it. He made an awkward throw that Bill Jones had to dig out of the dirt with his chest, but the play was too late and Seiling had their first base runner of the game, breaking up a perfect game and a no-hitter.

Vincent smiled. He knew a perfect game was improbable. Just as well. He knew that if he came out and pitched a perfect game, expectations would be enormous from then on.

Vincent settled into the stretch for the first time that night. He remembered what Grandpa Dean had said, that the runner wasn't important, only the batter.

With two outs, Tag McNugert stepped to the plate, victim of two strikeouts himself.

Vincent knew he had lost some velocity on his fastball. He had no idea how many pitches he had thrown at this point. He knew he had thrown well over fifty pitches by now.

Bacon Bob gave Vincent the sign to throw to first base and he did, rather slowly so as not to throw the ball away. His pickoff move was more infant than his fastball, and he wasn't about to let the game get away with an errant throw when he knew he couldn't pick off this little speed demon anyway.

When Vincent caught the ball again, he repositioned himself on the mound and got the sign from Bob: fastball, outside. He gave a glance toward first to check the runner and then looked back home.

Vincent reminded himself, *Don't worry about the runner. Concentrate on the thread!*

Vincent found the little thread hanging down in the webbing of Bob's glove and came home with the pitch as hard as he could heave it, only the leadoff hitter squared away another bunt along the first baseline that caught everybody off guard. Bacon Bob, Bill Jones, and Vincent all met at the same place and watched the ball bounce sideways off the infield turf and come to a rest right on the chalk.

"FAIR BALL!"

Vincent picked the ball back up and checked the runner at second. Just like that Vincent went from pitching a perfect game to having to pitch out of trouble.

Coach Grey called time-out and had a conference with his whole infield.

"Guys, we need to concentrate on the situations! Everybody knows those two guys on base are their fastest players on the team.

It makes sense that they would bunt, since they haven't been able to hit, huh? Now we got two outs and we're clinging to a one-run lead. Vincent, how's that fastball of yours holding up?"

Vincent looked at Bacon Bob and said, "I think I'm losing some velocity. My arm's getting tired."

"Bob?" Coach Grey inquired

"It's slowed down a bit Coach," Bacon Bob replied. "Five, ten miles-an-hour."

Coach Grey fingered his mustache and appeared to think for a moment.

"Okay. Establish the fastball early in the count. If you can put some movement on it, make it move outside. Remember what this guy did to that foul ball in the first inning?"

"Yes Coach," both Bacon Bob and Vincent said in unison.

"Okay," Coach Grey continued. "He's a pull-hitter, so we're going to keep everything outside. Bait him into trying to go opposite field, so be shading that way. Okay Seth, Quentin?"

"Yes Coach," the two said in unison.

"And only use that change up if you have to. Got it Bob?" Coach asked.

Bob nodded.

Coach said, "Okay, let's get this final out."

Vincent gathered himself as the other players ran back to their positions. Vincent wasn't nearly as confident as he had been and his attention began to stray. He looked to the parking lot and saw that bald guy from the Ford Explorer that he had seen the night after the Woodward game. Vincent remembered that the guy had given Jimmy something that night. The guy seemed to be pacing, and Vincent's inner voice was telling him that something was very wrong. He just couldn't put a finger on it.

Vincent shrugged it off and turned his attention to the plate.

Steven West stepped into the box. Vincent took mental inventory and remembered that Steven had grounded to second base last time up.

Bacon Bob gave two fingers and patted his outside thigh.

Vincent took a deep breath and thought about the verse inscribed on the underside of his ball cap. He took another deep breath in and held it through his delivery.

The ball would have hit the spot he was hoping for, but the batter was swinging all the way. The bat found the ball and the ball sailed high to center field. This was the first real good contact they had made off Vincent.

Vincent's heart skipped a beat, but only for a second. He realized Steven had gotten under the ball and that it should hang up for Jimmy to catch somewhere deep in the outfield. After all, there wasn't a worse place for a batter to hit the ball. It was the deepest part of the park, and Vincent knew Jimmy was probably the best center fielder in the state. But just as fast as Vincent felt safe, he turned around and saw that Jimmy was still playing shallow. Very shallow.

Jimmy stood there for a second and then turned his back and started running.

The ball cleared Jimmy and landed ten feet behind him on the way to the fence. He made his effort look good by picking up the rolling ball and heaving it toward the cutoff man, only Jimmy overthrew Seth and the ball rolled toward second. All the while the two base runners scored and the Seiling batter was rounding third and looking home.

Quentin ran out to greet the ball, and in one motion, swooped it up and fired it to Bacon Bob. The throw was a true strike, and Bob caught the ball with a half-second to tag out the opposing runner. It was a collision play at home that Bacon Bob won.

The runner bounced off Bob and was called out, but the damage had been done.

Vincent hung his head and listened to Seiling's crowd cheer incessantly.

The Stampeding Herd jogged in.

Vincent immediately did the math and knew Jimmy was throwing the game, and it burned him to no end. He decided right then and there that he would confront Jimmy, and it would have to be that night.

Augusta went three up, three down in their half of the sixth and Vincent managed to collect three ground-ball outs in the top of the seventh.

In the bottom of the seventh inning, Seiling put in their closer. Vincent knew the closer had a fastball, and though not as fast as Vincent's, it was still potent.

Bacon Bob led off the inning with a grounder to first.

Shawn Parker, who had calmed down at this point, held the ball and waited for Bob to get close before stepping on first to record the first out. Shawn also tagged Bob in the chest with his glove to put on his exclamation point.

Bob was jostled to the ground but picked himself up off the ground, and looked the other way.

Coach Grey blew his stack at the umpire in the field. This was the second time Parker had leveled an Augusta runner in as many years. Coach Grey went after the first-base umpire, kicking and screaming and putting up a good show for the hometown faithful, and Vincent saw that it was now the Seiling parents' turn to boo until Coach Grey sat down.

After Bill Jones went down swinging for the fence, Vincent was left as the final chance for Augusta.

The crowd chanted his name, and this brought Vincent goose bumps.

VINCENT! VINCENT! VINCENT!

Vincent stepped into the box and had one thing on his mind, taking that fastball and parking across Carroll Avenue. He was 2-2 in the game with that home run in the second inning and a line-drive single in the fifth inning, collecting two of Augusta's measly five hits in the game. He looked at the pitcher and saw him shake off a sign before settling on his pitch. Vincent wondered what that meant. *Change up? Curve ball?* Vincent didn't know what to expect and let the first pitch go. It came right down the pipe, a fastball.

"STRIKE ONE!" called the umpire.

Vincent stepped out of the box and smiled.

Mind games. Vincent thought. *That's fine. They can play their mind games.*

Vincent knew what was coming this time. He stepped back in and dug into the same spot. He made the sign of the cross with his bat and settled his stare on the pitcher. As a pitcher now, he found it increasingly easier to figure out the thought process of the opposing pitcher on the mound.

Again, the pitcher shook off the sign, but Vincent wasn't fooled.

Coach Grey didn't give him a sign, so Vincent knew he would be swinging if anything was close. The pitch came, and Vincent saw it tail outside, so he held up.

"BALL!" the umpire called.

Vincent readjusted himself, went through the same ritual, and watched two more balls miss outside. He stepped back in and gave some consideration to what the pitcher was going to throw next.

Three balls, one strike= hitter's count. Give me the heater.

The pitcher nodded with the first sign and went into his windup. He delivered the ball in the same place, only this time Vincent swung and belted a shot to right field. It had plenty of height and was tailing away from the right fielder toward the foul pole.

Vincent was running for all he was worth, fearing he didn't get enough of the ball to take it over the fence.

The fielder found the fence with his glove, and just as Vincent rounded first base, the fielder reached up and made the catch on the warning track for the final out.

Vincent heard the air let out of the stadium. He looked back up at the stands and saw Seiling's fans standing, mocking the Augusta fans. Vincent came to a stop halfway between first and second base and hung his head.

I am an idiot!

He knew he should have let the ball go and he would be on first base right now. As it was, he sent it for a ride, but it wasn't enough. Vincent knew the right fielder made a spectacular play.

Vincent stood in the same spot and watched Coach Grey walk for the dugout without saying a word. Vincent looked over at Jimmy, who sat with his face buried in his mitt. Vincent wondered if Jimmy might be hiding a smile. Vincent figured Coach Grey definitely was.

Chapter 11

After Coach Grey's weak speech to the team, the players split for thirty minutes to grab hotdogs and hamburgers. Jimmy trudged the hill toward the parking lot where his Corvette sat, and Vincent decided to follow him.

On the way up Vincent was obstructed by many well-meaning fans who wished to console him. By the time he caught up to Jimmy, he was already in his car and was pulling out of the parking lot. Vincent jumped in front of the car to stop him, and Jimmy groaned as he slammed on the breaks. Vincent walked around to the driver's side window and rested his hand on top of Jimmy's prized car. It was coated with the dust and dirt.

Jimmy smiled up at Vincent and said, "That was a nice game you pitched, Vincent. Pretty good for your first anyway."

Vincent thought, you're not getting out of this that easily.

Vincent moved in closer and put his other hand on the side of the car. "Cut the crap! Why did you do it, Jimmy?"

"You mind getting your hands off my Vette, dude? I try to take good care of it."

"Yeah, that's noticeable," Vincent remarked. He clapped his hands together. A cloud of dust dispersed into the air. On top of the car was a cherry red handprint. "So why did you do it?"

"Why did I do what?" Jimmy asked.

"You know exactly what I mean," and Vincent leaned in even closer, so as not to draw a scene. He wanted it to look like a friendly chat between two good buddies. "Why did you do it?"

Jimmy looked shocked. "Sorry, Vincent I figured they hadn't hit the ball out of the infield all game. Besides, I was trying to keep the lead runner at third base. I didn't know you were going to give up a near-gopher ball."

Vincent held tough with him. Just as Jimmy was about to peel out, Vincent grabbed Jimmy's jersey and pulled him in closer. "I know about the bald guy in the Ford Explorer," Vincent said, and he watched Jimmy's eyes widen fast. "Who is he, and what is he making you do?" Vincent asked.

"Man, get your hands off me! I don't know what you're talking about!" Jimmy tried weaseling out of Vincent's grip, but Vincent held on tighter.

"And the zip-lock bag he gave you at Stillwater?" Vincent said and stared Jimmy in the face.

Jimmy stopped short and then said, "Get in."

Vincent unleashed Jimmy and walked around the car and got in. Vincent's dusty uniform dirtied up the black interior, but Jimmy didn't seem to care much. They ripped out of the parking lot and drove toward the Eagle Chief River on the edge of town.

Once Jimmy felt he was a safe distance from the ballpark, he asked Vincent, "Okay, what do you know?"

"How 'bout you tell me everything, cause I think I pretty much got it figured out. Does your dad know?"

Jimmy appeared to search for the right words, then looked Vincent in the eyes and said, "Can I trust you?"

"I don't know," Vincent replied. "Can I trust you're going to tell the truth?"

The two stared at each other.

Jimmy passed the Davison Dealership and Salvage Yard. He drove to the bridge just south, pulled off the road, and parked his Corvette under the Broadway Street Bridge.

The two got out and made their way down to the water. Jimmy tried skipping a few stones across the Eagle Chief River, but with the drought, it was only about ten feet wide. The stones hit the water once and landed on the opposite bank.

Jimmy started, "You know, when I was a little kid my dad would take me fishing for channel catfish right under this bridge. We would pitch a tent over there by that huge cottonwood tree and hang a lantern on one of the branches that hung over the water. We would catch fish all night and when I would fall asleep, Dad would carry me to the tent."

Jimmy looked thoughtful, as if Vincent weren't even there. "This is the exact spot where I first decided I wanted to play," Jimmy said but turned away from Vincent. It appeared that Jimmy was about to cry.

"Look, Vincent," Jimmy continued, "I don't think you want to get yourself involved in this," and the urge apparently overwhelmed Jimmy. He put his hands to his face and wept.

Vincent didn't know what to do. He was faced with a situation he never thought he would be in. Should he console this guy? After all, the immortal Jimmy Grey was bawling like a baby.

Before he could say a word, Jimmy continued. "Vincent, I'm sorry I threw the game. That was one heck of a pitching performance, and I threw it for you." He wiped the tears from his face and tried to compose himself. "Don't worry. Everybody knows you threw the ball well, better than most. If there were scouts there, they would know you're good."

Jimmy moved a bit so he could get comfortable in the sand. "You don't want to know more. Trust me. I've gotten in over my head, and even though I know you shouldn't trust a thing I say, trust me when I say you don't want to know any of this."

Vincent decided not to back down. "Well, I'm already here and we both know your dad won't punish you for being late. Why don't you just give me the condensed version?"

"Didn't you hear me?!?" Jimmy shouted at Vincent. "Butt out! It's none of your business!"

"Well it seems like my business today, given that I pitched a gem and you lost it for me," Vincent said with an even voice.

Vincent sat next to Jimmy at the edge of the riverbank and part of the dry sand slid downward to its new equilibrium at the water's edge, causing both boys to move to higher ground, lest they end up in the water.

Jimmy wiped his eyes with his sleeves. He looked Vincent in the face. "It all started last year when this guy, the bald guy you call him, caught up with me after the game and offered me a joint if I ride around with him for a while. It was stupid, and I had never tried marijuana before, but for some stupid reason I found myself saying, 'yes,' and getting in with him. He drove a Suburban last year. He likes big SUV's. I'm not the only one he's lured into his car. He picks up underage girls all the time and gives them beer. The guy's sick, man! A real sicko!" Jimmy wiped the remaining tears from his cheeks and started turning red, holding his breath.

Jimmy continued, "I got high for the first time ever, and I didn't like it at all. Heck, I had never even been drunk before, but there I was in the front seat of this guy's Suburban, feeling like worms were eating my brains out and crawling out of my ears and all I wanted was to get out of there and get rid of the feeling. But the next day, I became a little curious about what happened the night before, because there were holes in my memory. I found his card in my pants pocket and called him up.

"He invited me to a pot party, and despite telling myself I wouldn't smoke any, I wound up high again, but this time it was a lot better." Jimmy looked at Vincent who was staring back at him.

"Anyway, he kept giving me free marijuana all through the school year and by the spring, he mentioned to me that it was time to pay my debt. The guy uses the money he gets from drugs, money that's not even his, and gambles with it. He turns a profit on the money before he has to ship it to his boss. That's where I came in. Since I was the best player on the team, and he was giving me free weed, he felt I owed him. When I told him, 'no way,' he reminded me that he could always bring the cops to my door. I have my suspicions that he has a few cops on his payroll also, so I had to agree. I felt I could control the action, that is until you came around."

"So which games have you thrown?" Vincent asked.

"I'm sure you can guess that. I never thought you would make a difference in ballgames. All the other guys, they're all good players, but if you haven't noticed, they kind of follow my lead."

"You mean everybody's in on this?" Vincent asked.

"No! That's not what I am saying at all. What I am saying is that I am the leader. When I am on, they, for some reason, are on also. When I am off, they lose their confidence. It's almost an exact science, except now they are looking to you for leadership, and you're providing it, and that's making my life hard in the process."

Vincent almost felt honored, receiving such a backhanded compliment from the kid with the golden key. But it still infuriated him.

Vincent wondered, *Jimmy isn't going to ask me to get in on the action, is he?* Vincent knew he would never get into that kind of trouble in a million years. Plus, there's nothing this bald guy had that he could lure him with. Still it worried him. *How powerful could this guy be that he could hold something this large over*

Jimmy's head? And also, was he himself now in the way? Was he going to be the bald guy's next target?

Jimmy continued. "Then, when you hit that grand slam against Ardmore, that's when I got in really deep. He had a lot of money staked on us losing. We were favored big time in that game. I could go to jail! I'm eighteen; I have a scholarship to UNCO. I turned down a major league contract because I want to be drafted higher. Look at everything I got going for myself! I could lose everything and become some guy's buddy in prison! You think I would do everything to keep that from happening? You better believe I would!"

"You gotta come clean!" Vincent interjected.

"And go to prison? Yeah right! You gotta promise not to tell anyone!"

Vincent thought for a moment. He thought the bald guy was hanging onto a thread, that the threats were baseless, and he didn't have a leg to stand on. He was bluffing Jimmy. "Jimmy, you know the longer you play this game, the deeper you get, right?"

"Yes, I know that. I'm trying to just tread water until I go away to college."

"And then?" Vincent asked. "You don't think this guy would like a contact in Ponca City?"

Jimmy appeared dumbfounded, as if he had never considered that.

"Are you still smoking?" Vincent asked without waiting for an answer to his previous question.

"No, I decided to quit."

Vincent smiled. "Well, that's the first step. Don't accept anything else from this guy."

"Trust me. He's not giving me anything anymore. I am in his debt."

"I also think you should call his bluff," Vincent said.

"Well, I can't."

"Why?" Vincent asked.

"Because I have $200 worth of the stuff in my car right now!"

Vincent was confused. "But you said you're not using it anymore."

"Don't you get it?" Jimmy yelled. "I have to sell the stuff for him now! That's what you saw in Stillwater. He gave me a bag and made me sell the stuff after you paraded around like a hero. He's not going to just let me off like that!"

A sound startled both boys. Vincent turned around and saw that another car pulled off the highway and drove up behind Jimmy's Corvette. Vincent feared that it might be the bald guy, but wasn't comforted any more when he saw that it was a cop.

The two boys walked back to the police car. The cop rolled down his window and said, "What are you two doing down here? Aren't you supposed to be playing Seiling tonight?"

"We're in-between games right now. Vincent and I just came down here to clear our heads after the loss. Did you hear the game on the radio?" Jimmy asked in a convincing enough voice. Vincent could easily see now what Jimmy's life was like, always covering his tracks.

The officer paused for a moment and said, "No, I'm probably the only cop who's not interested much in the game. So, did you two boys clear your heads?"

"Yes, sir. It was a tough loss," Jimmy said, continuing to speak for both boys. The officer looked at him, and then at Vincent who was particularly quiet.

"Did you get clean air, or did you breathe in some smoky air?"

Jimmy froze. "Oh no, sir! We don't do that. You can check the ground for any signs, or smell us if you'd rather. Trust me sir, we were just meeting alone to discuss the slide we're in. Trying to figure out how we can right our ship. We are the two best players on the team."

The officer smiled and turned on the radio. "Not too modest, are you?" The two radio personalities were discussing Vincent's pitching performance. The officer said, "Well, I guess you need to probably be getting back now, huh? Don't want to be late for the second game."

"Yes sir!" Jimmy said and the two got back into the car and drove back to the stadium.

Vincent had numerous questions, but the two didn't speak a word. Vincent had gotten an earful and was busy digesting.

They arrived back at the field just in time to run down to the dugout and hit the field. Vincent noticed that Coach Grey eyed the two with contempt and wonder.

*

The boys managed to salvage the split, beating Seiling 4-3. Jimmy played like a superstar, going 4-4 and blasting a shot into the yard across the street.

Vincent cooled off, going 1-3. Vincent just couldn't keep his mind on the game with the information he had been given. Many thoughts raced through his mind, mostly on how Jimmy could get out of his situation unscathed. After all, Vincent knew Jimmy was the victim. Vincent could see how this guy took advantage of Jimmy's ignorance and got him in so deep and so worried about losing his scholarship, or worse, that he would never dare try to rat him out.

It's not that simple. Vincent reminded himself. *Jimmy probably would lose that scholarship. Word would get around, and he might not be drafted. There was the court of public opinion that Jimmy would have to contend with, his father's disapproval...*

The more Vincent thought about the situation, the less secure he felt.

And besides, why should I help a jerk like Jimmy Grey? He has made my summer miserable.

228

But Vincent knew he was a better person than to just let Jimmy hang himself. He must do something to help, but the only thing he could think to do was tell the story to Mrs. and Grandpa Dean and seek their guidance.

Vincent left the ballpark to walk home.

A few blocks down the road, he noticed a Ford Explorer with tinted windows. It slowly crept up next to him. The window rolled down and the bald man stuck his head out the window. "Hey kid, aren't you Vincent Preston? You pitched a heck of a game tonight. You need a ride home?"

Someone else was in the passenger seat, but it was too dark for Vincent to make him or her out.

Vincent tried not to look. "Thanks, but no thanks."

"Oh, come on man. You must be tired from the doubleheader."

Vincent was scared. "Thanks, but the walk does me good. Gives me a chance to stretch my legs."

"I got beer in here," the man said. "You're welcome to all you want to drink. We'll call it a celebration for winning the second game."

Vincent looked behind him and saw no cars coming his direction. He was all alone and knew he was in for trouble. "Well sir, I'm underage, so I think I'll pass. Have a good night." He picked up the pace, his arms looking stupid in a power-walk he would expect to see out of a crew of little old ladies walking laps at the mall. His bat bag thumped his lower back and made it even more awkward.

The man picked up the pace to keep up with his new friend.

"Come on," the man continued, "I'm only going to ask one more time. Besides, Michelle was wanting to get to know the stud she saw pitching tonight."

Leaning across his lap from the passenger seat was a girl who looked to be about fourteen, too young for all the eye shadow and hot pink lipstick she wore. She licked her lips and gave a cute little wave that did nothing for Vincent.

"Thanks, but I really gotta be getting home," Vincent repeated.

"You don't want to ruin Michelle's night, do you? She really likes you."

Vincent stopped and found a little courage. "Look man, I don't want a ride home from you, so just leave me alone!"

"I don't think you understand," the man said and angle parked right in front of Vincent to cut him off. He stepped out and Vincent was petrified now. The man continued. "We can do this the easy way and you can get something you want in the process, or we can do this the hard way."

The man unzipped his jacket enough to bare the handle of his pistol. Vincent wondered how this guy kept from getting hot in the summer wearing a jacket. Then he looked down and saw the intended object and his knees turned to jelly.

Now I know how Jimmy was persuaded, Vincent thought. *Why can't another car be coming?*

Michelle smiled and sat back down in her seat.

The man just stared at Vincent, waiting for him to decide his fate. Finally a car's lights shone on the man's face and he zipped the jacket up just enough to conceal his weapon.

A mid-sized sedan pulled up to the two men and the window rolled down. It was Mrs. Dean!

"Hi Vincent!" She had on her teacher face. "And hi to you too."

"Hello, ma'am," the man said in his friendliest voice. "Lovely evening tonight, isn't it?"

"Quite lovely, sir. Pardon me sir, but I have some urgent business with Vincent." Mrs. Dean directed her attention to her young pupil. "Vincent, your mom wanted me to pick you up immediately! There's a family emergency! Come quickly Vincent."

Vincent stood there for one second, and the next he was getting into the car. They drove off and Vincent gave a sigh of relief.

*

Deuce stood there and watched the car pass into the distance. He thought, *The little old lady has impeccable timing.* He wasn't buying her story at all.

He stood there with his hands on his hips, wondering what to do next. Not having a clue, he threw up his arms in frustration and hopped back in his vehicle.

Deuce turned around and spoke to the person in the back seat. "He's not going to be easy."

From the backseat Coach Grey lit his joint and inhaled deeply. "Forget about it," he said and coughed a little from trying to keep the smoke in. "I got him on a leash."

Chapter 12

Mrs. Dean drove Vincent to his house. Vincent was silent the whole way. When they got there, she said, "Vincent, I've already talked to your mother. Why don't you grab some Sunday clothes and you can spend the night at our house tonight."

Vincent looked at her. "What's the emergency, Mrs. Dean?"

"I think we both knew what the emergency was back there. Come on. Be fast. I'll be waiting for you out here."

Vincent ran in and got a change of clothes and found his only pair of slacks and a nice button-down shirt. He forgot dress shoes and slipped on the same shoes in which he mowed grass.

When he got to their house, he was shown to the guest room at the back of the house by the kitchen. They both walked by Grandpa Dean who was sawing logs in his easy chair, the radio playing Elvis' "Love Me Tender."

As soon as Vincent's head hit the pillow, he went to sleep.

At 1:00 Vincent woke up with a ferocious thirst. He went to the fridge and pulled out a gallon of milk. At his house it would have been skim milk, probably outdated. He poured a tall glass. He took a swig and almost choked. When he checked the carton, it read *Butter Milk*. Whatever buttermilk was, he decided it wasn't worth drinking.

"What's the matter? Don't you like buttermilk?"

Vincent looked up and saw Mrs. Dean standing in the doorway in her robe. She had a smile on her face.

"I had the same idea that you had," she said, "but if you're not going to drink your glass, I'll take it from you."

"Yes, ma'am. It's a little rich for me."

Mrs. Dean smiled and flipped on the kitchen light. "I think you'll find grape Kool-aid in the pitcher. Grandpa Dean loves grape Kool-aid. He used to drink grape sodas, but the doctor put a halt to that. Doctor put a halt to a lot of things that he still does." She took the glass from his fingers and sat down. "Mainly I just want to keep him happy."

Vincent went to the fridge and got some Kool-aid. When he sat back down, he said, "You know Mrs. Dean, I don't know who that guy was tonight."

"Son, you don't have to explain. I trust you."

"I mean, I have a pretty good suspicion as to who he is, but I had never talked to him before," Vincent explained.

"He's bad news. But he thinks he's bigger than he really is," Mrs. Dean said and took a drink and smiled. "His father used to own the dealership on south Broadway between the two rivers. Now he runs it, and from what I hear from some of my students in the hallway, he doesn't deal much in cars. I'm sure you probably found that out tonight."

"Yeah, I got a pretty good idea. He offered me …" Vincent began, but stopped short.

He wondered, *How do I say this to her?*

He didn't know how to talk to Mrs. Dean. Mrs. Dean was his Senior English teacher, and here he was talking to her in his pj's and her in her bath robe like she was his best friend. He wondered, *should I use street slang?*

"Don't worry about it," she said. "I know you were trying to fend him off. If you don't mind me telling you, I was watching from the parking lot. Grandpa Dean keeps binoculars in the glove compartment. I hope you don't mind me looking after you, but if you'll recall, I told you Grandpa Dean and I have been at this game for many, many years. This isn't the first time we've seen a great prospect lured into a trap. You'll forgive me, won't you?"

Vincent felt stupid. She wasn't as dumb as he gave her credit for being. That was the weird thing about some teachers. They played dumb real well, but he knew that they knew more than the students gave them credit for.

"No, ma'am. You got there just in the nick of time."

"Looked like it," she said. "Just try to keep eyes in the back of your head. If you want, I can be your chauffeur. We can keep it secret, like meet in an alley by the ballpark so nobody sees you getting in with your teacher. I know how embarrassing that could be. After all, I'm not really that cool anymore. I haven't been hip with the youngsters for about ten years now."

Vincent laughed. "Mrs. Dean, that's really thoughtful of you, but I think I will decline."

"Well, keep it in mind," she said. "The offer stands." The two sat there in silence for some time. He looked up at the clock. It read 1:17.

"Insomnia," Mrs. Dean started. "I developed insomnia about a year ago when Grandpa Dean started really going downhill. As his wife, I really don't sleep well knowing… knowing it might be his last night."

She looked up and saw Vincent's eyes get really big, so she clarified. "Now relax, Vincent. It's going to be okay. I know you have a lot of questions about Grandpa Dean, and that's alright. It's only natural to have curiosity, especially about the people you care for. First you're probably wondering about his arm, how it became shriveled and useless. Yes?"

It took some time for Vincent to answer. The shock of her statement really caught Vincent off-balance. He knew Grandpa Dean was sick, but was it terminal? Vincent finally composed himself enough to say, "Well, ma'am, I have wondered a bit."

"Naturally. I'll leave it up to you," she said. "I can tell you the story tonight, or I can wait for another time. Are you awake enough?"

"Yes, ma'am. I would like to know."

Mrs. Dean took a deep breath and said, "What I'm going to tell you is something that Grandpa Dean never talks about. Slowly over the years I have gotten information out of him, but I think he has some ghosts in the closet, if you know what I mean. I wrote down the bits and pieces after talking to him so that someday I may tell the story, maybe write a book, but it seemed over the years that it would be disrespectful to him, or at least cheapen what he endured just to make a quick buck. So I decided to keep it to myself, but I have read my notes so many times that I have the whole story right here." She pointed to her heart, then removed her glasses so that she could clean the lenses on the lapel of her robe.

"Our country wasn't always like it is right now," she continued. "Right now you can live your life without the least fear of being sent to war. You have a promising baseball career in front of you, Vincent. So did Grandpa Dean. He was on the fast track to the pros, but then the war called in 1942, and he answered. That is why his arm is shriveled. Because one madman threatened the security of the world, Grandpa Dean's baseball career was cut off before it started. So you can understand why it is that he wants to help you so badly. He wants to see you succeed because you have the drive he had, and the gift he had, and he won't see you fail. You're curious about what happened to him in the war. I'll tell you the bits and pieces of what I know as long as you don't let him know I told you. Are you willing to listen to a long story?"

Vincent leaned in closer and said, "Yes, ma'am."

"Most of what you are about to hear is Gospel truth, Vincent. Some of it I've had to fill in with my own imagination."

"Grandpa Dean's War Story"

"It was early October of 1944. The Germans were retreating from the French occupied territory as Hitler was making mistake after mistake, spreading his troops too thin over the eastern front in Russia, and the western front which General Patton was steadily pushing back east. Basically Hitler's pride and arrogance led to his downfall.

"The front was now as far east as the Lorraine territory around the Forest of Gremecey by the Seille River in eastern France. It was only a matter of time before the Germans were pushed back to Germany and then all the way back to Berlin because the allied forces were now picking up steam.

"Grandpa Dean was a radio operator on a B17 that had been shot down on a bombing run to southern Germany. He was the only one to parachute to safety. I use the word 'safety' loosely. He was still in Germany.

"The German front line was sixty miles west of the French-German border, and Grandpa Dean was a good twenty miles into Germany. So he was eighty-miles behind enemy lines. He had to sneak across the western German countryside back into France and blend in with the locals before the Allied Forces pushed the German forces back to him. On top of that, there were patrols on his tail looking for him. Running through the rolling hills at night, he was definitely between a rock and a hard place.

"In the distance Grandpa Dean saw a farmstead with a solitary light. Down the hill he ran toward a ravine, looking back to make sure he wasn't being followed. He was cold and wet and was happy that the rain had finally stopped. He vowed to find a restful spot in the morning that was both secluded by cover and that had enough sunlight to dry him out. He wanted to ball up for warmth, but knew he had to keep on the move. It was too dangerous to move in the sunlight.

"The Germans had seen his lone parachute and had sent a team with a pack of bloodhounds after him. If captured he would be tortured until he gave up valuable information. And being an officer made him an even more valuable commodity to the enemy.

"He took to a small river. I think it was called the Kinzig, but my memory fails me in my old age. Anyway, he took this river because he knew sloshing through the ravine would be slow going, but it was his only chance to throw off the hounds.

"The irony of the situation was remarkable. Just three years prior, he was chasing coons with his own hounds on his father's farm in the Arkansas Ozarks. It was a simpler time then, not having to pay consequences for actions. Being on top of the food chain was the peaceful bliss that people in a free country like you and I take for granted when plopping our heads down on a feather pillow at night.

"Now the hunter had become the hunted, just like Rainsford became the hunted in 'The Most Dangerous Game' except this wasn't for sport and the men following him weren't gentlemen.

"You do remember the story, right?"

"Sure," Vincent responded. "He kills General Zaroff."

"Very good," Mrs. Dean said. This was much the same. This was purely survival against savage creatures that called themselves human and would eventually deny that they murdered six million Jews.

"Grandpa Dean had managed to trudge only a quarter of a mile of foot-deep water when he decided to climb the bank and head for the farmer's house he had seen in the distance. It rested on top of a hill. From the loft he would have the vantage point to see if he led the enemy off his path.

"He approached the barn with caution.

Sleep deprivation is a funny thing. His ears were playing tricks on him. He heard voices whispering his name and would turn from his left to his right with dagger in hand to see a bush moving in the wind or a pair of pants swaying on a clothesline.

"The earth still bore a sign of the weight of the reinforcement Panzers that had traversed the country toward the front.

"He ran around the back edge of the farm behind the wind block of thorn trees and peeked around the barn. Nothing was stirring so he slipped around to the front and slid through a crack in the barn door. Nothing. No chickens, no cattle, no sheep, no pigs, nor any other barnyard animal associated with a nursery rhyme. In fact when he got to the top of the loft he was disappointed to see that there wasn't even any hay. Part of living in Nazi Socialism. The farmer who lived there was a prisoner on his own farm, and Grandpa Dean deduced that the guy had to give away anything a Nazi soldier wanted or needed.

"He peered out the east window and saw two lanterns a mile off following the same path down to the ravine that he had taken an hour earlier. He prayed they would walk downstream, but after five minutes of deliberation, they apparently picked up the trail.

"It was a good try, but he knew he had to keep heading west. Now that they knew the path he was taking, there would be radio transmissions to field units ahead of him. His only hope was that they would be too occupied with the Allied attack to care much about him. After all, the German Army was in disarray at this point.

"He knew that he had to be close to the French Lorraine border. He was so tired at times, he started seeing things that weren't there. Like a recurring dream, he would see Elmer Fudd with gun in hand looking around for Bugs Bunny. Visions of his childhood didn't comfort him, but instead made him lonely and frightened.

"During the next two days, to stave off the visions, he would catch fifteen minutes of sleep here and there, but always there was the constant threat of the bloodhounds in the distance. He would outrun them, take a nap, get woken up again and run. He also knew that he had to keep changing directions, going northwest, southwest, northwest, southwest so he would stay ahead of the radio communications.

"The rain persisted throughout that time and he wished for a tornado to put him out of his misery. He couldn't let himself get caught, yet he wanted so badly to be back in his barracks. Eternal rest didn't sound too bad at that point. He didn't care if he ever got to play professional baseball or not. He just wanted this game to be over, but little did he know it would take six months before his head would hit an army standard issue cot.

"During the camouflage of night he would try to double-time it, but it was almost too dark to run. Plus there was the risk of running into enemy patrols. Still, survival pushed him.

"The Germans were being pushed around by General Patton and the German generals were split between those who wanted to push to Antwerp and then pursue peace and those who wanted to retreat. As it ended up, Hitler would try to drive all his soldiers to the grave in a narcissistic show of command.

"The clouds never parted, making it hard to see his way and even harder to be followed, much less seen. Elmer and Bugs stayed away during the night, but his energy level dropped to the point that he couldn't think straight. He would test himself with simple recall questions like his times tables or the books of the New Testament but would have difficulty remembering any of it, much less the jingles that went along with them.

"He offered up a simple prayer. He never told me what he prayed for, but I'm sure the answer's obvious. It was on this night that he recommitted his life to God and his energy was instantly restored like when that sick woman touched Jesus' cloak and was instantly healed from her affliction. That's all he needed really, a little faith. Faith is something that is tough to keep in times of utter despair. Times would get tougher for him in the next six months, but it was ultimately his faith that kept him going and kept him alive.

"On the fifth day he stopped hearing the dogs. He figured they gave up on him. That night he enjoyed the luxury of sleep. Six whole hours of sleep from midnight to dawn. He knew it was a selfish, guilty pleasure, much like stealing a cookie out of the cookie jar or sneaking out past curfew to chum around with the guys down by the river, but he felt such a steady peace that he knew it would be okay. He felt the presence of an angel watching over him.

"He slept with the burden of possible capture, but oh what a heaven-sent sleep it was! He told me he had never slept so soundly his entire life! His life and spirit came back to him in full force, despite having eaten nothing but the occasional shellfish he would find in the many creeks he traversed and a handful of grass now and then. After that week he swore he would never eat seafood again, and believe me, he hasn't!

"On the sixth day he came upon Strasbourg, which is a big town right on the French border, so he knew he would be encountering German forces. It was war-torn by the 8th Air Force.

"German soldiers walked around the ruins of destruction, heaps of rubble where great buildings and homes once stood.

"There wasn't a live tree within sight. Burnt conifer trees littered the horizon, still standing like stiff corpses.

"He wanted to avoid the town and its soldiers for some remote crossing, but he took a chance. With stomach growling he waited on the edge of town, holed up in a field of high grass that the war had spared. The rain stopped and the clouds parted as he left the safety of his hideout in search of food with the constant threat of sniper fire. As he snuck around, he pillaged the first house that didn't look occupied. He stuffed his pockets with cans of sardines. He once told me that the most important thing a man can carry around in a survival situation was his Air Force knife. That day, and many others, he used it as a can opener.

"He knew if he could make it to the town of Nancy he would be on the Allied side, but doing so meant sneaking through the Nazi front line from behind. Impossible. If he made it to Nancy, he wouldn't even have to use the Underground Railroad to Madrid. He would be free already. But he knew the idea was stupid. He felt God was leading him in a different direction, so he decided to sleep on it.

"Now it's not like God spoke to him like he spoke to Moses through a burning bush to lead the chosen few out of Egypt, but for the first time in his life he had stopped thinking and reacting, and simply opened his heart like a new set of ears. Like Moses, he was reluctant and fought with God through the night, or so I assume.

"He wanted to sleep but he tossed and turned. The longer he sat there, the more he knew what he had to do. He had to find a French connection in Strasbourg.

"The town had been used by the Germans for a rest and relaxation camp, but any able-bodied soldier was being thrown into the mix on the front not sixty miles west.

"He decided the Underground Railroad was his only chance. Tired as he was, he fell asleep on the cold dirt floor of the cellar and there he slept the entire day and night away.

"He woke twenty-four hours later with a big pain in his neck. When he looked up at the crack in the cellar door which shone day's first rays of light, he was startled to see a family of five staring right back at him."

Mrs. Dean paused and looked at her watch. "Well it's definitely getting late. Maybe we should finish this story some other time."

"Ah, come on!" Vincent begged. "What happened to him? Was it a German family? Hiding Jews? What? Come on, you gotta tell me. You can't just leave it at that!"

Mrs. Dean smiled. "We'll finish it on a rainy day."

"Please?" Vincent pleaded.

Mrs. Dean smiled. "Vincent, there's something more grave we need to discuss now before we go to bed."

"Yes?"

"Vincent, there's something Grandpa Dean and I have been keeping from you, but you deserve to know. You need to be strong when I tell you this. Okay?"

"Yes, ma'am."

"Vincent," Mrs. Dean started and her voice faltered. She quickly composed herself and said, "Vincent, Grandpa Dean, as I think you know, is dying."

He looked her in the eyes and then back down to the floor, the war story in the deep recesses of his mind now.

Mrs. Dean continued. "He and I have known for quite some time that his days were numbered. Last summer he started losing his appetite, and when we finally got around to going to the doctor in August, it was too late. Grandpa Dean has lung cancer and emphysema.

"You see, the cigarette companies would give free cigarettes to incoming GI's to try to get them hooked. Grandpa Dean chewed tobacco before the war, but chewing tobacco was hard to come by where he was stationed in England, so he started smoking. You can imagine his time behind enemy lines was tough on him without a cigarette.

"He finally quit eighteen years ago, but the damage was already done. If he hadn't quit, he would be long dead by now. They say each cigarette takes five minutes off your life. Well, Grandpa Dean was smoking a pack a day. I'm sure you can do the math. Then on one Christmas morning, he decided to quit cold turkey, and he's never had a puff since. He's pretty strong willed when he wants to be."

Vincent tried to smile, but all he wanted to do was scream in anger.

"Anyway," she continued, "last August he was given the option of going on chemotherapy or just living out his last days happily, without the agony and sickness that goes along with those nasty poisons they pump into a body. With chemo we were told he would have six to nine months, and we've already eclipsed that without using the poison, so we count our blessings every chance we get. The tumor hasn't shrunk or increased. It just stays the same. All the same, I fear it's spreading, which is why he is always in such pain."

Vincent didn't know how to react. He knew there was something wrong, but he didn't know Grandpa Dean was terminal. Vincent realized these might be his last days! It was too much to take in, too fast. He looked around the kitchen, hoping this was just a bad dream.

"Vincent," Mrs. Dean continued, "I wish I could have avoided this speech altogether, God only knows I do. I wasn't planning on telling you this soon either, but he's taken a turn for the worse lately. You'll notice he hasn't been able to be outside as much with you."

Vincent whispered, "Yes."

"Well, he has pain medication he takes, but he hates to take it because it makes him sleepy. He can't take his medication in the morning and work with you, so he's been getting tired a lot easier lately."

Vincent was feeling guilty now and Mrs. Dean quickly said, "Now that's not your fault. Don't believe that for a second. Fact is, this was Grandpa Dean's decision. He wanted his last days to be spent teaching someone what he knows, straight from his heart. You see, fathers always want their wisdom to be passed on.

Nobody wants his last words to be ignored, so he's lucky you came along."

This didn't make Vincent feel any better.

"Vincent," Mrs. Dean continued, "there's something else. When he came home from the war, we soon found he was infertile. We were never able to have kids, and Grandpa Dean always wanted to have a son. Vincent, you're as close to a son as he's ever had, and he's so proud of you. He only wishes he could watch you play, but he's not left the house in about three months now, save for his trips into the backyard. He was really disappointed that he couldn't see you pitch your first game tonight. It meant a lot to him. But he listened on the radio. You can be sure of that. He listens to every game on the radio."

Vincent felt more honored than he had ever felt in his life, that someone would care so much for him, that that person would weaken himself and shorten his life to help him. The anger was slowly melting away, but it still made him feel downright rotten.

"Well, what can I do? You know, to help?" Vincent asked.

Mrs. Dean smiled. "Vincent, you've already done all you can without even knowing. You help out with the yard work, and you put your soul and effort into becoming a better baseball player. You're a respectful young man in a country full of disrespectful youth. Sometimes Grandpa Dean wonders why he helped save this country when the kids turned out the way they have. Then one person comes around and changes his whole opinion of humanity. Grandpa is proud of you and that is the best thing you could have done for him. You made him feel like he's done his job. He helped someone who needed it. He's not trying to earn his way to heaven. He knows that's not how you get there. But it is his faith that has helped him fight this long." She paused briefly. "By the way, what book are you on right now?"

"Book?" Vincent asked.

"Yeah, of the Bible?"

"Oh, I'm in Exodus," he responded.

"Ah, you've got a ways to go. If you want to find out about heaven, read Mark and then read Acts right after that. It's not a bad thing to skip around and catch some highlights instead of reading it cover-to-cover. That's the only book you'll ever hear me say that about. You didn't hear me say that this year about anything we read from Charles Dickens, did you?"

"No, ma'am." Vincent admitted.

"Vincent," Mrs. Dean said, "do you know how to get to heaven?"

Vincent sat there in silence and shrugged his shoulders. He had been reading the Bible and enjoying the story that enfolded in front of him, but this wasn't an answer he had read about yet.

Mrs. Dean continued. "You'll find out that committing good works on earth won't get you there."

"So, being nice isn't enough?" Vincent asked.

"Unfortunately not," Mrs. Dean said. "Oh, I'm not smart enough to speak about the grace of God," she continued. "Nobody on earth is. What God decided to do, He will do, and we will never know His reasons why."

She looked at her pupil, "We are commanded in the Bible to accept Jesus as our Lord and Savior. Repent and be baptized. That's the only road to heaven. Grandpa Dean knows that and has taken the appropriate steps."

Vincent smiled. He, himself, had been feeling a tug that summer, something he couldn't understand, a void that needed filling. He felt Jesus working in his life, despite not having ever been introduced to the topic before. He saw the way Mrs. and Grandpa Dean lived their lives, saw the peace that filled Mrs. Dean's heart right now, despite the fact that she was about to be engulfed in the toughest struggle of her life.

"Vincent?" Mrs. Dean started.

"Yes, Mrs. Dean?" Vincent responded.

"Vincent, I knew you were special the first time I saw you walk into class last fall. I took a chance on you and you proved me right. Grandpa Dean took a chance on you and you proved him right also. Not because you have a gift, but because you have a love. You've made him feel better about himself. That's all you can do." Mrs. Dean smiled and took a drink of her room-temperature buttermilk.

Vincent could feel the tears coming again, but held them in. His anger resurfaced. He was mad that he finally found someone who believed in him, and that person was dying. It was so easy to be angry.

Mrs. Dean, perceptive as she was, said, "Vincent, I know this is hard for you, but I think you will learn to find peace in everything. Trust me. This is God's Will, just as it was God's Will that He brought you into our lives."

She got up and put a hand on his shoulder to console him.

Vincent couldn't hold it in any longer. He stood and hugged her and cried on her shoulder.

Mrs. Dean did not seem surprised at this act. She was strong for him. She patted him on the back, much the way Vincent figured she would have for her own son.

He didn't only cry for Mrs. Dean and Grandpa Dean. He also let out all his pent-up frustration about his parents, the abuse he had been through with a drunk for a father, the belts, the wrenches, the baseboard his dad had ripped right off the wall to use on his back one night, forgetting to take out the nails. He cried about how his mother didn't even care about him, how he had to basically care for himself since he was way too young to have to face such problems reserved for adults.

It was the first time he had ever let himself cry.

They sat back down at the table and he let it all out and she listened. Things he swore he would take to his grave, things that

247

felt like he was being unfaithful to his parents, but he wondered when had they ever been faithful to him?

His emotions ran the gamut that night, and Mrs. Dean was there for him for all of it.

When his tears subsided and he ran out of things to say, she said, "Let's get some sleep. Getting some of this emotion out ought to help cure our insomnia." She held him at arm's length. "Are you going to be alright?"

He wiped his eyes and said, "Yes, ma'am." He put his empty glass in the sink and closed the door to his guest room.

*

So that next morning Vincent had his first experience with church.

The Deans had been members of the church of Christ since marriage.

It wasn't boring as it was depicted on television, and the preacher made the lesson so interesting he felt he was at a college lecture on a fascinating topic. The congregation was nice to him, each member shaking his hand and welcoming him.

During the special needs part of the service, a prayer was raised for Grandpa Dean. Following the sermon the preacher gave an invitation for anyone who wanted to give his or her life to the Lord, and Vincent accepted the invitation.

On his way to church that morning, he didn't realize he would be making the most important decision of his life, but there he was, getting baptized in front of the whole church. Vincent walked away a different man. He felt like he had purpose for the first time in his life, that despite all the hardships that had come his way, there was…hope. He was full of energy and wished Grandpa Dean could have come along, but he sat at home listening to the First Methodist sermon on the radio.

The weekends went on like this. Mrs. Dean would pick up Vincent for church on Sunday mornings, and Vincent felt more and more at home in a place of God as he learned to walk the life of a Christian.

Though Vincent felt awkward about it, Grandpa Dean did the best he could to finish the lessons.

By the end of June, Grandpa Dean had to stay in bed and go on oxygen. He moved into the spare bedroom and needed twenty-four hour supervision, in case he choked, or worse.

Vincent was more than happy to sleep on the couch at night and rise whenever he heard Grandpa Dean ring his bell, indicating he needed something. The chores were gross, to say the least, but Vincent looked at it as his duty, much the way Grandpa Dean had sacrificed nearly sixty years prior.

Mrs. Dean took care of her husband during the day, but she was wearing out.

Vincent also had a hard time making it through work in the mornings at the park, teaching baseball skills to the future stars. He would sleep his afternoons away on the Deans' couch. His parents never asked, and probably never knew he was gone in the first place. Vincent considered his help part of his duty toward Grandpa Dean.

Vincent still went out in the backyard after breakfast and practiced, with Grandpa Dean watching out the spare bedroom window from his bed. Vincent would return to the house and take any criticisms Grandpa Dean could give. Vincent tried to tell Grandpa Dean to sleep instead to save his strength, but this only made Grandpa Dean mad. Grandpa Dean didn't like "being handled," as he so often put it.

By mid-July, Vincent had made his way through the gospel of Mark and was half-way through Acts like Mrs. Dean had suggested. He had a good handle on Jesus' life, death, and resurrection, and the formation of the worldly missions. Vincent even gave thought to doing some mission work that next summer.

He attended church with Mrs. Dean every Sunday and was growing in the faith.

In the backyard, he mastered the sinker and could make his fastball move any direction. He found out from the radio that he could throw ninety-seven miles-per-hour, but it didn't seem to matter as much to him. All he cared about was Grandpa Dean's pain, and there was plenty of it.

At times Vincent would pray for God to make the pain subside. Other times, Vincent was so stressed out and tired over the ordeal, he would pray for God to take Grandpa Dean.

It was a morbid, guilty thought, but Vincent knew Heaven was a better place. It hurt Vincent to see the old man strain to move his head enough to cough up mucus from his lungs into his bowl without choking. Grandpa Dean's lungs were filling with liquid, and he was slowly drowning to death. All Vincent and Mrs. Dean could do was watch.

By the time the State Regional Baseball Tournament neared, Grandpa Dean was a frail eighty pounds and near the end.

Augusta enjoyed a week off between its last twin bill of the year, a sweep against the lowly Franklin Braves, and the state tournament. By virtue of winning state the year before, Augusta had the pleasure of hosting the tournament this year and didn't even have to win a regional to punch their ticket. The team went into the state tournament with a 21-10 record and received the number two seed, second to Seiling, who kept up its winning ways, and was labeled unbeatable by the media.

In their home-and-home series with Augusta, Seiling won both of their home games to claim a 3-1 record against their arch-rivals.

Vincent read in the papers that the experts were picking, or more accurately hoping for an Augusta versus Seiling final, just like the year before. There were other teams that could win the title, but they were considered dark horses at best.

Vincent was leading the team with a .667 batting average. The only one even close was Dusty Redenbacher who was batting a sparkling .421.

Still, Coach Grey kept Vincent in the number six spot, and he managed a base hit every two out of three times to the plate.

Vincent wouldn't let Deuce persuade him to join in anything illegal, despite all of Deuce's efforts. Mrs. Dean was as good as her word and would pick Vincent up (despite his objections) a block away in an alley to keep him from having to deal with Deuce.

Augusta lost its fair share of games, and it was obvious to Vincent that Jimmy didn't play well in any of them.

Vincent tried many times over the summer months to talk to Jimmy about what was happening, but Jimmy was too far gone. Jimmy wouldn't speak to Vincent, much less anybody else on the team (including his former-best friend, Bacon Bob) and became an outsider on the team he used to lead. Vincent became the new unofficial team leader and in the choice moments he spoke, everyone listened. Vincent knew Jimmy needed help. The only solution he could come up with was to tell Coach Grey and hope the father would intervene. Given his relationship with Coach Grey, Vincent decided against it.

Vincent watched Jimmy slowly devolve. Jimmy's hair was getting shaggy, and he appeared to get less sleep than Vincent was getting.

Though Vincent knew about Jimmy's problems, he figured he hadn't the foggiest idea of the complexity of the situation, and he didn't want to know.

Heading into August, Vincent was worried about college. No college coach had contacted him, despite the queries he had sent to various in-state colleges per Mrs. Dean's request. Vincent figured he was out in the middle of nowhere, where true baseball players weren't grown very often.

Going into the year, Vincent was very aware that every coach knew Jimmy was the cream of the crop, and he was already taken. Vincent began to doubt his self worth, despite a .78 earned run average and 6-1 pitching record. He began to lose hope that he would go to college and began searching for a full-time job for the fall.

The week of the state tournament, the whole town started to prepare for the big event. The town mayor declared it Stampeding Herd Week. Businesses around town painted their windows with artistic versions of various players batting, or fielding, or just looking larger than life, while other businesses went for the general themes, like the herd of cattle busting down a farmer's fence in a Western-looking background.

That's the particular theme that appeared on the windows of Barbara's Boutique and earned her the first prize ribbon, which was given out by the local chamber of commerce during their weekly coffee hour. She also received a twenty-five dollar certificate to the Lazy R Restaurant toward the purchase of a steak dinner. All of this was chronicled on the front page of the newspaper and made Vincent laugh.

Vincent would walk downtown and see that flags were raised along the main drag depicting the team's mascot, while others that depicted the past state championships adorned the route to the ball field. All businesses held various "Stampeding Herd" sales. Vincent could feel the electricity in the air. He even overheard a conversation at the donut shop one morning where a bunch of old men complained that Augusta wasn't seeded first, despite being defending state champions.

As Vincent walked down the street, he would see tournament brackets stapled to light poles or taped to windows.

Oklahoma AA Double-Elimination State Tournament
1. Seiling Pirates 24-3
2. Augusta Stampeding Herd 21-10
3. Ada Royals 25-15
4. Vinita Dragons 24-8
5. Elk City Cougars18-12
6. South East Regional Bison 19-10
7. Altus Thrashers 17-15
8. Osage County Reds 12-18

Vincent visited the field and saw that during the week off, some of the wealthier town merchants pitched in to buy a new scoreboard, complete with a new pitch speedometer that would show every pitch's speed automatically. Of course it had room at the top to advertise not only the past state titles, but the merchants who put up the money.

Vincent and Bacon Bob held a meeting after every practice to go over pitch selection and were turning into pretty good friends. They rarely had conversations about Jimmy, about how he seemed to be spiraling out of control, about his scruffy look and dirty uniform, but Vincent knew Jimmy was on Bob's mind.

If there was one thing Vincent knew, it was that they would have a hard time winning the state championship without Jimmy's help. Still, Vincent couldn't bring himself to tell Bob just how deep Jimmy was in trouble because he didn't want to bum Bob out.

A few days prior to the first game, the team held a final tune-up practice. This time Jimmy didn't even care enough to show up. Though nobody mentioned it, Vincent knew it was on everybody's mind.

Coach gave a speech about not doing anything stupid like water-skiing or falling asleep in the sun, and he asked everybody take the next day off completely to relax and stock up on carbohydrates.

Despite Jimmy's absence, Vincent noticed that the team spirit was high as they joked around as they left. That left Bacon Bob, still wearing his shin guards, and Vincent.

They sat on opposite sides of the bench, and Vincent gazed out at the Little Monster, all the pennants that adorned the top. He looked through the fence and past the pennants to the big yellow house that would probably get plunked once or twice during the course of the tournament.

The evening's air was tepid. A slight southern breeze dried the sweat from their foreheads, and they sat in the shade from the stands. Vincent wished they could share a moment of silence without it being awkward, but that wasn't to be the case. He just knew Jimmy was on Bacon Bob's mind, and wondered how much Bob really knew.

Vincent knew well that Bob wore his emotions on his sleeve. As big, strong, and manly as Bob was, he was the kind to weep at a sappy movie. When tensions were high, Bob could always be counted on in a flash to lighten the mood. Vincent looked at Bob and knew the poor guy was about to burst. Vincent turned away and closed his eyes.

"Say, dude, how's your arm?" Bob asked not more than a minute later.

The words seemed to shock Vincent, who was trying to escape to a place far away, possibly on some barren beach in the South Pacific that he had seen on a postcard, or to the top of a snowy Colorado peak he had seen in a textbook. Maybe in war-torn France. These last days before the tournament should have been the prelude to the greatest time in his life, but his mind felt the urgency to relocate.

"My arm?"

"Yeah. Coach didn't have you throw too many pitches today, did he?" Bob asked.

Vincent rubbed his shoulder as if he had to figure out if it was sore or not. Not an ounce of pain surfaced when he rotated his arm in a clockwise motion. "Seems fine," Vincent said. "I counted thirty-five pitches. Just enough to keep the rust off."

Bacon Bob smiled for the first time now. "Good. We'll need it." He paused. "You thought about a curveball any?"

"A curveball?" Vincent asked, then shook his head. "Naw, I better hold to the KISS rule."

"Kiss rule? What the heck is that?" Bob asked and pounded on his chest to release a well-timed burp. Bob winced and said, "Chilidog with onions. Yuck."

In one of their conversations that summer, Bob had explained his thoughts on burps. Bob would rate foods according to their burp's frequency, stamina, and taste. While orange juice and cheese rated toward the top, onions, chili, and hotdogs definitely hit rock bottom. When he put the three together, he told Vincent, it was like adding baking soda to vinegar. The eruption that follows was roughly equivalent to half of the discomfort felt from the lethal combination of onions, chili, and hotdogs.

Ignoring the burp, Vincent said, "The KISS rule stands for "Keep It Simple, Stupid." I don't know where it came from, but an old man I know says it all the time, so it must be important."

"KISS rule, huh? I'll have to remember that," Bob said.

They both looked out past the fence to see a noisy black van race up Prospect Hill, and with its passing came that awkward silence again. Just as Vincent opened his mouth to talk about more nothing, Bacon Bob said, "Vincent," and paused.

"Yes, Bob?"

"You don't like Jimmy much, do you?"

Vincent exhaled. He really didn't want to have this conversation, but since Bob brought it up, Vincent told the truth. "Would you if you were me?"

"No. Probably not," Bob said. "You know, he used to not be like this. There was a day when we would ride our bikes down Prospect Hill towards the crick with a tackle box in one hand and two fishing poles in the other. Back then we would fish for carp all day, run over to the swimming pool to clean up and do a couple belly-busters off the board, then it was off to the game. Man, little league was great. Not because there wasn't any pressure, cause there always has been, you know, parents. What was so great about it was that we were..." and he stopped.

"Friends?" Vincent asked.

"Yeah," Bob said and sighed, "to skip to the point, we were friends. Jimmy wasn't this big hotshot with the Corvette, and no big league owner had ever heard of him. It was simpler then. KISS rule, huh?"

"So you're saying that Jimmy turned into this bad guy this year?" Vincent asked.

"No, it's been a gradual progression. He became the most famous kid at school sometime in junior high, and he's gotten worse every day. Shoot, I've just been along for the ride."

"But you're one of the most popular guys in our class," Vincent said. "Everybody loves you."

"Yeah, because I rode Jimmy's coattails. He just keeps me around to make himself look better."

Vincent patted Bob on the back and asked him, "What's on your mind, Bob?"

"I'm just wondering if I know the difference between right and wrong." Bob shook his head. "The cockier he got, the more I just went along with it, even if it meant putting other kids down, or giving a nerd a swirly. I didn't want to be the one put down by the popular crowd, so I just went along with everything, even though I knew it was wrong. What I saw him do to you at the beginning of the season--that was wrong. I knew it, but I never stood up to him.

I guess what I'm trying to say is I'm sorry. I wish I could take a lot of things back."

Vincent sat there in silence. He had no misconceptions about his social role in high school. Vincent knew he was among the unpopular and that anonymity was all he searched for when crossing the halls from first period to second. And as for lunch? Ha! Forget about it! He knew of a little nook behind the drill press in the woodworking room that he would hide at until the bell rang for fifth period. Anonymity. That was the key, but never had somebody apologized to him before for treating him badly.

"You know, you can kick yourself around all you want Bob, but a fact's a fact. Jimmy is the culprit behind being nasty. You had nothing to do with it. If I were in your position, I probably would have done the same."

Bob laughed and blew it off. "I doubt that. You would have done the right thing. You know Vincent, everybody looks up to you. You're the leader of the team and you're better than Jimmy ever thought about being. I want you to remember that."

Vincent shook his head to this.

"You want my advice, Bob?" Vincent asked. When Bob nodded, Vincent said, "An old man once told me, 'Who you are is who you hang out with.' It's as good a guide as any."

He looked over at Bob who was wiping tears from his eyes. "See, that's the problem, Vincent," Bob said. "I feel like I'm in a pickle. I should have left his side a long time ago. I knew we would grow apart once we went to our different colleges, but I didn't expect it to be this soon. I don't know if you've noticed, but Jimmy has changed this summer. I think he's into drugs or something. I want to help him, but I'm with you. I think that the farther away I place myself from him, the better off I will be. I mean, I don't know what the heck to think about him right now."

Vincent again wondered if he should tell Bacon Bob everything. Vincent knew more than he wanted to and didn't think he should share that burden with his catcher.

The poor guy looked as if he had enough to deal with at the moment, but on the other hand, Vincent didn't want Bob to get in over his head without first knowing what he was up against.

"Well, all I can tell you is that I know quite a bit more than I want to about Jimmy right now. Now whether you want to get involved in that mess is up to you, but I think you might want to think twice."

Bacon Bob looked up at Vincent and asked him, "Is it drugs?"

Vincent nodded. "And then some."

"Well, I've tried talking to him," Bob said. "It's like talking to a tree. I don't know. Maybe I'll try after the state tournament is over. Maybe then he will be thinking more clearly."

Vincent responded, "You know, an old man once told me, 'Absence makes the heart grow fonder.'"

"Is this the same old man who told you the KISS rule and that other thing you said about hanging out with bad people?"

Vincent said, "Yup, same guy." Vincent got up and stretched his legs. As if by a signal, Bacon Bob started unstrapping his shin guards and the meeting was officially over.

"Smart guy, huh?" Bob asked.

Vincent nodded and smiled. "Give me a ring tomorrow and we'll talk baseball. Okay?"

"Sure," Bob said. "Hey, Vincent?"

"Yes?" Vincent asked.

"What we just talked about, can you keep it to yourself? You know, until things get better."

Vincent had heard that one before. "Sure."

*

By the day of the first round games of the state tournament, Vincent was already sick of the pomp and circumstance, and only wanted to get out on the field and leave the world behind.

Vincent hadn't received a lesson from Grandpa Dean for over a week.

Grandpa Dean rarely did anything else but sleep. His voice had faded to short, hoarse whispers that seemed to zap all his energy.

That morning, as Vincent was heading out the door to catch the early games, already in uniform and bat bag in hand, Mrs. Dean caught him by the arm. "Vincent, Grandpa Dean wants to talk to you." She led him to the guest bedroom.

Vincent hadn't talked to Grandpa Dean in a week and was more nervous than ever. He loved this man, but given the circumstance, he didn't know what to say to him. It wasn't a position in which he had ever found himself.

When he opened the door, he noticed three things. First was the smell. He couldn't figure out what to call it, except the smell of death. It was in the air as thick as a Chicago fog, and it made him feel ill.

Second was the constant click of the oxygen machine helping Grandpa Dean take his last breaths.

Finally was the light. The only light in the room came from the window by the bed that overlooked his backyard.

Grandpa Dean lay there, gazing out the window at the pitching mound he had built many years before.

Mrs. Dean closed the door behind Vincent, and he walked up to the bed.

At first, he didn't know if Grandpa Dean was breathing or not until he saw him lick his lips. Automatically Vincent grabbed the ice water on the bedside table and put the straw to his lips.

Grandpa Dean took one small drink, only to have it come back up. Vincent held a rag to Grandpa Dean's mouth to catch the rest of it. This was something Vincent was used to doing. Nursing duties had come to him naturally enough.

He sat down on the bed next to Grandpa Dean and pondered what to say. Talk about the weather? How bad the Eagles were? Who's going to win the Super Bowl next year? All these topics were of little concern to a dying man and Vincent knew it, so he sat down and waited to be addressed.

Grandpa Dean could only whisper and took his time in between breaths.

"Vincent?"

"Yes, Grandpa Dean."

"Learn to use that sinker more."

"The sinker?"

Grandpa Dean coughed again and spit what came up into his bedside bowl. "Grounders are easier than strikeouts. Easier on the arm."

"Yes, sir."

"You pitching tonight?" Grandpa Dean asked.

"Yes, sir."

"Good, Grandpa Dean said, and added, rather cryptically, "They'll be coming for you soon."

Vincent wondered what Grandpa Dean meant by that.

Grandpa Dean looked at the water, and Vincent picked up on the hint and gave him another drink.

Vincent prayed Grandpa Dean would get this one down, and his prayer was answered.

After Grandpa Dean regulated his breathing, he again addressed Vincent.

"Vincent."

"Yes, sir."

"You got a gift. But..."

Vincent waited for him to finish.

"You need to be positive, but never cocky," Grandpa Dean finally said.

"Yes, sir."

Grandpa Dean continued, his breath labored. "You need to work hard. There's always someone out there working harder."

"Yes, sir."

"And one more thing, the most important," Grandpa Dean said.

"Yes?" Vincent asked, leaning in.

"Always keep your faith in God."

In such a moment, Grandpa Dean was looking out for him. Grandpa Dean's strength in his faith was something Vincent was going to have to strive for in his own life.

Vincent didn't want to cry. He had been holding it in whenever he was around Grandpa Dean.

"It's okay, son." Grandpa Dean reached for Vincent's right hand with his good hand.

Vincent offered it, and he held it there on top of Grandpa Dean's crippled right hand.

Grandpa Dean felt a surge of energy flow out of Vincent's priceless arm. Grandpa Dean knew Vincent would make it. That thought comforted him. He felt more positive about Vincent's future than anything he had ever felt in his life. "I'll be listening tonight. Save this for tomorrow."

Grandpa Dean held Vincent's hand for five minutes until he drifted off into a peaceful sleep.

Vincent released his grip from Grandpa Dean's hand and found another slip of paper in his palm. Respecting Grandpa Dean's wishes, he placed it in the side pouch of his bat bag and sat there and wept silently until he could collect his composure and bring himself to leave this man, a man he considered his father, helpless in the bed.

*

Mrs. Dean sat in a chair next to her husband, who looked so helpless. She cried as she watched his labored breathing. She thought about all the years they had spent living life together.

They traveled from one corner of the United States to the next, living out of their pull-behind Airstream when they were young. When they decided they were ready to settle down in one place, they moved into their home in Augusta, happy, content. They had each other, and they had lived life to the fullest, and that was enough for her. She was able to grow old with her best friend. What hurt the most was that Grandpa Dean was her life, and she was about to lose him.

The tears continued. She reached for his hand and held it. It was cold to the touch, so she pulled the blanket up to cover both of his hands.

Grandpa Dean cracked open one eye and coughed.

Mrs. Dean smiled at her husband through the tears and said, "Honey, the game is about to start. Would you like me to turn it on?"

She waited for an answer and received none. He gave no sign whatsoever that he heard her, only his breathing.

Mrs. Dean reached for the transistor radio that Grandpa Dean had kept by the bedside and turned it on.

The radio announcer was talking about how both Augusta's and Altus' teams were standing around, swinging bats and trying to loosen up. He mentioned that both teams looked nervous. He said that Vincent was warming up in the bullpen and was apparently not concerned with keeping any secrets, because he was throwing lasers. The announcer said that Vincent appeared to be "in the zone," which made Mrs. Dean smile.

Mrs. Dean fed an ice chip to her husband who choked on it, causing a series of spasms that terrified her.

After a few minutes a local high school girl sang the Star-Spangled Banner and finished to an audible applause.

The announcer let Mrs. Dean and all other listeners, the few who lived "in town that aren't at the game," as he put it, know that Vincent's first pitch was a strike at 97 miles-per-hour. Wild cheering erupted in the background.

Mrs. Dean held her husband's hand and the game acted as a welcome break from reality.

When the seventh inning rolled around, Vincent was still pitching a no-hitter, the score was still tied at 0-0, and Grandpa Dean was still asleep.

Mrs. Dean stroked her husband's face without response.

The announcer spoke about how Vincent threw sinkerball after sinkerball, and induced all three Altus batters to ground out to Quentin. The color guy did mention that it appeared Vincent's arm was tiring though.

At the bottom of the inning, Vincent was first up to bat, so Mrs. Dean decided to wake her husband.

"Honey, wake up," she whispered into his ear. He was lying on his back and appeared not to breathe.

The announcer mentioned that Vincent strode up to the plate and made the sign of the cross on the plate with his bat.

Mrs. Dean held her husband's hands in her own and listened intently.

The Altus pitcher threw a ball in the dirt on his first pitch.

Mrs. Dean wondered whether she should try again. After the second pitch in the dirt she tried to speak to her husband.

"Honey," Mrs. Dean whispered, "Vincent's up to bat. It's the bottom of the last inning and the score is tied 0-0."

She let out another round of tears as her husband looked so lonely, so helpless just lying there with the oxygen mask around his mouth and nose.

His chest spasmed in an effort to pump oxygen into his old lungs.

"Honey," she continued, "you did such a good job with him."

263

"Strike one," the announcer said.

"He has a no-hitter right now. He pitched a full game without giving out a hit," Mrs. Dean told her husband.

"Ball three," the announcer said.

"And it's all because of you," Mrs. Dean said. "You gave him the confidence. He will succeed. I made the phone call like you asked me to."

The announcer broke her concentration. "AND THERE IT GOES! HIGH INTO THE NIGHT! THE LEFT FIELDER HAS NO CHANCE TO GET THIS ONE! GOING, GOING, GONE! OFF THE HOUSE ACROSS CARROLL AVENUE AND BACK INTO THE GUTTER. A HOARD OF KIDS ARE RUNNING AFTER THE BALL. LADIES AND GENTLEMEN, VINCENT PRESTON HAS DONE IT AGAIN. HE'S ROUNDING THIRD AND COMING HOME. HIS TEAMATES ARE ALL THERE TO CELEBRATE. VINCENT PRESTON HAS DONE IT AGAIN. AUGUSTA WINS! AUGUSTA WINS!"

Grandpa Dean opened his eyes wide and looked straight up.

"Honey, did you hear? Vincent did it again!"

Grandpa Dean raised both of his arms in the air, reaching for something invisible to his wife's eyes.

The tornado sirens went off across town. Cannon fire was heard from miles around. It sounded like an air raid to Mrs. Dean.

Grandpa Dean held his hands straight to the sky with his eyes wide open, with a smile and a tear rolling down from his left eye. Then all at once, his arms fell down. His right arm stretched out from the bed, and lay there limply. His breathing subsided.

A moment later the sirens went quiet. All was calm.

His wife buried her head on her husband's chest and let out everything she had been holding in for the past two years.

In the background she could hear the announcer say that the whole team celebrated at the home plate.

It took some time, but Mrs. Dean pulled the covers over her only love's face and turned off the radio, all alone.

*

After the game, Vincent gave an interview on the radio and credited Grandpa Dean for taking a chance on a relative nobody and for being his mentor.

It was the happiest moment of his life. He had been carried off the field by his buddies to the sounds of honking horns and bursting fireworks in the air. The fans all seemed to want to greet him and shake his hand, and he even received a few hugs, which felt awkward to him, yet somehow okay.

After thirty minutes of celebration and fanfare, Vincent ascended the steps to the parking lot. He saw two people waiting for him, one, the middle-aged bald man with a jacket, the other a widow.

When Vincent saw her, he stopped right in his tracks. She wasn't supposed to be there. He figured she must be there to congratulate him in person, so he smiled a bit, but that faded when he saw her eyes. She approached him, held his hand and solemnly said, "I'm sorry Vincent. It's over."

The feeling wasn't relief like he had hoped. It was agony.

He hugged her, not caring about the bald man, or anybody for that matter, and escorted her back to her car before his emotions got the best of him.

The two drove away from the celebration together.

Chapter 13

Rick Strunk of Strunk Funeral Services came calling that night and Mrs. Dean and Vincent made the funeral arrangements together.

Vincent went to his own home and barely slept that night.

The next day word had apparently gotten around because his teammates tried consoling him, but it was of no use. The great ballplayer who was normally quiet was particularly quiet that day, going 0-3 against an underrated Ada Royals team that shut out Augusta and sent them to the loser's bracket. Vincent just couldn't concentrate.

The Stampeding Herd's next game would be against the number eight team, the Osage County Reds, who were bounced from the winner's bracket by Seiling and who barely held on against Vinita for a 12-11 victory in the first round of the loser's bracket.

Vincent had done his homework before the tournament started. He knew that Osage County had very little good pitching, a perfect team for the Herd to bounce back against, a team that probably didn't deserve to be in the tournament to begin with.

Vincent knew Augusta was the odds-on favorite to win the game--that is without any outside interference.

Vincent showed up for the game, but not much was different. He only wanted to keep to himself.

Coach Grey gave a weak pep talk and Jimmy played another poor game.

In the middle of the game and right in front of Vincent, Dusty pulled the team aside and gave a pep talk, telling them that they had to perform for Vincent, and not rely on him to provide the spark plug.

Other than Jimmy, the Augusta players took Dusty's words to heart, played well, and came out of their slumps. Ned Gasser threw fastball after fastball and blew away the under matched team 10-2, advancing them to a rematch against Altus the next day.

Though they were still alive, Vincent didn't care.

Vincent's mentor's funeral was the next day. He found he couldn't think straight or concentrate. He was burning inside. He would see Grandpa Dean's good hand, holding his, wishing for strength and only being able to muster up words to someone he fully expected to carry the torch. But how could Vincent perform under such circumstances to the level expected of him, a level that would seem impossible to the average American boy with dreams of playing in the pros? How could he accomplish these lofty goals without the man who made it possible for him to be the man he was?

A few months back he was a gutless kid with an untapped reservoir of potential and nobody to bring it out of him. He was destined for a lifetime with a shovel or a pickaxe. Then he became sure of himself, thanks to Grandpa Dean, and sought to reach for the stars. Now the sky was cloudy, the stars obscured. He stopped reading his Bible. No scouts or college coaches were scheduled to show up at the tournament. He had no hopes of being noticed, no hope of becoming what Grandpa Dean told him he would be, and only the vague realization that the shovel was going to become his best friend.

Mrs. Dean would be disappointed, that's for sure, but he could see no way out. Then there was another side that was pushing him.

Deuce had been giving Vincent more and more pressure toward the end of the season.

Try as Vincent might to avoid Deuce, Vincent would look out his window and see the guy waiting outside his house. Closer to the state tournament, Vincent's kitchen window had been broken by a brick, his father's car tires had all been punctured, and his mom had nearly been run over on her way to work by what she described as a "…big SUV with tinted windows."

Vincent knew it was Deuce, and Vincent didn't want to deal with it anymore. He didn't want to deal with anything anymore. He just wanted to bury his head in his pillow and wake up another person.

The lights around the park clanked off and the last headlights filed their way out of the parking lot. To the west there was a sound so unfamiliar to Vincent's ears that he had trouble recognizing it as that of thunder.

Coach Grey was the only one left, bagging up some equipment after having given his daily philosophical speech on the radio.

Vincent approached Coach Grey and waited for him to look up.

Coach Grey stole a peek at the kid who approached him, and then took a second look to make sure it was indeed who he thought it was. "Yes, Vincent? What do you want?"

Vincent hadn't known what he was going to say until that moment. "I'm sorry Coach Grey, but I won't be playing tomorrow."

Coach Grey turned his head away from Vincent's view and attended to a batting helmet. "And why not?"

"My pitching coach's funeral is tomorrow," Vincent replied.

Without turning around, Coach Grey said, "But you know we don't play until 2:00, and then again at 5:00 if we win. What time is the funeral?"

"2:00."

Coach turned back around and confronted Vincent. "I realize you were close to the man, and though I am disappointed you won't be able to play, I know it's important for you to have your grieving time. If we win tomorrow, will I see you for the championship games on Sunday?"

Vincent's visions of wearing that big league uniform and hurling from the mound in front of thousands of fans and ivy-coated walls in every direction faded with the summer night's last light. Instead all he saw was a shovel. He looked up at Coach Grey who looked like he was about to ask the question again. "No, I don't think so." Then Vincent looked down, disappointed. "Thanks for giving me a chance to play, Coach." Vincent walked past Coach Grey and up the old hill toward home. Vincent took one last look back at the ball field and saw Coach Grey on the phone, smiling.

Halfway home, the storm unleashed, and Vincent walked onward in the rain. No car stopped for him.

*

The next morning, Vincent rose at 11:00 and showered. He turned on the radio and the first thing he heard was the local sports talk show, mentioning that Vincent was not going to be available for the rest of the tournament. He switched off the radio before he could hear another sentence.

Vincent reached way into the back of his closet and pulled out his only suit, complete with clip-on tie. It was a dark navy suit that his mom had purchased second-hand for him four years prior to be used in a family picture. That idea was strange now to Vincent, as if he had a family with which to take a picture. If he had a picture taken with his family, it would have been with the Deans, but now his world was turned upside-down, and he now knew what it was like to lose somebody he loved. Worse yet, he lost somebody who loved him.

When Vincent put it on, the pants were a squeeze and rode a little high when he walked, exposing a bit of his white socks. He couldn't bring his elbows out in front of him for fear of the jacket ripping. His look wasn't pretty, but it was all he had. He didn't much care. He put on black dress shoes that didn't match the outfit too well and was on his way to Mrs. Dean's house.

The streets were wet and full of people wearing Stampeding Herd shirts and hats. Not a one recognized him in his dress clothes, Vincent figured without the "58" on his back. He had to hop puddles, but he arrived at the Deans' place in one piece, sweating and ready to take the jacket off.

Mrs. Dean had made breakfast for him as if it were any other day.

Both sat down to bacon, eggs, toast, and coffee, but neither ate.

Vincent did his best to make an effort at getting the eggs down, but his stomach felt greasy. He did finish his coffee, and the two sat in silence the whole time.

On the way to the funeral home, Mrs. Dean said, "Vincent, I just don't understand why you decided to quit."

Vincent looked at her, alarmed. "How did you know?"

"Heard it on the radio," she replied. "So it's true?"

Vincent looked down at his lap, the flow of the air-conditioner not really helping him sweat less. "It's true."

"So why did you quit?" she asked.

Because I am a loser. He thought.

Vincent didn't want to give her the truth, but she would see right through him if he lied. "Because there wasn't any point in playing anymore."

"And why not?" she asked.

271

Vincent growled, "Because I don't have a future."

"And why not?"

This line of Socratic questioning was getting on his nerves. His answer came as rage. "Because who am I going to play for? I don't have any scouts banging down my door. No college coaches are looking at me. I'm out here in the middle of nowhere where nobody looks for prospects! I have no future! I throw the ball in the upper-nineties and guys like Jimmy Grey throw games on purpose and get scholarships to major universities and I..." Vincent's face was red as he realized he was yelling at one of the two people on this earth that ever cared about him. "I-I'm sorry Mrs. Dean. I didn't mean to yell."

Mrs. Dean smiled a reassuring smile. "Son, it's okay to get mad. It's only natural. I'm mad right now also. Oh, I'm sure you're only deflecting your anger from losing Grandpa Dean toward me. It's okay. I don't mind. We'll get through this together." She paused, and then continued, "But to quit the team? Do you think Grandpa Dean would have wanted it this way?"

"But I can't do this without him!" Vincent blurted out.

"And why not?"

"Because I don't know how," Vincent said and stared at his mismatched socks and shoes.

"Son," she said as she pulled into the reserved parking, the regular parking lot had already filled up. "You don't need anybody to hold your hand. You were given a gift from God, and then given a mentor to bring out that gift. Now that he's gone, you are going to throw away all that he did for you? It's as if the last months of his life were for naught. Is that what you really want?" Mrs. Dean looked directly at Vincent, and he felt her stare.

Vincent didn't answer. He sat there in the sun, baking and wishing he were elsewhere.

When Mrs. Dean didn't get her response, she continued, "Well, something tells me you will see differently at the end of the day."

She put the car in park and sighed. "We have a few minutes before we have to be in there. How 'bout I tell you the rest of the story about Grandpa Dean and how he escaped during the war?"

Vincent nodded without looking up.

"Now where did I leave off last time?" she asked.

Vincent replied, "He was asleep in a cellar and woke up to see a family staring at him. You wouldn't tell me who they were."

"Ah, yes, he was still in Strasbourg." Mrs. Dean settled into story-telling mode. She took off her seatbelt and shifted in her seat to get comfortable, the blast from the air-conditioner working overtime.

"Let me tell you the rest of Grandpa Dean's war story.

"So he woke and saw a family staring at him. Immediately he saw that they posed no threat.

"They weren't afraid of him. The whole family looked as if they would blow away in a stiff wind they were so skinny. It wasn't an uncomfortable silence for long as the father handed him a bowl of soup.

"It was a vegetable soup with no meat in it, but just carrots and potatoes, and was as cold as the October morning, but it was a peace offering and tasted like a little slice of heaven. It was probably more food than they were prepared to eat as a family that day, but they gave it up for a total stranger.

"He never learned their names. All communications were through the oldest boy who looked to be about eight and spoke broken English. But it was enough to communicate to him that they were farmers and had helped a British soldier who was in the same predicament six months earlier. They were willing to help him also make his way down south to another town with friends who would also be willing to send him to the next check point.

"Now Grandpa Dean was a big man at six-foot, four inches and the farmer was well under six-feet, so he waited around for two weeks for the wife to sew him some clothes so he could blend in.

In the meantime, the eight-year-old taught him some basic French. Luckily the house wasn't checked by the Germans while he stayed there.

"They were the most humble, honorable people he had ever known. Having another mouth around to feed was hard for this family that had nothing to begin with, but they did it without complaining.

"He and the mother snuck out of town heading south in the morning, prepared to pose as husband and wife if they were questioned and providing the proper paperwork, forged to perfection with one of the only typewriters not found in the constant shakedowns.

"If a Nazi soldier were to question them, his name was Enzio Oliver Boisteau, a farmer from Montbeliard, a town to the south, and his wife's name was Adrienn Prescilla Boisteau.

"On their three-day journey to his first layover in the town of Mulhouse, forty-five miles south of Strasbourg, they encountered two checkpoints, one abandoned and the other with a few hungry soldiers who didn't even ask for paperwork, just took the bag of potatoes, lifted the gate and let them and their donkey-drawn wagon pass through. If only the rest of the journey would have been that easy.

"They arrived at their destination, a farm outside of Mulhouse, and the woman who answered the door showed no smile, just let them in. The two probably weren't related, probably didn't even know each other's first names. If they didn't know who they were, they couldn't give out information to the Germans in case of capture.

"He spent a week at that farm, sleeping in the barn which was cold now that it was November.

"The woman who accompanied him to Mulhouse left after the first day. She didn't say goodbye, just left without giving him a chance to say thank you.

"There would be many cases like this on his way to Madrid. Each stop he would learn a little more French until, by the time he reached the Pyrenees on the French-Spain border, he felt comfortable answering questions.

"And there were many questions by many soldiers, most of whom didn't know that they were on borrowed time, that their country was well on the way to losing the big war for the second time in thirty years. They were cut off from the rest of the world in their little assignments.

"The Allied Forces had broken through to Germany in places, but he wasn't lucky enough to be in the right place at the right time. He would have to make the entire journey to Spain to gain his freedom. Instead of things getting easier as he had hoped and anticipated, the farther south he traveled, the harder they got. And it was when he let his guard down that the big accident happened.

"It was now mid-January of 1945 and Grandpa Dean could see the Pyrenees in the distance. He knew that if worse came to worst, that if his cover was blown on the border with Spain, he could always get lost up in those mountains and fight a guerilla-style defense to stay alive. Really, how much fuss could they kick up for an American soldier now that word of Germany's imminent defeat was getting around to the furthest reaches of France? He didn't anticipate any problems.

"He was now with a girl named Mona. At least that was the name on the paperwork. He kept his paperwork and changed only the town of residence each time he made a stopover so that he wouldn't be asked about why he was so far from home.

"On the southeast part of the border with Spain was a gap between the Pyrenees and the Mediterranean Sea that was flat and very crossable, too crossable, and it was rumored to still be in the hands of a pocket of patriotic Nazi soldiers. Attempting to cross would be suicide. He had to cross over the mountain passes if he wanted any chance to make it out.

"By now there had been twelve girls accompany him as his wife. Mona, lucky number thirteen, had been one of the prettier girls, but he made a note of telling me that he cared only for freedom. Three months and nearly 300 miles later, he could care less for romance, and I believe him. After all, this was his life he was talking about. He had me waiting for him at home, and I was quite the looker back then.

"But Mona had a different idea. She was only nineteen, quite impressionable and had taken a liking to my husband. Her infatuation made it more believable that they were married, and he was only three years older than her at this point.

"He did his best to communicate that he was already married back in the states and that he appreciated everything she was doing for him, but she had dreams of becoming an American wife.

"At the next checkpoint, just south of the town of Foix in the northern foothills of the Pyrenees, things went bad.

"Now I don't know if I got the full story out of Grandpa Dean, and this part he was especially secretive about, that or he was fuzzy about it. Whenever I asked him about it, he merely said, 'It doesn't matter. It's in the past.'

"This is what I know. I know there were three soldiers. I know he was going to say good-bye to Mona when he got past the check point and brave the twenty-mile hike through the mountain pass by himself, but Mona had different plans.

"Mona said something to one of the soldiers in German, apparently blowing his cover. Shots were fired.

He doesn't know what really did it to him, if he got shot first, or if it was the shrapnel from a grenade, but he heard a big boom and he ended up on his back, head spinning without any sense of balance. That and he couldn't feel his right arm.

"Though he had no balance, he made another run and more shots were fired. Bark splintered all around him. He heard Mona scream and then it was cut short by another shot. He turned around to see her lifeless body fall from the cart and onto the ground.

"He got away without any food and only the coat on his back and his knife. A deep throbbing pain swept through his shoulder and felt like lightning arcing down what was left of his right arm. He wasn't anywhere near a mountain pass and was running through two feet of snow. The higher he got, the deeper the snow became, and he knew they would be able to follow his tracks. Using the laces from his boots, he tied some pine branches to his feet, which helped keep him on top of the snow better, sort of make-shift snow boots.

"He had come full circle. When his B-17 had crashed some three-plus months before, he was chased by bloodhounds through the west German hills. Having half-enjoyed a few months of forged safety, he was now on the run again with a bum arm and an alerted enemy on his trail, but his luck was beginning to change.

"First, he didn't lose much blood. In all the excitement and adrenaline, the body's natural reaction is to concentrate blood out of the extremities and into the core of your body. Anyway, it gave him enough time to get his arm tied up to his chest with the long sleeves of his shirt.

"Second, it seemed the German soldiers weren't putting in much of a chase. He never heard any hounds, and stopping to rest in a snow bank on the third day after the accident, he noticed nobody followed. It was true. Apparently they didn't care enough about one soldier to trek through those mountains in mid-January.

"It was a suicide march, but with only one arm and eating snow as he went, he found himself on the down slope after the sixth day.

"By the way, don't eat snow if you are ever in this type of situation. Melt the snow for water so your body doesn't have to work so hard to digest it.

"Anyway, half-alive and hypothermic one week later, he was in a hospital in Barcelona, where he stayed through February.

"There wasn't much they could do with his arm. Still, he wouldn't let them amputate it.

"He was taken to Madrid to the U.S. Embassy. One submarine ride back to England and the calendar read April 2nd. He had been gone five months and twenty-six days after flying the last mission of his career.

"His right arm was now as healed as it was going to get. It was shriveled like what you see now, completely useless.

"The Army sent him back to the states, and he served the remaining four months of his duty teaching survival school to soldiers.

"I was so happy to see him, after thinking he was dead for so many months. All they would tell me through the whole ordeal was that he was MIA. I don't know what was worse, what he went through, or what I went through, knowing I could do nothing but sit on my hands and wait. After some time I gave up hope. I never would have been strong enough to survive like he did.

"The Army wanted him to stay in, but as you know, World War II got in the way of his baseball career. All he could think about was getting back into the game. The war had taken his right arm from him, but it hadn't taken his heart.

"He tried for a whole year to rehabilitate his arm, but it was useless. Between the shrapnel and the frostbite, he would never use that arm again.

"The Eagles felt bad about what had happened and immediately offered him a position as a scout. It was bittersweet. Sad as he was, he jumped on it.

"We spent many years traveling around the country with a second lease on our marriage and his life. He kept the whole incident bottled up for many years, and it was only after about ten years or so that I managed to get a word out of him about it. I'm sure there are things he didn't tell me, and it doesn't matter to me."

She stopped here and took a deep breath.

Vincent was silent this whole time. He felt selfish for feeling the way he felt, for quitting the baseball team, for being alive.

Surely Grandpa Dean wouldn't be proud of his decision.

"Well Vincent, that's the whole story, as I know it. I suppose we need to get in there, get it over with." She exhaled and reached for the door. Both were very sweaty now baking in a four-wheeled metal oven under the hot Oklahoma sun. "But before you go in there, think about everything Grandpa Dean went through to give you the chance you've been given: the war, his lost dreams, and all the time he spent with you. You were always a very special boy. It's in your make-up. Grandpa Dean just helped bring it out of you. Now you get to choose how you honor him." Mrs. Dean walked into the funeral home and left Vincent behind to think. He followed a few minutes later.

Inside, Mrs. Dean was making small talk with some other ladies her age. They laughed and had a good time, as if they were at a party.

"We'll have to talk more afterward. It's so nice seeing you again!" She turned to Vincent who had just walked up and said, "Old friends. Thought I would never see them again." She turned and shook hands with the mortician.

Before anyone else accosted them, the mortician took her and Vincent to a privacy room on the side of the main room, with tilted slats in the wall like that of the blinds in a window.

Vincent had never been to a funeral and didn't know what to expect. Due to the angle of the slats, he could see the front where there was a pulpit, but could not see any of the seats that were now being filled with friends paying their respects, and they couldn't see Vincent or Mrs. Dean. To pass the time he read the program, wondering if he knew any of the names:

Pall Bearers: Brad Franks, Sonny Charleston, Bubba Banks, Jim Maynard, Tom Kuehn, and Dwane Niles

Eulogist: Sam Johnson

Prompted by the music leader, all rose and sang some song he had never heard before about peace somehow being like a river. Six elderly men pushed the coffin in on a cart. Each walked the same pace, each with a solemn look.

When they reached the front where Mrs. Dean and Vincent could see, the six men took a seat in the left-side front pew and the music stopped.

The minister followed the coffin and sat down in the front row on the other side.

A man rose from the audience and ambled up toward the podium. He wore a typical black suit that contrasted his white hair. He stood up at the podium and took out his reading glasses from one inside breast pocket, and a folded piece of paper from another. Looking up at the audience for the first time, he spoke in a low, patient voice. "I was asked to say a few words about Leonard Dean, and a few words is all I'm going to say, because Leonard was a man of few words himself, and I know he would frown on anybody tooting his horn. I just have a little story to tell about this one special man I used to know. Though I will probably stumble through it, it will have to suffice.

"As you may know, well you probably don't know, but I used to be up with the San Antonio Coyotes. I saw little playing time. But back in the post-war days, baseball was very important to national pride. Everybody wanted to forget about the terrible travesty to civilization over in Europe and the Pacific Theatre, me included. We know six million Jews died, and many, many men from many, many countries gave their lives to stop the threat of one madman. And no, it wasn't Leonard Dean who was the madman."

The audience politely laughed.

"Seriously, Leonard Dean was one of the men who answered the call when the nation was attacked at Pearl Harbor, and the President asked for the best. In Leonard Dean, he got the best.

"But Leonard had other plans he had to put on hold. He had to leave Elna back in the states to worry about him. He had to concentrate on the enemy instead of a blossoming baseball career. By the way, he had a heck of a fastball! He was going places with that arm. But in those terrible months when he was fighting the enemy, and in the very terrible months when his love, friends, everyone thought he was dead after his plane was shot down in Germany, he kept a dream alive that he would one day return to the states and play professional baseball.

"It was this dream that guided him out of Germany into occupied French territory, and eventually led him astray of German forces that sought to put an end to his dream. But unfortunately, as a bad joke, the arm that was to lead him to national greatness was wounded before he could make it out.

"Eventually he did make it out, but try as he might to rehabilitate it, he would never pitch a single ball in the big leagues, much less lift a fork with his right hand to eat his dinner. Yet most believe that it is this point where his life really began.

"Having known him while I was in the Coyotes organization before we were involved in the war, and having known him afterward, he should have been very bitter. Imagine, your only dream yanked away from you, never to be realized! This would ruin most people, but Leonard Dean definitely wasn't most people. Like the old saying, when life gives you lemons, make lemonade. It's a stupid, overused cliché I realize, but it holds true. Leonard Dean would not let his bitterness keep him down.

"This is when he spent the next third of his life working as a scout for the Eagles, finding talent wherever it lurked, helping other young men's dreams come true, men who were more fortunate than him. How humbling that experience must have been, especially when he knew he was better than most that he recruited!

"We met one day shortly after he accepted his consolation prize with the Eagles. I don't remember the year, as I am an old man. But that matters not.

"He decided to watch a game between us and, uh, well, I can't remember who we were playing.

"Anyway, I was getting down about my lack of playing time and about the inevitable truth that unless our starting first baseman broke a leg or something, I would be back in the Minors where I probably belonged anyway. I even tried pitching, but that wasn't my strong suit either.

"He came up to me and said, like he always did when he greeted me, 'Sammy, how's life treating you?'

"I didn't know what to say to the guy who had gotten a tough pill to swallow. I felt cheap not having defended my country the way he did.

"But as we talked about the weather, and the other stupid things two people talk about when they want to avoid a serious conversation, out of the blue he looked me straight in the face and said, 'Sammy, thank God every day for what you have, but don't ever be mad at Him for what you don't. There's a reason for everything. Besides, who are we to try to understand the will of God?'

"Now this came out of nowhere. No such topic had been breached. I was selfishly crying about my own little trivial problems, and this was a man who took a beating from the dark side of human nature and came right up off the mat swinging.

What I should have done was look him right back in the eye and thank him. What I did was chicken out and ask him about the prospect that brought him there.

"This was a man who was to spend his life in a capacity of serving others, helping others. I, on the other hand, couldn't see past my own nose and my own ambition. I regret chickening out to this day, but he knows I was listening. I should have known that I was more cut out for coaching baseball than I was for playing, but that's God's will.

"I found out that even after retirement, Leonard Dean was giving of himself. Apparently to the day of his death, he taught the great game that he knew to a local boy. From what I understand, their team is playing in the state tournament and could win it all tomorrow. We'll see."

Vincent was glad nobody could see him. He felt guilty about chickening out himself.

Mrs. Dean only looked forward.

The man with the white hair continued. "This is just one little story that is as insignificant to the world as Leonard Dean was to the masses of people who never got to know a great baseball player, a great coach of the game, and a great man.

"Well, when Elna called me and asked me to give the eulogy, I felt a little awkward. Why should I be given such an honor? But once again, I was thinking selfishly. After all this wasn't about me. This is about him, the man who never wanted credit in his whole life, the man who has no choice but to accept it now.

"Everyone here is a testament to the type of servant's life he lived. Everyone in this packed house could probably give a story that is similar to mine. That's because Leonard Dean earned it here on earth.

"He never gave up his faith in God, and to use his own words against him, 'There's a reason for everything.' There was a reason why God put Leonard Dean on this earth. And as each of us has our own memories of this wonderful guy, each of us knows that God's Will has been served, and now our brother can rest."

The old man stepped down from the podium and ambled back to his seat. Vincent sat through the rest of the funeral and didn't hear much of what the preacher said.

When it was over, Vincent got into the limousine with Mrs. Dean, who managed to keep her composure the whole time.

When the procession got to the cemetery, the coffin was taken out and placed over the burial site, and everyone braved the hot weather to try to get a standing spot under the tent canopy. The ground was muddy from the prior night's rain, and Vincent noticed many of the ladies had to take their high heels off to keep from sinking.

Prayers were given, friends passed by the coffin to console Mrs. Dean, and Vincent sat there next to her, uncomfortably.

When all had passed, the pall bearers came up to him. Each one took his turn to introduce himself to the phenom Mrs. Dean had told them about. Three of the pall bearers, Brad Franks, Sonny Charleston, and Bubba Banks were the result of Grandpa Dean's scouting efforts. Each had enjoyed a professional baseball career; each had their words of encouragement for Vincent.

The other three men, Jim Maynard, Tom Kuehn, and Duane Niles, spoke to Vincent about a time the four, counting Grandpa Dean, decided to take a trip up to Stonehenge while on furlough during the war and instead ended up in a Dublin bar a day later. This was the first time Vincent had smiled since Grandpa Dean had died.

Vincent listened to their stories with much interest as the mourners dispersed, one car at a time. He found that listening to these great men was easier than looking at the coffin and succumbing to tears.

The final person through the line was Sam Johnson himself. He gave Elna a big hug and consoled her. He turned to Vincent and shook his hand. "Sam Johnson. It's nice to meet you Vincent," the elderly gentleman said.

"Same here," Vincent whispered.

Elna said to the two, "Do you mind if I have a moment alone with my husband?"

"Go ahead," Sam said. "Vincent and I will just take a walk over to the fence and back."

Sam got up and Vincent obeyed. He felt like he was in a daze. The two walked for a time through the maze of tombstones before Sam said a word. "So Vincent, you know I talked to Leonard a few days before he died?"

"No sir, I didn't know that."

"Yes, it's true," Sam affirmed. We were friends, but mostly kept things on a professional level. He was always a man of few words, but by then it was from necessity. You know that. After all, you were taking care of him."

"Yes, sir," Vincent said softly.

Sam searched for his next word, and when the idea became audible, he continued, "Leonard was a servant until the day he died. You want to know what he said to me?"

Vincent's heart raced. "Yes, sir."

"He said, 'Sammy, listen carefully. I got a prospect for you. He's the real thing. I'll let Elna tell you about him.' That was all he said."

They reached the fence and looked past the road down the hill another mile away to where the Jack's Creek snaked its way across the grassy plains on an eventual meeting with the Eagle Chief River and eventually the Gulf of Mexico, many rivers along the way.

"I guess I should explain myself," Sam continued. "I think I alluded to the fact that I'm a coach in my eulogy. Well, that's true. I am the head coach at North Central Arizona State University. You've probably heard of us?"

Vincent perked up. "Sure! You guys were in the College World Series a few years back, weren't you?"

Sam chuckled. "Yeah, we make it every once in a while. Keeping a program competitive every year is difficult, especially when you're not in one of the big conferences. But we play against the toughest competition in the land, the California teams, certain teams from the deep South, all the Pacific coast teams, you name it. And we're always looking for young prospects."

Vincent stood there in disbelief. Arizona! It was a whole other state, and a long ways away from Augusta, Oklahoma. Heck, he had never been out of Oklahoma.

Sam continued, "Anyway, I understand you're in the middle of the state tournament right now."

"Yes sir." Vincent was sick that he quit the team.

"You're not playing today, obviously. This funeral's gotta be hard on you. You were close to him. But I heard on the radio that your team pulled out a close one earlier today, and they're about ready to play again."

"Yes, sir," Vincent managed to say, despite a frog in his throat.

"And if they win tonight, you play tomorrow?" Sam asked.

"Yes, sir."

Sam kicked a stone with his foot through the chain link fence and said, "Anyway, that's all I heard on the radio. The media always comes up with vicious rumors that turn the airways into a load of junk. I never had many good things to say about the media. Too many of them looking for a negative story. Any chance I'm going to see you pitch tomorrow? My plane back to Phoenix doesn't leave from Oklahoma City until Monday."

Vincent didn't know what to say. Should he plead Coach Grey for a chance to play again? Surely he would never let him play again. Vincent came out with the truth. "Well sir, I don't think I will be able to play tomorrow at all. I kinda quit yesterday."

Sam nodded and said, "Understandable. You're upset about Leonard. I'm sure your coach will understand. Are you going to talk to him?"

Vincent bit the bullet. "Yes, sir. I will talk to him, providing they win tonight."

"Provided," Sam replied, and paused. He watched a hawk making lazy circles in the sky. "Elna told me you were wanting to play baseball in college, but you garnered no interest from any local colleges. Is this true?"

Vincent nodded and said, "Yes, sir."

"You know Vincent, I don't know how many years I have left in this game. The game never changes, but the people do. I don't know if I'm getting too old to relate, or whether the kids today are too weak to work hard, but I want to be up front with you. I trust anything Leonard Dean says, and if he said you're the real deal, then you're the real deal. I will talk with you some more about this tomorrow after I watch you play, but just know that I don't take pansies. If you want to play for me, you will work your ever-livin' tail off. Are we clear?"

"Yes, sir," Vincent said with a smile.

"That is if you are interested in looking at our college," Sam said.

The two turned around. Mrs. Dean was on her way back to the Cadillac. "Well, you need to comfort Elna tonight, and be ready tomorrow," Sam said.

The two walked back as the cemetery workers lowered the coffin into the ground. From a distance, a friend, a student, and a wife said goodbye to a great man for the last time.

*

Vincent showed up in uniform an hour early. Butterflies circled his stomach, making him queasy. He walked the fence, admiring all the pennants along the Little Monster. They were quite impressive. He wondered if any of the players of the past championship teams had faced the trouble Vincent had faced, not only that summer, but in life. He bent down and grabbed a blade of grass and put it to his nose. He loved the smell of the outfield in the summer, and the solitude it now provided him. He let it flutter in the wind, which had been gusting out of the south all day. He squinted up at the sky and saw no threatening clouds.

The thunderstorm the other day was a freak occurrence for August in Oklahoma, and the games played the day before on the muddy infield tore it up. Field crews took four hours in the early afternoon preparing the infield to make it look as pristine as a professional park. The infield grass was even green from the rain, which was refreshing.

Vincent had spent the prior evening eating all sorts of baked goods that ladies across town and beyond had delivered to Mrs. Dean's house.

The house didn't feel so empty with vases of flowers and tin-foiled pans of food lying around everywhere. The house just felt... strange. It was strange staying in the house, but he knew Mrs. Dean needed someone to keep her company.

Despite her appearance, he knew her well enough now to know she was not well. They had listened to the Augusta-Ada game together to pass the time and keep their minds off other pressing issues.

Thankfully, the wind helped Fred Fingers pitch a complete game shutout of the team that had fed them their dinner a few nights prior.

Jimmy was also sensational, meaning the bald guy must not have had any money on that game.

Despite this, Vincent concluded there had to be money on tonight's games. He knew he would have to be at his best to off-set any plans that monster might have.

As he stretched his legs into a jog, the players came in one-by-one.

Coach Grey still had not shown up, and the butterflies increased in Vincent's stomach. He walked by Jimmy who sneered at him as the other players started loosening up their arms. Each player greeted him with warmth, except Jimmy.

Jimmy looked worse than he had ever looked in his life, and Vincent took note: uniform untucked, eyes blood-shot, hair a mess.

Jimmy didn't seem to have any earthly idea that there were other people on the earth at that moment. He appeared to be in his own little mood, and Vincent figured Jimmy was so high, he probably couldn't do his math times tables.

Coach Redenbacher gave Vincent a big bear hug and told him how happy he was to see him.

Vincent looked up and saw that the stands were filling up, and anyone coming remotely close to game time would probably end up standing.

Finally Coach Grey descended the steps to the dugout to a round of applause from the faithful. He raised his hand to accept the applause, but when he saw Vincent, he froze. The look on his face was not pleasure, but Vincent approached anyway.

*

Dan "Deuce" Davison put up the "CLOSED" sign in the Davison Motor's front window and walked to the back door to lock up. He grabbed a small wooden bat. It was time to do something about Vincent since Coach Grey didn't seem to be pulling his weight with the kid. Deuce had a distinct feeling that Vincent was too stupid to stay away. He decided that if Vincent dared set foot on that field, he would be taken to the salvage yard. There was just too much money staked on tonight's games. He never saw Police Sgt. Masterson's cruiser pull onto the dirt drive, along with the sheriff and his deputy, following close behind.

Deuce locked the door and went back to the showroom. He dropped the bat when he looked out the window. His first thought was to run, but his cool-headedness took control of him. The cops had nothing on him, did they? Deuce turned around with a big smile. His goods were hidden well, and he was just a local business owner closing up for the night.

Ten minutes later officers were tearing through his salvage yard and Dan "Deuce" Davison was cuffed and in the back of the cruiser.

The Drug Enforcement Agency brought the drug dogs who hit on car after car, in plain view of Deuce, before the speeder took him away. He took one last look back and started to cry.

*

Sam Johnson rang the doorbell and received a smile from Mrs. Dean when she opened the door for him. He entered and the first things that caught his eye were the pictures.

"You're over there," she said and pointed to a picture on one of the end tables of Grandpa Dean and a young Sam Johnson in a Coyotes' uniform, both leaning over a rail.

Sam smiled and said, "It's hard to believe we were ever that young."

"You're only as young as you feel, Sam," Mrs. Dean said.

He laughed. "Yeah, if that were true, I'd be dead. But it's amazing to think that I could play a double header in the July heat of the midday sun and not be sore the next day."

"Boys will be boys," Mrs. Dean said. "Would you like a drink?"

"No thank you. We need to be going."

Mrs. Dean nodded. "I just need to lock up." Mrs. Dean walked to the back porch, and Sam popped the question that had been on his mind all along.

"Elna, did you make the phone call?"

She came back into the house and smiled. She looked at him and said, "I'm sorry, did you say something?"

"Yeah, I asked if you made that call to the cops."

Mrs. Dean smiled. "I called a friend, a former student. It should be taken care of."

Sam chuckled. "Small-town thug. Will it make a difference?"

Mrs. Dean shrugged and said, "Well, I guess we'll find out. Should make for a heck of a show. Shall we?"

Sam offered his arm, and the two left for the game.

*

Vincent approached a visibly upset Coach Grey and spoke with ease. "Coach, I've had a change of heart. If you will have me back, I would like to play tonight, help the team out."

Coach Grey smiled really big and then hid it. "Son, I don't understand. Two days ago you wanted no part of this team. Now you want to play again? These young men around you worked their tails off yesterday to make it to the championship. What makes you think you're better than everyone else?"

Vincent looked toward the ground, then back up, determined not to lose to the guy. "Because any coach worth the price of his uniform would excuse a player for a funeral. That's why." Vincent wasn't sorry for saying it. It made him feel good. It was the first time he had let his real thoughts surface. It made him feel like a real man to stand up to the guy for the first time.

Coach's demeanor changed. "You talkin' back to me, boy?"

Vincent held his ground. "No, I'm not. I just want to play. I think I've proven myself this summer."

The other players stopped what they were doing to watch the power struggle.

Jimmy stood up and grabbed Vincent by the shirt and backed him up.

"Why don't you get your skinny little butt out of here? We don't need you!" Jimmy yelled and flung Vincent onto the infield with power Vincent never knew Jimmy had.

Vincent jumped back up and the fury he had been bottling up for so long surfaced. With the Coach haggling him, Jimmy being a jerk to him, trying to fit in with the team, Grandpa Dean dying, and his terrible childhood; steam was boiling out his ears. He took a step toward Jimmy, ready to pulverize him, but before he could do anything, Bacon Bob grabbed Jimmy from behind and got in his face.

"Buddy, that's a member of our team, whether you like it or not. Check your ego at the door! This is the State Championship!"

Everyone stared at Bacon Bob who appeared serious. Vincent looked into Bacon Bob's eyes and knew Bob was ready to fight for him.

Coach Grey stepped forward and got between Bacon Bob and Jimmy, who had his arm cocked back, ready to throw a punch at his old best friend now.

"I don't care what anybody on this team has to say! Vincent is no longer a part of this team. Case closed."

Lost in the mix was Vincent who was ready to throw a punch. Then another voice came forward.

"If Vincent isn't a part of this team, then I guess I'm not either." Vincent turned to see the words come out of Dusty Redenbacher's mouth. He took off his hat and dropped it at his feet, staring at Coach Grey.

Then Quentin followed suit. "The same goes for me, Coach."

Coach Grey's eyes bulged. "You boys better pick up those hats and start acting like seniors! This is the State Championship, for cryin' out loud!"

Bacon Bob let go of Jimmy and unstrapped his shin guards. "We need Vincent, Coach."

Coach Grey turned to Coach Redenbacher. "You going to say something?"

Coach Redenbacher looked back at his boss and said, "You never wanted my help before. You're not getting it now." Coach Redenbacher stepped back and folded his arms.

"In all my years! I've never!" Coach Grey searched for the right words to say, but nothing came out.

Vincent looked closely at Coach Grey and noticed his eyes were red.

Each player took off his hat and let it fall to the ground.

Vincent noticed now that the crowd was dead silent.

He smiled.

Jimmy stood by his father in a show of command, but it didn't work. The spell he had cast over Vincent, and now his teammates was broken forever. The superstar and his father stood alone in a sea of antipathy.

Then another voice came from above the dugout, a foreign voice to the regular dugout chatter.

"Coach Grey, Jimmy Grey, stand where you are. You're both under arrest!" Vincent looked past the fence that separated the dugout from the stands and saw two cops.

*

"Well I don't know what's going on ladies and gentlemen, but it appears that four cops have gone down into the Augusta dugout. What do you think Sol? Are they wishing them good luck?"

"That'd be my guess, but that still doesn't explain why Vincent is here in the first place, much less came flying out of the dugout and landing face-first in the dirt like he did. I would hate to speak so negatively, to say that the team was having a fight."

"Hopefully Coach Grey was wrong about him. Maybe he is playing tonight."

"Ladies and gentlemen, I'm not believing my eyes. Joel, do you see what I see?"

"Holy Cow! I think we're seeing the same thing! Ladies and gentlemen, we're five minutes away from the state championship game, and we're watching four cops escort Coach Grey and his son, Jimmy, out of the dugout in handcuffs! What on earth is going on here?"

"I'm speechless. Folks, we're gonna take a station break and see if we can sort out this mess. You're listening to Augusta Stampeding Herd Baseball."

*

Mrs. Dean and Sam Johnson arrived just in time to see father and son being stuffed into the back of the paddy wagon. It was a sight that made her smile in a time when smiles were at a premium. And it was all the better, knowing she had a hand in it all.

When they got to the stands, she saw that the only open seats were her reserved spot in the upper right-hand corner where she had watched many of Vincent's games without his knowledge.

As the two found their seats, Sam leaned over and said, "There's nothing like a summer's evening of baseball."

Mrs. Dean smiled.

*

Coach Redenbacher spoke up. "Okay guys, I don't know what that was all about, and quite frankly, I don't want to know. All I know is that if you are willing to play for me, I am willing to help us win a state championship tonight. Any objections?"

"No, sir," the team said in unison. Coach Redenbacher smiled. He said, "New game plan. Ned, you're still pitching game one. Fuzzy, you're in left field. Vincent, take over center, please? We'll save your arm for game two. I think I'll put you in Jimmy's spot in the batting order. You guys ready?"

"YEAH!" The team said in unison.

"Then take the field. Let's win ourselves a championship!

*

The local law enforcement, ten of them at this point, were standing around shooting the bull about what was being pulled out of the little nooks and crannies of the junk cars.

In Sgt. Masterson's hands were two bricks of marijuana

The DEA and their drug dogs continued their search in what would take a whole week before everything was found.

*

Vincent sprinted to center field, his mind relieved to not have Coach Grey and Jimmy affecting the team with their negativity. It bothered Vincent that Jimmy was carted off in hand cuffs and despite all the bad things that Jimmy Grey had done to Vincent, he didn't wish him any ill will. On the way to the outfield, Vincent hailed a silent prayer for Jimmy, then set his mind to doing his job.

Ned fired the ball as hard as he could from the mound. The infielders turned double plays and made sure grabs and throws to first when needed. The outfield was also tested by the timely Seiling bats, and Vincent found a love for center field and all the territory for which he was responsible.

Vincent went four-for-four in the game, blasting another shot into Carroll Street. The rest of the Augusta bats followed Vincent's lead in route to an easy 9 to 0 shutout in game one.

The P.A. announcer broadcasted that the starting pitchers for game two were Seiling's Lew Lassiter, who had beaten them earlier in the year, and Vincent Preston for Augusta. This was an all-star match-up, a winner-takes-all that would be talked about for years.

Chapter 14

Vincent looked up at the sky. Thin rays cascaded through the early evening cirrus clouds that painted the horizon, emitting pale hues. Pastels of yellow and pink and lavender led Vincent to thoughts of Easter and the ascension, and new life for an Augusta team he figured many would have given up for dead somewhere back in the loser's bracket.

With a loud clank, the lights came on in preparation of oncoming darkness.

As Vincent warmed up, he watched television crews from Oklahoma City set up on the hill on the first-base side to capture moments for the ten o'clock broadcast. He thought it would only add pressure, but he felt reassured by the spotlight and knew he was going to shine.

As Vincent threw in the bullpen, he left nothing to chance. He did not hide his pitches, and he would not try to be secretive. Both he and Bacon Bob agreed on this point. He knew Seiling was privy to his strengths, and it would just have to be a grudge match between two sworn enemies.

The starting lineups were read by the P.A. announcer, and at 8:55 the two teams assembled on their respective baselines and saluted the flag beyond the center field fence for the singing of the national anthem.

Before a single note of the national anthem was sung, the P.A. announcer told the audience, "Ladies and gentlemen, before the singing of the national anthem we would like to honor an Augusta great who passed away recently, Coach Leonard Dean, World War II veteran and former scout for the Oklahoma City Eagles organization. He will be missed. And now please rise and remove your caps for the singing of the national anthem and a following moment of silence."

Vincent stood there staring at the flag as the emotions grabbed him once again. Tears streamed from his cheeks as he visualized a scared man running through the occupied French Territory and evading the Germans, of a young man strapping his bad arm to a rafter in an attempt to strengthen it, of his mentor helping him learn the game from his backyard mound, and of the last words he spoke to Vincent,

It's okay son. I'll be listening tonight.

Then Vincent remembered the last piece of paper Grandpa Dean had given to him. Vincent hadn't looked at it yet. What was on it? Where had he put it?

The national anthem neared its end, and Vincent knew he had to look at that paper before he could fire a single pitch. Then he remembered his bat bag. He had put it in the side pouch.

"...and the home of the brave!"

Vincent remained standing for a moment of silence in Grandpa Dean's honor. He sent up a silent prayer and then scurried back to the dugout and quickly unzipped the side pouch of his bat bag. Sure enough, it was still in there, a white folded piece of paper. He unfolded it and read,

John 11:25.

Vincent opened his bat bag and grabbed the Bible Quentin had loaned him. Vincent took it with him everywhere he went.

He flipped to the page and read the verse to himself.

"Jesus said unto he, I am the resurrection, and the life: he that believeth in me, though he were dead, yet shall he live."

"Vincent, you're in the hole," Coach Redenbacher said as he stood over him. Vincent remembered that he was now batting in the number three spot, Jimmy's spot.

Vincent slowly closed the cover of the Bible and smiled.

Even on his death bed, Vincent knew Grandpa Dean was looking out for him, letting him know that all was well with his soul.

Vincent knew Grandpa Dean wasn't scared and was now in a better place. It made Vincent feel loved, a love he had learned to accept for the first time in his life. Grandpa Dean was to be a model for Vincent the rest of his life. "I'm gonna win this for you," Vincent whispered as he stood up and nodded at his new head coach.

Vincent hit the ball hard, but the line drive was snagged by Seiling's third baseman. After going three up, three down, Vincent and the Augusta players took the field.

Vincent took the mound. The lights, the TV crews, the crowd, every distraction that could cripple a pitching performance were in the deep recesses of his mind.

Vincent found his concentration. He controlled his breathing. He had pitched a near-perfect game against this team in his first start of the year and still managed to lose, the only loss on his record. It was now time to avenge that loss, and he was feeling good.

Tag McNugert, the first Seiling batter, came up to the plate.

Vincent didn't worry about pitching to trends. He wanted straight heat, and Bacon Bob was gracious enough to accommodate. Vincent went into his windup.

Lightning!

Thunder!

"STRIKE ONE!" the umpire called.

The ball crossed at Tag's knees and Bacon Bob heaved it back.

Vincent didn't bother to look to the scoreboard for his pitch speed, but he knew that everyone else had because an excited buzz ran around the stadium.

Vincent knew he had the advantage. Sixty feet, six-inches. That was a close distance not to see a ball. Add the myopia of the night to his heater and he knew he was going to be practically unhittable, as long as he kept his head.

Vincent again started his windup. As far as he was concerned, there was nobody in the batter's box. The first time he threw his fastball for Grandpa Dean, with the old man crowding the plate, Vincent was afraid to plunk him, but he had learned his lesson well enough. He didn't care who was in the box. His concentration was on the thread that still dangled from Bacon Bob's mitt, and that thread was located on the inside portion of the plate.

Vincent received the sign from his catcher. *Two seam.*

Lightning!

Thunder!

This time Tag bailed out of the box. The ball seemed to have a target on his hips, only to slide into the strike zone.

"STRIKE TWO!" the umpire called.

This time Vincent turned around and read 97 MPH on the scoreboard. He tried to ignore it so that his head didn't get too big.

Indeed, Vincent was dialed in, and he knew there wasn't much the opposing players were going to be able to do about it.

Tag stepped back into the box, this time determined to swing no matter what.

Bacon Bob gave his sign and Vincent delivered a sinker in the dirt. Tag swung so hard that he fell over on top of the plate. Bacon

Bob blocked the ball out in front of him when it skipped off the dirt. He picked it up and tagged out the batter.

The umpire, right on top of the play, yelled, "STRIKE THREE! BATTER'S OUT!"

Vincent looked up at the crowd, which was going wild, then over to Seiling's head coach, who was scribbling something down on a notepad.

Vincent refocused and then settled in on the rubber to take the next sign.

Steven West was next up to bat. He was the only one to really get much of a bat on Vincent's pitching the first game, but once again Vincent wasn't concentrating on the player. He just wanted to strike him out.

Bacon Bob called for a fastball on the inside corner, and Vincent delivered.

The umpire called out, "STRIKE ONE!"

Vincent preferred to get ahead on the count and wanted to throw a strike on every first pitch, but he knew he had to be careful. He reminded himself that if he got into a rut like that, the Seiling batters would have no problem figuring out all they had to do was swing on the first pitch. Sooner or later they would connect. Grandpa Dean once told Vincent, "The harder you throw it, the farther the ball will go." It was time to use his head and throw a change-up.

After shaking off Bacon Bob three times, they finally got their signals right, and Vincent delivered. Steven let this pitch go by, and it seemed to take forever to get to the plate. The ball crossed the outside part of the plate.

The umpire called out, "STRIKE TWO!"

Vincent turned around: 82 MPH.

He turned back toward the batter and watched him step out of the box and shake his head. Vincent knew that last pitch was going to be the only hittable ball he was going to throw this at-bat, and he figured he had the batter totally baffled at this point.

The batter repositioned himself and stared at Vincent, but Vincent only stared back expressionlessly.

Vincent knew the batter was looking for him to tip his hand, and that wasn't going to happen. Part of Vincent's invincibility was in hiding his poker hand.

Vincent directed his stare at Bacon Bob and waited there motionlessly, waiting for the batter to finish this silly little mind game which obviously wasn't going to work on Vincent. When the batter finally stepped back into the box, Vincent delivered a sinker that the batter easily swung over, just like the batter before him.

"STRIKE THREE!" the umpire called.

Bacon Bob started the ball around the horn and Vincent took off his cap to wipe the sweat from his forehead. He read his old reliable verse and refocused.

Shawn Parker stepped to the plate. This puzzled Vincent. For some reason, Coach Creek decided to switch Parker and Jas Foster in the three and four holes in the lineup for the final game.

It seemed to Vincent that his catcher must be questioning it also, because it took Bob a little extra time to come up with a sign. When he finally gave Vincent the sign, Vincent delivered a change-up that hit the inside corner.

The monstrous batter began to swing, but then held up.

The umpire called out, "STRIKE ONE!"

Vincent turned to check out his speed: 78 MPH. He was starting to enjoy knowing just how fast he threw the ball. He turned around and looked at Bob who appeared to be smiling. Knowing that he had only thrown one change up to each hitter, Vincent figured Bob wouldn't be expecting another one, so Vincent waited for the right sign, then delivered another one in exactly the same spot as the last one.

Shawn watched it go right into Bob's mitt.

"STRIKE TWO!" the umpire called out.

Vincent turned around and saw: 79 MPH.

"Dang it!" Parker said loud enough for Vincent to hear, which prompted him to put his glove over his face to conceal a smile.

As Vincent resettled, he knew he couldn't get away with another change up, or Parker might park one across the street. Both he and Bob agreed on the pitch, and Vincent unleashed a heater with a mighty grunt.

Vincent thought, *Lightning, Thunder!* And the ball cooperated. The batter was much too slow to catch up to the pitch.

"STRIKE THREE!" the umpire yelled. "HUSTLE IN, HUSTLE OUT!"

Vincent took off his glove and walked toward the dugout, the Augusta fans all on their feet cheering him. Again Vincent put his glove up to his face to obscure his smile.

*

Jimmy came out of the interrogation room with tears streaming down his face. He tried to hide them, but the local inhabitants laughed at him as the sheriff escorted him to his jail cell. He just couldn't believe this was happening. Hours before he was about to play in a game that meant nothing to him.

Now the door slid shut, the lock activated, and a deadly silence prevailed.

Jimmy would have given anything to be out there with the guys he used to call friends, receiving a standing ovation from the crowd as he made a diving catch, or knocked the skin off the ball, but life was no longer a game. It was real.

Jimmy had no idea what he was in for. He knew one thing for certain. As soon as Coach Milford at UNCO found out about this, he could kiss his scholarship goodbye.

The Feds had leaned on him, and he tried to mimic people on television, saying he wouldn't talk without his lawyer, but they weren't stupid. They knew he was just a scared little kid in a baseball uniform.

Disregarding his request, they threatened to put him in the same cell with a convicted murderer.

In the end, the Feds didn't need to. They leaned harder, threatened harsher penalties, and gave him the clincher: Deuce had already ratted him out when they bagged him earlier in the afternoon.

Plus, they let him know exactly what Deuce had said about his father.

With the cameras rolling, Jimmy could feel his jaw drop. He had no idea his father was in on anything illegal.

They asked him if he and his dad sold the stuff together, and he didn't lie. They asked him all sorts of questions about Deuce, and he sang like a nightingale with a setting sun.

Jimmy hoped for leniency. Now, as he sat there on the cold steel bench of his jail cell, it all came crashing home. He was in big trouble, and so was his dad. With lewd comments coming from his new neighbors, he wept like a little kid.

Then Jimmy overheard some of the officers from the other room talk about how they hadn't even talked to Deuce yet, and how the kid had ratted not only Deuce, but himself out. Overhearing this only made him cry harder.

Drifting from the front room was the sound of the radio, announcing the game he so wished he was a part of. His old teammates were still in the first game.

He heard, "...center fielder, Vincent Preston."

Jimmy's sorrow that followed was indescribable, wondering how a kid like Vincent Preston managed to beat him in the end.

*

With two dominant pitching performances, the game flew by without so much as a single run, and by the top of the seventh inning, the score was still tied 0-0.

Vincent watched Seiling's pitcher, Lew Lassiter be his usual dominating self, mixing an array of pitches to induce bad swings, pop-ups, and ground-outs. Vincent had lined out to the third baseman in both of his at-bats.

A few other players hit the ball hard. Despite Augusta's offensive prowess, Lew Lassiter had pitched a perfect game through seven innings. Not a single Stampeding Herd batter had reached base.

Normally this would be considered a great feat, but it was the other pitcher that was upstaging him, getting the consideration of the oohs and aahs. Vincent not only was pitching a perfect game like Lew was, but he had *struck out* every Seiling batter going into the last inning.

It took four innings before a Seiling batter was to even hit a foul ball.

Vincent had only gone to a full count on one batter and had kept his pitch count low. He was on his eighty-third pitch and the arm had only begun to feel tired the inning before. He maxed out at ninety-seven miles-per-hour in the first inning and had been slipping into the lower nineties. Despite this, Coach Redenbacher told Vincent that the game was his to win or lose.

In the top half of the seventh, Vincent ended the inning with yet his third line drive out to the third baseman. Three good looks. Three hard hits. Three good defensive plays. It was a tough break for Augusta and kept them on the defensive.

Vincent had to hold Seiling scoreless to force extra innings. He knew that if Seiling was going to score, this was going to be their best bet.

The top of Seiling's lineup was coming up. All Seiling batters had two previous plate appearances against Vincent tonight.

Vincent began to lose confidence with his slipping velocity. Sure, he had been mixing up his pitches and kept the Seiling batters off their feet, but his time was drawing to a close, and he knew it. Plus, this is where he had faltered against them the last time they played. Though it was only three outs, escaping this inning was a huge mountain for Vincent to climb. He would really have to concentrate, reach back and find his hidden strength.

Vincent took the mound, his fans cheering him on wildly. He took off his hat to wipe the sweat from his forehead and read his verse once again. He saw Grandpa Dean's face and could still hear his words of wisdom.

Concentration!
Balance!
Positive Attitude!
Lightning!
Thunder!

These were some that stuck out in Vincent's mind. He wondered which one was the key. Was there an answer for his aching shoulder? Could he increase the speed of his pitches? What if he threw as hard as he could and saved nothing for extra innings?

Then Vincent realized the answer. It was attitude. He had to clean up his attitude. If he had doubts, his play would reciprocate. He had to know he was going to beat them to get the job done. He knew that the confidence to know one's going to get the job done could be either the easiest thing to possess, or the hardest. The problem was knowing how to control it. Was it God? The devil? Was confidence ever spiritually related? He decided that it had to be. Of what could God not be in control?

He saw Tag McNugert in the batter's box, awaiting his first pitch. It was the top of the order again.

He thought, *Okay. Positive Thinking! I'm going to throw this pitch ninety-seven miles-per-hour. Concentrate!*

Bacon Bob gave him the fastball sign.

Vincent thought, *Lightning!*

He went into his windup, oblivious to the frantic fans, the honking horns, and all other distractions.

When the ball slapped leather, he heard, *Thunder!*

The umpire called, "STRIKE ONE!"

Vincent caught the ball from Bacon Bob and turned around to the scoreboard. He was amazed.

97 MPH

Okay! It worked! he thought, amazed.

The Augusta crowd came to its feet. Those listening at home could barely understand the radio, for the noise. Vincent turned back around to his catcher and bore down again.

Now I'm going to throw ninety-eight! he thought.

He went into his windup and released the ball with a louder grunt.

The umpire called out, "STRIKE TWO!"

Vincent turned around to see what he had hoped to see on the score board.

98 MPH

Vincent stepped up to the rubber again and took a deep breath.

He thought, *Okay, how about ninety-nine?*

Tag never had a chance. Swing as he did, he was under the ball by a foot and way behind it.

The umpire called out, "STRIKE THREE!"

Vincent turned around and saw 99 MPH on the scoreboard as his infielders threw the ball around the horn.

Vincent was on one heck of an adrenaline rush now. He was more mechanical than flesh and blood. Nineteen batters retired, he set his sights on number twenty.

After three fastballs, Steven West went down swinging for the stars. The scoreboard rang up one number each time:

99 MPH

99 MPH

99 MPH

With each pitch, Vincent gained confidence and focus. He was only vaguely aware that he had a shoulder, much less that it ached for ice.

Twenty batters down, one to go. Out of the batter's circle came the barrel-chested Shawn Parker.

Immediately it dawned on Vincent just why Seiling's coach moved Parker up in the lineup. It was just for this situation. Vincent figured the coach knew hits would be hard to come by and wanted to make sure Shawn got three looks.

This thought crossed Vincent's mind quickly, then exited his brain as fast as it showed up. Vincent was throwing laser beams. Nobody would be able to hit ninety-nine.

Vincent, who was in a groove, shook Bacon Bob off when he called for a sinker. Vincent couldn't understand what his catcher was thinking, calling for a sinker? Vincent wasn't going to throw a sinker when he was hurling smart bombs.

Bacon Bob looked upset, but then gave the sign for a fastball.

Vincent smiled and went after Parker.

Vincent grunted and thought:

Lightning!

Thunder!

The ball passed Parker at the waist, and he didn't even lift the bat off his shoulder.

"STRIKE ONE!" called the umpire.

Vincent turned around and saw 99 MPH on the scoreboard.

He turned back around and stood on top of the rubber to receive his sign. When Bob asked for another sinker, Vincent began to get mad.

Vincent thought, *Bob! What are you thinking?!?*

Vincent shook off his catcher again and got the sign he wanted.

Lightning!

Thunder!

The umpire called, "STRIKE TWO!"

Vincent caught the ball back from Bacon Bob and turned around to see 99 MPH on the scoreboard.

For the second pitch in a row, Parker made no effort to lift the bat off his shoulder.

Again, Vincent noticed, but gave it no thought. He did give thought to his catcher though.

Bacon Bob waited a moment or two to give Vincent the sign for the next pitch, then got up and headed for the mound.

Vincent, seeing this, motioned for him to go back. He didn't know what Bob could be thinking, wanting to have a conference when Vincent was in the zone like this. Vincent only wanted to throw another pitch. He could feel the blood concentrating in his arm and knew the adrenaline rush wouldn't last.

Vincent focused his energy into his concentration. He watched as Bob called for a slider. Vincent shook off his catcher and waited for another sign.

This time when Bob called for a change up, Vincent growled. He wanted to throw the heat and couldn't understand why his catcher was playing games.

Finally Vincent received the sign he wanted. He smiled, nodded and concentrated again. He couldn't hear the crowd, traffic from the street, or anything for that matter, the beating of his own heart in his ears. A meteor could have crashed in center field and Vincent would have ignored it.

Instead Vincent's thoughts drifted to his life. He considered all the memories of being an outsider, getting laughed at by his teammates, his father's beatings, and of an old man and woman picking him off the scrap pile and showing him that life was worth living. He heard his dead mentor's words screaming in his ears with his heartbeat in the background. These words coursed through his veins.

Strength through Christ.
Think positive.

Faith.

I'll be listening tonight.

Strength through Christ.

Strength through Christ.

Strength through Christ.

At that moment Vincent felt the world stop turning in order to allow this seemingly inconsequential event happen, an event that would possibly change Vincent's life forever.

He gripped the ball as hard as he could and stared at the thread hanging off Bacon Bob's mitt. Vincent knew he was going to blow this batter away. He went into his windup one last time, and with the utmost effort, grunted as he came home with the ball.

He heard, *Lightning!*

But it was a different kind of thunder that followed.

CRANK!

A voice entered Vincent's head a moment after the pitch. It was Grandpa Dean's again.

Remember, the harder you throw it, the farther the home run will go!

For the first time that night, Vincent's thoughts went mute.

He didn't turn to watch the ball at first. He knew where it was going. Vincent crouched down and put his head between his knees as the ball soared high into the dark summer sky.

Sound returned to Vincent's ears as he heard mixed results in the stands. Some cheered, and some yelled, "NO!"

As Vincent turned around, he watched the ball bounce off the roof of the house across the street and disappear into the back yard.

The player who was famous for towering home runs proved his valor one more time in the toughest of circumstances.

Vincent turned and saw Bacon Bob standing there in disbelief.

Vincent watched as Shawn Parker slowly jogged around the bases with his right hand in the air, his index finger pointed to the sky in a show of dominance. The hero strutted the last few steps, squeezing out every moment of pleasure he could, and stomped on home plate with his foot.

The Seiling fans erupted onto the field to join in the celebration at home plate, Vincent still on the mound watching the whole show. Last year Augusta had spoiled Seiling's home field advantage in the state tournament.

Vincent knew that turnabout was fair game.

He was but a young pup in the game and had a lot to learn. He knew he made a mistake. He shook off his catcher, which made it easy for Parker to read his mind. He threw too many pitches in the same spot with the same speed, never changing it up. Worst of all, he felt invincible. He now knew he wasn't.

Vincent turned around to see his consolation prize on the scoreboard:

100 MPH

Chapter 15

Vincent watched the rest of the show from the dugout, his fellow teammates patting him on the back as they filed past him, as if in a funeral procession.

Seiling's team posed for pictures on the mound with their championship trophy, then got their pictures under the scoreboard, the score still reading 1-0 and the dubious 100 MPH reminding Vincent of the unpredictability of life.

Parker made a second victory lap around the bases and made sure to stop and celebrate in front of the Augusta dugout with the trophy.

In the next few days Vincent overheard some Augusta fans comment that it would have been different if Jimmy was playing, that the team just wasn't as good without him. Vincent knew they may have been right. But as the story came out about the betting scandal in the weeks following, he figured most wouldn't believe a word of it. Not their golden boy and the hometown coach.

Mrs. Dean consoled Vincent afterwards. She mentioned to him that some prayers, no matter how sincere they are, or how hard a person prays for them, will be answered in a manner not understood. Some efforts, no matter how great a person tries, will not be rewarded. Such is life. Scientists can predict a solar eclipse with certainty as to the exact second the moon will cover the sun, and everybody knows that same sun will always rise in the east and set in the west. Death and taxes. Murphy's Law. What goes up must come down... including baseballs.

Mrs. Dean told Vincent that these are truths that can't be debated, that it doesn't make much sense to dissect happenstance and come up with truths. It will only lead to frustration.

For a fleeting moment, Vincent felt sorry for himself. He knew Augusta deserved to win, that he deserved to be the hero, but then another thought took over, that his story was still being written. Vincent's apex was yet to come. Right then and there he decided that despite what conventional wisdom might suggest, this one pitch would not define his career.

Mrs. Dean was also the one to let him know that there was plenty of baseball left in his future.

Coach Johnson had to leave directly after the game, but he had left with Mrs. Dean a full-ride scholarship for Vincent to sign. All of Vincent's college was going to be paid for!

Vincent had only a few weeks before he was to leave, but he wasn't going to go without telling Mrs. Dean goodbye. Before he left, he made sure the grass was cut and the structures were edged.

*

A few days before he and his friends were to part ways and go to their respected colleges for orientation, Coach Redenbacher called the players and families together for a cookout in the park. In the past this was an event that all media moguls were invited to for publicity, but Vincent knew that under Coach Redenbacher's watch, a lot of things were going to change.

It was a time not to look down in sorrow at their second place finish, but to rejoice in all the success that the season brought.

Since Vincent knew his parents would be too busy to attend, he invited Mrs. Dean, who was honored.

Coach Grey and son were noticeably absent, but this didn't keep Vincent and the players and families from enjoying their time together, one last time.

Instead of a long-winded speech from the coach about the importance of the off-season, Coach Redenbacher instead chose to let each senior stand and let the rest of the team know what his plans were for the next year, and to part by sharing some wisdom. The standard advice was given:

"Stay away from parties."

"It goes by real fast, so enjoy it."

"Stay in shape in the off-season."

"Enjoy the game, because it's a great game."

The small crowd cheered as each player spoke his peace.

When it was Vincent's turn to speak, this normally quiet boy-turned-man stood and addressed those who he could call his friends. He had everyone's attention when he spoke. "I'm certainly not the best person to be asking advice from, but if I could say anything, it would be this," and he looked up for a moment to stave off the tears.

Nobody spoke as he composed himself.

Vincent found the words, or it seemed to him afterwards that the words were found for him. "Through Christ, all things are possible. If you don't have a mentor already, find one. Find somebody who can teach you what is truly important in life. We like to think we know it all, but we don't. Sometimes we let things like a negative attitude, or even arrogance get in the way of our full potential. But with a mentor to guide you along the way, do what you can to make that person proud, to live your life not just to win, but to do what's truly right."

Vincent received a standing ovation which didn't quiet down until Bacon Bob and Dusty addressed the crowd.

Bacon Bob held a plaque in his hands, smiling big.

"Attention everyone," Dusty said and achieved their attention only after Bacon Bob stuck his fingers in his mouth and whistled. Dusty continued, "We would like to present the team MVP plaque now." A few cow bells came out, but quickly died down. Vincent held his attention on Coach Redenbacher's son.

Dusty continued, "This person is someone who has overcome a lot of obstacles to not only get where he's at, but to get where he's going. Nobody gave him a fair chance, myself included. But when he got the chance to prove himself, he was the best player to ever wear the Augusta uniform. He's someone I will always look up to as a hero, and someone I will try to model myself after."

Dusty's dad stood to the side, a proud man.

Dusty concluded, "The team voted and it was unanimous. The Augusta Stampeding Herd MVP is Vincent Preston!"

Everyone stood and applauded. Vincent, red from embarrassment, came up to the front to accept the MVP award.

The players, one-by-one, shook his hand and congratulated him. Bacon Bob gave him the plaque and then gave him a big bear hug which made the crowd laugh. It was a moment Vincent would remember for the rest of his life.

*

The day Vincent left on a bus for Arizona, Mrs. Dean made him one last greasy breakfast with coffee, something he knew he would miss.

Vincent didn't know what people from Arizona ate for breakfast. In fact he didn't know what to expect at all in a world so far away from what he knew. He also didn't know quite what to say to the only woman to ever give him a chance, so he started by thanking her.

On the front porch as the August sun blazed overhead and the grasshoppers flew around, finishing off what green was left for them by an arid summer, Vincent said, "Mrs. Dean, I don't know how I'll ever be able to repay you."

Mrs. Dean smiled and said, "Make good grades in college. Have you decided on a major yet?"

"Yes I have," Vincent replied. "I've decided since I can speak the language, I might as well major in English."

"That's my boy," Mrs. Dean smiled. "But I have two more requests of you."

"Yes, Mrs. Dean?"

"You are no longer my student, so call me Elna now."

Vincent nodded. "And the second?"

"Write me often, okay?"

Vincent smiled and looked past her to the front room that still bore the pictures of the past. One picture was of a smiling Leonard Dean teaching the greatest game on earth to a willing pupil in their humble backyard. Vincent considered himself the luckiest man in the world.

"Yes, Mrs. Dean. I promise."

Mrs. Dean chuckled and gave him a box.

"What's this?" Vincent asked.

"I understand you had to give that Bible you were borrowing back to your friend," Mrs. Dean said.

"Yes, ma'am. That's true."

Mrs. Dean straightened up and put on her teacher face. "You're about to go on a journey. It will be full of trials and tribulations, but now you have your own guidebook. I hope you cherish it."

Vincent took the lid off the box and pulled out a beautiful white hardback leather Bible with gold trim on the pages. When he opened the inside cover he read what she wrote.

Dear Vincent,

Remember, life is a tough journey. If you ever run into trouble and can't find a way out, the answer is in here. "Then they cried unto the LORD in their trouble, and he delivered them out of their distresses." -Psalm 107: 6

Keep the faith son,
Elna Dean

Vincent smiled and gave her one last hug before he took off for the West. He was good to his word and wrote to her once a week. Playing for Coach Johnson was very hard, as college ball should be. And he thought the sun shone hot in Oklahoma! It was a dry heat in Arizona, but a strong heat all the same.

Best of all though, the only reputation that preceded him was that of his ability, that he had one heck of a fastball. He had no past, no rotten parents, no doubting coaches, and nobody to tell him he couldn't do the job.

Mrs. Dean kept Vincent up to date with the happenings back home, like the trial of Dan Davison. Unfortunately, the DA couldn't bring up enough evidence to charge him with anything concerning the young girl in his car, or anything concerning the rigging of the outcomes of the high school games, but the drug charges were a foregone conclusion.

Anything Mrs. Dean didn't tell Vincent, he caught up on by reading his hometown newspaper online. The situation was such big news that the small-town newspaper became very popular throughout the state of Oklahoma and beyond.

The DEA searched the salvage yard and found all the marijuana Deuce had stowed away, plus some other hard-core drugs and a freezer full of dead rabbits.

Before Christmas, Dan "Deuce" Davison started the first of his eighteen years of straight time, with no chance of parole.

Mrs. Dean wrote to Vincent and told him that, as expected, Jimmy lost his scholarship, and as part of a plea bargain for testifying against Deuce in court, was sentenced to ninety days of time already served in jail.

She also told Vincent that when Jimmy got involved with Deuce, he was still a minor, which was taken into consideration. Also taken into consideration was the fact that Jimmy was a victim of a very persuasive man who liked to wield a gun to make his point. Ironically, the authorities found out that the gun Deuce used to intimidate young kids was actually an old cap gun made to look real. His fellow prison mates thought that last point was comical, and Dan Davison was teased mercilessly for it.

Not only did Jimmy miss out on his big break, but so did his dad. It soon came out that Coach Grey was planning on quitting his head coaching job at Augusta and taking an assistant's position at UNCO, that is until the scandal hit the newspapers. The news didn't surprise Vincent in the least.

Coach Redenbacher, innocent as the other boys on the team, was the logical replacement for the man who betrayed his adoring fans.

Coach Grey didn't let the rumors of his fixing games keep him down. Like most lucky men, he would eventually land on his feet. Poetic justice could only keep Coach Grey down for so long.

As soon as Jimmy was released, he followed his father to a small college in Missouri. Coach Grey was their newly hired bench coach, a favor that the head coach, one of Coach Grey's old buddies, apparently granted him.

Vincent was happy to find out that Jimmy would get a second chance.

The newspaper also reported that, though not convicted, Coach Grey was banned for life from coaching in Oklahoma.

Mrs. Dean told Vincent that Coach Grey left town one day without a word.

Vincent would forever reminisce on the summer following his senior year of high school. He learned that most people were sheep, and would follow anyone who stood up to lead, good or bad. But he also learned that a few people in this world were indeed good-hearted, and all it took was for someone to care about another more than himself. All it took was love, and he now knew where to find it.

Vincent would have other challenges in his career, and other challenges in his life, but he never confused the two, and in the end, the answer always lay on the inside bill of a dusty, old baseball cap.

ABOUT THE AUTHOR

Ryan's passion for writing began with his first letter to Santa. He's been writing in some capacity ever since and especially loves to pen stories about the great outdoors and sports. He earned his bachelor's degree from Northwestern Oklahoma State University and teaches high school English and coaches tennis. A family man, Ryan is active in his church and loves to serve his community. Ryan can be seen booting routine ground balls on the dusty softball fields when he's not on a river, changing his daughter's diaper, or helping his boys with their Pinewood Derby cars. Ryan, his wife Angela, and their three children live in Ponca City, Oklahoma.

The Mentor is Ryan's first published novel.

Made in the USA
Charleston, SC
28 February 2013